Treasure in a Field

Cover designed by Sharon K Connell
Book Cover image of Pirate courtesy of Mysticsartdesign / Pixabay

Editing Services from Above the Pages

Treasure in a Field is a work of fiction. Names, characters, places, and incidents are products of the author's imagination or used fictitiously. Any resemblance to actual persons, living or dead, or events is entirely coincidental.

Printed in the United States of America

ISBN: 978-1-7329237-3-7

Dedicated to my Lord Jesus Christ who has given me the ability to write and guided me through the story.

Acknowledgements

My thanks to all listed on this page for their contribution to the details of this story with professional information, critiques, support, and so much more. I am ever so grateful.

Nathan Arneal, President, North Bend Area Chamber of Commerce, Nebraska

Waylon Fischer, Fire Chief, North Bend Fire Department, Nebraska

Arnold C. Hauswald, U.S. Army (Ret.)

Faye Hamilton, RN, over 30 years as an ER Trauma Nurse

ACFW Scribes Critique Group

And the many members of the Christian Writers & Readers Facebook Group Forum for their encouragement.

But lay up for yourselves treasures in heaven, where neither moth nor
rust doth corrupt, and where thieves do not break through nor steal:
Matthew 6:20

There Abideth Hope

Sharon K Connell

Chapter One

University of Colorado ~ Boulder

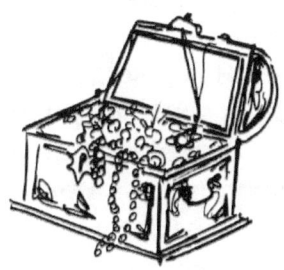

H aley MacKenna sat on her dorm room bed, head propped in one cupped hand with her elbow on her knee, focused on the notepad. She brushed a lock of shoulder-length red hair away from her eyes. What had she written during the afternoon lecture? She shook her head in disgust. "Chicken scratches. I can't stand it when my scribbles come out worse than a doctor's signature."

Pointing to the middle of the page, she held the spiral pad out toward her roommate, who sat at a desk against the wall. "This word. I can't figure it out. Did Professor Duncan mention something about a treasure in that lecture? Here. See if you can read it." Haley tossed the pad onto Kayla Ross's lap.

Kayla laughed and examined the paper, then glided to Haley's bed. "You have the worst handwriting I've ever seen, girl." She squinted at the page. "I think...I don't know...but I think it says treasure." She flipped the pad onto the comforter in front of Haley and sauntered back to her chair.

"Yes, siree. Don't you remember? He talked of nothing but gold and jewels for a few minutes when he went off on a rabbit trail again, just as he usually does. He gave details of his vacation last year when he and his wife had gone to Florida to see if they could find buried treasure on the beach after he'd read of interesting discoveries. But why notate that?" She resumed reading her geological engineering book.

A moment later, while Haley scratched out the undecipherable note from the paper, Kayla shut her textbook and turned back to Haley. "Professor Duncan carried on and on about the gold coins. I thought it would pique your interest after the story you told me our first year here. The MacKenna legend. Do you plan on a trip to Florida to hunt for gold yourself?"

Haley glanced up at her and sighed. "Must have zoned out after I wrote this word. For most of my life, I've been spoon-fed that old family myth. To be honest, if I never hear another story with a connection to treasure, Spanish galleons, or pirates, I'll be a happy camper."

She jumped at the loud knock on their door. Her hand flew to her chest. Rapid taps followed. "What on earth?"

Kayla ran to the door and peered into the hallway through the peephole. "Haley, I think it's your brother." She turned with her brows furrowed, pointed to the picture on Haley's nightstand, and shrugged. "Doesn't he live in California?"

"Yes. Well...let him in."

As Haley leaped out of her chair, the door swung open. "Hi, big brother. What brings you to—"

Aiden wrapped his strong arms around her in a tight hug. "Sis, I have bad news."

As Kayla helped her pack, numbness spread through Haley's body. This had to be a dream. *A nightmare.* Mom and Dad...gone? "They can't be gone." Sparkles floated around her peripheral vision, and she sank to her knees.

"Haley!" Her brother scooped her up and laid her on the bed. He shoved the clothes still on hangers to the foot. "Are you okay?"

"No." A flood of tears burst from Haley's eyes. "This can't be happening. There must be some mistake."

Kayla slid Haley's suitcase from the bed to the floor, sat next to her, and rested her hand on Haley's back. "You'll be okay. You've had a shock." She winced and glanced at Aiden. "Sorry. I'm just so inept in these situations. Easier for me to discuss rocks." She launched herself off the bed. "I'll get her a cup of tea from downstairs. Maybe it'll help."

He handed Haley a handful of tissues from the box on her nightstand. "Sis, I'd better check with the airport and make reservations for a flight to Omaha. When I received the news, all I thought of was getting to Boulder...to you. Will you be okay while I make the call?"

Haley sat up and grabbed the tissue box. She nodded and dabbed at her tears. Words stuck in the back of her throat like a half-baked biscuit. As her brother phoned the airport, she finished packing a carry-on for the flight home. She plunked back down onto the edge of the bed in a daze.

The door squeaked open as Kayla reentered their room. "Here's your tea, Haley." Kayla placed the steaming cup on the nightstand, eased next to her friend, and swiped a stray tear from Haley's red eyes.

"Wish I was more help. But you know my heart and prayers are with you and Aiden. Your parents were two of the sweetest people I've ever met. After they found out my folks died in that plane crash during our first year at college, they always treated me as if I were one of the family. If there's anything you can think of for me to do, just ask." She slipped her arm around Haley.

The waterworks resumed. Another nod was all Haley could manage.

Aiden reentered the room. "The only flight available to get us from Denver to Omaha is tomorrow morning at 4 a.m. We have to allow at least an hour for the drive to the airport, two hours for check-in, security, and everything else. So we'd better leave here around midnight, just in case."

He pulled the desk chair to the bed and turned it to face Haley. Aiden lowered himself onto it, taking her hands in his. Dilated red veins from lack of sleep showed in his dark green eyes. "Did you hear me?"

"Yes. I just don't understand. How could this have happened to Mom and Dad? He's such a good driver. He never took any chances. What happened?"

"The details are sketchy." He ran a hand through the bright red curls on his head. "But apparently they were driving home by Carter Lake near twilight. There's that section of road around the water, heading west, where it seems as if you'll drive straight into the lake, but the road veers off to the right."

"Yeah. Mom's favorite way to come home after visiting the park or airport." Her voice quavered. She pressed her lips together and grabbed his arm. "But *what happened?*"

"According to Aunt Deb, the deputy said it looked like Dad lost control when he neared the turn. The car crashed into a clump of shrubs and went through the guard rail. They said he was going so fast, the car took flight and landed in the water. It sunk. The Fremont Sheriff Department is still investigating why Mom and Dad didn't get out of the car when it hit. But with the electric windows up, everything might have—" Aiden's voice hitched, and he swallowed. "We'll have to wait until they figure out the details. Once we get to the farm, I'll contact the sheriff's department and see if they've learned more."

"How can that be? You know what a careful driver Dad is...was." The dam broke again. Haley snatched a pillow from the head of the bed, buried her face in it, and wept.

Kayla wrapped her arms around Haley and held her. Aiden rubbed her back and spoke, but sobs muffled his words.

"Come on, Haley." Kayla touched her roommate's chin. "Drink your tea before it goes cold. It's chamomile. It'll help calm you."

Haley lifted her head and stared at Kayla's glistening eyes. "Nothing will calm me until I find out what happened to my parents." She pinned her brother with a searching gaze. "You don't accept their deaths as an accident either. I can tell by your expression. Can't you find out the details right now? Isn't there someone you can contact? You being a lawyer?"

Aiden pulled her into an embrace. "That's exactly what I intend to do, Sis, as soon as I get you home to the farm. No, I don't accept it. Something's not right about this so-called accident. I'm sure the sheriff will see that after their investigation. They just haven't had time to find out what happened. I'm not going to badger them with questions they can't answer yet."

He pushed her gently from him and looked at her. "You'd better freshen up and rest." He glanced at his watch. "It's seven already. I'll run out and get burgers since we've missed dinner. After we eat, we'll sleep a couple of hours before we head to Denver. I can crash on the floor. Be right back." He let go of her and rushed out.

Kayla took the half-emptied cup of tea from the nightstand. "Haley, you need to rest. The next few days will tax your nerves. I've gone through funeral preparations myself. Plus, the unsettled fears you and Aiden have."

When she reached the door, she turned. "I'll take my study materials to the common room, so I don't keep either of you awake. Your brother can use my bed. I'll be up at least until midnight, studying. Besides, I want to see you off."

5

"You don't have to go. With a ton of questions going through my mind, I probably won't be able to sleep anyway. And your being here is comforting. My brother can snore through a hurricane." She smiled. "You've been my best friend since we met. Please stay."

"All right, gal. But promise me you'll rest?"

Haley stretched out on her bed and pulled an Afghan to her shoulders. "Okay."

Kayla turned off the nightstand lamp and returned to the desk. She took a sip of the tea Haley had left and drew out a clip-on book light from the drawer.

Twenty-five minutes later, Kayla answered a soft tap on the door. Aiden stepped in. The smell of burgers and fries followed him and filled the room.

Haley hopped out of bed, took a card table from the closet, and placed it between the twin beds. Kayla rolled her desk chair to the open side of the table. The girls sat on their beds, and Aiden seated himself in the chair.

After asking the blessing on their food, he opened the bag he'd set on the table and passed out hamburgers and fries. They ate in silence.

When they finished, Kayla stuffed wrappers and napkins, along with Haley's half-eaten burger, into the sack. "I'll dispose of these downstairs."

"But you'll come right back, won't you?" Where had this insecurity come from? Haley touched Kayla's arm. "I'll feel better if you stay."

"It'd help Sis to have you near, so please come back, Kayla." Aiden patted Haley's hand. "You won't bother me if you're in the room. I can sleep anywhere, on anything, and like a rock. Sis has written to me many times about how close you've become. She always did want a sister." He glanced at Haley and smiled.

"Okay, I'll be right back." Kayla scooped up the remaining trash and went out the door. Before it closed, she stuck her head back in. "Aiden, you sleep on my bed. I'll be studying until midnight, so you may as well be comfortable." The door clicked shut before he could answer.

Haley gazed at her brother. "Thanks for understanding. She is more of a sister to me than simply a roomy...or even a friend. I wish she could come to Omaha with us." She sighed. "But she'd have her first round of tests to make up when she got back."

Hope I don't miss any important classes, tests, or lectures while I'm gone. They'd already started out rough this year.

Several minutes later, Kayla bounded through the doorway. "Okay, you two. Lights out." She tossed a huge comforter from the end of her bed at Aiden. Then she reestablished herself at the desk.

Haley curled up on her bed, tears seeping from her eyes. She pulled out more tissues, dabbed at the corners, and blew her nose.

"Try to rest, Sis. I've set the alarm on my cell for eleven-thirty. That'll give us two and a half hours of sleep." He laid his head back on the pillow. "Trust me. We'll get everything straightened out when we reach Omaha."

She closed her eyes, but her imagination took over. An image of her father's car swerving out of control on the road alongside Carter Lake flashed in her mind. Haley pinched her eyelids together, trying to erase the scene. It just couldn't be. There had to be another reason for the crash. *Oh, Mom...Dad...*

When a hand touched her shoulder, Haley jerked awake. The dim light from the bathroom showed Kayla bending over her.

"Haley, it's midnight. Your brother has everything in the car ready to go. I threw a few goodies from our stash into your tote for you to munch on during the flight, if you get hungry." She turned on the nightstand light and held out the bag.

Haley's purse and computer sat on the card table next to the door. She smiled at her roommate. "You're one of the best friends I've ever had."

Kayla plopped down on the bed and hugged her. "And you mine. I'll miss you while you're gone, girl. Text me when you get there, okay?"

"I will. Wish you were going with us, but you need to stay in class with the load you're taking this last year. When I get back, I'll have to pick your brain on our joint classes to catch up. If only all our classes had been together." Haley rose and finger-brushed her hair.

Kayla ruffled Haley's hair back up. "With your smarts, it'll be a piece of cake for you to catch up. You should check to see if you can get any work done online while you're gone. Just in case you don't get back right away." She hugged Haley and walked with her out the door. "Look, don't let this get to you. Remember, I'm here if you want to talk. I'll be praying for you."

Haley forced a smile. "Right. I'll text you later in the morning. You take care of yourself, Kayla. And don't worry about me. I'll be fine."

Then why do I feel things will never be the same again?

Chapter Two

Omaha, Nebraska

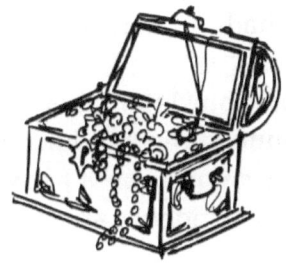

aley's eyes burned as the plane landed at Eppley Airfield in Omaha. She glanced at her cell. Only six-thirty a.m. She and Aiden made their way through the concourse, out of the terminal, and down the walkway toward the rental car customer service. "Aiden, are they open?"

"Yes. Since six this morning. I checked yesterday and reserved a vehicle. We'll reach the farm in no time."

"That's good." As she pulled the carry-on behind her, it seemed to gain a hundred pounds. "Did you fall asleep on the plane? How do you feel?"

"I'm okay. Alert enough to drive anyway, if that's what you mean. Did you rest at all, Sis?"

"Not really. Every time I shut my eyes, I had horrible visions of the crash."

Aiden took her carry-on from her and flipped it sideways on top of his. Then he slipped his arm around her shoulders and squeezed as they walked. "It's understandable, considering."

Before long, they left the airport en route to the farm. Haley reclined the rental's passenger seat to rest, but sleep still eluded her. Had Dad's car malfunctioned? Had an animal jumped out from the brush and caused them to veer off? Mom had a soft spot for animals. Or had Dad had a heart attack...and lost control? How could they be gone?

A little more than an hour later, they pulled onto the MacKenna family property and rounded the bend in the driveway. A dozen cars and trucks dotted the large open area between the white farmhouse with its black shuttered windows and the new traditional white-trimmed, red barn.

"Aiden, what are all those vehicles doing here? What's going on?"

"I'm not sure. One belongs to Aunt Deb. She said she'd stay with us and help with the funeral preparations. It was something she had to do. But I think more so you'd have a woman to talk to." He patted her hand, which gripped the seat as though braced for impact. "The other vehicles...I have no idea."

Haley gave him a half-smile and nodded. She drew in a deep breath to calm her nerves. *Didn't work.* It'd be nice to have Auntie here. Not that Aiden wouldn't be a comfort, but she had a special relationship with her mother's younger sister, almost like a second Mom.

"Maybe Aunt Deb needed help with something Drago couldn't handle." Aiden chuckled. "Although it's hard to believe there's anything that burly farm manager wouldn't tackle. He'd all but run this farm for Dad since we were kids. Or, perhaps she called a prayer meeting. Guess we'll find out." He pulled the car next to the red barn and hopped out.

Haley grabbed her purse and opened the passenger door. She followed Aiden toward the house. Aunt Debbie burst out the front door, down the porch steps, and enveloped both of them in her arms. A flood of tears drenched her face.

After greetings, they headed to the house.

The tight bands around Haley's heart loosened. Auntie had left her home in Council Bluffs to be with them at the farm. Just like her. She'd give her advice on what to do. Even though Aiden's wife and son would be here in a day or two, he'd have to return to California and his practice at some point. And he had no interest in the farm.

The farm, college, her degree…her career. She shouldn't worry over those things now. It was time to focus on what had to be done.

As they ascended the front porch stairs, her heart ached, and her eyes blurred. *What am I going to do?*

Aiden lugged the bags upstairs. He set Haley's in the master bedroom. Would she want to stay in Mom and Dad's room? He sighed. He'd bring them down again if she decided on her old room instead. But she'd probably want to be with everyone else upstairs for a while.

He turned and dragged his own carry-on down the hall to the room he'd used before he left for college. Char and Everett would arrive tomorrow. Aunt Deb occupied the guest room. He'd let his wife sleep in here while he and his son camped out on the floor of Dad's study. A twinge of pain hit Aiden's heart. Man, he sure needed Char to bolster his spirit. He missed them. Even more so than when he attended the conference for the firm earlier this year. But his heart hadn't hurt then, like now.

Aiden tossed his bag onto the crazy quilt that covered his twin bed. It landed with a whoomph. Mom had made that bedcover when he was ten. His eyes misted.

He headed downstairs to join the others in the living room. His mother had always referred to it as "the parlor."

Standing in the archway, he watched as Aunt Deb and Haley conversed with his childhood friend, Jason Schumaker. Decked out in a deputy uniform complete with sidearm. Guess he'd finished the requirements. "Hi, Jason."

The deputy hurried to Aiden and grabbed him in a fierce hug. "So glad to see you again, buddy. Although, I wish it was under other circumstances."

Aiden took a step back. "In law enforcement now, huh?"

"For over two years, man." His brows furrowed. "I'm sorry about your folks. If there's anything I or the family can do to help you and Haley, please don't hesitate to ask."

"You can tell me you found out what happened to Mom and Dad."

A look of puzzlement filled Jason's face. "Didn't your aunt tell you? Your dad lost control of the car, and it landed in Carter Lake. It appeared that he and your mom couldn't get out of the vehicle when the electrical system got wet."

"Yes, Aunt Deb told us that, but Haley brought up a good question. How is it possible for the car to have launched out over the water? You know what a careful driver he was. The car had to be going really fast. And he never drove fast."

Jason rubbed the stubble on his chin.

A five o'clock shadow at eight in the morning? Aiden pursed his lips. Poor guy must have been up all night.

His old friend blinked a couple of times. "Say...you've got something there. No one's mentioned mechanical failure as yet, but the investigation is ongoing. I'll talk to the chief and find out what they've learned."

"Thanks. This accident doesn't sound right." He thumped Jason on the shoulder and leaned in closer to whisper. "Who are these people?"

He shrugged his shoulders. "Just got here myself. End of my shift. Thought I'd drive by and check if everything was okay with your aunt since she was alone. Saw these cars, so I decided to come in. She said they're a prayer group from her church in Council Bluffs. Nice bunch of people to have driven all the way over here for her."

"This early? It sure is. They're probably close friends of hers. Let's join them."

Haley turned as Aiden approached the gathering Aunt Debbie had already introduced to her. She closed the gap between them and smiled at her brother. "You were right. This is part of Auntie's prayer group. They've been here since the wee hours of the morning to pray for our safe trip home and for comfort."

She pulled Aiden closer to the strangers. Aunt Deb introduced him to each prayer partner. Hands were shaken as words of sympathy were extended.

Jason shook Haley's hand. "I really need to get home for some shut-eye after my night shift, so I'll leave now. Hope you, Aiden, and I can get together soon."

"Thanks for checking on our aunt. I'm sure we'll all get together before Aiden goes back to California." Jason had always put her in a good mood when they were kids.

As the group broke up, Aiden followed Jason and the church members to their vehicles. A few minutes later, the front door swished opened.

Haley's jaw tensed. *No. Not him.* Surely *he* wasn't part of the prayer chain.

Aunt Debbie smiled. "Robert, thank you for stopping by. I know you and your dad are still busy with the soybean harvest." She latched onto Haley's arm. "Sweetie, you remember Robert Sheffield. Weren't you two in the same class in high school? When we lived here in North Bend, he mowed our lawn. He used to help Uncle Jeff with all kinds of odd jobs too. And now he and his parents drive to Council Bluffs on occasion to attend our church."

"He was a year ahead of me, Auntie. Rob was Aiden's friend, not mine." She grimaced and looked away.

Aiden came back in and shouted from the front door. "Rob, didn't see you arrive."

As they shook hands, Rob glanced at Haley. "Haley, Aiden, I can't tell you how sorry I am about your parents. Hard to believe this happened." He turned to Aiden. "A member of the prayer chain from church phoned Mom after the accident. I decided to stop by today to find out if your aunt needed anything. We've prayed about what your dad told us has gone on over here." He glanced at Haley again. "Your aunt got in touch with my mom this morning and told her about the dark figure she saw run from the house into the field last night. Mom said her voice sounded shaky on the phone, so as soon as I could get away, I drove over."

Aiden whipped his head to Haley and back to Rob. "What's going on? Dad's never said a word of this to me. And neither did Aunt Deb when she called yesterday."

Haley's gaze traveled from Rob to her brother. Then settled back on Rob. "What are you talking about?" She peered over his shoulder at her aunt, who looked up from the last member of the prayer group as he made his way out the door. Aunt Debbie's dark brown brows wrinkled.

"Auntie?" Haley rushed toward her. "What's happened here? Does it have something to do with the accident?"

Aunt Debbie hurried to meet Haley, who was followed close behind by her brother and Rob. Her lips tightened as she glanced at her niece and nephew. "I'm sorry, Aiden. I didn't tell you this earlier because I didn't want to add more stress to either of you while you were so far away. I planned to explain everything to you tonight. Your mom told me things have been strange around here. She said it started weeks ago. Let's go into the kitchen and talk, now that everyone else is gone."

Chapter Three

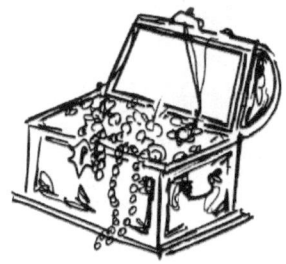

aley, Aiden, and Rob followed Aunt Debbie into the kitchen. Haley glanced around the all-white room. It was as immaculate as her mother had always kept it. Would she ever be as good a housekeeper as her mother? She sighed and lowered herself into a chair while her aunt poured a cup of steaming hot coffee for each of them. She could use the caffeine after so little sleep.

The chairs screeched on the floor as the men and her aunt sat. Haley stared at Aunt Debbie. "So...what happened last night?"

With taut lips, her aunt folded her hands in front of her and took a deep breath. "Thursday night, while sleeping in your old room downstairs, I heard noises outside the window. When I pulled the drapes aside and looked out, I saw a shadow run from the house to the back field." She gestured toward the back of the house where the fallow field lay eighty feet behind Haley's bedroom.

"It disappeared in the dark. Minutes later, rolling smoke appeared where the figure had gone. Sent chills through me. I thought whoever it was set fire to the debris in the field. Then the smoke vanished, and a light...no, a glow took its place and grew larger." She placed her hand over her heart.

"I called the sheriff's office and the fire department. They came out to investigate the area." She shook her head. "They found nothing. No evidence of a fire, no footprints. Nothing."

Aiden covered Auntie's hands with his own. "It's okay. Only a prank by a teen, using a flashlight and amateur magic trickery, no doubt."

"I'm not so certain, Aiden. Not after the things your father talked about that had happened recently and the old legend. One night, when I had dinner here with your parents, your father told me of weird goings-on at night. Visions appearing in the field behind the house, noises that couldn't be explained, and the blood."

With a gasp, Haley bolted from her chair. "What blood? Did you tell the sheriff?"

"No. The incident rattled me, and after your parents' accident, I was too distraught over their deaths. But your father said he had told them."

Aiden pulled Haley back into her seat. He glanced toward Rob, who shrugged his shoulders. She narrowed her eyes at her brother's friend.

After a sip from the steaming mug, her aunt said, "Your dad thought the same thing you did, Aiden. At first. Kids. But the incident with the blood seemed to unnerve him."

"Auntie...what blood?" Haley gulped. "Exactly what things did Dad say were going on?"

"Sweetie, he said none of the noises or anything else upset him. He figured the kids would tire of their pranks. Trying to play out the legend of the Indian burial grounds and were having their fun.

17

But when he went out there last week and found that blood on the ground, it gave him a start. It was inside the edge of the field, on this end. He assumed it was an animal attacked by a larger one and carried off. But that night, screams came from out there. He called the sheriff."

"We need to get Jason back out here and tell him about this." Haley started to rise again, but Aiden stopped her.

"Sis, Aunt Deb said Dad reported it."

"Yes, and when he did—" Aunt Debbie's hands shook.

Aiden leaned toward her and again covered them with his.

After another deep breath, she continued. "They found nothing. The blood was gone. Because of the rumors that a burial mound used to be where the field is now, the deputy may have figured it was your dad's imagination." She glanced at Aiden. "They took samples of the ground where your dad said he thought he'd seen it. But as far as I know, he hadn't heard a word about the results."

The chair almost toppled when Haley rose again. She paced the kitchen floor. "They probably assume everything is Auntie's imagination too." She glanced at Rob, sitting across the table from her. He hadn't made a comment. Probably thought it was all in Auntie's head. Haley's eyes narrowed. *Why is he really here?*

"I'm sure they don't." Aiden's gaze traveled from Haley to Aunt Debbie. "I'll talk to Jason. What did Drago say?"

"Oh, you know Cary. He's thoroughly convinced it's a ghost from the burial grounds. He tries to hide it, but I think he's scared out of his wits. He just keeps working anyway, good man. And, Aiden, you need to stop using that awful nickname for him. You're grown up now. I can't imagine how he feels when you refer to him as a dragon."

Picking up the receiver on the wall phone their mom had refused to update, Haley pressed the numbered buttons. "What we call the farm manager is not the issue here, Auntie. I'm phoning the sheriff's department to find out what they know."

Later that evening, Haley opened the front door to Deputy Schumaker. "Hi, Jason. Thanks for coming back. Aunt Debbie may have neglected to tell you everything that's gone on around the property. You're aware of the person who ran away from the house and the smoke in the field the other day. And she says Dad reported the rest of the incidents. But what's been done?" Haley folded her arms across her chest.

Jason entered the foyer and removed his cap. "The captain thinks they're related to what happened last night."

Haley held out her hand and motioned for Jason to enter the living room. "With the old Indian burial grounds legend and the stories Dad used to tell us, Auntie and I are worried the sheriff's department won't take this seriously.

"Take a seat while I tell Aiden and Auntie you're here. We made a fresh pot of coffee. Do you still take yours half and half, coffee and milk?"

"Sure do. Gotta keep those dairy farms in business." He snickered. "I meant to tell you this morning. You're looking pretty, as always. How's school?"

"It's fine. I'm hoping to graduate next spring, but I'm not certain what will happen now. Excuse me." She turned to leave.

The sound of footsteps descending the staircase stopped Haley mid-step. She glanced toward the foyer.

Aiden landed with a thud at the bottom of the stairs. Her brother would never grow up when it came to hopping down those stairs.

"Hi, Jason. Thanks for returning."

"No problem, buddy."

Haley stepped into the dining room to head for the kitchen. "I'm getting coffee for Jason. Do you want some? I'll ask Auntie to join us."

"I could use a cup." Aiden grinned as he moved into the living room. "So, deputy...it sounds odd to call you that. But I'm glad you're working the case."

Haley hurried to the kitchen. Would Jason consider these happenings and Dad's tales of them a joke? He used to listen to Dad, eyes as big as saucers when they were all kids. Maybe he always thought the MacKenna family history was a joke. She took in a sharp breath. Were the stories true? They couldn't be. But now specters and blood?

Where could the blood have gone?

As Jason lowered himself to the overstuffed chair, Aiden settled on the couch. "These other incidents Aunt Deb told us of have me worried. Haley's already stressed from the deaths of our parents, but these weird occurrences are making her a wreck. Were you one of the officers who came out when Dad reported the blood in the field?"

A slow nod and Jason's pursed lips made Aiden's hands clench. They hadn't believed Dad. "Jason, you know my father was never one to exaggerate. Even when he told us that legend about the buried treasure our ancestor found, he said he never put any stock in it. Said it was a good fairy tale. But this is different. Aunt Deb said it upset him."

"The night I came out here, your dad was shaken by what he'd seen and heard. It wasn't my place to go against my superior. I checked out the field but didn't find anything. But I figured something wasn't right. I haven't stopped looking for an answer yet and won't. Same with the accident. You can count on me."

"Thanks, man. I was hoping I could. I'll be here for a couple of weeks, but I have to return to California soon. I'm concerned about

Haley staying here on her own. Aunt Deb can stay for a week, but she has her job to consider at the church office."

"Won't your farm manager be here? What's his name?"

"Drag—ah, Cary. Yes. He'll be here, but he's scared, according to Aunt Deb. And that's saying a lot because I've never known anything to bother him. I talked to him right before you came. Never knew he was superstitious. He said he'd considered quitting over this, but after what my folks had done for him, he couldn't leave. He also told me other strange things have happened."

The aroma of freshly brewed coffee preceded Haley as she entered the room with a carafe, mugs, sugar, and creamer on a tray. Aunt Deb followed with napkins, plates, and a pile of scones.

"Bless you, Haley." Jason grinned up at her. "You must have noticed my stomach complaining the minute I walked in."

She returned his smile, poured him a mug of the steaming brew, and then turned to Aiden. "Did you say there's something else to worry about? As if we don't have enough?"

Everyone prepared their coffee and took a scone.

Aiden took a sip. "It seems Drago...sorry, Aunt Deb. Old habits die hard. Cary said a few weeks ago, small things, tools, started disappearing from the stable."

Tears flooded Haley's eyes. "This has been the MacKennas' family home since the early eighteen hundreds. Nothing like this has ever happened here."

"It's okay, Haley. It's okay. We'll do everything we can to find out what's going on." Aiden faced Jason. "Doesn't all this sound odd to you? First, the weird stuff around the farm, blood in the field that disappeared, tools and other equipment missing, and then the so-called auto accident. Someone's running around at night, playing pranks. And don't tell me you believe in that haunted burial grounds nonsense."

The deputy shook his head and narrowed his eyes. "Your dad was not given to theatrics or superstitions. Neither am I. I don't intend to give up on my investigation of these incidents. I'll keep a close eye on everything out here." He smiled at Haley, finished his scone and coffee, and rose from the seat.

"If you need anything, call me. Thanks for the goodies, Haley." He nodded, holding four extra scones she'd wrapped in a napkin for him. "Always loved these orange-cranberry things, and I remember them as one of your specialties. I'll share with Mom and Dad when I get home."

Aiden walked Jason to the front door and shook his hand. "Thanks, buddy. Be careful out there on patrol with all this nonsense happening."

Chapter Four

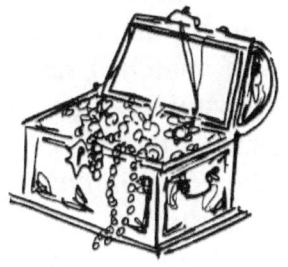

Monday morning, Haley finished loading the breakfast dishes in the dishwasher and went to her old room at the back of the house. Exhausted by the stress of the last four days, she reclined on the bed. A midday nap might help with the fatigue that had overwhelmed her. She took a deep breath and closed her eyes. They popped open again. "What on earth?" The odor of smoke drifted into the room.

She sprung from the bed and gaped out the window to the field behind the farmhouse. Flickers of crimson and gold reached up from the ground. How could the debris left from last year's harvest be enough to cause a fire? That field had lain fallow this past year and with all the rain...it should be too damp. If enough chaff remained from corn stalks, it might spread. "Aiden! Aiden, come quick!"

Haley grabbed her cell from the nightstand and pressed 9 1 1.

As her pulse increased, Aiden rushed into the bedroom. "What's wrong, Sis?" He joined her at the window. His jaw dropped. "I'll call nine-one-one."

"Ringing." She pointed to the cellphone at her ear. "Get Aunt Debbie."

Aiden ran from the room.

When the dispatcher came on the line, Haley blurted out, "We need help. There's a fire in the field behind the house." With the phone still to her ear, she snatched her purse and followed her brother. "I think Auntie's upstairs taking a nap."

As they ran up the stairs, Aiden yelled, "Get up, Aunt Deb, get up. *Fire.*" He banged on the door. "*Aunt Deb.* We need to get out of the house in case the wind shifts."

She threw the door open, her eyes wide. "Not again."

Seconds later, the three of them fled out the front door. Aiden jumped into the rental car while Haley and their aunt rushed to each of theirs. They drove the vehicles away from the house and parked on one side of the long dirt drive. A wail of sirens filled the air.

Once the fire engine drove past them and around the house toward the field, Haley, Aiden, and Aunt Debbie leaped from their vehicles and ran to the side of the house. They stood frozen to the spot while the firemen hosed down the field. Haley glanced at her aunt. "What did you mean, 'Not again'?"

"Remember? One of the 'incidents' your father mentioned to me was a fire in this field. The fire department attributed the first one to spontaneous combustion from the dry mulch of cornstalk left in the field during the last hot spell. But two fires?" She gazed wide-eyed at Aiden.

Aiden rested his hand on Aunt Debbie's shoulder. "Let's not add to—"

Aunt Debbie placed her fists on her hips. "To what? Hysteria? Is that what you think I am? Hysterical? I suppose you think your father was making things up in his head too."

"Speculation, Aunt Deb. Not hysteria."

Haley slipped her arm around her aunt's waist. "Auntie, we don't think you're hysterical. We only want to wait until the professionals tell us what they think happened. We don't want to add any *fuel*, so to speak, to that old tale about Indian ghosts who want their land back."

"But a few people in North Bend have always believed the legends." Their aunt dropped her hands to her side. "This will only promote more belief in them."

"You're probably right." Haley pursed her lips. "They made great fireside stories, but I've never believed in ghosts. Neither did you, as I recall."

After a sigh, Aunt Debbie smiled at her. "You're right. But this talk from your dad, the incidents he couldn't explain, has upset me more than I realized. I started to consider the stories."

Fingers of smoke were the only evidence left of the fire as the fire chief approached. Trailed by Haley and their aunt, Aiden strode to meet him. "What happened out there? It's not hot enough to have caused spontaneous combustion. Besides, isn't the ground too wet after all the recent rain?"

"I'm not entirely sure what happened here, Aiden."

"You remember me, Chief?"

"Of course I do. You think I'd forget the young man who persuaded my son to join him in trying a cigarette in the basement and almost burned down our house?"

Aiden's chin dipped as he rubbed the back of his neck. "What a thing to remember me by. I didn't sit for a week after Dad finished with me. Haven't touched the evil things since."

Haley bit her lip. He was right. Dad had walloped Aiden good that time. The first time she'd seen her brother cry. Afterward, she'd gone into his room and cried with him. He hugged her and said thank you. They'd been super close ever since.

The chief chuckled. "Boyish pranks. But in that case, a serious one. Glad you and my son learned your lesson. I guess I have you to thank for that, although at the time I sure was peeved. We've all had lessons to learn before we grew up." He headed for the firetruck. "But that's not what you're interested in right now."

"No, sir. Why aren't you sure what caused the fire?"

"Something didn't look right out there. I'm going to refer this to the investigator, and I want to talk to the sheriff before I say any more. In the meantime, be on the lookout for anyone lurking around your property. We heard what happened to your folks and the reports of odd occurrences out here. News like that gets around in a small community. So be careful. Will you stay here at the house or elsewhere?"

"I'll be here at the house for a couple of weeks. Haley's home from college, but she's not sure what her plans are at this point. We're taking one step at a time."

Once the smoke died, and the firefighters assured the chief the area was safe, they left the property. Haley, Aiden, and Aunt Debbie stood at the edge of the field and stared at the black char.

Haley crouched and picked up a half-buried cigarette filter, black and brown from dirt. The firefighters must have kicked it up from the ground while making sure the fire was out. Must be from Drago when he used to smoke. She stood. It was a good thing they made it out here so fast. The fire had spread only to around a thirty-foot circumference.

With lowered brows, she gazed toward the woods at the end of the field. "Why did the chief say he wasn't sure of the cause?"

Aiden glanced at her. "He obviously suspects someone started the fire on purpose."

After Aunt Debbie stooped to pick up a withered corn leaf, she straightened and faced him. "An animal sure didn't start it." She spun and walked back to the house.

Haley continued to gaze at the trees. "Aiden, why would someone do this? The fires, the mysterious events." She turned to face him. "Why?"

A couple hours later, Haley and her aunt sat in the kitchen, mulling over a shopping list. "Aunt Debbie, there isn't too much we need from the store. Mom kept the pantry well-stocked. But we do have to make a trip to the butcher. There's not much meat in the freezer."

"I noticed that when I made dinner last night."

"Okay, the list is complete. Auntie, are you ready to go?"

Aiden breezed through the kitchen and out of the back door without a word.

In a flash, Haley was on her feet. "Aiden, what's up?" She ran out the back door and caught up to her brother.

"Just thought of something. Have to check the stable." He hastened his stride.

When they entered the structure, Drago was feeding the horses. "Drag—I'm sorry, Cary. I'm so used to that name we gave you when we were kids. If we upset you, it was unintentional."

"Yes, Cary. Auntie made us realize you might not appreciate being called a dragon. We meant no harm by it. It was only a childish thing because you smoked." Haley smiled at the burly man.

He turned from his work and grinned. "Not a problem, kids." He chuckled. "But you're not kids anymore, are you?"

The stocky man's laugh sent a warm cozy sensation through Haley. She used to sit on the lap of a much younger Drago when she was a child. He'd told her tales of the Indian mounds in the burned back field. Drago had always been good and protective of her and Aiden.

Their dad had hired Drago even after learning about the trouble he'd gotten into as a teen. How parents could turn their backs on their own son for making one mistake, hanging with the wrong crowd, she'd never understand. He'd been a model prisoner during his short sentence and changed his life completely when he got out. Still, his folks had nothing to do with him. *Oh well. Their loss is our family's gain.*

Drago hopped up and sat on a stall rail. "I kind of enjoy the name you gave me, even though I don't smoke anymore. Nasty habit. Gave it up when my doctor showed me some pictures of lungs from people who smoked. He told me it would be my future if I didn't quit." He waved his hand in the air as if to disrupt the thought.

"My friends at the chess club got a real chuckle when I told them the name you'd given me. Now they call me Drago too. So please, don't change it now. You'll confuse the tar out of me." He laughed and jumped down from the rail. "Never did like Cary, anyway."

"Okay, Drago." Aiden held out his hand to him, and the man clasped it. "Do you know any more than our aunt about the strange things happening around here? And, where were you this morning when the field caught on fire? I didn't see you come out of the bunkhouse."

"I wasn't here. We had our chess meeting in town during lunch." He smiled at Haley. "For your sake, I wish I'd been here. I'm not gonna let one of those haunts get to you, Miss Haley. No matter what. You neither, Aiden. Even if you can take care of yourselves now that you're grown."

Good old Drago. He must be near forty by now, and yet still assumed ghosts were real. But what a sweet guy. He'd always reminded her of a teddy bear with that black wavy hair, fuzzy arms, and bearded face. Built like a barrel and solid, but the gentlest creature she'd ever met.

"Aiden." Drago's eyes rounded. "You don't think I had anything to do with the fire, do you? Or the other things that've happened?"

"No. No. Of course not. That's not why I asked. It only occurred to me that you didn't come out when it happened. And that maybe you saw something we didn't this afternoon. Surely, you don't still accept that old Indian story as real."

"Now, don't scoff at that legend. If you'd seen the things I've seen through the years." He sat on a wooden tack box. "These things aren't to be made light of. Fortunately, these old Indians from the past had a lot of respect for horses. They've never once tried to damage the stable or hurt your father's horses. But Indians aren't the only ghosts around, you know."

Her brother sat on another box across from him. "That is strange. About the stable, that is." He rubbed his chin.

What was Aiden thinking? Did someone want the horses? She gazed at Drago's almost black eyes. Did Aiden suspect him? But Drago wouldn't have mentioned the horses and the lack of attacks on the stable if he were the one responsible for the fire. And Drago loved her parents, almost as if they were his own.

When Haley and Aunt Deb returned from the store, Aiden carried in the packages and set them on the kitchen table. He ran his tongue behind his lower lip as he pondered. "Aunt Deb. Was Drago here the first night you stayed. When you saw smoke and the glow in the field?"

"Yes, he was. Why do you ask, dear?"

"Just wondered." He helped the women put the groceries away and got a cup of coffee from the pot he'd started. The chair squealed as he pulled it from the table. He lowered himself to the seat. "Did Dad reveal his suspicions when the incidents began? Did he say anything about Drago?"

Aunt Deb pinioned him with a stare. "Tell me you don't suspect that nice man. He's always worked so hard for your father. No. That can't be what's in your head."

Haley and Aunt Deb sat at the table after getting their cups of coffee. Haley's brows furrowed.

"It's crossed my mind." He glanced at Haley. "It's crossed yours too, hasn't it?"

She wrinkled her brows. "I didn't want it to, but it did when we were in the barn. But why would Drago do any of this? What would he gain? The farm's ours, so he couldn't sell it even if we decided to leave."

"I don't know. I guess I'm frustrated and grasping at straws. Who'd want to harm Mom and Dad, or cause such strange incidents?"

Haley took a sip from her mug. "Has the sheriff's office called? The fire chief?"

"Kids, it's only been four days since the accident...if indeed it was an accident. We'll have to give them time."

A loud knock on the front door echoed down the hall to the kitchen.

Chapter Five

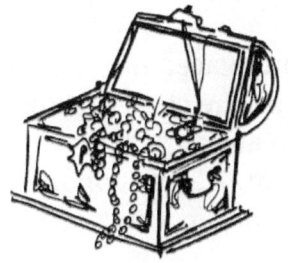

*A*s Haley opened the door, her stomach sank to her toes. There he was. He'd grown into a handsome man—tall, broad shoulders, perfect curly hair, *and so irritating.*

Aiden came up behind her. "Hi, Rob. Come on in."

Drat. She grimaced. Guess she'd better get used to seeing her brother's best friend, even if he did antagonize her. She did an about-face and scooted back to the kitchen.

As she entered, Aunt Debbie raised her cup to her lips. She looked up from the newspaper she'd spread across the table. "Who was at the door, dear?"

"Only Robert." Haley slumped into the chair opposite her aunt and sipped her coffee.

"Didn't you have a crush on him at one time? I recall you saying his deep blue eyes and light brown curls were dreamy. What did he want?"

"Who knows?" Haley sneered.

"Why Haley MacKenna, do I detect a note of annoyance in you? Are you mad at him?"

With a thump, Haley lowered her cup to the table, splashing the contents. She rushed to the sink for a dishcloth. "Yes, after the terrible thing he did to me in high school. But he's always irritated me." She scrubbed the table as though she were cleaning up dried pancake batter.

Aunt Debbie stood and placed her hand over Haley's. "It's clean now, dear." Her aunt took the cloth and tossed it in the sink. "What did he do to make you so angry?"

After resuming her seat, Haley supported her head in her cupped hands, elbows stretched out in front of her. She squeezed her lips into a tight line.

"Come on, dear. It'll be good to talk. Something tells me you haven't told anyone, and it's long festered. Does Aiden know how much you dislike Robert?"

"No. They've been friends forever, I didn't have the heart to tell him."

Her aunt's brows lowered. "Rob hasn't...um—"

"*No.* If you mean—he's never touched me. Not *that* way."

Aunt Debbie blew out a breath of air. "Then what has you so upset with him?"

"It's too embarrassing."

She tilted her head and smiled. "You've always confided everything to me."

"Rob always teased me, even when we were little."

"And...?"

Haley sighed. "Then I'd forgive him. But in his last year of high school...he was in the class ahead of me...his cousin, Chad, who was in that class too, asked me to their prom. I was thrilled to have been invited to the senior prom by the star quarterback." Her eyes grew teary. She rose and tore off a paper towel to blot the tears, then sat again. How could she tell her?

"Auntie, I really don't want to go into this. Can't we save it for another time?"

"Not if you still hold a grudge against Robert. He's a sweetheart. You need to get it out and forgive him for whatever happened. It's not good for you to hold on to anger."

"All right. I—"

Aiden and Rob's voices traveled through the hallway. As they entered the kitchen, they laughed.

Glad they're having such a wonderful reunion. Haley sucked in air between her teeth, popped up from her chair, and put the half-full mug in the sink. She turned. Rob's tan face, from long hours of work in the sun, smiled at her.

Aiden motioned for him to take a seat at the table.

"Aunt Deb, I invited Rob to have dinner with us. He wants to—"

Haley brushed past her brother and hurried to her room. She shut the door harder than intended and collapsed on her bed.

Father, Auntie is right. I need to get over this, but it hurts. Why does it hurt after all this time?

After the loud bang reverberated into the kitchen, Aiden looked at Aunt Deb. "What's wrong with her?"

"You should talk to her. She has old issues she needs to deal with, but it's not my place—" she glanced at Rob, "—to tell tales confided in me." She rose and took two mugs from the cabinet.

Aiden sidled up to her at the counter. "She told you what's eating her?"

"She didn't get to finish, but it's something she apparently can't get over." She glanced back at Rob.

Aiden followed her line of sight. Rob fidgeted in the chair. Why was his friend so nervous? A chill swept through Aiden. "What happened between you and my sister?"

Rob's brows furrowed. "It was a long time ago."

"What did you do to Haley to make her so mad? She's been cold toward you ever since we got home."

Rob peered at Aunt Deb. "What did she tell you?"

"Not much of anything. She mentioned your senior prom and your cousin but was reluctant to discuss it. When the two of you entered the hallway, she stopped talking."

After a deep breath, Rob frowned. "She hates me."

Aiden's eyes met his aunt's. He grabbed the full cups of coffee. As he sat at the table, he pushed one of the mugs in front of Rob. "Maybe you'd better tell us what happened."

Aunt Deb joined them.

Rob folded his hands around the mug and gazed into the black liquid. "She hardly spoke to me afterward."

Leaning forward in the chair, Aiden fixed his gaze on Rob. "After *what*? What did you do? You two never dated, but she used to like you."

"Back in high school, I—no, I was *always* attracted to your sister. Even as a little kid. It's why I teased her." He pursed his lips. "Never had the guts to tell her or ask her out. Then Chad, my cousin, asked her to our senior prom. He found pleasure in provoking me. The way he talked about Haley made me furious. He was the star quarterback, and the girls loved his attention, but he took advantage of them. Haley didn't show any interest in him, so he decided to go after her."

"Okay." Aiden's index finger tapped the table. "But why would it make her hate you?"

Rob took a drink and cleared his throat. "I wanted to ask her to the prom myself but had the idea you wouldn't like it. You were protective of her even when you were in college." He shot Aiden a hesitant glance. "If only I'd gotten up enough nerve."

Aiden slapped his hand on the table. "What does this have to do with Haley resenting you?"

"When I found out Chad asked her, and she'd accepted, I couldn't stand it. That rat had bragged he'd get what he wanted from Haley on prom night, one way or the other. You had such a temper where she was concerned, I was afraid of what you might do if I told you his plans. So...I—" He gritted his teeth.

"You what?" Aiden and Aunt Deb chimed in unison.

"I told Chad I'd already had the pleasure." He winced. "That Haley and I had been dating secretly because we didn't want you to find out. I told Chad the only reason she agreed to go with him was because we had an argument a few days earlier, and she wanted to make me jealous." He scrunched up his face and furrowed his brow like he expected a blow.

Aiden's jaw dropped. "How could you say such a thing about my sister?"

Aunt Deb's posture stiffened. She clasped Aiden's arm.

Rob opened his eyes and blinked at Aiden, then glanced at Aiden's aunt. "I'm so sorry. It was the first thing I thought of to make Chad call off the date and stop what he had in mind. I was afraid he'd go through with his plan to take her even if she resisted. He'd boasted of his conquests. I figured if there was no *conquest* to make, he'd cancel the date and take his regular girlfriend to the dance. Turns out, I was right."

Staring at his childhood friend, Aiden leaned back in the chair. "Why didn't you tell Haley what Chad said to you?"

"Stupidity. Didn't know how. Didn't think she'd believe me."

Aiden clenched his teeth. "It still doesn't tell us why Haley is mad at you. Did she find out what you said, and if she did, how?"

"Chad was a master at vindictiveness, which I hadn't considered at the time. He told Haley he had no use for used goods and decided to take Cicely to the dance instead. When he told me what he'd said to Haley, I decked him. What I should have done in the first place."

Steam radiated through Aiden. His jaw twitched.

His aunt touched his arm again. "Calm down, dear. It sounds more like Rob was trying to protect Haley in his own misguided way."

Aiden crossed his arms over his chest. "So I suppose word spread through the entire school that my sister was *easy* because of what you said. Were you out of your mind?"

Rob nodded and then rubbed his forehead. "Stupidity, pure stupidity. I didn't think, period. But honestly, I never presumed my cousin would say what he did to her. I expected him to break the date, but that's all. Then he started boasting about how he devastated her. After I slugged him, he said he didn't tell her what I'd said to him. And I never heard anyone else mention it. Chad didn't either." Rob dropped his head into his hands. "I should have confessed to Haley long ago, but I was ashamed of what I'd done. And now she hates me for it."

He stood and turned to leave. "I'm so sorry."

"Wait." Aiden rose from the chair. "If Chad didn't tell her, you never did, and there were no rumors. How did she find out?"

Rob stopped and turned. "I have no idea."

Aunt Deb stood. "The problem may not be this at all. I'll talk to her. But, Robert, you need to explain everything, including how you feel about her."

"Sit down, Rob." Aiden pushed the chair out further for him.

"I wish I could erase what I did."

"Even if it was a horrible idea, I understand why you did it. But you should have told me what was going on. You should have trusted me to take care of things."

"I realize that now. But you did have an Irish temper."

Aiden stifled a laugh. "I did. Still, the point is, you should have *trusted* me. Will you stay for dinner?"

When a light tap came to the bedroom door, Haley wiped her eyes with a tissue. Auntie's knock. "Come in."

After Aunt Debbie closed the door behind her, she sat next to Haley on the bed. "Are you okay, honey?"

"I will be. As soon as Rob leaves."

"Robert told us what he said to his cousin to get him to call off your date to the prom. He feels terrible."

"Sure he does. I've never been so humiliated in my life." She pulled another tissue from the box and blew her nose. "He actually told you what he said?"

"Yes. He also said he's never told anyone else. He was unaware you knew." She rubbed Haley's back. "Dear, Rob said there were no rumors, and his cousin hadn't revealed it. So, who did?"

Haley stood and paced her room. Heat rose from her neck to her face. "My heart was shattered. Not because I wouldn't go to the dance, but because someone I trusted slandered me. When Chad said he was taking the other girl instead of me, I shrugged it off and felt relieved because of his reputation. But up until then, he'd treated me with respect. Then he called me damaged goods and said I was nothing but a tease and a hypocrite. I was shocked. It was his way of getting out of the date, I assumed. I never dreamed Rob could tell him such a lie."

Aunt Debbie patted the bed. "Please sit down, dear. My vertigo is acting up with you walking back and forth. Tell me how you found out what Robert told him."

"The day after the prom," Haley dropped to the edge of the bed, "Lucy and I went to a movie. You remember her, don't you? Tall, short light brown hair, big hazel eyes, and always laughing?"

Her aunt nodded. "The girl who had a terrible crush on Aiden."

"Crush isn't the word. But he was head-over-heels for Charlotte, with her jet-black hair. Aiden always had a thing for girls with shiny black hair." A soft giggle escaped Haley.

"Anyway, Lucy and I were at the movie. Before it started, she told me how sorry she was that Rob had told such an ugly lie about me. I almost choked on my popcorn. She said she was sitting on the grass around the corner from where he and Chad talked. Chad boasted...what he'd planned for me. Then she heard Rob say it was too late, he'd already—" She clamped her lips shut with her teeth. "He makes me so mad."

Haley shot from the bed and kicked her beanbag chair. Tears surfaced and ran down her cheeks.

Aunt Debbie rose and pulled her into her arms. "There's more to the story."

"What do you mean?"

"Robert has cherished you since you were both very young, but he didn't have the nerve to ask you to the prom. When his cousin did and then bragged over what he planned for you afterward, Robert told the lie. It was the only way he could think of to make Chad leave you alone. But when Robert learned what the scoundrel said to you, he hit him."

Haley paced again. "So. This is his plan to get Aiden on his side? Don't believe him. It's a lie."

Aunt Deb sighed. "Dear, was there any gossip after what Chad said to you? Did anyone mention your supposed affair?"

"Outside of Lucy, no. I braced myself, but it never came." Haley leaned her ear to the door. "Is Rob gone?"

"No. As I left the kitchen, Aiden was chewing him out for not coming to him. I'm sure Robert will be at dinner. Why don't you and he talk after we eat? Give him a chance. You're both grown up now and can work this out. He needs to apologize, and you need to forgive. Don't you see he cares for you?"

"No, I don't. If the story got out, his reputation had just as much to lose as mine. So, he probably threatened Chad to keep him from telling anyone. If he didn't have malicious intent in what he said, why didn't he make things right? He never tried. He's a liar. And I don't trust him."

Chapter Six

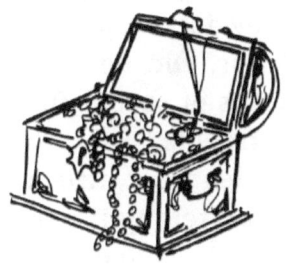

iden and Rob burst into the kitchen after their short walk in the barnyard. Aiden glanced around the room. "Where's Haley, Aunt Deb? Why isn't she helping you?"

"She's not feeling well. As you can expect." Aunt Deb laid her hand on Rob's shoulder. "Give her time. Right now, she's got her back up about your rash behavior in high school. She's been harboring that hurt for five years. All we can do is pray for Haley right now that her heart will soften, and she'll listen to reason."

"She doesn't believe me, does she?" Rob's eyelids drooped.

Aiden stepped toward the hallway. "She's got to eat, Aunt Deb. I'll get her." His aunt slid between him and the doorway.

"Let her be, Aiden. You don't know anything about a woman's broken heart." She blocked her next words with Aiden's frame and whispered. "She doesn't believe him. She doesn't trust him for some reason, best friend of yours or not."

He'd never understand that woman thing, as long as he lived. He pivoted and pulled out the chair from the table. "I guess she's not hungry. Doesn't mean we can't enjoy dinner. Have a seat, Rob."

As Aunt Deb placed the platter of meatloaf and the bowl of mashed potatoes on the table, Aiden fumed. He hadn't gotten angry with his sister many times, but he couldn't understand why she'd decided not to trust Rob. Surely, Aunt Deb had told her how remorseful Rob was. Tomorrow he'd talk to Haley...alone.

"So Rob, you heard my father was having difficulty with the crops this past few months. Did he tell your dad why? It seems strange, after all these years of successful farming, that Dad would suddenly have a string of trouble."

As they ate, Rob told Aiden what little he knew. "Don't know the details. Dad felt out of place telling me that much. He has to work on our farm, but he said if I wanted to help out here, it was fine with him. Our dads go back a long way, both having been raised on our pieces of land. Do you know any more than what I've told you?"

"No. I didn't know that much, but then, Dad wouldn't have discussed it with me. Ever since I was in high school, he knew I didn't have any desire to farm or raise horses. He recognized my interest in law as early as my freshman year and never pressured me to follow in his footsteps. Sis always had the heart for it. So, it's odd he didn't mention it to her." Aiden placed a forkful of meatloaf and gravy in his mouth.

Rob picked up his fork and stabbed a chunk of meat. "Maybe for the same reason he didn't tell you. You'd worry."

"Yeah. You're right. He'd kept everything under wraps while Haley worked so hard on her studies all last summer." Aiden glanced at Rob. "You know, her plan was to come back after graduation and use her skills to help Dad with advertising for the farm."

"Mrs. Moye, would you pass the salt and pepper?"

Aunt Debbie moved the shakers closer to Rob. "Sorry, I got used to keeping the seasonings on the low side for my late husband. He was a plain meat and potatoes kind of guy. Do you need any ketchup or steak sauce?"

Rob smiled at her. "The meatloaf is great, but if you don't mind, I could use ketchup. I put it on most of my meat."

A guffaw came from Aiden. "Remember how we used to tease you about your ketchup soup when we were in the lunchroom in high school? You used to drown everything in it."

"Ha! That was because most of the time, we were eating mystery meat."

Laughter filled the room for the first time since Aiden and Haley returned home. That felt good. Sure wish Sis would join us. Like old times. But it'd never really be like old times again. Not with Mom and Dad gone. Why hadn't the sheriff's department called yet?

Haley entered the kitchen as Aiden was helping their aunt clean up. "Has your *friend* left?"

Aiden scowled at her. "Yes. Rob went home. You beat all, Sis. Rob didn't have to tell us what happened between you two. But he did because he feels terrible about it, and even more so because you're still hurting from what he said. Can't you cut the guy some slack?"

Tears rushed to her eyes. "You have no idea how it felt. How it still feels." She spun on her heel and left the room.

Before she reached her bedroom door, Aiden came up behind her. He clutched her shoulder and made her face him. "Look, Sis, I'm sorry." He opened his mouth a couple of times, but no words came out.

Tears slid down her cheeks, and her brother enveloped her in his arms. "Can we talk?"

She nodded.

He let go of her, and they entered her bedroom. Aiden sat on the desk chair in the corner, and Haley hopped onto the bed. Several seconds of silence passed. The air hung heavy as they gazed across the room at each other.

"Haley. I've known Rob all our lives. He'd never intentionally hurt you. What he told Aunt Deb and me was that he said you and he had already...that you were—"

"I know what he told his cousin. Lucy had been nearby and heard what he said. She was shocked but didn't believe it. She waited until the next day to say something to me because she didn't know how to tell me."

"It must have been gut-wrenching to hear it. You and Lucy have been as close as Rob and me. She knows your character, so it's a good thing it was her who overheard it, if anyone had to. But just as much as she knew you well enough to not believe what was said, I know Rob. And I believe him that he said it without any thought to the consequences. He knew what Chad had planned to do to you after the prom, and it was all he could think of at the time. Stupid as it was. He figured Chad would just break the date with you, but he never thought he'd say what he did."

Anger burned in Haley's chest. "What right did he have to say anything? Why couldn't he just come to me and say something? Tell you. I think he was just being his old mean-spirited self again."

Aiden rose from the chair. "You've got that set in your mind and won't listen to anyone. You are the most stubborn redhead ever." He stormed out of her room, slamming the door.

There'd only been a couple of times in her life when she'd suffered the brunt of her brother's anger. She hated it when they fought, but she wasn't going to back down this time. It had always been her who asked forgiveness and compromised with Aiden. He was wrong this time, dead wrong.

His buddy Rob was a chameleon. He could change from person to person, depending on what he wanted. For as long as she could remember, he'd be nice to her one minute and the next, he'd say something to make her mad or even cry. But not with Aiden. With Aiden, Rob had always been the same, always there for him.

Why did she have to fall for that two-faced—no matter how he treated her? He was no better than Chad, except...no one ever spoke poorly of Rob.

The waterworks started again. Why couldn't she have met a nice guy at college? Someone she could have relied on and had fun with without the garbage that always started. All these years, Rob had never left her heart. And yet he broke it. She'd never forgive him for what he'd said. *Never.*

Footsteps traveled across the floor above her. Aiden had gone to his room. She glanced at the clock on the nightstand. Auntie was probably reading in the master bedroom by now. Haley's stomach growled. If she didn't eat, she'd probably wind up with a headache.

She quietly opened the door and tiptoed to the kitchen. After she sliced a piece of meatloaf and placed it on a dish, she added mashed potatoes and green beans. She'd zap it and take the food to her room.

By the time she'd put the rest of the leftovers away, and the microwave dinged, the room had filled with the aroma of her aunt's savory meatloaf. Her mouth watered.

With plate in hand, Haley headed for the hall. She snapped her fingers and stopped. *Forgot the milk.* She placed the plate on the table and took a glass out of the cabinet. With the refrigerator door open, she poured milk into the glass and then allowed the door to shut.

Facing the back door at the other end of the mudroom, she closed her eyes and took a sip of milk. When her eyes opened, a white face stared at her from the back door window—and disappeared.

Haley screamed. The tumbler slipped from her hand and dropped to the floor. Shards of glass and milk flew everywhere.

Chapter Seven

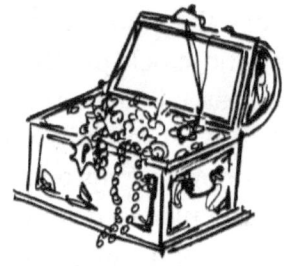

aley froze in place. *What was that?* She couldn't drag her eyes off the window where the strange face had appeared and then disappeared. Her heart raced.

Crunched glass behind her and a hand on her shoulder made her jump. She whipped around, ready to strike at whatever it was. "Aiden! It's you." She exhaled. "Did you see that face?"

"What face? Why did you scream? You scared the wits out of me."

Haley shook her head, attempting to erase the image, but lost her balance. She grabbed the back of the chair. So woozy. She glanced down to where her aunt knelt to gather large pieces of glass. When had Auntie come into the kitchen? "I'll get those, Aunt Debbie."

Her aunt threw the broken glass in the garbage. "Child, what on earth happened here? What made you scream like that?"

As her aunt grabbed the broom from the broom cabinet, Haley sucked in a deep breath. "A face." She turned and pointed to the backdoor. "Out that window. Staring at me. And then it disappeared."

Aunt Debbie's jaw dropped.

Aiden lowered his brows. "You're as pale as a ghost. Whose face?"

"A white face. That's all." Haley's body shook as she turned and buried her forehead in her brother's chest.

"What do you mean by a white face? Caucasian?" He wrapped his arms around her and led her to a chair. "Come over here and sit."

"No...no..." Her shoes crunched on bits of glass. "I have no idea what he...or she...was. But the face was white. Ghostly white—" *Was it a ghost?* "—as if covered with flour." She sat and peered at him. "But not pure white. More of a dead-person white."

Aunt Debbie picked up a few smaller pieces of the broken tumbler and discarded them into the garbage can, then swept. "Be careful, there's still a little glass left." She ran down to the cellar, returned with a handful of rags, and tossed them in the sink. After she wet and wrung the cloths out, she placed two on the floor and moved them back and forth with the broom.

Her aunt disposed of the glass-embedded material and used more rags to gather the remaining fragments from the floor. Haley watched as though everything moved in slow motion. She dropped her head to the table. "This can't be real." Had she lost her mind?

Sleep...she needed sleep. Haley lay back on the bed. She hadn't slept well since Aiden picked her up from college. Fatigue was the problem. She'd be fine after a good night of peaceful slumber. Hopefully, nothing else would happen.

After a soft knock on her door, her brother stepped into the room. "Aunt Deb said you might need this." He walked to her bed and placed a steaming cup on her nightstand. In his other hand, he held the plate she'd prepared for herself. He pushed the hot meal toward her.

Haley sat up in bed and took the offered food. "Thanks. I'm sorry I scared everyone tonight."

Aiden eased onto the edge of the bed and handed her a napkin. "It's okay, Sis. This has been such a strain on all of us. Maybe Aunt Deb only thought she saw things out there," he pointed to the window on the other side of her bed, "like you did in the kitchen."

"But, Aiden. I *did* see a face. And Auntie didn't imagine what she saw either. I'm sure of it. It may not have been a ghost or even a person, but something was there. When I glanced at the door, two eyes stared back at me, and just like that," she snapped her fingers, "it was gone."

He shook his head and gazed at the floor. "I ran outside as soon as you headed to the bedroom but found no evidence that anyone had been there. The sky's clear, so it wasn't likely a weird lightning flash. And no objects were near the window, only the mat at the back door."

After she'd taken a bite of the meatloaf, she eyed her brother. "You don't believe in ghosts. I don't either, no matter how adamant Drago is about them. There has to be an explanation for this. Something or someone looked in. I promise you."

Aiden leaned over and placed his elbows on his knees. He turned his head to face her. "Do you suppose Dad had made somebody mad at him, and these pranks are their way of getting even? Sounds foolish, though. Perhaps it's kids playing games. He might have chased them off the property, and this is their method of retaliation."

Haley sipped her tea and put the cup down with a clink, making a face. Why does everyone think tea solves everything? "How could kids manage these things without a trace?" She took a small bite of potatoes and glared at the window, which faced the back field. "When I was in the kitchen, I thought I'd lost my mind from the stress of Mom and Dad's deaths, but there's too much going on for this to be hallucination. And we *all* can't be imagining things—me, Auntie, Mom, Dad, and Drago. No. Someone's pranks are getting out of hand. That was definitely a face. And certainly not a ghost."

"You're right—too many incidents. Besides, kids would have left evidence. Has to be a clever adult. You may be on to something. I'll find out if anyone's made an offer to buy the place recently."

"Mom and Dad wouldn't sell our home." Haley lifted a forkful of meatloaf. "Not for anything. Remember Dad's stories about our ancestors who came here and worked so hard to get this piece of land from the Indians? How they struggled to survive until the farm became profitable. He inherited the place and planned to leave it to us. There's no way he'd sell."

As she placed the meatloaf into her mouth, she could visualize the gears turning in Aiden's head.

Slowly, he straightened. "The question is, who would go to such lengths?"

"Yeah. Also, how? And why?"

He rubbed his chin. "I can't think of anyone who would do something like this. Can you?"

"Off the top of my head, I can think of two people who might benefit from the sale of this property. Both live adjacent to us. If either acquired this land, they'd double their prime real estate."

Aiden stood. "Haley, you're talking about people we've known all our lives."

"People change. Rob's a *perfect example*, excuse the expression."

"Sis, his father would never do anything to hurt our parents or us. They were there for each other through the hardest of times over the years."

"Rob may have his own plans. After all, he'll inherit someday. Maybe he wants to expand."

"*Enough*, Haley. He made a terrible mistake, a bad judgment call. But just because you're mad at him and refuse to forgive him, that's no reason to accuse him of something so underhanded. Get— over—it!" Aiden rose and strode to the door.

She flinched and put the plate on the nightstand, then moved to the window. "I'm sorry." She viewed the field in the moonlight. Quiet tonight, so far.

He hadn't opened the door. She spun. "If it's not Rob or his folks, what about Mr. Lowell? He's never been friendly, always accused Dad of letting horses stray onto his property, and he even tried to claim the old stone barn on the border of our land, remember? Claimed his property line was several feet on our side of the building. Dad's lawyer won the case. Old Mr. Lowell might be at the bottom of this."

Haley resumed her position on the bed and watched Aiden. He removed his hand from the doorknob, turned, and leaned against the doorframe.

"I do recall that mess. After the battle, I decided to become an attorney so I could help people like Dad. But I thought Mr. Lowell died this year. I'm sure Mom mentioned it in one of the emails last spring."

"Okay, what about his family? Who inherits Mr. Lowell's property?"

"I'm not sure. After his wife left him, she took their only son to Italy. That must have been around twenty years ago. Mr. Lowell never remarried, so I guess his son is the heir. But why would he want to start trouble? He'd already have an immense estate. And he's a stranger here. He'd no doubt want to sell the house and land, then move back to Italy. He's lived there since he was five or six."

At another soft tap on the door, Aiden pushed himself off the frame.

Aunt Debbie stuck her head in. "Are you feeling better, dear?" She walked to the bed and grimaced at the food with only two bites taken. "You need to eat." She picked up the plate and held it in front of Haley until she took it.

"Okay." She took another bite of potatoes and swallowed. "Auntie, what do you know about Mr. Lowell, who lives on the east side of this property...and his family?"

Aiden pulled a desk chair to the bed. After their aunt sat, he lowered himself onto the bed next to Haley.

"Not much. Your parents had mentioned Mr. Lowell's death this spring, but nothing else. Why?"

While Haley ate, Aiden repeated her suspicions. "So, we wondered if the son has returned from Italy to claim the property."

"I have no idea. But I'll bet Cary does. People say women are gossips and busybodies, but he's got them beat hands down. Not that he's a gossip, but he stays apprised of everything that goes on everywhere in town, the country, the government. I'll wager everyone's personal business too." She chortled. "I haven't a clue where he gains his information, but if anyone wants to know something, they go to Cary." She gave them a quick nod.

Aiden popped off the bed. "Okay. We can ask Drago tomorrow."

Auntie pressed her lips together. "You'll have to wait until he's back. He went to Omaha to check on the orders your dad placed before the accident. Cary said he'd be back Thursday evening."

Three days. Haley sighed. And still no more word from the sheriff's department about Mom and Dad's *supposed* accident.

Chapter Eight

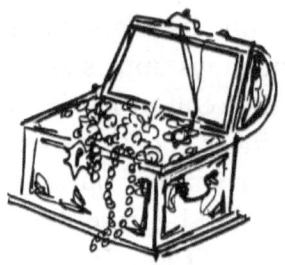

After their parents' funeral on Friday, Haley, Aiden, and Aunt Debbie conveyed their gratefulness to neighbors and friends who came to the house. Aiden excused himself to help his wife pack for the flight home to California, leaving Haley to see the guests off.

Haley's heart filled with gratitude for their friends and neighbors as they offered words of comfort and condolences. Would she be able to live up to the legacy her parents left? They'd been such a blessing to the community. "Thank you, everyone. Your kindness means more to us than you know."

As the last guest pulled out of the farmyard drive, Haley waved from the porch. She re-entered the house and shut the door.

Aiden descended the staircase, parking his wife and son's bags on the foyer floor. "Sis, I need to get Char and Everett to the airport, so they don't miss their flight to California."

Haley nodded. "Wish they could have stayed longer."

He returned her nod.

Char descended the stairs, her carry-on in one hand, and Everett's hand in the other. A small baby bump had blossomed on her otherwise trim sister-in-law.

Haley rushed up the steps and took the bag from her. "Char, it was great having you here even for only a couple of days. I know Aiden found comfort in you and Everett. I did too. Hope your mom feels better soon."

"Thanks, Haley. We'd stay longer if it weren't for Mom's surgery. She's so nervous. Outside of when she had us kids, she's never been in the hospital. But we'll be back for Christmas."

Aiden's arm circled Charlotte's shoulder. "Honey, I'll be home as soon as Haley's settled."

"Don't worry about us, dear. We'll be fine. This long drawn out business from the accident and the investigation has been hard on you and Haley. You take care of your sister right now." She smiled and kissed his cheek. As she turned to Haley and hugged her, Char retrieved her carry-on.

With a *whoomph*, Everett rushed to Haley and wrapped his arms around her legs as if she were his teddy bear. "Auntie Haley, wuv you."

"Awww, I love you too, little guy." She tousled his hair. "You be good and take care of Mommy. Okay?"

He nodded his little towhead and ran out the front door.

As Aiden and his family drove from the farmyard, Haley's eyes misted. She and Aunt Debbie waved until the car rounded the last bend in the long drive.

"Come on, Haley. Let's have a cup of tea. You can tell me which online courses you have, now that you've set them up, and how you plan to use what you've learned to improve the farm."

How did she always know when a distraction was needed? Just like Mom used to. Haley dragged her eyes from the driveway and smiled at her aunt. "Sure, Auntie. But make it coffee for me. I'm not much of a tea drinker."

For the next two hours, Haley and her aunt drank coffee and tea in the kitchen. Haley talked about the classes she'd complete for graduation in the spring. "I can't believe the last three years have flown by so fast. And yet, this past week has felt like an eternity. Auntie, will things ever feel normal again?"

"With God's help, I'm sure they will, dear. It'll take time, and things will never truly be the same, but you'll be okay. We learn to deal with life one day at a time."

The sound of tires on gravel surprised Haley. "Aiden must be back already."

He strode into the kitchen. "They're on their way to California." He ran a hand through his auburn curls.

His sad eyes made Haley's heart pinch.

Auntie rose and hugged him. "You'll be with them soon. From what Haley's told me, she has a good handle on school, and I'll come and help her whenever she needs me. Can I get you a cup of coffee?"

"No, thank you." He squeezed her shoulder. "Now that everyone's gone, I want to talk to Drago. What do you say, Sis?"

She agreed and followed Aiden out of the kitchen. In silence, they strolled to the stable. Letting his wife and son go home without him had been so hard on her brother. Best leave him to his thoughts.

They entered the building and searched front to back. How she had missed the fresh-cut grass smell of oats and hay while at Boulder. Not so much the other odors, though. She chuckled to herself.

As they passed the last stall, Haley stopped. A white substance scattered across the straw in the back corner caught her eye. "Aiden, look at this."

"What? It's just powder."

"Powder in a horse stall? Remember what I told you about the face in the window? Pale, as if flour covered it."

"I thought you said a dead-person white. Wouldn't that be more of a gray?"

"I was a little stressed at the time, but the exact color is beside the point." She bent to examine the substance. "How did this get here? Who'd use powder on horses?"

"What's going on, kids?" Drago came up behind Aiden.

Haley shot upright. Where had he come from? Quiet as a...ghost. "What's this stuff on the floor? And where are the horses?"

"Not sure, miss. I came in this morning and found it there. It might be the horse supplement we've given on occasion, but we haven't used it in some time. The horses seemed jittery this morning, so I put them in the corral. Figured I'd clean this up before I brought them back in."

Her lips tightened. Was he hiding something? Could *Drago* have been angry at Dad over something and wanted to get even?

Aiden bent and fingered the powder. He held it to his nose. "Smells like baby powder." He turned to Drago.

"Baby powder?" The farm manager's face scrunched.

Haley's brows rose. His response seemed a bit dramatic.

As Aiden brushed off his fingers, he glanced at Drago. "Where were you Monday night around ten o'clock?"

With his brows furrowed, Drago stared at the powder on the floor and then at Haley and Aiden in turn. "On my way to Omaha. Why?"

Haley tilted her head to the side and gazed at Drago, trying to recall who the white face might resemble. "Someone watched me through the kitchen door window. Scared me half to death. Whoever it was had a very white face." She stooped down to the powder again. "Maybe from this."

Drago's face turned ashen.

"Don't get superstitious on us, Drago." She rose again. "We know you believe in ghosts, but we don't. If ghosts did exist, they wouldn't need to put powder on their faces."

He blew out a long breath. "Miss Haley, Aiden, I haven't the foggiest about that white stuff, but no one can convince me there aren't haunts that roam around here. I've heard those legends your dad told all my life. And I've seen things."

She opened her mouth to protest, but Aiden's quick shake of the head told her she'd best leave the subject alone. No sense stirring the pot. "*Someone* was outside the kitchen that night, and *someone* put this here. I want to know who."

Her brother grabbed her arm. "Haley, let's take a look around. Drago, thanks for explaining what that white stuff might be."

"You two be careful out there." Drago latched onto the stable broom leaning against the tack box and entered the stall.

After a nod, Aiden pulled Haley out of the stable.

When they cleared the building and rounded the corner, Aiden stopped. Had Drago really gone to Omaha? "Haley, Monday night after you left the kitchen and I checked outside, there was a light on at Drago's, and a shadow passed by a downstairs window. Auntie said he'd gone to Omaha. If true, who was in the bunkhouse?"

"Good question. Let's go ask him." She turned and headed back into the stable.

"No. Let it go for now. If he hadn't left yet, and he's the one who scared you, we won't get a straight answer. I don't want to believe Drago's responsible, but I need to find out if he went to Omaha or not. And when. Just to settle the question in my mind."

"But we didn't ask him about Mr. Lowell's son yet."

Aiden grimaced. "The powder got us sidetracked. Come on." He led her back to the stall where they found the powder. The white substance was gone, and Drago was nowhere in the building. Now where'd he go? Aiden pushed the door to the corral open, and they stepped out. Only the horses were there. Where could he have gone so fast? Movement across the field caught Aiden's attention. A shadow disappeared into the woods.

He grabbed his sister's hand. "Come on." They sprinted across the corral. When they reached the back, he released her and vaulted over the top of the fence.

Haley doubled over and slid between two rails, then continued her dash after him across the field. "Aiden, where are we going?"

"The woods. Someone ducked into them. Couldn't make out who, but we'll find out. Hurry."

As daylight sent shafts of light through the canopy of dried leaves above, they ran past the clearing where Drago cut wood and deeper into the grove. Aiden halted and surveyed the area while catching his breath. They had to be in the middle of the woods. He searched the ground for a trace of the direction the individual had taken. "That's just great."

"What?" Haley asked as she panted.

"No footprints, thanks to the thick carpet of leaves. No way to tell if they turned toward the Lowell place or the stone barn at the corner of our property."

She stepped between two saplings. "Why don't you go to the Lowell farm, and I'll go to the old barn? That way, one of us should discover who's out here, and why. But if it was Drago, why would he be out here? He was never fond of Mr. Lowell and hates that barn. More of his superstitions."

Aiden frowned. "I've no idea. Haven't a clue about much of anything lately, but you'll not traipse off into the woods alone. That's for sure. We'll both check the barn, and if no one's there, we'll cut across to the Lowell property. If it wasn't Drago, then whoever it was is probably long gone by now anyway. Hopefully, it was just Drago, and he has a good reason for being out here. If we find him, we can ask about Lowell's son."

Haley and Aiden approached the old stone barn. She shook her head. This place hadn't changed. Still creepy, even if it was beautiful in its own way. "Remember when we used to play cowboys and Indians out here? We never did tell Mom and Dad. We'd have been skinned alive after they'd warned us against playing up there." She pointed to the hayloft door. "But the structure sure appears sturdy for being well over a hundred years old."

"Yeah, I remember. Dad said things were built to last back then, but he still didn't want us in the loft, or in the barn." He stepped closer and ran his hand over the weather-worn ten to fifteen-inch gray boulders used to construct the lower left side of the barn. "Check out these stones." He pounded on the rocks with his fist. "Still solid. Can you imagine the work it took to put this up? I'll bet the loft floor is undamaged too. I wonder what's up there."

"You are *not* going up there, Aiden."

"Nah, just wondering."

Haley touched the dark brown doors. "Why is it called a stone barn when most of it is made from wood?" She stepped back and inspected the second floor where the loft would be.

"I guess because of these stones. Someone started to call it that, and it stuck."

When a twig snapped behind them, Haley jumped and spun. Rob stepped from behind a clump of shrubs.

"Hi, Rob." Aiden held out his hand. "What are you doing out here?"

Haley's jaw tensed. Exactly what she wondered. "Yeah. Why *are* you here? This isn't your property."

Rob's eyes grew wide. "I know that. Your folks said they didn't mind if I wandered the woods when I needed downtime. When things trouble me, I come out here where it's nice and quiet...and *usually* peaceful. I sit on the old stone fence in the rear of the barn. Imagine what life must have been like back when this was built."

He sauntered to the barn and laid his hand on the stones. Then he turned. "Sorry we had to leave so soon after the funeral. Mom had one of her sinus headaches and needed to go home, but I'm sure she'll call when she feels better."

Haley bit her bottom lip. She shouldn't have jumped down his throat. He'd always loved this place. Said he'd write a story about it someday, but that would never happen if he still planned to be a farmer. There'd be too much work to do...unless...he expected to have enough profit from a *bigger* farm. And get a lot more help.

Aiden sat on a stump. "Did you see anyone else out here a little while ago? Someone entered the woods from the other side, and we decided to see who. Was it you?"

"No. I came from our farm and followed the back section of trees. Didn't come across anyone out here."

Haley glared at Rob as if she could read his mind by staring at his skull. *Quit.* Maybe Aiden was right. This anger over Rob's actions in high school didn't do her any good. But she doubted she'd ever be able to forgive him.

She lowered herself to the ground next to the stump where Aiden rested and crossed her legs.

Rob leaned against a tree across from her and gave her a half-smile. "Haley, I—"

Her hand flew up to stop him. "I don't want to talk about it."

With a sigh, he closed his mouth.

"Rob," Aiden picked up a yellow-green ash leaf and inspected it, "we need information on the Lowell family. Weren't your dad and Mr. Lowell friends at one time? Can you tell us anything? Has the man's son come back from Italy? Have you met him?"

Haley peered at Rob, who dragged his eyes from her to Aiden. Her heart pounded.

"Dad and Mr. Lowell were friends, but just before I left for college, they had a falling out. Dad would never talk about it, but as far as I know, they never spoke to one another after that. Mom wasn't fond of the man, but she never said why. Haven't seen the son. A few months back, Dad mentioned that Mr. Lowell's son had returned. Is something wrong?"

In one easy motion, Haley rose from the ground. Good thing she'd kept up her exercises the past three years at school. She'd need strong leg muscles now that she'd come home to stay and work.

Aiden stood. "Let's take a walk to the edge of the property and see what's going on at the Lowell place."

Chapter Nine

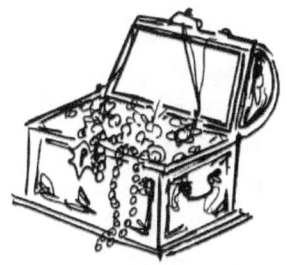

aley, Aiden, and Rob arrived at the edge of the woods where the MacKenna land ended and the Lowell farm began. They walked across the old dirt road. Haley hopped over the shallow ditch on the other side. She squinted against the sunlight to view the buildings across the harvested field between them and the Lowell house. Could that shadow have been Mr. Lowell's son?

When the sound of Aiden and Rob's footsteps stopped, she turned. "Aren't you coming?"

"Not me." Rob shook his head and raised his brows. "You shouldn't go any further, either. Mr. Lowell was adamant that people stay away from his place. Don't know what his son's like, so I won't take a chance at getting shot."

"You've got a point." Aiden nodded. "The father was rumored to be trigger-happy, even if the shots went over people's heads. The apple may not have fallen far from the tree, as they say." He motioned for Haley to return.

She frowned and backed away from the wire fence surrounding the Lowell field. "People have cut across everyone else's property around here for ages. When we were kids anyway. Although...I don't recall going near the Lowell farm in the last several years." She studied Rob's face. It was out of character for him to be afraid of anything.

She searched her brother's face for any sign of fear. "Aiden, were you ever on Mr. Lowell's property?"

"No. Dad warned us to stay away from here when we were young. I'm not sure why, but I didn't want to make him angry."

A slight snicker escaped Haley's lips. "You were always such a good little boy. Never got in any trouble."

"Not that I got caught for, miss smarty-pants." He laughed. "I was careful when I did something I shouldn't have. But when it came to this place, Dad spoke in such a serious tone, it scared me out of any desire to venture here." He glanced at Haley. "You, on the other hand, little tomboy, were always in trouble."

She threw a clump of sod at his stomach.

Rob laughed. "I remember you got in Dutch with your Mom a lot, Haley."

The smile on her lips drooped. She glared at him. Again with the teasing. *Don't let him get to you.* "So, what are we going to do, just stand here? This won't get us any information." She focused on the barn across the field. "Aiden, look." A man strode toward them from the building.

A hand grabbed Haley's arm and pulled her back to the ditch. "Let go of me."

"Hush, Sis. Rob just pulled you behind the property line." Aiden leaped over the ditch to join them.

She eyed Rob's hand still on her arm. Guess he wasn't too afraid of Mr. Lowell.

As the man wearing snug charcoal gray slacks and a half-unbuttoned light blue shirt neared, he drew a cigarette from his lips. A mop of pale blond hair fluttered every which way in the breeze. "Can I help you?" A plume of smoke billowed upward.

Her brother stepped forward and extended his hand. "Hello. Aiden MacKenna. We were walking in the woods and lost our bearings. Didn't realize it until we wound up here at the old road."

The man's eyes pinned to the hand thrust out to him. He took it in his and stared at Aiden as they shook. "Nice to meet you. I'm Craig Lowell. I came back to the States a few months ago when my father died."

Haley stepped up beside her brother and held a hand out to Craig. "I'm Aiden's sister, Haley. We heard your dad had passed away—our condolences. I understand you lived in Italy. It's too bad it had to be these circumstances that brought you back. Can we do anything for you?" Handsome, even if rather thin. Late twenties, maybe? Those were the palest blue eyes she'd ever seen.

As he shook her hand, he stretched his neck and peered over her shoulder. "And you are?"

Haley wiggled her hand out of his tight grasp. What a clammy hand. Her hand would reek of nicotine. She peeked at Rob. His eyes narrowed. What was wrong with him?

Without offering his hand, he stepped up to Craig. "We met in town a month ago. Though you neglected to give me your name then."

Craig smirked.

Haley narrowed her eyes at him. The man did smile. But she'd hardly call it friendly. What was up with these two?

"Oooh, yes. I remember now." He shook his index finger toward Rob. "You're the son of that man who swindled my dad out of his land. The piece of land you walked through to get here if I'm not mistaken." Craig pointed to the forest and took a drag on his cigarette. He exhaled. "No, wait. It had an old relic of a barn on it. Must be on the other edge of the woods." He threw the burning butt on the ground near Rob's foot.

Haley stiffened. He must have meant their land. The Sheffield's farm didn't even touch his. *Hope Rob doesn't get mad.* "Mr. Lowell is mistaken, of course. Your dad's property line is well away from his." She laid her hand on Rob's forearm.

As Craig crushed the glowing cigarette with his boot, he snickered.

Rob gazed at Haley's hand on his arm and then at her face. He smiled and placed his hand over hers. "That's right. And my father never swindled anyone."

Haley withdrew her hand.

Rob turned his attention back to Craig. "You should check your facts before you make accusations like that. And, you should be careful with those cigarettes before you start a fire." He spun on his heel. "Need to get back to my work at home."

She watched as he disappeared into the woods. He could've flattened Craig with one blow. She'd seen him do it to a guy who got physical with him in high school. Even when they were little, he was strong from the work he did on the farm. She let out a sigh of relief. *Get your mind off him.* "Maybe we should go too." She turned back to Aiden.

He didn't move or acknowledge her. His eyes were glued on Craig's. "What do you mean swindled out of *his* land?" Aiden's eyes narrowed. "This is our land, including the old barn...as well as this road my dad had put in."

Heat rose in Aiden's neck. This son of Mr. Lowell's was trouble.

Craig cocked his head and glowered. "I suppose you think that land and barn are on what you call *your* property. But it's not."

"It *is* our property. That matter was settled in court years ago."

"Of course, it was. A court in a town run by your family who's been here since before the Indians left. Honest and above board all the way, right?" He turned and stomped away.

"Aiden, what's he saying?"

Taking Haley's arm, Aiden led her back into the woods, gulping deep breaths to calm his ire. When they were well within the privacy of the trees, he stopped and faced her. "Haley, he claims the court settlement from years back wasn't fair. Dad told me Mr. Lowell never gave up on his allegation that the stone barn was on the property his family bought from our ancestors. Now his son argues the court ruled in favor of our father because our family runs the town and everyone in it. This guy's trouble."

"He can't have the judgment overturned, can he?"

Aiden resumed his quick pace through the thicket toward the house. "Not sure. Hard to tell what he has in mind. I'll have to research the issue. He reminds me of the last lawyer I faced in court. Nitpicked everything."

Haley smiled at him. "Did you win?"

He returned her smile. "As a matter of fact, I did."

"Then we don't have to worry." She hurried past him and broke into a run as they neared the edge of the woods. "Beat 'ya home."

Haley reached the house first. She always could outrun her brother. *Mmm.* As she opened the back door, the aroma of cake filled her nostrils. "Smells wonderful in here, Auntie. But aren't there enough goodies from everyone who came over after the funeral?"

Aiden came in and stood behind his sister.

Aunt Debbie's eyes shone red. "I had to stay busy to keep my mind off this morning. It's hard to believe my big sister won't be here anymore."

The siblings rushed to envelop her in their arms.

"It's okay, Auntie." Haley kissed her cheek. "You've held the pain in to be strong for us. Let it out. And remember what you told me. One day at a time."

Aunt Debbie laid her hand on Haley's cheek. "You're such a dear. Thank you."

For a few minutes, the three of them stood next to the table and nibbled from a half-emptied platter of lunch meats. Then Aunt Debbie placed her hands on her hips. "At this rate, I'll be as wide as I am tall. Now, where'd you two go earlier? I thought you wanted to talk to Cary, but when I saw him out with the horses, neither of you were with him. You were gone longer than I expected."

With a slight shake of the head, Haley shot a warning glance at Aiden. *Don't tell Auntie someone was snooping on the property. Not now while she's upset.*

He nodded. "Haley and I decided to take a walk to check out the old stone barn. We wanted to see if it still stood. Haven't ventured out there for several years."

Auntie moved the tray of meat to the back counter. "I haven't been out there in years either. Does it?"

"It sure does." Haley pulled out a chair from the table and took a seat. "That old barn'll last forever. Solid as a mountain. Whoever built it sure knew what they were doing."

Her aunt turned her head and shook a finger. "Don't you test that theory. I remember how your dad warned you two to stay out of that barn. He said the walls may be solid, but that didn't mean the upstairs floor was."

Aiden chuckled. "Don't worry, Aunt Deb. Neither of us is a kid anymore, and we've no desire to climb around in an ancient barn."

"Good!" She placed the lunch meat into a storage container, returned to the table with a pot of coffee, and set it on a trivet. "I'll put the rest of this food away after a break. Besides, it's lunchtime. Do you mind if we eat this?" She motioned to a large bowl of salad on top of an ice-filled dish in the middle of the table.

Haley grinned. "Not at all. Someone has to, and there's so much of it. With this and the food everyone brought over and packed into the fridge, we won't need to buy groceries or even cook for a week."

While she passed out paper plates, Aiden gave them each a set of flatware from the jars still on the table. Aunt Debbie handed out napkins.

Aiden eyed Haley and then their aunt. "Aunt Deb, Monday night when I asked if Mr. Lowell's son had returned from Italy, you told me to ask Drago, but I'd have to wait until he got back from Omaha. Did you see him leave that night?"

"Yes, I saw him go. He returned very late last night, but he's back now. He was at the funeral, remember. Didn't you see him when you went out?"

"I did—we did. He talked with us for a while at the church. And a little while ago. But I need to know if he actually did go to Omaha."

"I'm sure he did. Let's see. I walked him out to his truck and watched him drive away. Oh! I almost forgot. This morning he handed me receipts. Hang on." She reached into her purse on the corner of the counter and pulled out several papers. "Here, Haley. He said you'd need them for taxes." She glanced at Aiden. "Why do you ask?"

Haley took the receipts and laid a hand on Aiden's forearm. Aiden patted his sister's hand. "I wondered if he'd left later, and I missed my chance to talk to him that night. That's all."

"Oh. Would you give the blessing, Aiden?"

Haley's brows pinched as she closed her eyes for prayer. The receipts were from Omaha and time-stamped. *So if it wasn't Drago that night in the bunkhouse, who was it?*

Chapter Ten

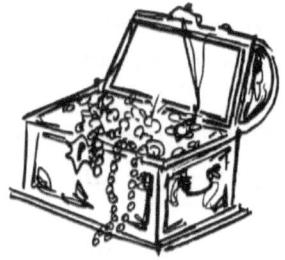

Rob finished his chores and cleaned up in the barn. He hadn't thought about it until today, but why was Craig Lowell in the lawyer's office in town last month? He'd have thought the legalities of Lowell's inheritance would have been settled by now. When Craig barreled out of the building that day, he almost knocked Dad into the street.

Did Craig plan to have the property-line case reopened? Rob wiped his face, hair, and arms with a towel, and strode to the house. He and his father had introduced themselves to Lowell, but the snob just turned and walked off. That Lowell really thought he was something.

Seemed way too interested in Haley today, but she saw through his suave demeanor. Rob bounded up the back steps of the late nineteenth-century clapboard house and swung the door open. He had his own plans for her...if he could ever convince her to forgive him for the lie he'd told in high school. What a mess. Had he found his way into her good graces this morning? Shivers had skittered across his skin when she touched his arm.

As he entered the kitchen, his mother peered over her coffee cup. "Robbie. I didn't hear you go out after we got back from the funeral. I thought you were in your room. Where'd you go?"

"Sorry, Mom. I had to meditate, and you know me. I do it better on my feet. Didn't plan to stay out that long. Is your headache gone?" He turned a kitchen chair backward and straddled it.

"Yes, thank you. Almost gone, anyway. My sinuses give me a fit at this time of year. Speaking of seasons, the corn maze in Fontanelle promises to be lots of fun. Prizes to win and everything." She rose and patted his shoulder. "You should invite Haley and Aiden to go. It'd do them good to get out and relax after this tragedy with their parents."

Yeah, right. As if Haley'd go anywhere with him. Maybe Aiden could talk her into it. "You're right, Mom. Thanks for the suggestion."

His father lowered his newspaper, took a drink from his mug, and looked at Rob. "What's got you thinking so hard these past couple of days, boy? Someone with strawberry-colored hair?" Tongue-in-cheek, he leaned back in the chair and eyed Rob. The smile on his dad's face grew.

Rob laughed. "Several things were on my mind."

"Nice to have Pete's son and daughter home." His dad folded the paper and put it aside. "I can't understand how an accident like the MacKennas' could happen."

While his father expanded on his opinion, Rob's mother took a hamburger from the refrigerator, placed it on a plate, covered it with a paper towel, and slid it into the microwave. She placed the bottle of ketchup in front of Rob. "You must be starved after loading all that hay before the funeral." While the burger warmed, she poured him a glass of milk.

"Mom, don't make anything for me. I ate enough at the MacKennas' to last the entire day."

"Nonsense. You'll be hungry within the next hour even after you've devoured your hamburger and the rest of these chips." She tossed the potato chip bag from the counter onto the table. It landed with a crunch. "Boys are never full. You and Dad will be back out in the fields this afternoon."

Dad laughed. "Son, I learned a long time ago not to argue with your mother when she decides to do something. Just eat your burger."

Rob grinned at his father. "What did you say about the MacKennas' accident?"

"Huh? Oh. I said it sounded strange to me. I've ridden with Pete many times, and he's the most careful driver I've ever seen."

"Aiden wondered the same thing. He's convinced it wasn't an accident and talked to Jason Schumaker about it. Jason said the sheriff's department is still investigating."

"Does Aiden suspect anyone in particular? Who'd want to harm the MacKennas? Never heard anyone speak ill of them, and nobody could've asked for nicer neighbors."

The earlier scene at the edge of the MacKenna property popped into Rob's head. Old man Lowell was someone who had a grudge against them. His son probably talked to the lawyer about the old land dispute. "What about old man Lowell? He had a beef against them. His son might have one too."

Rob's dad took a gulp of coffee. "Yes, Tom Lowell did. But it was a while ago. You kids were still young, in high school. And the claim was settled in court."

As the reheated hamburger was slid in front of him, the aroma of grilled beef and onions made Rob's mouth water. "Thanks, Mom."

She patted his cheek and left the room.

Between bites of food and sips of milk, Rob explained the encounter with Craig Lowell at the edge of his farm. "I was so mad I could have strangled the guy when he accused you of swindling his father. But then Haley said he was mistaken. I left right away because I didn't want to mention the dispute between their dad and Lowell's father."

Rob's dad nodded. "Just as well. Let him find out on his own."

After Rob swallowed the last bite of hamburger and washed it down with the remains of the milk, he wiped his mouth with a napkin. "You never told me why you and Mr. Lowell had a falling out."

His father rubbed his chin and shook his head. "Your mother didn't want me to tell anyone. Mr. Lowell had his eyes on her. Whenever she'd run into him in town, he'd make a pass at her. She told him she was a happily married woman and wasn't interested in his attention. But it didn't stop him."

Rob's dad lifted his mug and swallowed a mouthful of coffee. "One night, when she left the mall, and no one else was around, he came up behind her and attempted to pull her into his car. She jammed her elbow into his ribs, stomped his foot with her spiked heel, and jumped into our vehicle. Then she sped out of the parking lot before he even got into his car. Didn't stop until she was home. Not even for the red light in the middle of town. Fortunately, no cars were at the intersection. When she got home, she finally told me she was afraid of him."

Heat rose in Rob's neck. "That *rat*."

With a stack of dishtowels in her arms, Rob's mother stepped back into the kitchen.

"No wonder you and Mom never spoke to Mr. Lowell again."

His mom dropped the towels onto the counter and stared at her husband. "You told him?"

"Honey, he's old enough to know."

"But it's so embarrassing."

Rob smiled at her. "It should have been for him, Mom. Not you. I love the way you handled the situation, though. You should teach self-defense methods to other women. Hope you stomped him good."

She turned and snickered. "I did."

His dad snickered too. "It tickled me to see Lowell limping around for a week afterward."

"But what did you do, Dad? Call the sheriff?"

"When your mother told me it wasn't the first incident, I wanted to knock his block off. She calmed me down and said she thought there was something mentally wrong with him."

She sat at the table and folded her hands. "Narcissism is what it's called. I'd read about it. He didn't think he'd committed any offense. People like him don't. Everything they do is okay, and they have a right to do what they want."

His dad affectionately patted her hands. "Later, I paid him a visit. Told him if he ever bothered my wife again, he'd regret it. He stayed clear of us after that."

"Good." But if he remembered right, Mom despised Mr. Lowell even before that. As soon as his wife left him. It may have been what started his pursuit of Mom in the first place. "You did report it to the sheriff's department, though, right?"

"I talked your mother into filing a complaint, but there was nothing the authorities could do. No witnesses. Her word against his. They hadn't had complaints from anyone else."

She stood and put the towels in the cabinet. "After that, I made sure to always stay around other people."

"But, Dad, getting back to what happened this morning, I don't understand how Mr. Lowell's son would've known about the property dispute between his father and Mr. MacKenna when he's been in Italy for years?"

"I overhead Tom Lowell tell the bank manager he'd kept in touch with his son. He probably mentioned it to him." Dad tapped his finger on the table for a second and then bobbed his head. "Yeah. In court, Tom and his lawyer said Pete MacKenna had *swindled* him out of the land."

Rob ran the tip of his tongue across the inside of his bottom lip as he thought. If the sheriff's department had completed their investigation and determined the crash *not* to have been an accident, Craig Lowell would be a likely suspect.

Early that evening, Rob and his dad returned from the barn to the house. Nuts, he'd forgotten to call Aiden about the corn maze. "Wow! I'm soaked in sweat. Sure wish we'd get some cooler days, but I suppose I'll complain it's too cold when October comes."

His father nodded. "You're right. We both will. A shower'll feel real good. Got any plans for this evening, or will you stick around home for a change?"

"I meant to ask Aiden if he and his sister wanted to go to Fontanelle for the pumpkin festival. They could use something to lighten their spirits. Hope you don't mind."

A hearty slap on his back from his dad gave the answer.

As they entered the kitchen, the aroma of Mom's spaghetti sauce with garlic and herbs greeted them.

Rob shut the door behind him. "Wow! Smells great in here. I'm as hungry as an old bear."

"Don't be silly, Robbie. I doubt an *old* bear would be all that hungry. As for a young one," she glanced over her shoulder and winked at him, "he'd be ravenous." She giggled and stirred the pot of sauce.

His father slapped Rob's back again and guffawed. "She's got ya there, Son."

"Eeuuu!" She covered her mouth and nose. "Showers. Both of you. Now. And use plenty of soap. You brought the barn in with you." She shooed them away.

Rob raced up the back stairs to the bathroom. No way would he want to smell like a barn when he called on Haley tonight. He stuck his head into the shower stall and turned the hot water tap. Then he headed to the dresser to pick up his cell to see if he'd missed any calls while working. None. Rob punched in Aiden's number.

The phone rang twice and connected. "Hi, Rob, what's up?"

"I wondered if you and Haley want to run over to Fontanelle with me this evening for some fun. The 4-H group has the Great Pumpkin Patch Festival going. You two need to relax. They have a terrific corn maze, and this year there's a hayride with a country music sing-a-long. Your sister has such a beautiful voice. I've missed hearing it."

"Sounds good to me. I'll ask her." Footfalls echoed through the cell. "Hey, if you have time, what do you say to fishing tomorrow?" A firm knock sounded next. "Hang on, Rob."

Their voices were muffled. Aiden must have the phone pressed against him.

"Rob? Haley isn't done with her online work yet."

"Oh." He knew it. She refused.

"What time do you want to go? We haven't eaten dinner yet."

A smile spread across Rob's face. She did want to go. "Tell her to take her time. I haven't eaten either. I'll swing by around six. Okay?"

"Sounds good, buddy. We'll be ready."

Rob ended the call and pitched the cell onto the bed. Maybe she'd forgiven him after all.

Haley racked her brain, trying to figure out the answer to a question at the end of the session's online quiz. Her professor had covered this only a month ago. How could she have forgotten it already? She stuck her tongue in the corner of her lips. "Of course!" She typed in her response and submitted the test.

"Whew!" These online courses wouldn't be so bad. But she sure missed Kayla. Phone calls just weren't the same. Funny how people could get so close to you. Even their first year as roomies, Kayla had become more like a sister. Lucy had filled that role until she moved away. Then they'd lost touch. They used to talk online all the time.

It was hard not having another female her age to chum around with. *Sure hope Kayla can visit soon.*

As Haley closed the laptop, Aiden sauntered in. "Aunt Deb said dinner will be ready in a few minutes."

"Good. I was hung up on the last question in the quiz, but then it burst into my head. These online classes will work out fine. It's just lonely. And I should have helped Aunt Debbie with dinner."

"Hey, it's okay. Aunt Deb wants to do everything while you settle back in and get used to things. There'll be plenty to do once she goes home."

Haley stood and stretched. "I suppose you're right. Hope there's something on TV tonight. Or we can watch a DVD and eat popcorn. We could use the downtime."

"Sis, I told you Rob is taking us to the pumpkin festival at six."

Her mouth dropped open. "And I told you I had to finish an assignment."

"Yes, and you did."

"No. I don't want to go anywhere with him." She peered at Aiden's face and bit her lip. "I'm sorry."

"Sis. It's been a stressful few days. Can't you ease up and allow us to have a fun evening? He said there's a corn maze...and a hayride. Oh, and a country music sing-a-long. You love to sing. You'll have a good time. I promise."

Haley sighed. Aiden was right. They'd been stressed since the news about their parents. He deserved to relax, and Rob was his best friend. If she didn't go with them, her brother would worry about her the entire evening. The sheriff's department had a patrol car in the area to ensure no more mischief went on at the farm, so he needn't be concerned. But knowing him.... "Does Auntie want to go?"

"No. I asked. She said she wanted to read this evening, not traipse around a cornfield or pumpkin patch." He laughed. "But she said to have a good time."

There was nothing she could do. She'd have to go and endure Rob's company. For her brother's sake.

Chapter Eleven

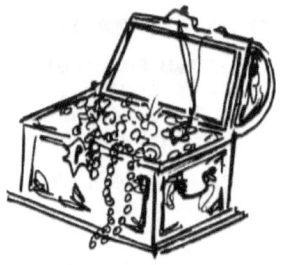

A s Rob pulled his parents' car into the field used for parking at the Murphys' farm, squeals and laughter met Haley's ears. Kids ran in every direction. She giggled to herself as they passed a petting pen with young animals the children could touch.

A little boy thrust his hand between the wires just short of a calf. The baby cow turned its head and licked the pudgy hand. "Eeuuu! He's cute but yukky, Mom." His mother pulled a handkerchief from her purse and wiped off the slime. As soon as she released him, he darted off as fast as a pony, running across the field toward the castle-shaped bounce house and slide.

If only life could feel that light and carefree again.

Her eyes locked onto Rob as he parked the car. It was thoughtful of him to suggest an evening like this. And to borrow his parents' brand-new Impala instead of driving his truck. She didn't have to squeeze into the little space in the back...or sit between him and her brother. Aiden would have insisted on that.

Rob sacrificed the little bit of free time a farmer has during harvest season to take them to the pumpkin festival.

As Aiden swung the door open for her, his hand ran over the shiny metallic blue. "Man, this is a beaut of a car."

Rob sprinted around the front of the vehicle and joined them. "Isn't it, though? Sure beats my ten-year-old, blood-red rattletrap of a truck." He glanced at Haley.

She looked away and suppressed a smile. That old truck had always been a favorite of hers in high school. Rob had driven her home often. Aside from his teasing, he'd always been so sweet until—

Haley shook her head. The atmosphere here should lighten the heaviness she and Aiden had on their hearts for the past week. Tonight, she'd do her best to believe Rob was sincere in his apology for the hurt he caused her in high school. They all did stupid things back then—things they regretted.

Rob peeked at her from the other side of her brother. She smiled at him, and he grinned.

He waved his hand toward the moving crowd of people. "Come on. Let's get into the maze. I hear it's a pretty good one this year. They've included more dead ends where there's a clue to find the prize. The Murphys advertised the treasure to be dinner for two at one of Omaha's best steakhouses. When the maze closes at the end of October, all the winners' names will go into a drawing for the grand prize of a trip for two to Hawaii."

"Wow!" For the first time since they'd come back to North Bend, Haley's heart lightened at the prospect of something fun to do. "That's quite a prize and incentive."

"Makes me want to try harder to find those clues." Rob laughed and walked backward as he spoke. "They've set up some dead ends as outdoor rooms with benches and tables, like a patio, but I heard they're hard to find. In each one, we'll search for a hidden clue.

Only after we've found all the clues, do we leave the maze. If we can find our way out." He chuckled and spun to walk forward again. Next to Haley this time. "Then, we solve the clues and find the treasure. It gets harder every year to find your way out of the maze, so let's stay together."

Not another treasure. Haley rolled her eyes. Aiden had mentioned it, but she'd only half-listened back at the house. Oh, brother. Haley slapped her palm to her forehead. "Is this community *treasure-happy*?" She glanced at Aiden.

He laughed and squeezed her shoulders. "Sis, I know what you think of the old family legend, but let's not let it spoil our fun for tonight. Okay?"

She bumped the side of her head against his arm. "Okay. But I'm so tired of that story. When we were growing up, every family get-together turned into a *treasure*-fest. Always the traditional rundown of how the treasure was buried by the pirate," she spun her hand in circles over her head, "and how our ancestor dug it up and reburied it where the farm is now, but no one's ever found it."

Aiden caught her hand. "Calm yourself, grasshopper. That isn't entirely true, and you know it."

"Oh, yes, it was found and rehid, and *now* no one knows where it is. It almost made me glad I was away at school for most minor holidays." She frowned. "Why'd you call me grasshopper?"

"Sorry, I guess I picked it up from my father-in-law at the firm. He's always saying that. He says he got it from some old TV program about a Kung Fu something or other he used to watch. He says it when an employee gets upset over something. It makes me laugh."

"Oh. Oka-a-ay." She giggled. "So, all right, I'm game for this hunt. I'm good at puzzles...or clues, in this case."

Rob gave her a thumbs-up and nodded. "You were. I remember when we used to put those thousand-piece jigsaw puzzles together. You found ten pieces to Aiden's and my one."

She remembered those times. But it was Rob who was so good at them. He was trying to butter her up. *Quit. They were both good at the puzzles—something they had enjoyed together.*

"This sounds like fun." Aiden drew Haley along until they reached the corn maze entrance.

She counted the people in line. "Nine people ahead of us. Nice turnout tonight."

"Yeah." Rob surveyed the area. "Thought there'd be fewer here tonight. Glad more didn't show up. We'll have a better chance to find and solve the clues. Remember, stick together, so we can find them that much faster. The three of us will get out at the same time too. What do you say, Aiden?"

"Sounds good. Right, Sis?"

"Yes. Staying together is a good idea." She sure wouldn't want to run around in a cornfield by herself in the dark. Even with the floodlights the Murphys would turn on soon, it'd still be spooky in there.

Craig kept his eyes on Haley MacKenna and her companions as they broke into a jog across the path leading to the corn maze. This was his lucky day. The only pretty woman he'd met since he'd come to this farm town. She'd be worth the pursuit for more than one reason. However, after the remarks he made earlier today, he'd have to make amends to her and her brother. But why was that Sheffield guy with them? Must be...what was the brother's name...Aiden. Must be Aiden's friend.

He threw down his half-smoked cigarette and took a step. An older man approaching from the opposite direction stopped and stared at the smoking butt lying on the straw-covered ground. His brows rose, and he peered at Craig over his wire-rimmed glasses. Craig crushed the cigarette butt with his heel.

When he finished smashing the butt into the ground, he looked toward the threesome who stood in line at the maze. From the way Sheffield responded to her touch on his arm this morning at the property line, he must be in love with her. But was the feeling mutual? A tingle surged through Craig at the idea of Haley's touch. He quickened his steps and closed the gap between them.

As he crept up behind them, Craig eavesdropped. Sounded like Haley wasn't keen on getting lost in the maze. This could prove interesting. With a little luck, she'd wind up separated from the men, and he'd make sure he was nearby when she did.

While Haley and her companions were focused on the people in front of them, Craig stooped. If only he could loosen the lace on her shoe, she'd have to retie it at some point. She might fall behind her brother and his friend.

Haley leaned on her brother's arm. She slid one foot behind the other and rested the toe of her shoe in the dirt. "Hope the line starts moving soon."

A girl around the age of five or six ahead of them turned to her mother. "I feel sick, Mommy." Her face turned red. The mother laid a hand on the child's forehead. "You're burning up. Let's get you home."

"Poor little thing," Haley said. She, Aiden, and Rob watched as the mother hurried away with her daughter clinging to her hip.

Perfect. Craig grinned. *Thank you for distracting them, my dear little one.* Carefully, Craig extended his hand and tugged gently on Haley's shoelace. He couldn't loosen it too much. Just enough so it would untie while she was in the maze. He snickered to himself and stood.

Craig cleared his throat.

Haley glanced behind her. "Hello, Mr. Lowell. Out to enjoy the local sights?" She cocked her head and smiled.

"Yes, I am. And they are a joy to see." His gaze roved to her neck, but he quickly brought it back to her eyes and returned her smile. "When I was in town today, someone mentioned this festival. It intrigued me, especially the corn maze. They have a few in Italy, but I've never experienced one. So, here I am. May I join your party?" He winked at Haley.

She opened her mouth, but Sheffield stepped between them. "I invited the MacKennas tonight. You can invite them another time."

Haley pulled on Sheffield's arm, but her brother stepped in front of her, next to Rob, as if building a wall to hide her. "The three of us plan to find the treasure. Rob's right. We can get together another time."

Craig clenched his teeth. So, the brother was hoping she'd hook up with Sheffield. Okay. Understandable. *But it won't stop me from getting what I want.*

After another forced smile, Craig nodded. "Another time, then. Like you said." He stretched his neck to peer over their shoulders and see Haley's face. "If that's what the lady wants."

Haley pushed her brother and Sheffield out of her way. "You two don't mind if I'm a part of the decision-making here, do you?" She gave them both scathing glares. Then she turned to Craig.

"Mr. Lowell. Thank you for the offer, but since Rob invited us, maybe another time would be better."

Craig held out his hand, and she placed hers in it. He lifted her fingers to his lips and kissed her knuckles. "Fair lady, your wish is my command. Perhaps we can have dinner one evening."

Before she could answer, Aiden pulled on Haley's arm. "Come on, Sis. It's our turn."

The threesome stepped up to the young woman collecting admission. Haley looked back at Craig. Her cheeks bloomed to match the sunset.

So she's interested. Nice.

Craig stepped up and gave the striking young woman at the admissions booth the once-over. So there were other pretty women around this backwoods place.

As she explained the clues and the prize offered to the first person who found the treasure, Craig's pulse increased. He paid the fee, and she held out a flyer. He enveloped her hand with his, but she pulled hers away as if it was a common occurrence.

After she went over the rules of etiquette in the maze and participation in the contest, the girl lifted the entrance bar to let him through. "Have fun."

He gave her a half-smile. "Thank you, young lady. I intend to."

When he entered the first path in the corn maze, Haley and the men were out of sight. Craig concentrated on the sounds from the cornfield. He couldn't tell which voices were theirs, not with kids' ear-piercing squeals filling the air. From the sound of it, a lot of people were in this thing. If he hurried, he might spot Haley. He couldn't care less about this farmer's game or treasure. The only prize he wanted was Miss MacKenna.

Craig entered the next path and jotted down his pattern of turns on the back of the brochure the girl gave him. But half an hour later, he had no idea which way he'd come from or which way he was headed. From the sound of voices in the distance, everyone was lost. And he'd lost control of the situation. Which turn should he take? How far away was Haley?

If he didn't find the way out soon, he'd plow through the corn walls, rules or no rules. Of course, that wouldn't help him score points with the community. Much less Haley. He kicked the dirt.

He had to find a way out. Then he'd wait for her. When he caught her alone, he'd talk her into joining him for a drink. Craig stood still and listened again. Was that her voice? It sounded like she was calling her brother?

Chapter Twelve

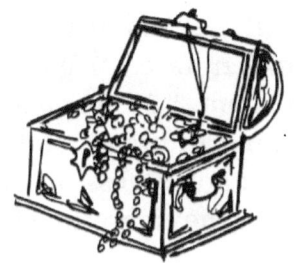

aley sucked in air as if she needed an inhaler. They'd run through this corn maze for at least half an hour and hadn't come across one room. Were they going in circles? She stopped and bent over. "Hey guys, I don't know about you, but I need a breather." Oh, brother, how long had her shoe been untied? She could've broken her neck. "And I have to tie my shoe!"

When she looked up, Aiden and Rob were gone. "*Aiden?*" Great! Bet they had no idea she wasn't with them anymore. Like little kids, those two. It was all about the game. Had they gotten too far away to hear her? "That's okay. Leave me alone in here. See if I care." Typical men. Oh well.

She knelt and tied her left shoe, then pulled the right shoelaces and retied them. As she rose, something slammed into her. "*Hey.*"

Arms wrapped around her, and someone rolled with her into the cornstalks. When they came to a stop, Craig Lowell's cool gray-blue eyes gazed down at her. His jaw lowered. "Haley, I'm so sorry." But he remained on top of her.

A tingle ran through her arms as she pushed him over and wiggled to get out of his embrace. He'd held her so tight. "*Off.*"

Craig let her go and hopped to his feet, but a wide grin replaced the astonished expression. "Where's your brother and Sheffield? Are you as lost as I am?"

Haley sat on the husk-strewn ground and made sure her laces were tight. She could still feel his arms around her. Heat flowed into her neck and up to her face. "I guess so. I mean, no." She listened, but the air was silent. "Everyone else seems to have found the way out. When I ran out of breath and stopped for a second, I was right behind Aiden and Rob. Guess they didn't notice."

She wrinkled her nose at the cigarette odor from his clothing. He must smoke a lot.

"So, did you find the clues to the treasure?" Craig thrust out his hand to help her to her feet.

He was a gentleman, at least. She'd give him that. Haley bit her lip and took his hand. She bounced to her feet and brushed off her clothes. Her tangled, shoulder-length hair fell into her face. She pushed it back.

Craig pulled a piece of cornhusk from her hair and handed it to her. "A souvenir?"

She laughed and took it. "We haven't found any clues."

As she twirled the sliver of cornhusk between her fingers, Craig scanned the path in both directions. He held a hand to his ear. "Do you suppose everyone's gone home?"

"I doubt that. It's a very large corn maze. Aiden should have realized I'm missing by now. He'll be looking for me." Wish he'd hurry up about it. She didn't like being alone out here with this man, even if he was polite.

Craig brushed off his clothes. "How big is this thing anyway? I've been walking forever."

"Rob said it was over twenty acres, and they make it bigger every year." She looked down the path in both directions as he had. "Now, which way do I go? That tumble disoriented me."

"May I suggest we stick together until your brother locates you, or until we find a way out? Who knows, maybe *we'll* discover the clues and figure out the puzzle without them." He smiled.

A tickle ran through her stomach. She hadn't felt that sensation for so long. Not since she'd first realized her feelings for Rob—*forget him*. This evening might turn out nice, after all. With his chiseled features, Craig was handsome in a trim, male model, fashion magazine sort of way.

He extended his elbow. "Shall we?"

And such good manners. Must be a European thing.

Rob glanced over his shoulder. "Hey, Aiden, wait up. Where'd Haley go?"

Aiden peered past Rob down the long path of cornstalks. "Man, when did we lose her?"

"I don't know. Right after we came around that last corner, I checked behind me, and she wasn't there. Guess she got tired of the pace we were keeping. We should go back for her. It's getting dark even with the floodlights."

Aiden bent and rested his hands on his knees. He took in a couple of deep breaths. "She's not afraid of the dark. Never has been. But we need to find her. We agreed to stay together."

As they backtracked through the paths, Rob stepped into the right path at a fork and stopped. It didn't seem right. "Which way?" He stared at Aiden.

With his brows furrowed and teeth clamped on his lower lip, Aiden shrugged. "I'm not sure. We were running so fast I can't remember if we turned left or right."

Rob cupped a hand on either side of his mouth and tilted his head back. "Haley!" He listened. "Not a sound out there. Everyone must have left the field. Why don't you call for her? I don't think she'll answer me."

Aiden tried next but still no reply. "Oh, boy. Am I in trouble now. My little sister is missing in another cornfield. Happened when we were kids, remember? She was four years old, and I hid from her in the tall corn stalks one afternoon in the field behind the house. While she searched for me, a corn snake crawled past my feet, and I followed it deeper into the field.

"When I realized she'd stopped calling my name, I looked for her but couldn't find the imp anywhere. I had to get Mom and Dad. Mom was in tears. They found her asleep on a hay bale in the barn. Dad tanned my hide for losing her."

Rob laughed. "This isn't quite as serious. But I do recall when my parents packed me into the car to help in the search. We were five and six at the time, right?"

"Yeah. I almost didn't live to see seven."

A burst of laughter broke the tension.

When they stopped laughing, Aiden yelled again. "Haley! Awww, come on, Sis. Answer me. She's remembered that time, too, and decided to get even. The brat!"

Rob shouted for her a couple more times, but stillness filled the air. A chill ran up his back. "Where did she go? The temperature's dropping, and our jackets are in the car. Call her cell. I left mine in my jacket."

Aiden palmed his forehead. "Why didn't I think of that?" He punched her speed dial number, but the call went to voicemail. "She must've left her phone at home, or it's in her purse under the car seat. Since we hadn't found the first room, she may have decided this quest wasn't worth the energy and went back to the entrance. Let's keep going. We'll find our way out, and if she's not waiting for us, we'll have the Murphys go in for her with their map. Too bad we aren't at the tall, raised stand in the middle of the maze. We might spot her from there. Not sure where it is, though."

"They sure made this year's corn maze a hard one." Rob followed his friend back the way they'd come. This wasn't the way things were supposed to go. He had to find Haley. Besides helping Aiden and Haley relax, the whole point of the trip was to get her to be comfortable with him again. And now this. She'd blame him for it for sure. "Say."

"What?"

"I have an idea. Why don't you find the exit, and I'll head back and find Haley? If we don't make it out in a reasonable amount of time, send in the Marines."

"Good plan, Rob. At least that way, Haley won't be alone. And I've seen enough cornstalks today to last me a long time. But we'll come back and hunt for the treasure another day. Since it's my fault I lost her again, I'll spring for admission next time."

"No need. This is my fault, too, for not paying attention." The treasure was the last thing on his mind at the moment. He wanted to find Haley. The image of Lowell ogling her before they entered the maze popped into his head.

A twinge skittered up his neck as he ran back through the corn maze.

Craig and Haley strolled through several paths in the maze until they entered what looked like a dead end. He spotted a narrow gap to the left. *Hmm, a hidden doorway to a secluded room?* They made it almost undetectable. And it didn't look like anyone had been through the opening.

He led her into the space, which led into an outdoor room, complete with a table and two chairs. Nice and cozy. Craig pulled out a black wrought iron chair for her. "Let's take a breather before we continue. I'm surprised we haven't run into your brother yet."

Haley appeared none too happy about her brother and Sheffield leaving her.

As he sat down, she lowered herself into the other seat and crossed her arms. "Aiden and Rob were moving so fast, they're probably out of the maze by now. I still can't believe they left me."

He smiled at her. "I'm sure they were preoccupied with the treasure."

Eyes narrowed, she peeked at him from under her long lashes.

Oh yeah, she was upset with them.

She tilted her head back and gazed at the stars. "Even with floodlights bathing the area, the heavens are bright. It's a beautiful sky tonight."

"Right now, I'm enjoying an even more beautiful sight."

Haley bit her lip. Her brow wrinkled. "I've heard men from Italy are terrible flirts."

"I know, but truth is truth." Even in the dimness of the night, he could see her blush. He laughed inside.

She gazed upward again. "See the bright light there." As if she could touch the orb, she stretched her arm out and pointed.

After he'd dragged his chair closer, he leaned his head next to hers. His line of vision followed her finger. "That's quite a star."

She lowered her hand, backed away from him, and gave a soft laugh. "It's Jupiter, not a star. Now observe the twinkling white one up there."

He leaned toward her until the heat from her body warmed his skin. Her flowery fragrance tantalized him—intoxicating—nothing like the women he'd known in the past. He wanted more. *Take it slow. Savor the moment.* "I suppose that's Saturn, right?"

"Wrong again. That one *is* a star. Aldebaran, to be exact. It's in the Taurus constellation. The stars twinkle. Planets don't."

"I'm impressed with your knowledge of the galaxy. Studying to be an astronomer, are you?" He slipped his arm onto the back of her chair.

"No, my brother was in an astronomy club through high school. We'd sit in the backyard at night, and he'd point out everything to me."

He wasn't interested in her brother. Craig fingered a lock of her soft hair. "Haley, once we get out of this maze, would you care to go somewhere for a drink?"

She jumped to her feet. "At this hour? I'm not sure we'd find anything open for coffee now. Besides, I have to find my brother and Rob. We should get going."

Coffee? He stifled a snicker. Who was thinking about coffee? He hopped up from the seat and pointed toward her chair. Something hung from the back leg. "What's that?"

Haley leaned the seat forward onto the wrought iron table. "It's a clue to find the treasure." She pulled a slip of paper out of the plastic holder and tucked it into her jeans pocket. "I'm sure someone's already found it for tonight, but it can't hurt to hang onto this." She set the chair back on its legs.

"Aren't you going to read it?"

"No, I'll save it for when I catch up with Aiden and Rob. In case they missed this one."

"What about me? I thought you and I were going to do this."

"*You* said we'd find the treasure together. *I* didn't agree. Aiden, Rob, and I planned to work on it. I'm not one to go back on my word."

Craig bent, retrieved a clue from the plastic envelope. "In case I happen to find the rest. I respect you for keeping your word to your brother. Family's important. They add so much to our lives. Sometimes even when they've passed on." Especially when they'd left important information for him to find. Very valuable information.

He held the clue between his index and third fingers. "Or it could be my souvenir from spending a night *alone* with a beautiful lady." He locked onto her sea-green eyes as he stuck the clue into his shirt pocket and grinned.

Haley's face flushed again.

He winked. "My dear lady, what direction shall we take now?"

Chapter Thirteen

aley wrapped her arms around her middle and shivered. She'd catch a cold in this damp air if they didn't get out soon. Why had she left her jacket in the car? Because she didn't think they'd be in this crazy maze this late, that's why. She peeked at her watch. Nine-thirty. A breeze swept up the path and through the weave of her sweater. She shivered.

Craig discarded his leather jacket, revealing a dark blue, short-sleeved shirt with the top three buttons undone. He handed the jacket to her. "You must be cold."

"No, thank you. I'll be fine." She couldn't take it. At least she was wearing a sweater. She'd feel terrible if he got sick.

"Okay, but don't hesitate to tell me if you change your mind." He swung the jacket back on. "Please allow me the liberty of keeping you warm this way." He slipped his arm around her shoulder. "Do you feel the heat?"

She shouldn't let him do that. As he pulled her close to his side, warmth radiated from him. His smile held nothing but kindness. She didn't want to offend him by pulling away. And she didn't want to get sick. Why couldn't Rob be thoughtful like this?

Several turns in the path later, Rob careened around a corner and skidded to a stop. Haley's heart skipped. "*Rob.*" While a different kind of heat rose in her face, she gazed past him. "Where's Aiden?"

Rob didn't answer. He scowled at the arm wrapped around her shoulder.

Haley spun out of Craig's hold, planted her hands on her hips, and glared at Rob. "Where's Aiden?"

"Your brother went to locate the exit. I told him I'd find you."

Craig smirked. "I guess you found *us.*"

She pressed her eyes shut for a moment and shook her head. *Men.* What was it with these two? Nothing but sarcasm between them. She opened her eyes. Rob's expression reminded her of a hurt puppy. "We've been searching for the way out. When I bent down to tie my shoe, you and Aiden kept on running. Didn't either of you hear me call?"

Rob wedged himself between Haley and Craig. "We didn't hear anything. Not sure how far ahead we were, but when I glanced back and saw you weren't there, we called for you. I'm really sorry, Haley. Aiden tried your cell, but you must not have it on you."

"It's at home. The last thing I imagined was needing a cell phone out here in the middle of a corn field or being left alone in a cornfield by my brother a second time."

"We were too focused on finding those clues to win the prize. Again, I'm sorry. Now, let's get you out of here." He took her arm and hustled her away from Craig.

"Rob. I can walk on my own, thank you. Did you find any clues?"

"No. Once we discovered you weren't with us and you didn't answer our calls, we gave up on them. I started back for you. Let's speed up the pace. You have to be chilled in this dampness. I know I am."

They took off as if in a walking race. Craig followed.

Haley placed her hand on Rob's forearm. "Wait." Using his arm to push herself up, she jumped as high as she could to peer over the cornstalks. "I can't spot the exit. Do you know which way to go? All I see is corn tassels."

"I'm not sure. We were confused about which direction we had come from when we first turned back to find you. That's when I said I'd catch up with you while Aiden went for help...if we needed it."

Haley eyed Rob. Just what kind of help did he think they'd need?

Aiden marked the time on his watch again. He'd been standing there for more than half hour. Surely Rob had found Haley by now. Maybe he should alert the Murphys, so they'd go in and search for them. They must have a map in case someone couldn't find the exit. Oh, yeah. *Great idea, Einstein.* Haley'd scalp him if he embarrassed her that way. He'd better give them a few more minutes. The maze would close in another half hour anyway. Then the family would go through and shoo everyone out.

Five minutes later, he turned to walk toward the booth where a Murphy family member sat reading a book. As Aiden opened his mouth to report his friend and sister missing, Haley called to him from the edge of the corn maze. He spun and ran toward her.

Next to her, Rob grinned with satisfaction. Aiden slapped his friend on the upper arm, then spoke. "Haley, what happened to you? And, Rob, thanks for finding her. I was about to send out the bloodhounds."

Before either could say a word, Craig Lowell came out of the exit. Aiden gaped at his sister. "Was he with you?"

With a frown on his face, Rob came alongside Aiden and whispered, "They were together when I found them. He had his arm around her."

Aiden put a hand on each of Haley's shoulders to read her face. If that jerk did anything to his sister— "Are you okay?"

"I'm perfectly fine, outside of being chilled to the bone. Can we go?" She turned to Rob. "Thanks for coming after me." Then she addressed Lowell. "Thanks for the warm arm and staying with me in there."

"Any time, fair lady." He headed for the parked cars, but after three steps, he turned back to smile at her. "Remember, we have a date. I'll get in touch next week. *Ciao*." He broke into a jog toward the parking area.

Rob scoffed. "Chow? That's what he calls a *date*?"

Haley laughed. "He doesn't mean chow as in dinner. It's the way Italians say good morning, hello, goodbye, see ya later."

While the threesome watched, Lowell strode between the few cars left at the festival to a black Mercedes. He drove away.

When they reached the Sheffields' car, Aiden opened the rear passenger door for his sister, and she slid into the back seat. He got into the front while Rob eased himself behind the steering wheel. Aiden shifted his body so he could view Haley. She put on her jacket and attached the seatbelt, then leaned her head back.

"Sis, what's with Lowell? His rudeness this afternoon...downright hostility even...and then he takes care of you back there. What did he say to you?"

"Not much. We were too busy trying to escape that monster. I don't remember the maze being this huge when we were teens."

Rob chuckled. "It wasn't. They keep making it bigger and went all-out this year."

She nodded. "Oh." After fumbling in her jeans pocket, she pulled out a piece of paper, handed it to Aiden, and laid her head back again. "I picked up that clue for you while we were stuck in there. Not that it matters now since you didn't find any."

"Little sister, don't change the subject." He puffed air out through his nose. "What did you two talk about while tripping the light fantastic in the corn?"

"Oh, really, Aiden." She whipped her head up from the seat. "You sound more like Dad every day with those clichés." She winced.

Aiden sighed. He did sound like their father, who had used that phrase often to tease Mom when she was out shopping for longer than he expected. He'd have to choose his words with care for a while. Haley didn't need to recall their loss any more than he did. "So...what did you and Lowell talk about?"

"You're relentless." She glowered at him. "I told him I couldn't believe you left me alone out there. Craig defended you." She shifted her attention to Rob. "*Both* of you. He said you two were probably so intent on the treasure you didn't notice you'd *left* me. I'm sure he was right. Do you realize how uncomfortable I was...alone out there as it got dark...until Craig showed up?" She giggled. "While I tied my shoe, he came flying around the corner and tripped over me." She bit her lip. "Then, we rolled across the path into the corn."

Aiden furrowed his brows at her. "He rolled with you, huh? And then what happened."

"We got up, brushed ourselves off, and started to search for the exit." Her brows knit together.

As Rob fiddled with the car heater, she crossed her arms and stared at Aiden. "Any more questions, Mr. Attorney?"

"I have one." Rob glanced back at her.

"Oh, why not? Sure, Rob. Your turn to interrogate."

"No interrogation. Just wondered why Lowell was holding you."

Aiden's lips pressed together in a firm line. He'd forgotten that.

Haley took in a deep breath as if she'd blow out candles on a birthday cake. Then exhaled. "I was cold. He *noticed*. He put his arm around my *shoulders* after I refused to take his jacket. Which he offered. *Enough*. End of topic." She glared at them. Her eyes dared either of them to say another word.

That Irish temper of hers was as bad as his used to be. Aiden faced forward in the seat. A jacket had better be the only thing the guy offered. And what was all that about a date? He'd drop that question for now. For tonight, anyway.

Rob fumed as he drove. Fine, just fine. What a great evening this had turned out to be, thanks to Craig Lowell. Rob gritted his teeth so tight his jaw ached. He tightened his grip on the steering wheel. Too bad it wasn't Lowell's neck he was gripping. Rob's knuckles grew white. Here he'd been working on getting back into Haley's good graces, on getting her to forgive him and be friends. Who was he kidding? He wanted more than friendship from her. But this new guy swooped in and already had her in his arms in one day.

"Rob, slow down." Aiden grabbed the dashboard. "We're not kids anymore, and we don't have a curfew."

"Sorry, man. I guess I'm a bit heavy on the pedal." He slowed the car to the speed limit. "Still want to go fishing tomorrow?"

"Sure, but it'll have to be later. Not sure we'll be up before dawn as we planned." Aiden turned to Haley, who had laid her head back against the seat once more. "Sis, you're up for fishing, aren't you?"

Rob waited, expecting to hear a resounding no from her lips.

She murmured.

Aiden grinned at Rob with raised brows. "Now that she's warm, she's fallen asleep. I'm sure she'll go. She always tagged along with us when we were kids."

He took another peek at his sister. "Look at her. So sweet...when she's sleeping." He snickered and faced Rob. "What time should we head out tomorrow?"

Rob glimpsed the sleeping red-haired beauty in the rearview mirror and smiled. She'd always been sweet, even when angry at him for teasing her. Despite the recent rejections, he wanted her to be his.

Aiden nudged his arm. "What time?"

"Not sure we'll catch many fish, but how does noon sound? That'll give you more time to sleep after all this fresh air. I'm used to it, but I'll bet neither of you has spent as much time outside lately. Like we all did as kids."

"That's for sure."

Rob raised his thumb from the steering wheel. "I'll ask Mom to pack us a lunch, and we'll make a day of it. You think Haley will go?"

Aiden nodded.

Hope he's right. She had to go. Rob grimaced and peered into the backseat once more. His gut told him Lowell was up to no good. He had to find a way to keep her away from that guy.

Chapter Fourteen

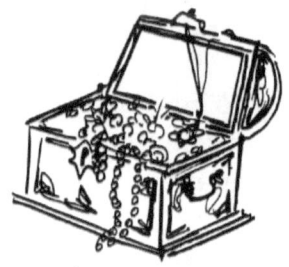

Craig sat in the living room of what was now his lavish home and let his eyes rove the Spanish décor. His family had been wise to acquire this vast piece of land from the MacKennas so long ago. Craig grinned. And now, the house, land, and money were his, as well as all his father's investments. But he wanted more.

The question was, did he want to stay in the States or go back to Italy? He had serious thinking to do. Although it hadn't been his plan, now that he'd met Haley MacKenna, she'd be a real prize to take with him. He narrowed his eyes at the large painting of his mother, which still hung over the fireplace. But, if he went home to Italy, he'd have to deal with his mother's family and their accusations. He pursed his lips. No, he'd stay in this country. Besides, he still had unfinished business to take care of.

He leaned his head back on the leather armchair. That Haley was a knockout. And what a shape. An appreciative whistle filled the air. He'd find an impressive place to take her for dinner.

The glance she gave before they entered the corn maze last night came to mind. When he'd tripped over her and rolled into the cornstalks with her, he shouldn't have let go. Too bad she'd pushed him away. But she was interested. His pulse increased.

Still, it couldn't hurt to make a bigger impression. Be the gallant suitor for a while. It'd be easy for him to get her mind off that hick, Sheffield.

Craig strutted into the old-world kitchen, its stainless steel appliances as sleek as ever. His gaze traced the stone and tile walls. A smile flickered across his lips. When he was little, he used to imagine it was a castle. He'd often visit to sweet-talk the old cook into giving him the treats his mother denied him.

That was before—Craig's smile evaporated. Before his mother took him to Italy and reduced his relationship with his father to phone conversations for the past twenty-two years.

Craig sucked in air to quell his anger. He ran his hand over the countertop. Haley would be proud to be the mistress of this house. He prepared a ham sandwich and returned to the living room.

As he ate, he flicked on the television. His pulse increased again as he eyed the voluptuous female reporter. "Investigators have found nothing suspicious about last week's fire in the MacKennas' field."

"That's good news." He snickered and switched off the channel to watch a DVD.

An action movie caught his attention from the collection in the bookcase. "Now, this is interesting. Not like tramping around in a field of corn for a good time. Although, that too had its exciting moments." Another snicker escaped.

Half an hour later, he turned off the machine. "I take it back." His company last night in the corn maze provided much more entertainment than this. Too bad Sheffield had shown up when he did. Things were moving along quite well up to that point. All alone. Secluded.

Craig slid a second flick in and settled back on the armchair. Cars blowing up in the streets of New York eventually changed to sensual scenes. He smirked and licked his lips. His mother had kept him too busy with the financial aspect of her business to watch movies in Italy. He'd barely had time to breathe. But she was gone now. With him in America, what happened there will be forgotten. She deserved what she got, and he deserved to be happy.

After a trip back to the kitchen, Craig kicked up his feet on the hassock and munched on chocolate cake. "Food's tasty here too." The longer he stayed in the States, the more he favored it. Even in this backward town. Although he could search for a better place to reside. He'd take Haley with him. Craig's eyes roved the room, the antiques, the sculptures, the furnishings, and their richness. His father had lived in luxury.

Haley stared at the screen. Here it was Saturday, and she was studying again. Same as in Boulder. The only difference, she didn't have Kayla to bounce questions off of from across the room. Oh well. It was only until she graduated next spring. She could do this, even if the farm work did cut into study time.

Drago had taken over the care of the horses so she could study. As much as she loved them, she knew nothing about their needs. And he loved doing it.

"*Haley*," her brother shouted from the living room.

She hopped up from her desk chair and hurried to him. As she entered the room, Aiden laid the house phone receiver into its cradle.

"Who was that?"

"Just got off the phone with the Fremont Sheriff's Department. They found evidence that someone tampered with the brakes on Dad's car. But that's *all* they've found so far. No indication of who might have done it. They had the nerve to ask me if Dad worked on his vehicle himself." He dropped into the armchair next to the phone table.

A vein enlarged on the right side of Aiden's forehead. It always swelled when he was anxious. *That's not good.*

Aiden rubbed both temples and laid his head back.

Haley's hand rested on his shoulder. "Of course, Dad worked on the car himself. He worked on all the farm equipment, including the vehicles. But don't let it upset you." Her brother had tried so hard to hide his stress.

Aiden jumped up and paced. She could almost see the fumes spewing from the top of his head. He'd seldom lost his temper like this anymore. Their parents' accident and the situation on the farm had taken a toll. He needed to talk. "Aiden. What did they mean by that? Do they think Dad messed up his brakes?"

His teeth clenched so tight his muscles twitched. Oh boy, Aiden was really mad. She had to calm him down. But how? She was upset too.

"Yes!"

Heat rose in Haley's neck and flooded her chest. How could anyone who knew their father believe he'd mess up brakes he'd worked on for years? Dad could fix anything. "No! There must be evidence that someone else tampered with them. They'll find it, eventually. But why, Aiden...why would anyone want to harm Mom and Dad? It makes no sense."

"The sheriff said they have nothing else to go on. Jason told him the idea that Dad messed up was off. But his supervisor said everyone makes mistakes."

Tears burst from Haley's eyes. She couldn't stand any more of this. "There has to be a way to find out who tampered with the brakes. There has to, Aiden."

"I'm not sure how. If the sheriff's people say there's no concrete evidence, what can we do?" He enveloped Haley in his arms. "It's okay, Sis. I shouldn't have upset you. Jason came on the line after the sheriff and said he'll continue his investigation."

Aunt Debbie stepped into the room and rushed to Haley. "What's wrong, dear?"

After Aiden filled their aunt in on his phone conversation, she led Haley to the couch and sat holding her, rubbing her back.

With a deep sigh, Aunt Debbie rose from the sofa and headed through the dining room into the kitchen. She called over her shoulder. "I'll start lunch. I can at least do that before I head home to Council Bluffs."

Auntie felt as helpless as they did. Haley sniffled. *Here I was going to calm Aiden down...and look at me.*

Her brother sat on the couch and held her until the sniffles stopped. He stood, grabbed her hand, and pulled her to her feet. "We need to pray harder for answers. But right now, let's give Aunt Deb a hand."

When they entered the kitchen, their aunt's head was in her hands, elbows propped on the table. Her mouth moved, but no sound came from her lips. Aiden and Haley waited at the door until their aunt peered up at them.

Auntie smiled. "The only way whoever caused your parents' deaths will be brought to justice is through prayer. After I called our church's prayer chain to get things started, I had a good talk with our Lord."

Haley whisked herself to her aunt's side and hugged her. "Aiden was just saying we needed to pray harder. Thank you, Auntie."

Aiden dragged two chairs closer to Aunt Debbie. He sat in one. Haley took the other, and the three huddled together in prayer, taking turns. When they finished, a collective peace filled the room.

"Can you feel that?" Haley sighed and glanced at Aiden, then at her aunt.

"You mean the peace surrounding us." Auntie laid her hand over Haley's on the table.

"I sense it too." Aiden's smile reached into his eyes. "What an incredible sensation. I've never known it before."

Aunt Debbie beamed. "Matthew eighteen twenty. 'For where two or three are gathered together in my name, there am I in the midst of them.' He's here. God's right here with us."

Tickles ricocheted through Haley's insides. "Wow!"

A hard knock sounded from the front door.

A few minutes later, Rob followed Aiden into the kitchen. "Aiden here tells me you two forgot our fishing trip this afternoon." Rob gazed at Haley. "Not because you're sick from last night, is it?" His brows lowered. If she caught something, it would be Lowell's fault. He'd kept her from the exit in that damp air to hunt for clues so he'd have her to himself. Rob recalled glimpsing over his shoulder in the maze. If only he and Aiden had noticed when she stopped.

"I didn't forget." Haley turned her back on him, stepped to the counter, and poured herself a cup of coffee. "I told Aiden I had no interest in going." She added cream to the mug and sat down at the table next to her aunt. "I'm not a kid anymore. You two will have a much better time without me." She grinned at her brother.

He tapped Rob on the head. "Told you she'd say that. I tried to tell her we'd have fun, but no soap."

Rob tightened his lips. He had to convince her to go. He needed to spend time with her. Alone if possible. "Look, Haley. If you're still sore about us losing you last night, you can blame me, but you and Aiden still need downtime to relax. Do something fun. You used to love fishing. Later we'll have a picnic lunch, and you can tell me what you've been up to at college for the last three years."

She shook her head.

Aunt Debbie lifted Haley's chin and peered into her eyes. "Honey, Rob is right. You and Aiden do need time to relax and enjoy yourselves. That didn't happen last night, so take advantage of it this afternoon. It'll only take me a few minutes to put a picnic lunch together for you three."

"No need, Mrs. Moye. Mom made enough for an army. She still thinks we guys eat like horses. Refuses to accept the fact we're grown up and won't get any bigger. Leastwise, not taller."

Aiden burst out laughing. "Only wider, I suppose."

Haley giggled.

"Go ahead, honey. Go with the boys. Relax. Get some fresh air and sunshine. It's a beautiful day. You can always lay out on a blanket and read while they fish."

Rob stepped closer to Haley and cocked his head. "I promise not to talk to you if you don't want me to." Even though he was dying to find out what happened between her and Lowell last night. She'd cut Aiden off when he asked yesterday.

Haley glanced at her aunt. "I suppose I could take a book with me and enjoy the peace and quiet."

"Guess I won't have to get lunch out after all. I'll eat when I get home." She patted Haley's back.

Yes! Rob restrained a grin from popping out. Maybe he could figure out a way to be alone with her at the pond.

Chapter Fifteen

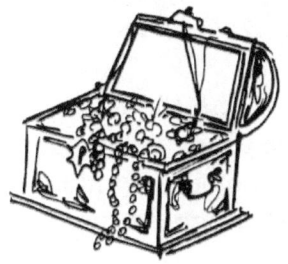

*H*aley hopped into the cramped extended cab of Rob's beat-up 2008 Ford pickup. She stretched her legs and wiggled back onto the pillow he'd brought for her. What a thoughtful thing to have done. He'd been trying hard to make up for the past.

"Sorry I couldn't get Dad's car today, Haley. He needed it for a trip to Omaha for a church meeting."

"It's okay. If I fit, I sit. Like those cats that can get into the most unusual places." She'd let him know she was trying to forgive him.

"Aiden offered to drive the rental car, but it wouldn't be good to turn it in smelling of dead fish."

She stifled a giggle and smiled. "Rob, I said it's okay. Thanks for the pillow."

Aunt Debbie moseyed to Rob's truck while Aiden deposited her suitcase in her car. She leaned against the passenger side. "Now remember, dear. If you need me, call. My boss will understand if I have to leave again. I've kept him updated."

Haley gave her a thumbs-up. "I've held the fort alone many times. And Drago's here."

While her aunt made her way around the truck to talk to Rob, Haley watched Drago saunter from his bunkhouse to the stable. Could she rely on him? Her family always had. She sighed.

Her brother strode to the truck and hugged their aunt. "Thanks for the help, Aunt Deb. Drive safely and relax for the rest of the weekend."

"I will." She circled around the front of the vehicle. "Next week, I'd love to have you three young people over for dinner."

Haley stuck her head out the window, and her aunt kissed her cheek. "Thank you for staying with us, Auntie. You've been a great comfort."

"I'm glad I could be here." She gazed into her niece's eyes. "Remember...I'm only an hour away."

"Don't worry. I'll be fine." No matter what happened next.

As their aunt stepped away from the truck, Aiden got in on the passenger side. "Drive slowly, Aunt Deb. We'll call you when we get back."

"Of course." She walked to her car, slipped behind the steering wheel, gave a quick wave, and then drove away.

Rob started the engine. "Okay. Off for a day of fun." He glanced at Haley in the rearview mirror. Happiness showed in his eyes.

Several minutes later, he pulled the red truck down a dirt road to the pond at the far side of the Sheffields' land. It had been their favorite fishing hole since they were kids.

Haley's jaw lowered. There was that old rowboat tied to a tree, floating on the edge of the bank. That boat had been there for as long as she could remember. Fond memories of swimming with her brother and Rob flooded her mind. Even Lucy and Jason had spent many summer days here in their company. Lucy sure had been smitten by Aiden back then. Haley giggled to herself.

Too bad her friend had chosen a job that took her so far from home and all over the country. She recalled the day Lucy told her, *"After I graduate high school, I plan to travel everywhere."*

When had she last heard from her? At least a year ago, when she called to say she'd be a tour guide at the Wisconsin Dells. Then nothing. Haley bit her lip. She'd missed her so much before her own departure for college two years later. Then Kayla became her roommate in college, and she'd gained another sister. But also far away now.

The truck stopped with a jerk next to a thick clump of trees and shrubs, interrupting the sudden onset of gloom. She took Rob's offered hand and jumped down from the extended cab. "Thank you."

"You're welcome." He joined Aiden at the rear of the truck and helped him remove their fishing gear from the bed. "Before we start, what do you say we eat? I skimped on breakfast to hurry through my chores and get to your place."

Haley poked him in the ribs. "You mean you had six eggs instead of your usual dozen?" She smirked.

"Hilarious." Rob laughed. "Seriously, though, I'm starved. Aren't either of you?"

With the poles hoisted onto his shoulder, Aiden nodded. "Sounds good to me."

Haley gathered the blankets in one arm and tried to pull the ample picnic hamper to the tailgate with the other.

Rob removed her hand from the handle. "I'll get that. With all the food Mom packed, this weighs a ton." He slid it to the tailgate, lifted it to his shoulder as if it were a hay bale, and followed her to the old silver maple tree where they'd spent hundreds of hours as kids.

She spread the blankets across the grass, and Rob placed the heavy basket at a corner, then plopped down on the blanket and stretched out his long legs. "This is a perfect spot."

"It always has been." Her thoughts drifted back to Lucy. She should get in touch with her to tell her what happened to Mom and Dad.

As she gazed into the branches, Haley smiled. "I've missed this old tree. Brings back a lot of good memories."

Rob rolled onto his side and peered at her. "Very good memories. I'm glad you recall those. We had great times at this pond...and in it. Remember the day I lost my swim trunks when I dove in?" He grinned.

She dropped to her knees on the blanket next to him and chortled. "Yes, we did, and I do. It was a good thing Aiden came to your rescue and found them." Had Rob ever guessed how she'd adored him back then? Until he messed up. *Let it go, Haley.* She frowned, opened the third blanket, and smoothed it out beside the first two.

Something rustled in the woods behind them.

As Craig Lowell stepped from a tall clump of bushes, Rob jumped to his feet. "What are you doing here?"

Craig glanced at Haley, then at Aiden, who was heading back from the water's edge. "I was taking a walk." Craig focused on Haley.

"That's quite a walk." Rob eyed Craig. "We're about ten miles from your place."

As Aiden approached, Craig extended his hand. "Afternoon, neighbor."

"I'm not your neighbor. The farm isn't mine, it belongs to my sister now. Did I hear you say you were out for a walk?"

"Yes. I walked everywhere in Italy. Good exercise."

Rob scowled. "Ten miles?"

"What can I say? I love walking. It's a farther distance than usual, but I was enjoying the scenery. Is something wrong?"

Haley rose and gave him her hand. "Nothing's wrong, Craig. It's nice to see you again."

He took her hand in his and kissed the back of it. She could get used to this treatment.

After he released her hand, he faced Rob. "Have I intruded?"

Haley glowered at Rob. "The pond *is* Sheffield property, but I'm sure Rob doesn't mind company. Do you?" She raised her brows.

Rob's neck burned as though his collar were on fire. "Company's always welcome." He expected to have a fun day with Haley and Aiden. Now, this jerk showed up with that hand-kissing stuff?

Haley invited Lowell to sit, and he joined her on the blanket. As Rob resumed his spot, he glared at Lowell. So he just happened to walk *here*? Had he attached a GPS device to Haley? Could have planted it last night when he'd hung all over her.

Rob grimaced. He'd seen too many spy movies. Better change his attitude if he didn't want Haley mad at him again. "Since you're here, join us for lunch and fishing afterward."

Haley rewarded him with a pleased expression.

"Sure, thanks." Lowell pointed to the cookie container Haley had opened. "Bet you made those?"

Rob handed him a stiff paper plate. "My mom made the food, but she always makes more than enough."

Aiden hadn't spoken a word since he told Lowell he wasn't his neighbor. Guess he wasn't too pleased this guy was here either, and he'd always been a good judge of character. Rob's eyes shifted from his friend's twitching jaw muscle to Haley. She was awfully happy to see Lowell. Probably why Aiden was upset.

With a flick of his wrist, Rob sailed a paper plate into his friend's chest. "Aiden, why don't you pray over the food?" Rob's glance moved to Lowell, who sneered.

After the blessing, Haley pulled containers out of the large picnic basket and cooler. Aiden passed out soft drinks.

Haley scooped potato salad onto each plate alongside a piece of fried chicken and an assortment of fresh fruit pieces. "Pass that container of brownies and chocolate chip cookies, will you, Rob?"

He handed her the open container.

Half an hour later, Lowell wiped his mouth and hands with a paper towel and tossed it onto his plate. "That was very good. Please give my compliments to your mother, Sheffield."

"Thanks. I will."

Lowell leaned back on one elbow, facing Haley. "I understand your aunt is staying with you right now. Didn't she want to join the picnic?"

"No. She went home this afternoon. Auntie lives in Council Bluffs. When our parents died, she came to stay with us and help with funeral arrangements. Aiden will return to California next week."

A twinge shot through Rob. Wish she hadn't told him that.

"Oh. I see." Lowell helped himself to another cookie.

Rob's lips stiffened. What had Lowell seen? Haley...alone at the farm?

As she cleared the remains of lunch, Rob and Aiden rose and headed to the rowboat. Halfway there, Rob spun and clenched his teeth. Lowell hadn't followed them. He still reclined on the blanket, eyes fixed on Haley. "Hey, Lowell. Time to fish."

"I'll pass. Never have been interested in fish."

Rob gaped at Aiden. "So, you'll just stand there and let that jerk make moony eyes at your sister?"

"Easy, buddy. You don't want to embarrass Haley." Aiden strode back to the blanket. "Sis, you coming?"

"Okay, let me put this food away."

Lowell stood and glanced at Rob, then at Haley. "Guess it's time for me to leave. Thanks for lunch. I'll have to have the three of you over soon."

He lifted Haley's hand to his lips and planted another kiss. She smiled.

Rob's insides burned as if a volcano were about to erupt.

Haley ground her teeth. As soon as Aiden stopped rowing, she laid into them. "What was that back there? The glares, the remarks? What's wrong with you two?"

That glow on Rob's face wasn't from the sun. She stared at Aiden. "An explanation, please?"

After he'd baited his hook, Aiden answered. "I don't trust that guy. He's after something. Too smooth. We know nothing about him except that he's old man Lowell's son. Try to understand this, little sister. Next week, I'll be gone, and I don't like the idea of his knowing you'll be by yourself on the farm. He met you yesterday, and already he's had his arm around you, kissed your hand, and has a date with you?"

Before she could respond, Rob added his opinion. "*Twice*. And what is it with that hand-kissing stuff anyway? Thinks he's Don Juan, or what?"

"For your information, Mr. Know-it-all, Don Juan was Spanish, not Italian. You must have meant Casanova. But what's it to you what Craig does? At least *he's* a gentleman." *Great!* She'd promised herself she'd let the incident with Rob in high school go.

His face inflamed.

"As for the *date*, I never said yes."

"Look, Sis. My gut tells me this guy has an agenda. Don't let this feigned chivalry go to your head. He's no Sir Galahad in shining armor...who wasn't Italian either."

Rob snickered from behind Aiden's back.

As she stifled a giggle, Haley rolled her eyes. This conversation had gotten out of hand. Maybe they were right. She stole a peek at Rob. His nose sure had gotten out of joint. Warmth spread through her. He used to do that in high school. Always when another guy paid her attention. She drew in a quick breath. Could it be jealousy? But he'd always treated her more like a little sister.

Aiden cast his line into the water. Rob's line followed. He laid his pole in the boat and leaned forward to look past Aiden. "Haley, can I bait a hook for you? Or are you still mad at me?"

I guess he's trying to be a gentleman. "Thank you, yes."

An hour later, after not one nibble on any of the three poles, Aiden rowed to shore. As the bow hit the ground, Rob jumped out and secured the line to the maple tree. Aiden stepped onto the grass and pulled the rear of the boat to the bank with his other foot.

Rob extended his hand to Haley. She placed hers in his and rose, tripped over the seat, and fell forward. The boat wrenched away from Aiden, and he landed on his backside.

As Haley stumbled into the water, Rob caught her in his arms and pulled her to shore. "Whew! That was close. Did you decide to take a swim with the fish since we didn't catch any?"

He held her tight. Her heart pounded. His deep blue eyes held hers with a magnetic pull and reflected the sparkle of sun from the water. She gasped. "I'm okay now. Let go."

"Oh." He dropped his arms and stepped back.

Aiden's laughing? She glared at him as he rolled to his knees. When he stood and faced her, his lips clamped together, but his shoulders bobbed.

She hit him in the arm. "You'd better let that cackle out before you cause interior damage. Glad you thought it was funny. First, you lose me in the maze in the middle of the night, and now you find it hysterical that I wound up in the pond."

"Sorry, Sis. The entire scene was just too much for me. And it wasn't in the *middle of the night.*"

Rob's lips clamped shut, and he shook.

A rush of joy surged through Haley. Laughter sliced through the air. "I guess it was pretty funny. Thanks for the rescue, Rob."

"Any time." He bowed at the waist.

As one side of his mouth lifted, a tingle spread inside her. Aiden thought *Craig* had an agenda? What about Rob's sudden change of attitude toward her?

Aiden grabbed the poles from the boat, and they strolled back to the maple tree. "Hey, Rob. I forgot to tell you about the phone call this morning." As they stretched out on the blankets, Aiden relayed his conversation with the sheriff and Jason. "Remember when we used to help Dad as teens? He always double-checked our work on the car. He rechecked everyone's work, including his own."

While the discussion between the men continued, Haley watched Rob's expressions. He'd always been very good with cars. He would know how to cause brakes to fail. She glared at him. And he'd have a lot to gain...*Stop it. There you go again.* She closed her eyes and shook her head. There was no way he'd have tampered with Dad's brakes? *What's wrong with you, Haley?* Rob would never do something like that.

Chapter Sixteen

One Month Later

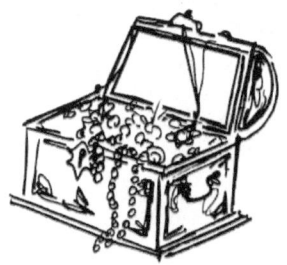

Haley listened to the ring on the line. "Come on, Aiden. Answer your phone." Voicemail clicked on. "It's me. Call back when you get the message." She dropped her cell onto the coffee table.

As she rose from the couch, the phone rang. Her brother's image grinned at her on the screen. That was fast. "Hi, big brother."

"Nice to hear from you, Sis. Is everything okay?"

"Things on the farm have settled to a workable routine with my studies and chores since your last call two or three days ago." She laughed. "You need to relax and realize I'm not a little girl anymore."

"He-e-ey...you're the one who phoned me this time." He chuckled.

"Yes, but you told me to, or you'd hunt me down." She giggled. "Nothing out of the ordinary has happened since you left. Perhaps Drago and his nightly patrol have scared whomever away. And Aiden, don't worry about Drago having been involved in Mom and Dad's accident or any of the strange episodes here. I don't. He's been an enormous help to me. Even taught me how to care for the horses, although I leave the major work for him. It's fun to learn, though."

"I'm glad. I hated to think he was implicated after our parents had done so much for him. He's proved himself over the years. Made up for the mistakes he made in his youth."

"Right. Drago told me to call his cell at night if I need to. He'd keep it handy. He's like another older brother."

"What did you find out about those mysterious trips to town he keeps so hush-hush? Has he mentioned them?"

"Not a word. Maybe he's got a girlfriend he's not ready to reveal. And it's not my place to ask about his love life."

Laughter came through the line. She loved her brother's laugh. Such a deep throaty sound...like their father's had been.

"He needs a good woman, Sis. Speaking of which, has Aunt Deb been over?"

"No, but she phones every other day, like you. She wants me to come to Council Bluffs to spend the weekend with her. I guess I will. Drago says it's no problem for him to handle everything here." Haley sucked in a breath.

"Oh. I've decided to hold Thanksgiving dinner here at the farm like Mom always did. Auntie will help me. I hope you, Char, and Everett can come."

"Sounds great. I'll talk to Char. She hasn't mentioned the holiday yet, so I'm sure we can make it."

Everett's squeal echoed through the phone. "What on earth was that, a banshee?"

"*That*, my dear little sister, was *your* nephew escaping from a bath."

Haley giggled. "So now he's *my nephew*? What a fuss."

"Oh, you've no idea. And yes, *your nephew*. He takes after you. Wait until you get married and have a little dickens like him." Aiden paused. "What's a banshee?"

"You know. That story Grandma used to tell us. The banshees of Ireland. Those Irish spirits who wailed, warning of impending doom. I imagine Gram's eyes would've been like saucers if she'd heard Everett's distress call."

Her brother's banter had been sorely missed after he went home last month. "Aiden, do you remember Lucy?"

"How could I forget her? It was almost as if I had another sister until she left for Chicago. What about her?"

"We finally connected. She's still up in Wisconsin. I invited her for Thanksgiving too. She'll bring Shaun with her. You remember her little white ball of fluffy energy called a dog? The Bichon."

"Yes, I remember. Everett will love the little guy. So, who else did you invite? Rob?"

Always pushing his best friend on her, but he didn't need to, not since her one-eighty-degree turnabout where Rob was concerned. They were good friends again. But just friends.

"Haley?" Aiden broke into her thoughts. "Haley, you still there?"

"I'm here."

"Are you mad at me for mentioning his name? Aren't you over that by now?"

"Yes, I am, and your buddy will be here with his parents. Mrs. Sheffield has insisted on roasting the turkey, and I acquiesced." That word should impress her big-time lawyer, brother.

"Acquiesced, huh?" He chuckled. "So, you've softened toward him?"

"Don't start. Rob and I are friends again. But I haven't much time for more than an occasional chat now that the farm has been placed in my hands. You sure you and Char don't want Everett raised in the country instead of California? Why'd you give up your share? Nebraska needs lawyers too."

"Sis, I appreciate it, but I'm not cut out to be a farmer...nor a rancher. I love the law, and I've gotten used to city living. But perhaps we'll move to Omaha sometime in the future, if I decide to open my own office. Then Everett can spend all the time he wants on the farm with his auntie. Hold on for a moment."

She'd adore having the little rascal hang around with her. Every girl's dream was to be a mother someday. But for now, she'd be content with her nephew. Besides, she had to find the right guy...who thought she was the right girl...before she could start a family.

Rob's face floated into her mind, but the image morphed into Craig Lowell's face with his pale blue eyes.

"Hey, I'm back. Speaking of spending time with someone, tell me you haven't spent any more with Lowell."

What was he, psychic? "Oh, Aiden. We've run into each other once or twice when I've gone to North Bend. I had coffee with him at Pete's Café a week ago. He'd just come out of his lawyer's office and bumped into me. Please don't worry about him."

"I'd rather you stayed away from him."

She shook her head. When would he realize she could take care of herself? "It's not like we're dating. Besides, I don't have time for him or any guy right now. The only one I see occasionally is Rob, and usually because of my classes. He helps me with agricultural information I need."

Another squeal came through the line. "Char needs me in the bathroom, Sis. Everett's giving her a hassle over something, so it's time for Dad to lay down the law. I'll phone you again next week. Say hi to Rob and his family for me, and stay safe."

"Will do. Bye."

Haley stashed her cell in her purse. She didn't get a chance to tell him she was going out with Rob tonight. *Oh, well.* She'd better get dressed. He said he'd pick her up at six-thirty. Why on earth had she decided to go with him to his cousin's wedding rehearsal and dinner? He'd claimed not to like Chad after the way he treated her in high school, and yet Rob agreed to be an usher? Didn't make sense.

If Chad brought up what he did to her back then, she might haul off and hit him, fiancée present or not.

Rob stepped back when Haley opened the front door. "*Wow.* You look great." This woman grew more beautiful every time he saw her. He took a deep breath to steady his racing pulse. "Are you ready to go, or do you still need a few minutes?"

"All set. Let me grab my jacket. Come on in."

As he entered, she ducked into the living room and snatched her evening bag.

"Wear a warm coat. It'll get colder."

Haley breezed back into the foyer and lifted a fake-fur jacket in shades of gray from the coat stand. He took the wrap from her hand and laid it on her shoulders. She was gorgeous in that navy-blue dress. It made her light green eyes more striking. He'd always thought she was one of a kind, even in high school. Should have told her long ago.

She lifted her keys from the clutch bag and locked the door after them.

He'd find the right time to make up for the things he'd never told her. Later. "Thanks for going with me to this rehearsal and dinner. I wasn't sure you'd say yes." But things had gone well between them since he started helping her with her studies.

As he held open the passenger door on his father's Impala, Haley slipped in. The door latched with a solid thunk. Rob ran around the front end and seated himself behind the wheel.

She glanced at him without a word.

"You're not worried that Chad will mention what I told him in high school, are you? I confessed the truth to him. He's changed a lot since then. I think it has to do with Stacy, his fiancée. She makes him toe the line, and he's found he gets in far less trouble that way." Rob snickered and started the engine. "We get along now. I suppose it's why he asked me to be an usher. We're not best of friends, not like Aiden and me, but good enough to laugh together once in a while."

Haley smiled and toyed with her purse.

"When I told Chad you were coming, he was glad. I also warned him against bringing up the past, and he agreed. He's sorry for what he said and how he treated you."

"Thanks, Rob. I did have second thoughts, but I feel better now."

When they arrived at the church, Rob scanned the room and found Chad waving at them. *Lord, please don't let him say anything about high school.*

His cousin strode toward them and extended his hand to Rob. "Hi, Cuz. Ready to catch me if I faint tomorrow?" He chuckled.

"If you need me to." As they shook hands, Rob dipped his head toward a tall blonde beside the minister. "Stacy doesn't seem one bit nervous."

"She's not. Always has everything under control, including me." He laughed again and held out his hand to Haley. "Thanks for coming."

She placed her hand in his and gave him a wary smile.

"Let me introduce you to my soon-to-be wife."

Rob took Haley by the elbow and led her to the front of the church. Chad slid his hand around Stacy's waist and excused them from the minister. She beamed at him.

Rob glanced at Haley. If only she'd look at him that way. Maybe someday."

"Honey, you've met Rob, my cousin. This is the lady he—"

"Lives next door to," Rob added quickly. "My neighbor, Haley MacKenna." He knew he shouldn't have confided his feelings for her to Chad. *Way to go, Cuz.*

As Rob gave his cousin a sideways glance, Chad lowered his brows. "Yes, neighbor. My cousin's farm runs up to theirs. We were all in high school together." His face flushed, and he bit his lip, then turned toward the minister at the pulpit. "Ah, let's see if Pastor wants to start the rehearsal." He scurried off.

Stacy gazed at Chad and shook her head. She faced Rob and Haley. "He's more nervous than any man I've ever seen about to acquire a ball and chain." A chortle bubbled out of her. "And I've seen many. I wondered if I'd ever be a bride after the numerous weddings I've attended. Who'd have guessed I'd marry a catch like Chad?" She sashayed to his side.

Rob let out a relieved breath.

Haley peered at him and seemed to stifle a laugh. "I see what you mean. They're a good match."

He could think of a better one.

After the rehearsal and dinner, Haley finished her goodbyes to everyone and found Rob and Chad in conversation at the church activity hall entrance. She strolled up to them. "Are you ready to leave, Rob?"

Chad turned to her. "Thanks again for coming tonight. Believe it or not, it means a lot to me." He turned to Rob. "As I said, take good care of this sweet thing. See you in the morning, Cuz." He punched Rob in the arm and smiled at Haley. "You will attend the ceremony, correct?"

"Yes. I'll be there." She returned his smile. What had they been so deep in conversation about?

Chad joined Stacy and a group of guests inside the foyer.

"I can't get over the change in his personality, Rob. He's so easygoing. None of the egotistical attitude he had in school." She grinned at him. "Thanks for asking me to come with you tonight. I had a pleasant time, which did me good."

"Shall we take the long way back to your place? The night should be beautiful with the full moon and frost forming on everything. Strange, we haven't had any snow."

"Don't worry. Snow's on its way. You haven't checked the *Farmer's Almanac*, Mr. Sheffield." She giggled.

He narrowed his eyes at her. "Okay, Miz Farmer. Takes a few classes, does a few farm chores, and now she's an expert."

Haley elbowed his ribs. "Only because you've helped me with my studies. I appreciate the time you've taken away from your own work to do that. Your dad has been gracious."

"He understands how much it means to you. Besides, he's always had a soft spot for a certain strawberry-haired girl on your farm."

After they drove through the countryside, Rob pulled into the MacKenna farmyard. They exited the vehicle and hurried to the front porch. Their breath hung like clouds of mist in the cold night air.

She unlocked the door. "Thanks again for inviting me. It was fun."

"Haley?" He looked at his feet. "You know—oh, nuts. Always could talk to anyone else without getting tongue-tied, except you." He gazed into her eyes. His glistened from the security light over the drive. "It's why I never asked you out when we were in high school. I wanted to but could never get up enough nerve."

He'd wanted to date her back then? She thought he viewed her as a sister—one to tease mercilessly. She pressed her lips together. Did he mean it? For years, she'd wanted him to ask her out. Now that she was home again, her feelings for him had grown stronger.

"Haley, may I take you to dinner and a movie next Friday night? You know, a real date? I'd ask for tomorrow, but the wedding and reception are in the morning, and Dad needs me at the farm for the rest of the day. Mom asked me to go with her into Omaha on Sunday afternoon. Then there's evening service, and—"

Haley put her fingers over his lips. "Dinner and a movie next Friday will be fine, Rob." A flutter traveled through her stomach. As long as he and Chad hadn't planned a prank to play on her. They did have their heads together tonight over something. No, they wouldn't.

Chapter Seventeen

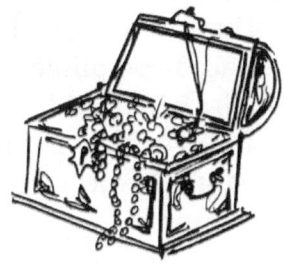

id-afternoon Saturday, Craig drove the Mercedes into Haley's yard. He'd planned to take her to dinner weeks ago but never could get her to commit.

As he approached the front door, he glanced toward the barn where a burly, dark-haired man jumped into a beat-up, two-door truck and pulled out of the drive. He had to be the farmhand. Good. A chance to be alone with Haley. And no interruptions. They hadn't been unaccompanied since they were lost in the corn maze last month...when that fool Sheffield made an untimely appearance. Craig sneered.

He should have called first, but every time he did, she'd end the conversation before he'd had a chance to ask her out. Craig grinned as he raised his hand to knock. The restaurant he'd found in Omaha was perfect for dinner tonight. She couldn't refuse his invitation now that he was here. They'd make a big night of it in the city and then go to his place. He rapped on the door.

After a few seconds, he cursed under his breath and turned. She might be in the barn or stable. As he stepped down from the porch, the front door opened. He spun.

"Craig, what are you doing here? Oh." Haley half-smiled. "Sorry. That didn't come out right. I only wondered *why* you're here."

"Surprise? I thought I'd show up since you're always too busy to talk on the phone." What a knockout. His eyes roved over her every curve. "Your fancy green dress shows off—" He dragged his gaze to her face "—your eyes." They could spend time right here before dinner. A few more well-placed compliments would entice the lady into a romantic mood. "You're beautiful."

"Thank you." Color flooded her cheeks. "This morning, I attended a wedding and just got home a few minutes ago. I haven't had time to change. Please, come in."

Exactly what he wanted. The two of them alone without interference. He entered the foyer and spotted an older woman sitting in the dining room. *Great!*

"Aunt Debbie, this is Craig Lowell."

The tall, thin, middle-aged woman approached him without a smile. "You're Tom Lowell's son from Italy. Aiden told me about your escapade at the pumpkin festival last month."

I'll bet he did. What was she doing here? At the fishing pond, Haley said she'd gone home.

Haley touched his upper arm. "Have a seat, Craig. Would you care for coffee? I'm afraid I can't make espresso or cappuccino." She led him into the living room.

He lowered himself onto the armchair as Haley's surprisingly good-looking aunt watched him from the foyer, her arms crossed over her bosom. "Coffee is fine. Thank you."

"I'll be right back." Haley hurried into the dining room and disappeared from view, her aunt on her heels.

The aunt must have come back from wherever she lived. The troublemaking woman ruined his afternoon plans. Craig grimaced as he gazed around the room. Old-fashioned. Nowhere near as lavish as his new home. His survey stopped at the corner fireplace. Now there was a cozy spot with the loveseat in front. He grinned. Yes, he'd love to spend time there with Haley in his arms, if her aunt wasn't here. The corners of his mouth drooped.

Murmurs reached his ears from the direction in which Haley and her aunt had headed. Their words sounded heated. What else had MacKenna or Sheffield said to the woman? He rose and inched into the dining room.

Craig strained to make out the conversation. No doubt, the brother had given her an earful after that night in the maze. *Sheffield would have told him he found Haley with my arm around her.* Craig smirked. Haley belonged in his arms. She was his.

Perhaps he could find a way to get the aunt to leave. Or...Haley could come home with him after he finished his coffee.

Haley poured coffee into two mugs. Why was Auntie so uptight? She placed the cups for Craig and her on a tray with the sugar bowl, spoons, napkins, and creamer. "Are you sure you don't want to join us?"

"What I *don't* want is to sit in a room with that young man. He came here uninvited and thought you'd be alone. If I hadn't met you and Rob in town after the wedding and followed you home—he certainly didn't know I was here with my car parked by the barn." She crossed her arms and blew a rush of air through puckered lips. "Aiden's right not to trust him. Tom Lowell couldn't be trusted either, from what Mrs. Sheffield confided in me last week at church. She's worried about you, too, after what Robert told her happened at the pond."

Haley's head jerked toward her aunt. "What did Rob's mother tell you?"

"We can talk about that another time. This young man shouldn't have shown up here when he thought you'd be alone. Can't you see that, dear?"

"Maybe they don't worry over such things in Italy when a woman is grown. Besides, he's proved himself to be a gentleman every time I've met him."

The look on Auntie's face told Haley that didn't matter to an overprotective aunt. Not now that Mom and Dad were gone, and her brother was in California. *Dear Auntie.*

Haley lifted the tray from the counter and gave her aunt a quick peck on the cheek as she passed. "If you're so concerned about our being alone, sit with us. I'm sure Craig will be delighted." She swept through the kitchen doorway, across the dining room, and into the living room where Craig stared out the front windows.

When she placed the tray on the coffee table, he turned. "I thought I saw a man leave when I pulled into the yard. Is he your ranch hand? Does he live on the property?" He sat on the couch next to Haley.

A short burst of laughter came from her. "Drago's hardly what you'd call a *ranch hand.* This is just a farm—a large one, but nonetheless, a farm. We mostly grow crops. Although we do have livestock—cows and goats, chickens. And Dad had started to breed horses." A twinge of sorrow hit Haley. She shook it off and handed a steaming mug to Craig.

Haley held out a napkin to him. "I know nothing about horses, except how to mount one and ride. But Drago grew up on a horse ranch. He's been a blessing to us."

While he sipped his coffee, Craig peered over the rim of the cup. "Drago. That's an odd name for an American. It's the Italian form of Latin, meaning dragon."

"Yes, so my aunt reminded my brother and me not long ago. Drago's real name is Cary. Aiden and I named him Drago when we were little kids." She giggled. "When Aunt Debbie told us he might not appreciate that name, we apologized to him. But he said he'd grown fond of it. Could be it made him sound tougher."

Craig's brows rose. "And he's not tough?"

"Not really. He's strong, but he's not mean. Always willing to help, even strangers." She smiled. "But I sure wouldn't want to tangle with him. I've seen him wrestle down a bull calf without raising a sweat when it slipped the rope on branding day. He's not someone to go up against."

A somber expression darkened Craig's face, then disappeared. "So, does he live here on the ra—farm?"

"Yes, he does. He has the old bunkhouse all to himself. It's his home. Why do you ask?"

"Just that...it's a good thing he's here at night since you're alone."

Aunt Debbie stepped into the room, cup in hand. She slid in between Haley and Craig. As Haley scooted over, Aunt Debbie turned to him. "It's true. Cary is *always* here. And he's very protective of *our* girl. He treats her more like a niece than the boss's daughter. I'd hate to see what happens to *anyone* who tries to mess with her."

Haley's mouth dropped open. What on earth had gotten into Auntie? "Do you truly believe I need Drago to protect me?"

Aunt Debbie took a sip of coffee. "I suppose not. You did win first prize in rifle shooting at the fair four years ago, didn't you?" Before Haley could answer, Auntie had swung her gaze back to Craig. "She'd won first place for three years in a row and would have continued to win each year if she hadn't left for college."

Haley shook her head. "Okay. I think he gets the picture."

Craig finished his coffee and stood. "Guess I should leave. Thank you for the coffee. Would you walk me to my car, Haley?"

"Sure." She glanced at her aunt. "I'll be right back."

After Haley closed the front door, Craig stopped on the porch. "I have to admit, I was surprised to see your aunt here. She lives in Omaha, right?"

"On the other side, Council Bluffs." The hair on Haley's neck rose. Why was he so interested in where her aunt lived? Hadn't she already told him at the pond?

"Oh. Does she visit often?"

"She works full time, so whenever she can. She decided to spend this weekend with me. Why?" Haley narrowed her eyes at him.

He chuckled. "Don't get nervous. Just making conversation. The reason I stopped by was to invite you to dinner. Since you have company until Sunday, we can make it another evening...after your aunt leaves. I'd planned to take you to a nice restaurant, but I have a better idea. I've hired a cook, and she's fantastic."

Haley gulped.

"Don't worry about being in the house alone with me either. The cook moved in yesterday."

A tingle joined the risen hairs on Haley's neck. She bit her lip.

"Haley?"

"Umm. I'll have to think about this. Do you have a church to go to, Craig? Have you visited ours?"

Craig clenched his jaw as he steered the car toward home. *Church.* He'd have to endure people who acted as if they were better than anyone who wasn't a member. Hadn't he met enough of them in Italy? He shouldn't have promised to meet Haley there tomorrow. He had no use for church. But if he hadn't, he wouldn't get anywhere with her.

He gritted his teeth as he drove through the long driveway that led to his house. These locals weren't any better than him, far from it. But okay, he could pretend with the best of them.

When he parked in the three-car garage, he shut off the engine and laid his head back against the headrest. She said she'd consider dinner with him another time after he'd gone to a service or two. What was it with women? They just had to drag a man to church. He'd play the game to please her...for now.

Craig strode from the garage to the front entrance. When he opened the door, his mouth watered at the familiar aroma of Italy. He dropped his keys on the table in the foyer and continued to the kitchen.

As he entered the room, Mrs. Yonge stirred an oversized pot. She jumped. "Oh, my stars, you scared me, Mr. Lowell. I didn't hear you come in. Supper won't be ready for another three hours. I'm afraid I forgot to ask what time you wanted the evening meal served. Is five-thirty right?"

Good thing he'd forgotten to tell her not to make any. "That's fine. What are you cooking? It smells terrific. Reminds me of the ravioli our cook in Italy used to make."

"That's what I'm preparing now. It's probably the oregano and garlic you remember. I've made enough so you'll have plenty to snack on, when you'd like after I leave each night and for my days off. I'll make frozen dinners for you too. All you need do is pop them into the microwave on the frozen meal setting."

Him? Cook? He wasn't about to fix his meals, microwave or otherwise. That's why he'd hired a cook. When she wasn't here to make the food and clean afterward, he'd go to the roadhouse outside town, as he had been doing since his return to the States. No sense in dirty dishes when there wasn't anyone to pick up after him. Someone else had always done that. "Call me when it's ready."

"Yes, sir."

"I'll be in the living room." He left the kitchen.

After he turned on the TV and set the volume to low, he stretched out in the brown leather recliner in the room off the foyer and closed his eyes.

A vision of Haley in the emerald green, curve-hugging dress filled his thoughts. He grinned. What a woman. Too bad he wouldn't have her with him alone tonight. His body surged with excitement as he let his imagination wander. He ran his tongue over his lips in enjoyment. He had to have her.

Chapter Eighteen

Thanksgiving Morning

*A*s Haley rose from her bed and gazed out the window toward the field behind the house, she giggled with glee. *"Wow."* That blanket of snow makes it look more like Christmas than Thanksgiving. She'd talk Aiden and Rob into a snowball fight after dinner. She laughed. Craig, too, if he joined them tonight.

Lips pulled to one side, she let out a sigh. When Aiden came down to breakfast this morning, she'd better tell him she'd invited Craig. "That ought to begin the day on a cheerful note." She'd better be prepared for another lecture on her brother's gut warnings too.

But she was right to invite Craig to join the family. Otherwise, he'd spend Thanksgiving alone in that humongous house. She'd not gone on a date with him yet, putting him off each time he'd asked her out. But then he'd made an excuse each Sunday not to come to church. Still, she felt obligated to invite him. Everything would work out fine.

Things had worked out for Lucy to be here. Haley smiled. After the long drive from Wisconsin yesterday, she'd probably sleep until noon.

Haley made her bed, washed up, and headed for the kitchen to start on the big family meal. At least this year she didn't have to head back to school the following Sunday. Although she'd gladly accept that sadness in exchange for the pain in her heart over her parents' deaths. She pushed the thought from her head.

As Haley neared the kitchen, Aunt Debbie swooped through the dining room wearing her jacket and stocking cap. "I'll collect the eggs for you, dear." She breezed out the back door before Haley could reply.

Auntie loved those chickens. They must bring back happy thoughts of when she and Mom lived on a farm years ago.

What fun they'd all have with everyone here for the holiday.

After Haley put away the clean dishes from the dishwasher, she pressed the start button on the coffee maker. A loud rap sounded, and a dark figure showed through the nine-paned window of the back door. She wiped a circle of fog from a pane and grinned. *Drago.*

When she swung the door open for him, he dangled two pheasants from his hand. "Thought you could fix up one of these for Thanksgiving dinner tonight. To go with the turkey."

"Where...how...?"

The stout man chuckled with a sparkle in his dark brown eyes. "Rob invited me to go hunting with him and his dad early this morning. We had a great time, and I bagged two."

She'd never gone hunting when Dad and her brother went with the Sheffields. It wasn't her thing. Give her a plain old non-living target, and she'd have a ball. But to kill something that beautiful...she just couldn't. Yet, she'd not hurt Drago for the world. Good thing Auntie was here. She'd know what to do with the birds.

Haley peered into his eyes. Her lack of response had already hurt him. "I'm sorry, Drago. I slept late this morning. Just woke up a while ago, and I'm not quite cognizant. Thank you. Come on in. Put the pheasants in the sink."

He complied. "That coffee smells good."

Without asking, she poured him a cup and motioned for him to have a seat at the kitchen table. "You plan to join us for dinner tonight, don't you?"

After he'd sipped the steaming brew, he sighed. "I wouldn't miss it for the world. Your family has always treated me as if I'd been born into it. I don't know where I'd be today if it hadn't been for your daddy. He gave me a chance at a decent life. I hope my kid brother Markus has done as well. "

Haley's heart pinched. "Your brother?"

Drago drained his mug, rose, and set the cup in the sink. "Thank you, Miss Haley. Nothing like hot coffee on a cold day. I'll run the snowblower in the circle out front. How many cars should I allow for?"

He didn't want to talk about it. "Let's see. The Sheffields' and Craig Lowell's car will need spots."

Drago snapped his head back to her. He frowned.

She shouldn't have mentioned Craig. "Good thing Aiden's rental, Aunt Debbie's, and Lucy's vehicles were here yesterday before it snowed." She laughed. "Less work for you."

"That son of old man Lowell's? Why is he coming here?"

"Oh, Drago, not you too. Why does everyone think he's such a bad person? He's done nothing to deserve such scrutiny."

Drago shook his head. "Something about him doesn't meet the eye, Miss Haley. You mark my words. When I was in town last week, he came strutting out of that shifty lawyer's office. What's his name?" Drago drilled darts into the kitchen floor tiles with his eyes. "Doty. Yeah, that's it. The New York city-slicker lawyer. He set up shop here a couple'a years back."

She tried not to laugh at his exaggerated facial expressions as his bushy black brows with touches of silver furrowed. "I'm sure Craig still has legal affairs to handle since the death of his father." Again her heart pinched. "And if his father used this lawyer...that would explain it. Wouldn't it?"

"Even so, I'll keep an eye out with young Lowell hanging around."

Drago turned the doorknob, shook his head again, and opened the back door. "See you in a while. Thanks for the coffee."

Haley watched him traverse the slick steps. "Drago," she called after him, "Can you salt these and the front stairs before anyone arrives?"

"On my list, Miss Haley," he answered as he waved back at her.

She shut the door and returned to the kitchen. Noises from overhead signaled her brother and his family were awake.

Seconds later, the back door opened, and Aunt Debbie stepped in with a basket of eggs. "Your chickens aren't worried about a little snow. The sturdy coop your dad built has made for a bunch of happy egg layers." She laughed, laid the egg basket on the washing machine, and hung her jacket and hat in the mudroom before she stepped inside the kitchen. Aunt Debbie deposited the basket in the left well of the sink. "I'll take care of these pheasants for you. One to roast and one to freeze."

"Thanks, Auntie. I appreciate your help. Did Drago tell you he brought them in?"

"No problem. I love to gather eggs. I can't keep chickens where I live now. So this makes me feel like a farm girl again." She grinned. "I'll have some of that coffee if you don't mind."

"Me too. It smells great." Lucy followed her words into the room. Her dog, Shaun, scampered in right behind her. He slid to a stop at the water and food bowls Haley had placed in a corner. Lucy dropped into a chair. "So, what can I do to help today? I've had a good night's sleep after that drive from Wisconsin, and I'm raring to celebrate Thanksgiving."

Haley pulled down three mugs from the cabinet and filled each with the black liquid. Why didn't Auntie answer when asked if she'd seen Drago? Must not have been paying attention.

As Haley set the steaming cups on the kitchen table with the creamer, her mind shifted to what Drago had told her about Craig. Now that she thought about it, the paperwork for his father's estate should have been settled months ago.

As the Sheffields arrived that afternoon, Rob spotted Craig Lowell's Mercedes-Benz parked next to Mrs. Moye's snow-covered vehicle. Rob gritted his teeth. What was that guy doing here?

Rob's mom asked, "Whose car is that next to Debbie's?"

Rob's blood seethed as he eyed Lowell's pale mop of hair behind the steering wheel. "It's Lowell's. Aiden said he inherited it from his dad along with everything else."

With raised eyebrows, Mr. Sheffield glanced at his wife. "This will be an interesting evening." He stepped out, then circled the front of the vehicle.

Rob hopped out of the back seat and opened the passenger door for his mother.

His dad took her hand to help her stand. He gazed toward the barn. "Whose pickup is next to the silo?"

"That's one of those GMC Sierra Denali's I mentioned, Dad. I'd love to trade my old heap in for one. Must be Lucy Craft's truck. Haley told me Lucy bought one when she accepted that job in Wisconsin. She's here for the holiday."

As they left their vehicle, the driver's door of the Mercedes opened. Lowell slid out and shoved the door shut with a loud thunk. Without a smile, he gave a curt nod to Rob.

Wasn't enough for him to horn in on their picnic last month, now he'd crash Haley's family Thanksgiving dinner? A slow burn rose in Rob's neck. Was that a bottle of booze under his arm? Aiden would take care of him fast enough.

Pumpkin and spices filled the air. Rob's mouth watered. He'd already savored the aroma of his mother's turkey as the roasting pan rested on the seat next to him. Now the pie. Dessert first tonight. He snickered to himself.

Craig made it to the top of the stairs before the Sheffields reached the bottom step.

All thought of food left Rob's mind when he caught the smirk Craig threw his way. If this weren't Thanksgiving, he'd—

The front door opened just as Lowell raised his hand to knock.

Like a Christmas angel in an off-white dress that made her deep strawberry-blonde hair glow, Haley smiled. "Welcome, Craig. I'm happy you took me up on the invitation. No one should be alone on Thanksgiving. Come on in."

She'd invited this creep? Rob expelled a rush of breath.

Lowell held out a bottle to her. "I brought this as my contribution to the party. One of Italy's finest, Moscato d'Asti, from the town of Asti. And my cook made cantucci before she left for the holiday." He handed her a large plastic-wrapped plate.

Haley's expression was priceless, with her brow wrinkled and mouth hanging open.

Lowell tilted his head to the right and gawked at her. "You're confused by the Italian. Ah. That's right. You call these biscotti here." He pushed the platter toward her.

She held out her hands to receive the plate. "Thanks to you and your cook..." she peeked at the bottle, "...but we don't drink alcohol. Dad never allowed it in the house."

As Rob stifled a laugh, he followed his mom and dad to Lowell's side. Way to go, genius. He'd lost points with this blunder. Rob glanced at his father, whose gaze traveled from Haley to Lowell to Rob.

Lowell's brows lowered. He stuck his tongue in his cheek, then smiled. "I'm sorry, Haley. I should have asked what to bring. Let me put this in the car." He turned and bumped Rob's arm as he passed.

Haley smiled at Rob and his parents. "Thanks again for roasting the turkey, Mrs. Sheffield."

She kissed Haley on the cheek. While still in the doorway, Mr. Sheffield wrapped his arms around her and his wife's shoulders.

"Hey, Dad. Can you move inside before you make out with *my* girl?"

Haley's head whipped around to Rob. "What?"

"Just teasing," he said under his breath. He hoped Lowell heard it loud and clear though. They stepped into the foyer, and Rob seized the door handle. "It's freezing out there. Let's not let any of these good aromas escape."

As he pushed the door closed, Haley grabbed the edge. "Wait a minute. Craig's on his way up the stairs." She pulled the door open wider.

After he'd entered the foyer, Lowell removed his overcoat. Dressed in a tailored two-piece black suit, light gray shirt, and a diagonal-striped black and light blue tie, he looked out of place with the rest of the men. Where did he think he was? A job interview? A tie? Really? Rob peered at his four-year-old dark brown sports jacket and tan slacks with a new beige shirt.

Haley took their coats and hung them in the hall closet. Everyone followed her into the living room, while Rob's mother took the roast turkey to the kitchen.

Rob grimaced. This would be a disaster of a holiday.

As Craig entered the living room, he noted Haley's aunt seated on the couch next to a beautiful woman with shiny black hair and curves in all the right places, except for her stomach. His gaze roved over the younger woman and then traveled to Aiden on the other side of her, his arm draped across her shoulders. She was his wife. Nice, even though pregnant.

Aiden observed Craig as if he were an insect that had crept into the house. Haley took his arm and pulled him toward the couch.

"Auntie, you remember Craig."

The look in her eyes wasn't any warmer than her nephew's. "Nice to see you again, Mrs..."

"Moye."

She didn't offer her hand. What a bunch of icebergs.

Sheffield and his father stepped up to Aiden, who shook hands with them.

The front door opened, and a stocky man with dark hair strode in and through the dining room as if he lived there. Must be that farmhand. He had nerve tromping through here. The hired help should use the back door.

Aiden's curvaceous wife stood and waltzed to the staircase. "Haley, I'll check on Everett, then see what still needs to be done for dinner."

As she ascended to the second floor, Craig watched her legs until they were out of view. Slim and trim outside of the swollen stomach, and well-endowed.

His gaze left the staircase and landed on Aiden, who glared at him. Craig sat in the overstuffed armchair next to the brick fireplace. Must have struck a jealous chord. Fearful she'd enjoy someone else's attention, was he?

Haley switched on the stereo system. Soft classical music played in the background as she exited the room. An attempt to soften the atmosphere, no doubt. Much needed with these characters.

Mrs. Moye got up and followed Haley. Rob took up the spot Aiden's wife had vacated, and Mr. Sheffield filled Mrs. Moye's place. That left just the men...with nothing to say. The atmosphere in the room sure turned frigid. Craig smirked again.

He closed his eyes and pretended to listen to the gentle music. If looks could kill, he'd have bled to death by now. Muffled whispers came to his ears, then footsteps sounded, moving away. He opened his eyes. Only the Sheffield men remained, with Rob glaring and Mr. Sheffield buried behind a newspaper.

This would be an evening to remember. Craig closed his eyes again. Better than an empty house with nothing to do but stare at the walls or watch boring TV. He killed a snicker before it erupted. Being near Haley and that raven-haired beauty would be worth it. Yes, an evening to remember.

He settled back in the chair and gave his imagination free rein.

Chapter Nineteen

aley placed a stack of dishes from the china cabinet on the dining room table. What a fantastic idea, everyone together to celebrate this Thanksgiving. She was so excited. It would be a chance for Craig to show his neighbors he wasn't the villain they assumed him to be.

As she turned to get the water goblets out, Aiden came from behind and grasped her arm. "Come with me." He dragged her into the kitchen.

"What are you doing? I need to set the table."

"Why is Craig Lowell here? He's not family."

Their aunt and Mrs. Sheffield spun from the stove.

Oh boy. Haley's cheeks grew warm. She knew she should have told Aiden ahead of time. "Neither is Rob nor the Sheffield's. Nor

Lucy. Not really." She stood her ground, leaning on the side of the kitchen sink.

Mrs. Sheffield removed a large pot from the stove and poured steaming water from it into the drain. She dumped the sweet potatoes into a colander, ran cold water over them, and began to peel the skins away.

Aiden grimaced and broke the silence in the room. "You know what I mean, Sis. The Sheffields are family to me, and they used to be to you too."

Haley's jaw dropped. How could he say such a thing with Mrs. Sheffield right next to her? Haley wrapped her arm around the woman's shoulders. "I was referring to blood relatives. My brother wants to make a scene just because I invited Craig to dinner. You and Mr. Sheffield are as close to me as my own family."

Mrs. Sheffield leaned her head against Haley's. "Yes, dear. And we think of you like family too. But I can't help but wonder why you invited Mr. Lowell's son either. His father stirred up so much trouble for all of us in the past."

Haley dropped her arm and sighed. "I'm sorry everyone is disappointed, but I had to invite him after I found out he'd be alone for Thanksgiving." She faced her brother. "He lost his father. His mother is in Italy. He's an only child with no family in the States. Wasn't it the Christian thing to do?" She held out her hands, palms up.

Lucy entered. "Ahhh...am I interrupting something?" Her brows rose.

Haley smiled at her. "Not a thing. We were having a discussion about Christian values. That's all." If Aiden's jaw tightened any harder, he'd crack every tooth in his mouth. She glanced at her aunt.

With eyes glued to the folded napkins she had shaped into swans, Aunt Debbie puckered her lips and drew in a deep breath.

Mrs. Sheffield put her hands on Haley's shoulders. "Yes, Haley. It was the right thing to do. Under the circumstances." She hugged her.

Aiden left the room without another word. Aunt Debbie continued to fold napkins.

Rob kept his eyes on Lowell. What were his secret plans for this evening? The smirk on his lips surely meant the guy was up to no good. He was not to be trusted.

Everett ran down the stairs, through the foyer, and plopped himself at Rob's feet. He dumped an armful of assorted tractors and wagons on the carpet and spread them out on the floor. Oblivious to anyone else in the room, the little boy moved them in a circle as though they were in a race. Rob chuckled to himself. *Kids.* He leaned over and ruffled the boy's flax–blond hair. In a peaceful world of his own.

Sitting back on the couch, Rob watched Lowell open his eyes and sneer at the boy. So, he didn't like kids. Another strike against him since Haley adored them.

"Say, Craig. I hear you had some business in town with the most unpopular lawyer in the area. Many people don't like or trust him."

Lowell glared at Rob. "Are you trying to warn me? Or infer something? I don't see where my choice of an attorney is any of your business, Sheffield. Mr. Doty was my father's lawyer, and he set up my trust fund. He also handles the estate. Does *that* satisfy your curiosity?"

Without a rattle of the pages, Rob's father continued to read the newspaper.

Rob uncrossed and crossed his legs in the opposite direction. "Excuse me. Didn't mean to pry. There are many good attorneys in the area. Doty is fairly new in town, as are you. I thought maybe you weren't aware of the rumors." But Craig Lowell *had* heard of the unfounded grievances over his neighbors' property line, which Doty filed on behalf of old man Lowell. Craig had mentioned the old stone barn on the edge of the MacKenna farm the day they met him at the edge of his field. *Oh, yeah.* This guy knew exactly what kind of attorney Doty was.

With arms folded in front of him, Lowell continued to glare, his chin sank to his chest like a bad-tempered child. "Sure, you did."

Aiden strode from the dining room to the foyer and turned. His head motioned for Rob to follow him upstairs.

Rob rose and tailed Aiden. "What's up, buddy?"

"Shhh." Aiden led him into his old room and shut the door. "Thought I'd tell you why Haley asked Lowell over for Thanksgiving dinner. Besides his status as an only child, he has no other family here in the U.S. With his mother still in Italy, he's alone for the holiday. My clever sister pulled the *Christian-thing-to-do* card."

Aiden sat on the edge of the bed. "But I suppose she's right." He stood again and went to the window. "I just don't like having Lowell around. There's something off with him. Can't quite put my finger on it, but something's not right."

"Yeah." Rob leaned on the closed door. "I guess so. But why are you telling me?"

A smile stretched across Aiden's face. "Quit the act. You don't think I know how you feel about my sister? And always have? Now with this interloper around—"

"Hey, slow down. I..." Rob pressed his lips together so hard it hurt. "When did you figure it out?"

Aiden burst into laughter. "Subtle as a brick through a window, man. The teasing you did every time she came in sight?" He shook his head and continued to laugh.

Heat rose in Rob's face. "Did you ever say anything to her?"

"Not sure. I may have teased her about it, but then she might not have taken me seriously." He chuckled.

They both stepped over several toy vehicles scattered across the floor and lowered themselves to the edge of Aiden's old bed.

"*Yeowch!*" Rob jumped up when something sharp threatened to stab his buttocks. He handed a small metal tractor to Aiden.

"That son of mine is destined to be a farmer. Never plays with citified toys. Always farm animals and equipment. When we got him a firetruck, he pouted for the whole day."

"Do you think you'll leave California and come back home?"

"No. I've no intention of doing that. This area already has well-established attorneys. I'm not a farmer. Haley's the one who loves agriculture. Not me. Sure, Drago could manage the farm for me, but why trade in a good-paying job in California and struggle to start a business here with such competition?"

Aiden pointed the tractor at Rob. "Wait'll you and Haley have your own kids. You'll get used to stuff like this." He snickered. "And wait until you step on one in the middle of the night."

"Our kids? You mean you expect us to get married? We've only been on one date so far."

"Of course, I do. I know you love her. It was crystal clear from the day you came clean about what you told your cousin back in high school. Aunt Deb knew it too. She told you to let Haley know how you felt about her."

A rush of joy filled Rob. He grinned. They'd be one family someday. The grin died. But it was all up to Haley. Lowell was in the picture now, and he had her fooled. Had she only felt sorry for him and acted with Christian charity when she invited him to be with her family? Or, had she fallen for him? "Aiden, I got the same vibe you did about Lowell. What are we going to do to protect her?"

"All we can do is keep an eye out, and that'll fall on you when my family and I go back to California." Aiden slapped Rob on the back. "It's like that verse in Second Corinthians where it says Satan is transformed into an angel of light. She doesn't see what we see...or what our intuitions tell us. But she'll come around."

Char's voice traveled up the stairs. "Dinner's ready."

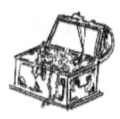

Craig's jaw and facial muscles stiffened as he sat across from Haley in the dining room. Rob lowered himself into the chair next to her, her nephew on her other side. Aiden took the seat at the head of the table, with his knockout wife to his right.

As Drago pulled out the chair beside Craig, his jaw tensed even more. The hired help sat at the dinner table around here? *How rustic.* At least Lucy was on his other side. Perhaps he'd focus on her for the evening to see if he could spark a bit of jealousy in Haley.

Craig thanked his lucky stars the farmhand separated him from the frozen-faced aunt. At least he didn't have to endure her glares. He'd never seen such a hodge-podge assembly of people at the dinner table.

Mr. Sheffield seated himself at the other end of the table with his wife to his left.

Rob took Haley's hand in his. One by one, everyone at the table reached for the hand of the person on either side of them. *Now what?* There was no way he'd touch the *farmhand.*

Lucy held her hand out to Craig, then leaned toward him and whispered. "Aiden's going to say the blessing over the food."

He grasped hers but kept his left hand in his lap. The farmhand they called Drago did the same with his right. While everyone else closed their eyes, Craig watched. After "Amen" was repeated by everyone but him, he sneered.

Cheerful conversation filled the room as platters of food were passed around the table. The mixed aromas of turkey, pheasant, hot vegetables, sweet potatoes, and buttered corn made Craig's mouth water. But his eyes remained glued to Haley and Rob.

Heat rose from Craig's collar. His gaze left Haley and traveled to Aiden's wife. Nice name, Charlotte. He ogled her as she engaged in a conversation with her son concerning the amount of sweet potato he could have. Craig glanced at Lucy and back to Charlotte. Too bad he hadn't sat between the two of them. Now *that* would have been enjoyable.

He turned to Lucy. "I understand you work as a tour guide in Wisconsin. What do you do during the winter months when it's so cold?"

"Wisconsin is a great place year-round. There are always things to do. Take, for instance, the Wisconsin Dells. They offer a holiday train, cross country ski and snowshoe trails, winter camping, sledding and snow tubing, and lots more. Currently, I work at The Cave of the Mounds, which is open all year. It's an hour or so south of the Dells. You should visit someday."

Interesting woman. Pretty, smart, and so far friendlier toward him than anyone else here, except for Haley. *Hmm. I wonder if she knows anything about the treasure.* "You used to live in this town, right?"

Chapter Twenty

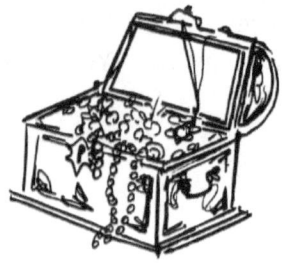

After dessert, Craig strode into the kitchen to refill his coffee cup while the rest of the guests and family read, watched television, or played a board game. He would need all the caffeine he could drink to stay awake at this dull party. Where had Haley disappeared to? He had tried to catch her alone the entire evening. Sheffield had gone missing too. Maybe the oaf went home, but his parents were still there.

Soft voices filtered through the closed door at the end of the kitchen. Must be the hallway to the back door. He moved closer. Haley's voice. And *Sheffield's*. The clown beat him to her. Craig gritted his teeth.

At the sound of Haley's giggles, heat rose in Craig's neck. He glanced into the dining room to see if everyone was still busy. Like a bunch of mushrooms stuck to the forest floor. He hurried back to the door and leaned his ear on the wood.

Did that yokel tell her he loved her? Sheffield had his nerve. *She's mine.* Craig closed his hand around the doorknob and slowly turned. That interloper must have her pressed against the door.

The voices quieted. Craig leaned to listen again and waited. Not a sound. He removed his hand from the knob. *Go ahead, Sheffield, have your fun.* He'd deal with them later.

Rage filled Craig as he rushed to the foyer, snatched his overcoat, and flipped it over his shoulders. Without a sound, he opened the front door and exited the house. No one in this place would miss him. Not one of them wanted him there, anyway. Haley had kept herself busy with everyone but him all day. He descended the stairs and stomped to the trunk of the Mercedes.

She didn't belong to Sheffield. Craig unlatched the trunk lid. He had his own plans for Haley.

After a long silence as Rob leaned on the mudroom door, he took Haley's hand in his. He drew her into his arms and gazed into her sea-green eyes lit by the porch light flooding through the backdoor window. They'd had a sweet few minutes alone talking things out, and sharing one expressive kiss. Even if it was in the mudroom. His pulse raced. He drew in a deep breath to settle it. "So, now do you realize how much I care for you?"

"Yes." She nodded.

"You're not mad at me anymore?"

"No." She shook her head.

"And you'll trust me?"

Haley's eyes narrowed. "That depends on what you want me to trust you about. I'm here alone with you in this tiny room, ignoring the rest of my guests. Doesn't that prove I trust you, Mr. Sheffield?"

He kissed her nose. "I want you to believe me regarding Craig Lowell."

She pushed away. "What? Craig! Oh, don't start. You and Aiden have set your minds." The pitch of her voice rose. "You both assume Craig is untrustworthy without giving him a chance."

"Shhh, let's not disturb the others." He pulled her back to his chest. "It's not in our minds but our guts, Haley."

"Your guts." She lowered her brows. "You've watched the Marine Gunny on that investigative TV series too much. The one who always talks about his gut. I don't think there's any such thing as trusting your gut. You've simply taken a dislike to Craig. Are you jealous of him?"

Rob kissed her fingers and grinned. At least she didn't pull away again. He pressed their hands to his chest and held them against his heart. "Since I've already told you that I love you, and you let me kiss you a moment ago..." And what a kiss. "...even if you won't admit you love me back yet, yes, I'll confess. I do get jealous when he's around you, and you pay attention to him. What red-blooded man wouldn't? But that's not what makes me leery of the guy."

A smile tickled at the corners of her mouth. Her gaze ran from their hands to his eyes. "What is it then?"

"Many things put together. The business with that shady lawyer. The accusation he made against my dad and then yours in the matter of the lawsuit over the land. His arrogance. Asking people in town questions about you and the farm. Showing up when he thought you were alone in the house."

Her brows furrowed. "What kind of questions did he ask?"

"How long your family's lived here, about changes made to the house, and if Drago stays on the farm all the time. Among others."

Haley's eyes widened. "Why did he want to know? Who did he ask? How did you find out?"

"He mostly questions people he meets at the roadside lounge where he frequents for dinner. Do you remember Bob Chancy from high school?"

"Your old friend on the football team?"

"That's him. He busses tables there at night, part-time. Several times he's heard Lowell pump people for information. Yesterday morning, I ran into Bob at the feed store in town. He was curious. Asked if I knew why Lowell was so interested."

Haley's lips parted. "I don't understand."

"Nor do I. I told your brother. He's worried. My dad said it sounded fishy."

Haley backed away. "I'll ask Craig, but I'm sure he has a good reason." She reached around Rob and grabbed the door handle.

"Wait, Haley. Let's not let it spoil the evening. It's the first time we've been alone together since we went to the movie and dinner weeks ago. We'll get to the bottom of it. I promise. But not tonight. Please?"

She let go of the doorknob and nodded. "You're right. I don't want to ruin anyone's Thanksgiving."

He kissed her on the forehead and wrapped her in his arms. "What do you say we go for a walk in the snow while everyone's busy in the house?"

"Good idea. I'm still not cooled off from cooking today." She giggled.

Rob beamed. Or from that kiss he'd given her? He hoped.

Haley grabbed her mother and father's old work jackets from the pegs beside the back door. "If we're super quiet, we can slip out, and no one will be the wiser."

"Sounds like a plan, ma'am." When she turned toward the door, he spun her back into his arms and covered her lips with his. She molded into his embrace. He'd waited so long for this.

Haley hung onto Rob's arm as they traversed the icy backstairs. She was so happy to finally know Rob loved her. At the bottom step, she lost her footing. "Whoa! I thought Drago had salted these."

Rob grabbed her arm and pulled her to him. "It's okay, I've got you and won't let go." He pointed to chunks of cloudy crystals on the edge of the steps. "You hit a patch that didn't melt, but I'm not complaining." He kissed her cheek.

"You can let me go now." She'd have to plan another slip on the way back. So many times, she'd dreamed of Rob holding her this way.

"Not a chance. Don't want you to fall in the snow now, do we?" He squeezed her tighter.

She should have admitted her love for him when he told her he loved her. But it would serve him right to have her tease him for a change after all his teasing through the years. She wouldn't make him guess for long, though. Surely, he could tell how she felt by the way she'd returned his kisses.

They shuffled around the back porch toward her bedroom. She tugged away from him, and Rob pulled her back. They played their game of catch and release until they reached the bedroom window where Haley lost her footing again.

Her leg sank knee-deep into a hole. "What on earth!"

Rob lifted her out of the two-feet-deep depression, then brushed the snow and dirt off her legs. "Where did that come from?"

"I've no idea." She bent to inspect the dark open space, but it was pitch-black. "Look, it goes under the house. Do you suppose some animal burrowed its way under there?" Just as well she couldn't see anything. If two shiny eyes peered out at her, she might scream. How would she sleep tonight, knowing something was under the floor?

She watched as Rob extracted a penlight from his pocket and searched the ground. "What are you doing?"

"Checking for tracks. I don't see any. Only footprints." He turned to her. "Haley, it was a two-legged animal that made this hole. If it had been four-legged, the dirt would have been flung straight out behind the critter as it burrowed, not dropped here in a pile. Has Drago said anything to you about needing to get under the house?"

"No. Why would he dig under my bedroom?"

"I'm not sure, but let's get him out here and ask."

After entering the house, they discarded the jackets in the mudroom and nonchalantly strolled across the dining room. Haley hoped no one would notice their red cheeks.

Lucy, Aunt Debbie, Charlotte, and Rob's mom paid no attention as they played their board game on the table. Haley waited in the foyer, as Rob entered the living room where his dad and Aiden were engrossed in a football game on TV. Drago, with his legs stretched out from the couch, perused the newspaper.

Rob eased himself next to Drago and spoke in a hushed tone. The burly man's eyes widened, and he dropped the paper to his lap. Rob held a finger against his lips and motioned for Drago to follow him.

The three of them made their way to the kitchen and out the mudroom to the back porch.

Drago stopped right outside the door. "What's this about a hole under your bedroom window, Miss Haley?"

"Come with us." Rob helped Haley down the stairs, and they headed for the hole. Drago followed.

Haley held out her hand and pointed to the deep well. "I take it you didn't dig this?"

"No." He squatted and examined the black channel extending under the floor of the house. "This had to have been hollowed out tonight. There's dirt on the snow, and you can smell the fresh earth. The ground hasn't frozen yet. Who would have done it? And for what purpose?" He looked up at Rob and then at Haley.

She studied both men's faces. They were as baffled as she. Who and why? Rob's words returned to her mind. *"How long your family's lived here, changes made to the house, and if Drago stays on the farm all the time."* A chill zigzagged along her back, neck, and scalp. Her parents had added this room to the house.

"Rob, we need to talk to Craig. *Now.*"

Chapter Twenty-One

Friday before Christmas

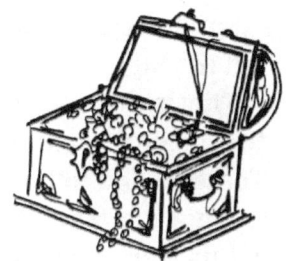

aley wiped a tear of frustration from her eye. Here it was Christmas weekend, and still, the culprit who had dug the hole under her bedroom window hadn't been identified. Craig insisted he didn't know anything about it. The sheriff's department had gotten no further in the investigation of other incidents around the farm, which had started up again. Nor had they found anything new about her mom and dad's car accident. She slammed the morning newspaper on the kitchen table.

She sat back in the chair, and a smile grew across her face. On the bright side, it was great to have Lucy come in from Wisconsin again last weekend to stay for the holidays. Sure was nice to have someone else around the house when the strange occurrences had started. Drago promised to keep his eyes open, but he still figured the missing things around the farm had something to do with that creepy old Indian legend. "The *creeps* involved were definitely two-legged," she muttered.

Lucy breezed through the kitchen door. "What did you say, Haley?"

"Oh, nothing. Just complaining because the Fremont Sheriff's Department is so baffled by these *pranks* pulled out here. Whoever's been messing around leaves no evidence."

Her friend poured herself a mug of coffee and stepped to the table. "It has to be frustrating." She lowered herself to a chair. "They're quiet too. They don't even arouse Shaun. And I thought he'd hear a *ghost* if it floated through the house." She giggled.

Haley's eyes widened. "That's not funny, Lucy. It's almost as if those Indian ghosts in the legend want to scare me out of my house. Not funny at all." Tears welled in her eyes.

"I'm sorry, hon." Lucy got up and hugged her. "Those old stories your dad used to tell us were real hair-raisers. In particular, that one about the Indian burial mound out there." She pointed toward the back of the house as she reseated herself, took a sip of coffee, and leaned back in her chair.

Shaun bounded into the kitchen, took a few nibbles of food, and scuttled out again. His feet slipped and slid across the tiles. It was as if he had to get back to the living room before the TV commercial ended. Haley and Lucy burst into laughter.

"At least your little dog is good for a laugh."

"He is that." She gave Haley a puzzled expression. "Whatever possessed your family to settle on this piece of land?"

"You've heard the story."

"Not for a long time. How 'bout it? Refresh my memory before we begin our preparations for the big Christmas Eve party on Monday." She leaned in and peered into Haley's eyes. "It's been so long since I heard the tale." She winked.

Haley narrowed her eyes at her friend. Would she never hear the end of these stories? Aiden, Rob, even Jason kept them alive whenever anyone wanted to hear them.

"Attention. Earth to Haley. Are you going to tell me that story or what?"

"Sorry. I was thinking about something."

"Yeah, and I'll bet he has deep blue eyes and brown curls." Lucy took a sip from her cup, and a plume of coffee sprayed out as she laughed. She choked and coughed.

"Easy, girl." Haley slapped Lucy on the back.

When the coughing died, Lucy wiped her face with a napkin, then cleaned the table. She grinned. "Wish I could find a guy like Rob. All the good ones are taken."

"I don't think you have to worry. With your looks and super personality, the right man will come along. God has someone special in mind for you."

Lucy glanced at Haley. "What do you think of Craig Lowell? He might be a bit reserved, but I thought he was nice when I was here for Thanksgiving. I didn't talk to him much. Although... while we sat together at dinner, he showed interest in what I did as a tour guide." Her brows fell. "But after a while, he switched to questions about you, your family, this house... which was strange. I suppose he's the nervous type. Seemed distracted too."

Haley bit her lip. Craig, nervous and distracted? More inquiries about her and the farm? But why? Strange how he left without a word Thanksgiving evening. And he hadn't come around or attempted to contact her since that night. Probably because the sheriff's office questioned him about the hole dug under her bedroom window.

"There you go again, Haley...off into that never-never-land of your mind. Quit stalling. Tell me how your family wound up with land that has a burial mound on it. I want the whole story."

After Haley gave her mug a warm-up in the microwave, she retook her seat at the table. "Allegedly *had* a burial mound. Okay. The details on genealogy are scarce. All I know is one of my ancestors, so the tale says, was on a ship which sank after an attack by pirates in the Gulf of Mexico off Florida. He was the sole survivor and made it to shore on a broken piece of the hull. But before the pirates killed everyone, they searched the ship and hauled everything of value onto their vessel."

"Wow. But what does that have to do with the farm being on an Indian burial mound?"

Haley pulled her lips to the side and sighed. "You said you wanted the entire story."

Lucy giggled. "I did, didn't I?" She held out her hands toward Haley. "You have the floor. Proceed."

"You sound like a lawyer. Coffee first, if you don't mind." Haley took a long drink. "Mmm, it's good this morning."

Lucy's fingers drummed on the table as she grimaced.

"*Patience!*" Haley snickered and lowered the cup. "After the guy crawled onshore, he crept away from the water into the underbrush. The pirate ship was still in view. A few minutes after he collapsed behind a clump of brush, voices neared his hiding place. He peeked through the bramble and saw two pirates carry a chest toward him. The captain followed. My ancestor recognized the box as one he'd brought on board the ship. It contained the family's fortune."

Lucy's face perked. "That's right. This is a treasure story."

Haley glowered at her, then continued. "His father had feared the English would confiscate what remained of their wealth the way they had the family's land, so they hid the treasure box in with the belongings they took with them. Things were dangerous in Ireland at the time."

"Don't head off on another rabbit trail. You can tell me that story later."

Haley nodded. "Right. The pirates buried the chest while the captain and my ancestor looked on. The captain killed his men, then rowed back to the ship alone."

"What? Didn't the rest of the crew wonder what happened to the others?"

"We'll never know that part of the story. After the ship sailed away, my ancestor dug up the chest and reburied it farther inland. He remained in Florida until his children set out for Nebraska. He retrieved the treasure, and they took it with them."

"They never spent any of it?"

Haley sat back in the chair and narrowed her eyes. "Lucy...you ask questions I can't answer. As far as I know, none of this was written down anywhere, only passed from generation to generation, word of mouth. Details can be lost and changed over time. Especially in a *fictitious* story."

Another puzzled expression formed on her friend's face. "How many centuries ago did this happen?"

"I've no idea. If these events really did happen, maybe the eighteenth, nineteenth century. I told you I couldn't give you the genealogy. Family records have been lost through the years because of floods and fires, etcetera. Most of this farm's history is hearsay, except the most important documents, deeds, and the like. They're kept safe in town."

"Haley! Your ancestor may have come face-to-face with the infamous Jean Lafitte."

"Wouldn't *that* be noteworthy." Haley chortled. "But I've never heard his name mentioned."

"So, go on with the story. I'm intrigued."

"Ever the historian. No wonder you're such a great tour guide." Haley took another sip from her mug. "Let's see. Where was I?"

"The ancestor came to Nebraska from Florida and brought the treasure with him."

"Ahhh...they came here when this land was still Indian country. A local tribe befriended them, and they acquired this huge tract for the family farm."

"The Indians gave him their burial mound?" Her brows rose as she peered at Haley over the top of her cup. "That's rather unusual, isn't it?"

"Lucy, remember...it's a legend. A *legend*. There's never been any solid proof the back field was a burial mound. First of all, the land is flat. Granted, one of my ancestors probably plowed over the ground, and it gradually flattened, but the only thing ever found out there were a few bones dug up a long time ago. You know how people are. They acquire a piece of information and blow it out of shape. Like the news reports sometimes. Actually, a news reporter could have heard this story. *Voilà*, a legend is born."

"Yeah. I can see that. But where did the treasure go?"

Haley shrugged. "If I remember correctly, said ancestor buried the chest in what's now the back field, and over the years, the treasure was forgotten. The map with one of those traditional ex-marks-the-spot disappeared for a long time until another family member found it when he was a boy. That was the one piece of evidence regarding the legend, or at least part of it, supporting the story's validity. Then again, the map may have been the creation of who-knows-whose imagination years ago. My great-great-whatever-grandfather might have come across what looked like a drawing to find a treasure and made up the tale. We MacKennas are known fabricators of fanciful tales of unfounded intrigue." She giggled, then grinned. "It's the Irish in us. But the paper has gone missing again, again, as far as I know."

"Did this grandfather ever search for the chest?"

Haley shook her head. "You won't give this up until you hear every single detail I can recall, will you?"

"Nope." Lucy crossed her arms. "As I said, I'm intrigued. This is better than a movie."

As she stared at the ceiling, Haley wracked her brain to remember what came next in the legend. She pinched her eyes shut. Dad had told the story so many times, she should've written the details down. It *would* make a great book or movie.

"Let's see. I think, after the boy found the map, he and a neighbor located the treasure in the field behind the house."

Lucy pointed toward Haley's bedroom. "Out there? In the burial mound?"

Haley tilted her head and pursed her lips. "*Le-gen-dar-y* burial mound, and it's hardly a mound anymore. Yes, out there. But they'd discovered the chest at night and decided to wait until daylight to dig the thing out of the ground. In the meantime, the neighbor boy went home. But before the next morning, his mother packed their bags and left her husband, his father. They moved to another country. And..." That sounded familiar, and not from the old legend either. Haley bit her lip.

"And what?"

"Oh. The neighbor never returned. My ancestor dug up the treasure himself, reburied it, and to my knowledge, no one has ever found the box or another map again. The last time I heard Dad tell the story was years ago, so my version may not be totally accurate. Whenever we had a family get-together, someone would ask him to tell the legend. I excused myself from the room."

Lucy shook her head. "That's quite the tale. So the chest of jewels is still out there, but no one knows where."

The chair screeched on the tile floor as Haley rose to get another cup of coffee. "Lucy. As I keep telling you, this is a family *legend*. And there's no telling if the treasure was jewels, or coins, or something else. My bet is there never was a treasure. But supposedly, the neighbor boy was someone back in old man Lowell's family line." *Strange coincidence.*

Chapter Twenty-Two

Christmas Eve

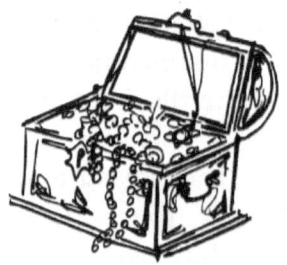

R ob fingered the box he'd stuffed in his pants pocket. Would Haley like it? His mom thought it was perfect. When should he give it to her? Not with everyone standing around looking on. She still hadn't told him she loved him. He sighed. But everything about her told him she did. Her expressions, her tone, and mannerisms. Why hadn't she said it?

Maybe Christmas morning, when Haley and everyone came here for breakfast. That might be a good time to give her the ring. Or later, when they were alone? Yes, that'd be better. Or should he give it to her tonight? Better be prepared in any case. No way could he wait until Valentine's Day.

He tightened his dark blue tie with the silver and gold paisley print and took one final look in the mirror over his dresser. Not bad. New dark blue suit, pale blue shirt. "Even if I say so himself." He chuckled.

His heart pounded when the kiss he'd given Haley on Thanksgiving night came to mind. Busy with post-harvest chores, he hadn't had a chance to repeat the euphoric experience. Hmmm, she'd have mistletoe hung in the foyer—at least she used to when they were teens. He'd make sure they spent time under it tonight. Rob grinned.

With a nod to his reflection, he spun and headed downstairs to join his parents. Haley's party would be fun. All the immediate neighbors had been invited—*except for one.*

Lowell had his nerve digging up those old disputes his father had over the property lines between his farm and the MacKennas'. What a fool to think he'd win. Good thing Aiden had his firm contact the best lawyer in the vicinity to represent Haley.

Better to lay that ugly mess aside for the holiday, though. It was Christmas. And what a Christmas. He wanted to make it special for Haley.

As he reached the bottom step, his mother greeted him with raised brows and a smile. "You look very handsome, Son." She straightened his tie and kissed his cheek. "Dad went out to warm the car."

"I'll take my truck. Chances are, I'll want to stay later than you and Dad."

She nodded. "I thought so." She headed out to the car.

Rob locked the front door behind him and followed.

After his mother lowered herself to the passenger seat, he closed the door, and she rolled down the window. "Thank you, dear."

"See you there, Son." His dad pulled away.

Rob gazed upward. A million stars twinkled. Even the sky was happy tonight. He strode to the barn and opened the door to the section where he parked his truck. A thump sounded at the other end of the structure. He was sure he'd locked that door after he stored his tools earlier.

He strode to the back of the building. As he reached for the door handle, the wind slammed the door shut. Careless of him. Too many other thoughts had flooded his head. He must have left it open. But could anyone blame him with Haley on his mind? He gave the door an extra tug and latched it.

When he turned, movement to the right of him caught his eye. What was that? He surveyed the dark end of the barn as he fumbled in his pocket for the penlight. *Nuts.* He'd left it in the truck. Rob tuned his ears to listen for any sound. Nothing but the wind.

As he stepped toward the truck, something ran across his polished black shoes. One of the feral cats. He gulped in a breath. "Kitty, you scared the freckles off my arms. Stinker!" Must have been the cat he saw. "If you don't get out now, you'll stay in here for the night. Happy mouse hunting."

He slid behind the steering wheel and turned the key in the ignition. Purred like brand-new thanks to Dad's help with the tune-up. Rob pulled out of the barn, jumped out, and closed the doors. As he hopped back into the cab and shifted into drive, his peripheral vision caught movement at the edge of the corral. What now? "Whatever it was, it's bigger than a cat."

Rob aimed the truck so the headlights lit up the area. Nothing there. Maybe he had the jitters. Proposing to Haley was the most important thing he'd ever planned, if the opportunity arose tonight. "Calm down, give your imagination a rest, and get to the party."

He turned the truck around and drove toward the MacKenna farm. Why did he have the sensation someone had been watching him? A tingle snaked through his neck.

After her guests had eaten their fill from the buffet and settled in the living room to watch a Christmas movie on DVD, Haley and Rob ambled to the fireplace. Char was such a dear offering to help Aunt Debbie clean the dining room. Haley glanced at Rob. Now she could sit with him and rest for a while.

Haley seated herself on the loveseat in front of the ember-filled hearth. Rob sat next to her. The Christmas tree to their right rotated on its base with a soft hum, while traditional carols from the movie on TV created a peaceful background.

As she gazed at Rob, happiness bubbled inside her. Sparkles from the decorations and lights glittered in his deep blue eyes like moonlight dancing on ripples in a lake. His smile sent a surge of tingles through her arms and heart. *Yes.* She loved this man and would tell him tonight. Why was she so nervous? How hard could it be to say a simple I love you to the man she'd known her entire life? And why was he as tense as a cat under a rocker. "So, have you enjoyed yourself, Mr. Sheffield?"

Too bad the tree didn't block them from everyone's view. Why couldn't her guests decide to take a walk outside? Then she and Rob could be alone.

He took her hands in his. "This has been the best Christmas Eve party ever. You're quite the hostess." He kissed her fingertips.

If he didn't stop, the butterflies in her stomach might carry her off. "Maybe I should hand out gifts now."

His arm slid around her waist. "We have an audience right behind us, but they may not notice. So...if you insist." He moved closer, leaned in, and his lips nearly met hers.

"Whoa!" She pushed him back. "Cool your jets, Mr. Sheffield," she whispered.

Rob laughed. "What? You've been avoiding the mistletoe in the foyer. I thought you were saving the kiss for now. You did say you should hand out gifts."

She slapped his arm. "I was referring to presents...and you know it."

"Rats!" He snapped his fingers, then snickered. "Eventually, I'll catch you under that plant."

Haley narrowed her eyes and shook her head. What a character he'd become. The awkwardness she'd felt between them when she first came home was long gone. So much had happened this fall. She recalled the kiss he'd given her in the mudroom on Thanksgiving night. Her pulse sped into overdrive. He hadn't kissed her since. How she wished he would. But not here. Not *now*. She sprang from the loveseat. "We should interrupt the movie."

Rob rose and followed her to the other side of the living room, where she pressed the pause button on the remote. "We can resume the movie in a little while. Gather round, everyone. Aiden and I have tokens of gratitude to pass out for all your support this year. Who wants to play Santa Claus?"

A flurry of green rushed to her, and Everett grabbed her legs. "Me, Auntie, me."

Laughter filled the room. Haley kneeled. Her nephew lifted his arms to her neck. "I'll be Santa, even if I'm not *fat* like him." He grinned.

"Apart from that, you'd make a perfect Santa, sweetie. But can you read?"

Aiden sauntered their way and took his son's hand. "I'll help the apprentice Santa with the gift tags." He winked at her.

What a joy to have everyone here with her. Except Mom and Dad. The familiar twinge of pain stabbed her heart. She took a deep breath, filling her lungs with the scent of evergreen, and released it. *Don't spoil the evening with tears.*

Rob extended his hand and helped her stand. He led her to one of two empty chairs near the tree. She sat, and he plopped into the other.

As Haley gazed around the room, her joy returned. Smiling neighbors, family, and friends filled the couch and chairs. This was what Christmas celebrations were about. Relaxation, celebrating Christ's birthday with loved ones and close friends.

Everett chose a small package. Aiden lowered to a chair between Haley and the tree. He held out his hand to receive the gift from his son. A frown formed on her nephew's face. "I'll do it, Daddy. I'm *not* a baby."

Her brother stifled a laugh but didn't withdraw his hand. "I know, Son. But you still can't read, remember?"

"Oh." He placed the package in his father's hand and leaned over his leg. Everett's nose almost touched the tag.

Haley giggled.

Aiden pointed to the name as he pronounced it. Everett jumped up. "Thanks, Daddy." He scampered off to deliver the gift to a gray-haired neighbor who had raised her hand.

Rob squeezed Haley's shoulder but didn't say a word. Did he imagine the same thing as she? Someday they'd have their own little boy, if...*dratted butterflies.*

When the guests had opened their trinkets, Haley served dessert and coffee. Rob helped Aiden and Char refill the punch bowl and eggnog pitcher, then joined Haley at the piano.

She touched the keys. "Rob, will you sing for us? I love your tenor voice."

"In front of everyone?"

"Yes." How can a man so sure of himself and bold in every other way, be shy when it comes to singing carols with neighbors and friends around? "You have a talent, and it needs to be shared. Now come on." She tinkled the keys on the right end of the piano, then began to play "Silent Night."

Rob opened his mouth, and mellow tones floated through the house. The chatter around the room ceased, and guests migrated toward the piano. She loved the way he'd always sung from his heart.

When he finished, applause broke out. Rob's face turned red. "Please, don't thank me. Give our Lord the praise for His unspeakable gift."

Haley gazed at him and smiled. "Well said. Let's all sing." She played "Hark, The Herald Angels Sing." After so much sadness this year, the house was flooded with jubilant music. Tears of joy edged Haley's eyes as blended voices, both on and off-key, filled her ears.

The last of the guests said their goodnights and left. Drago wished everyone a pleasant night's sleep and headed out the back door to the bunkhouse. Only Rob, Aiden, Char, Aunt Debbie, and Lucy with Shaun in her lap remained in the living room.

Haley searched the room. "Char, where's Everett?"

"He's been tucked into bed for at least a couple of hours. It's eleven o'clock. He was too tired to even say goodnight to his Auntie." She chortled.

Where had the evening gone? Haley shook her head. "I had no idea it was so late."

After the women loaded the dishwasher and stored the leftovers, everyone except Haley and Rob meandered to the second floor.

As she let out a yawn, Rob stepped behind her and wrapped his arms around her waist. He pulled her against his chest and lowered his chin to the top of her head. "One gift didn't get passed out this evening."

Haley rushed from his embrace to the Christmas tree, Rob right behind her. "I don't see anything left here." She turned to him.

He grinned. "It's not *under* the tree. It's here." He patted his pants pocket.

Her brows furrowed. "What? But we planned to exchange gifts tomorrow with the family."

Rob placed his hands on her shoulders, spun her, and guided her to the mudroom. "This one's special."

He closed the door behind them and kissed her as he had Thanksgiving. Sparkles danced like fireworks through her. When he backed away, she opened her eyes. He flicked on the nightlight and held up a small gift. She glanced at the box and then his eyes, which twinkled with glee.

Rob slipped the red ribbon off the black velvet box and flipped it opened. He lowered to one knee. "Haley MacKenna, will you marry me?"

She gasped.

Rob's stomach did somersaults as he kneeled on the cold tiles and waited for Haley's answer. Would she say no? "Haley?" He held his breath.

Her eyes were round as saucers. Her mouth fell open. "Rob—"

"Yes?"

"Rob—"

"Haley, are you okay?"

She blinked.

"What's wrong?" He rose from the floor with the ring box still held out to her.

Her gaze traveled from the ring to his eyes. Tears welled.

Rob snapped the box shut, stuffed it in his pocket, and gathered her into his arms. "It's too soon, isn't it? I should have waited at least until Valentine's Day. I knew I should have, but I just couldn't. We've gotten so close since you came home. It's not as if we just met. I mean. We grew up together. But I'm—"

Haley placed her fingers on his lips. "Shhh."

He gazed at her tear-filled eyes. "I'm so sorry, Haley."

"Sorry that you love me?"

He backed away from her. "Of course not. Why would I ask you to marry me if I was?"

She smiled. "Just checking." She snatched a towel from the stack of folded linens on the table beside the dryer and wiped her face.

"Okay, so what's the deal here? You don't love me? Is that what you're saying?"

Haley grabbed him by the tie and pulled him to her. She planted her lips on his. When she stepped back again, she said, "Yes, I love you. I've loved you since we were little kids. Even though I didn't *like* you very much through high school. Still, like and love are two different things." She paused and furrowed her brows. "I think."

His brows lowered. "You love me...but you don't *like* me."

As she blew a puff of air, her bangs flew upward. She narrowed her eyes. "*Men.* I said I *didn't like you* in *high school.* You teased me so much, how could I? And then there was the thing with the senior prom."

Guilt seized Rob's heart, and he shut his eyes. "Can we not mention that again? At least not right now." He reached for her and closed the gap between them. "Haley, I love you, and you love me. So...again, will you marry me?" He let loose of her arms, drew the box out, and reopened it.

Tears filled her eyes again. She tightened her lips.

Rob snapped the box shut and put his fists on his hips. "I'm confused. Will you please say something?"

Chapter Twenty-Three

Haley rested her cheek on Rob's chest. She shouldn't have teased him, but she needed this payback for all the times he'd tormented her in the past. Or thought she did. She whispered, "I do love you, Rob. And I will marry you."

As he lifted her chin, butterflies took off in Haley's stomach like jets. He lowered his lips to hers. Fireworks ignited in her head. Her dreams had come true. Their kiss deepened. When they parted, she sucked in a long breath and clung to him for fear she'd faint.

"*Wow!*" Rob took in a gulp of air. His grin spread from one side of his face to the other.

"I'll say." She blew out a stream of air that could have heated the mudroom.

After he'd turned on the overhead light and switched the nightlight off, Rob snatched her hand. He pulled her to the kitchen door. "Let's go tell everyone."

"Wait." Her hands flew to her cheeks. "My face is flushed. I'm not going to call them downstairs now. Aiden will start in on me. He will. And everyone will laugh. Let me get myself together...and cool off."

Rob chuckled. "I need to cool down too." He opened the back door, and chilled air seeped into the room. His gaze focused on the field behind the house. His brows lowered.

"What's wrong?" Haley looked outside.

"Nothing, I guess. My mind's been playing tricks on me this evening. Guess from the anxiety over your answer to my proposal." Rob explained what happened in the barn and corral at his home. "And now, a shadow ran out toward the field. But I'm not sure what it was."

Haley wrapped her arms around his waist. "Maybe your head's foggy." She giggled.

He bent to kiss her. "Probably."

She backed away. "Don't start again, or we'll never get to tell everyone our good news."

"Okay, but I plan on more before I go home tonight." He closed the back door. *"Oh!"* He reached into his pocket again and pulled out the engagement ring. "Now, Miss MacKenna. Let me try this again." He lowered himself to one knee and held the open box in front of her. The emerald–cut diamond sparkled in a shaft of moonlight through the window. "Haley MacKenna, will you do me the honor of becoming my wife?"

Rob removed the ring and slipped it on her finger. He kissed each fingertip.

"I will," she said in a wispy voice. "It would be my pleasure to become Mrs. Robert Sheffield."

Several minutes and kisses later, Rob and Haley emerged from the mudroom. Her face still glowed. No doubt, his did too. They'd have to accept the serious ribbing they were in for. But it was worth it to have heard Haley say she loved him.

As they entered the foyer, Haley called up to the second floor. "Hey, everyone. I have news you'll want to hear. Can you come down here?" She turned to Rob. "I'm not sure anyone will still be awake. It's almost midnight."

He'd bet Aiden clomped down the stairs first. Rob snickered to himself. When he'd confided in his soon-to-be brother-in-law tonight, he said he'd do his best to get everyone upstairs and wait for news. "There are footsteps aloft." Rob winked at her.

When the rest of the adults returned to the living room in robes and slippers, Haley lifted her left hand to display the engagement ring.

Aiden pumped his fist and arm backward, then grabbed Rob and gave him a bear hug. Char pressed her lips together as if she held back a shout, then wrapped her arms around Haley. Mrs. Moye and Lucy joined Char in the hug-fest.

The tip of Haley's tongue stuck out of the right side of her mouth as she was squeezed. She bit her bottom lip and pinched her eyes shut. Rob laughed. They'd better let go before she passed out.

Mrs. Moye released the girls first. "Haley? Where were you? Out in the cold? Your face is red." She tilted her head to one side.

"Oh, I don't think she's one bit cold, Mrs. Moye." Lucy giggled. "Overheated, maybe."

As he clamped his lips together, Aiden's brows rose.

Rob took a deep breath. "We did open the back door to—"

The room plunged into darkness.

Aiden grabbed Char's hand, and she plastered herself to his side. Now what was going on? "Take it easy, everyone. I'll check the breaker."

"I'll go with you." Rob flicked on his penlight. After he'd guided the women to seats, he led the way across the dining room, kitchen, and mudroom to the back door.

Aiden threw on an old jacket from the pegs next to the door and tossed another to Rob. They stepped out into the night air.

When they reached the box at the far end of the porch, Aiden opened the small metal door while Rob aimed his penlight at the breakers. Aiden scratched his head. "The main breaker tripped." He glanced at Rob. "What could have caused that?"

Rob shook his head.

Aiden touched the breaker. "Cold." His brows lowered. "That's odd. It should be warm." He turned off the individual breakers, reset the main one to the on position, and turned each circuit back on, one at a time. A stream of light from the kitchen shown through the back door window. "Guess we're back in business."

Rob doused the penlight. "Aiden, something...or someone ran from the house to the field tonight when I opened the back door after Haley and I...ah, after I proposed. Somebody's messing around."

After retrieving a large flashlight from the mudroom, Aiden flashed the light across the yard and field. They walked to the far right corner and scanned the area from the road in front of the house, back across the field to the woods, and across the back of the house to check the corral. He shined the light on the stable, the bunkhouse, and across the left of the house to the yard and barn. The two men walked around to the front of the house, searching for movement, then returned to the back porch. Everything was still. "Nothing's moving out there now."

He glanced at Rob, who grimaced. Aiden headed for the back door. "Let's get out of this cold air."

"Aiden, I tell you something's not right. I saw shadows earlier at our place while in the barn and again when I left. Now here? I also couldn't shake the sensation that someone was watching me as I drove away from home."

"That *is* weird." Aiden led the way into the house, but before he closed the door, he stepped back out and gazed toward the bunkhouse. Drago's lights were out. "In the morning, I'll ask Drago if he heard any noises tonight. We were so involved in your engagement, a herd of horses could have run through the yard, and we wouldn't have noticed. We'll check for footprints tomorrow morning too. If someone tampered with the electrical box, there should be a sign of it."

"Good idea. I hate that this has started up again. I'm worried about Haley."

Aiden closed the door, and they entered the kitchen. He was worried about her too. "So, you proposed. And she said, 'Yes.'"

Rob pushed past him as they stepped into the dining room. "Yup. You're getting a brother."

Aiden gave him a sound thump on the back. "Congratulations, bro."

"Thanks. And I'm glad you'll be here for at least the next week. Will Haley freak out?"

"My sister? Freaked by the thought of being hitched to you, buddy?"

"Not *that*. The circuit breaker and another shadow. I told her about the shadows both here tonight and at home."

Aiden reached out and caught Rob by the shoulder. "What did she say?"

"She thought my eyes were still foggy." A grin sneaked across his face.

They laughed.

"Don't worry, Rob. She'll be fine. My sister doesn't fear much." He hoped. These strange occurrences were as if someone wanted to frighten them away. Had somebody tried to scare their parents before they died? He hadn't found out about anyone trying to buy the farm when he checked previously. But now...he had to tell Haley.

In the living room, Aiden sat next to his wife. "The main circuit breaker tripped. We're good now." He glanced at Rob, who nodded.

As Rob settled back onto the couch next to Haley, he slipped his arm around her.

Aiden stared at the lit tree as it revolved. "I didn't want to bring up the subject this evening, but now that we're wide awake, I may as well tell you." He looked at Haley. "Craig Lowell and that shifty lawyer of his are up to no good."

Haley dropped her head against the back of the couch. "You've already told us Craig has reopened the old claim of his father's. The one about the property line where the stone barn sits."

"Not only that, Sis, but this entire piece of real estate. The lawsuit over the property line by the barn came after an initial claim by old man Lowell that his family originally owned this land. It never got anywhere, so he started in on the old barn. That guy was real trouble."

Rob's jaw muscles worked back and forth. "And the entire time he planned to open that case, he tried to get somewhere with Haley. What a reprobate."

"You've got that right, Rob. But Lowell better keep his distance. She's spoken for, and he'll be in big trouble if he gets your dander up. Your temper just might rival an Irishman's." Aiden laughed. "But it's the legal stuff that bothers me. Of course, his claim is bogus, but it'll be time-consuming and cause a lot of anxiety. We have ancestors buried in this ground. I'd hate to have it fall into Lowell's hands."

"They're not Indians, are they?" Lucy's eyes widened.

Aiden chuckled. "No. We're not of American Indian heritage. The story goes that the local tribe welcomed our ancestor who came to Nebraska around the seventeen hundreds. He farmed their land, worked hard for them, and later the Omaha Indians told him it was his. The details have been long lost, but Dad showed me the deed for the property before I left for college. He never said the Lowells had owned any part of it at any time."

"When she arrived, Lucy bugged me until I told her the story again." Haley chortled. "At least what I remembered. But why does Craig even want this land? It's not as if he doesn't have enough of his own. Why go through all that trouble and cost, when he won't win anyway?"

Rob shook his head. "Who can tell what goes on in that guy's head? He's a skunk if ever I got whiff of one. And that lawyer of his is no better, from what Dad told me. But I'm sure God will work this out."

"I'm sure He will too." Aiden smiled. "But we all need to pray in earnest about this lawsuit. Haley will have enough stress as she finishes her classes this spring."

Rob nodded. "Because of what it means to both of you, I'll pray it doesn't come to that. But so you know…if for some reason God chooses to take this tract, we'll be okay. Dad told me he plans to sign over our farm to me when I get married. He and Mom want to move into town and retire. Haley and I will still have plenty of land, even without this farm. And if you ever decide to come back, Aiden, there's enough room on our property for your family too."

With tears in her eyes, Haley hugged Rob.

"Thanks, Rob." Aiden stood and shook Rob's hand. "Let's hope and pray things don't get to that point. For the sake of our family's heritage."

Chapter Twenty-Four

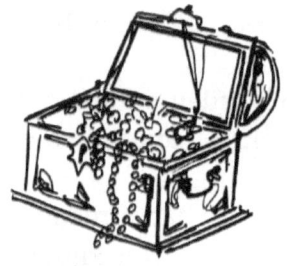

ob held Haley in his arms at the top of the front porch steps and kissed her once more. This last hour had flown by. He had to leave. "Someday we won't have to part anymore. Promise you won't make me wait too long. Please?"

She hugged him and snuggled her head under his chin. "I promise. Tomorrow we ladies will put our heads together and figure out an appropriate date. I'll call and run it by you and your folks."

"Sounds good." Man, it was hard to leave her. Rob dragged himself down the stairs and turned at the bottom. Haley blew him an air kiss. "You'd better get back inside before you get a chill, Sweetheart. Can't have sneezes and sniffles delay our wedding." He winked at her.

"All right." She stepped inside the house, reappeared at the front window, and waved.

After he returned the wave, Rob crossed the circle drive and slipped behind the truck's steering wheel. He started the engine and pulled away. Better take it slow after that mule deer ran across the road earlier this evening. Wouldn't want to hit one of those big boys in the middle of the night.

As he eased the truck onto the road at the end of Haley's drive, he pressed the brakes to slow the turn. "That doesn't feel right." He'd have to check the brakes first thing in the morning before the Christmas breakfast get-together. Funny. He thought Dad tested them when they did the tune-up.

Only two miles to go. No critters so far, but he'd still better be careful. Haley'd never forgive him if he hit one.

He crested a slight incline in the road, then stepped on the brake to slow down before descending to the last turn. Mushy brakes? His foot stomped to the floorboard. "Oh, great!" Rob pumped the pedal, but there was no resistance. If he tried to pull into the dirt, the truck could roll with the sharp drop on either side of the road. *"Lord, help!"*

Haley's cell rang. Who could it be at this hour? Her eyes opened to a pitch-dark room.

She yawned and swung her legs over the edge of her bed, then turned on the lamp. "Three o'clock in the morning?" Better not be one of those carousers from the country bar who've misdialed again. She'd give *them* a piece of her mind. She stood and reached for her cell on the dresser. "Hello."

"Oh, Haley."

"Mrs. Sheffield? What's wrong? Why are you crying?"

Mr. Sheffield's voice came on the line. "Rob's been in an accident. We're in the emergency room. Thought we'd better call and tell you. Can Aiden bring you here?"

"*Emergency room! Accident?*" Haley's head swam. But he'd just left not long ago. The room spun, and she fell back on the bed. She clutched her forehead and took a deep breath.

"Haley? Are you okay?"

"Yes. Yes. I just don't—let me. You're at the hospital?"

"Yes. The ER. But don't come alone. Have Aiden drive you."

"Right. Is Rob...is he...?"

"He's in the ER. They haven't told us anything yet."

Haley dropped the phone onto the bed and ran to the master bedroom. "*Aiden, Aiden, wake up.*" She banged on the door. "Rob's in the emergency room. I need to get to the hospital. *Aiden!*"

Footsteps rushed to the door, and it flew open. Aiden stood in the darkened doorway, zipping his jeans. "What happened, Sis?"

Char sat straight up in bed, panic written on her face.

Tears flooded Haley's eyes. "I don't know. Rob's in the ER. His dad said they haven't told him what happened. I've got to get there. He doesn't want me to come alone."

Aiden turned to his wife. "Honey, I'll call you from the hospital. Get Lucy and Aunt Deb, and start praying for Rob. Phone Drago." Aiden pointed to the dresser. "His number's on that notepad."

As he threw on his shirt, Aiden stepped out the door. "Tell Drago about Rob, and ask if he'll stay with you women until we get back. After the thing with the lights last night, I'd feel better if he were here."

Haley gulped in a breath. *Oh, Rob. Please, Lord, let him be okay.* She ran down the stairs with Aiden on her heels.

Aiden paced the waiting room while Haley and the Sheffields kept their heads bowed in prayer. He pulled out his phone. After four a.m. He and Haley had been there for an hour. The Sheffields had been here for three. Why didn't someone come out and tell them something?

The ER was overrun with people. Accident victims, no doubt. Because of drunks on the road. Drinking yourself stupid was no way to celebrate Christmas. Mr. Sheffield said Rob never made it home last night. A drunk might have hit Rob.

A doctor emerged from the double doors, which led to the back rooms. He strode across the main room to the Sheffields with a grim expression on his face.

Haley jumped from her seat, and Aiden rushed to her side.

The physician gave Mr. and Mrs. Sheffield a tired smile. "Your son's regained consciousness. He'll be all right, although he won't do any pushups for a while."

Mrs. Sheffield's relieved sigh sounded like she'd held her breath for the last hour. Haley broke into tears, and Rob's mother put her arms around her. Mr. Sheffield wrapped his arms around both of them. "Thank you, doctor."

Mr. Sheffield followed the physician back to the double doors with Aiden behind them. "Are you sure my son will be okay?"

"We'll keep him here under observation, but I'm sure he'll be fine."

Rob's mother hurried to the physician and grabbed his arm. "What happened to our son? All we've been told was his truck overturned. The Fremont Sheriff's Department didn't say any more except that he was brought here."

"Mrs. Sheffield," the doctor placed his hand over hers, "you can relax. Let's step through here." He opened the double doors.

Aiden, Haley, and the Sheffields followed the doctor into the back hallway. "We'll take good care of him. The officer who came to the ER told us it appeared that your son's brakes failed. When he tried to make a turn, the truck ran off the road and struck a tree. Your son flew forward with the sudden impact."

The doctor continued. "Thank God, he had his seatbelt on, and the airbag deployed. But his momentum caused him to make hard contact with something, and he suffered a substantial cut on the forehead. We stitched the wound, put an ice pack on it, and gave him something for the pain."

Haley's face turned pale. With an unsteady gait, she sidled up to Aiden. Several times she gulped in air. Her tears slowed, but her posture stiffened, and she lost her balance. He caught her and led her to the chairs lining the wall. "Take it easy, Sis. Rob'll be fine. You know what a hard head he has." He smiled at her.

She clamped her lips together and stared as if in a trance. Her brows wrinkled as she looked at Aiden. "How? Rob's a careful driver. Why?"

"We'll find out more later, dear." Mrs. Sheffield sat down and reached her arm around Haley's shoulders.

"I should have made him leave earlier." Haley's tears resumed. "If only I hadn't teased him for so long last night."

Mrs. Sheffield's red eyes gazed at her. She lifted Haley's chin with her hand. "This isn't your fault. Let's pray for Rob again." They bowed their heads while Mr. Sheffield spoke with the doctor for a few more minutes.

After the physician continued down the hall, Mr. Sheffield led the group back to the waiting room and sat next to his wife. "The officer on the scene told the doctor Rob ran into the old tree on the corner of our property. The ground's very low at that intersection, so the vehicle went airborne before it hit. Then it rolled before it came to a stop. We can thank God he put thick underbrush in the bend, which made the ground softer. Praise God for the vehicle that came along right away too. The driver who saw Rob's headlights flash across the tree in the distance had just pulled onto the road. As he approached the intersection, he saw Rob's vehicle on its side and called nine-one-one."

Aiden glanced around the room. "Where's the officer? Who was it? Had to be Jason. I thought it was him who drove away in a patrol car as we arrived."

Mr. Sheffield laid his hand on Aiden's back. "He must have gone back on duty. I'm sure he'll get in touch with us."

Heat rose in Aiden's neck. At the party last night, Rob mentioned he and his father had given the truck a complete tune-up. Another suspicious accident? The sheriff's department had better find out what was going on. Someone must have tampered with Rob's brakes just as they had with Dad's car. *Lord, please help us find out who's responsible. I'm beyond frustrated.*

Chapter Twenty-Five

Spring 2019

H aley settled herself in the swing on the end of the front porch and peered out over the water-soaked pasture. The March flood waters had receded, and people worked hard to bring life back to normal around North Bend. She sighed. But the devastation had affected so many—farms flooded, livestock lost, roads, houses. Her eyes teared. Thank the Lord Rob had recovered from his accident before things got bad.

The Sheffields were fortunate that their track of farmland was mainly on higher ground and had less damage. Good thing the

MacKenna land was too. Rob and his parents had done what they could for others who weren't as fortunate. She was so proud of him.

Now the wedding plans for June were back in progress. A tickle skittered through her. Soon, she'd be Mrs. Robert Sheffield.

She glanced at her cell and dialed Kayla's number.

"Hi there, Haley."

"Hi, yourself. You know, every time I call you, I get homesick. The way I used to when we were roomies, and I called home." What a blessing to have had a wonderful person like Kayla for a roommate.

"After living here on campus like you did for over three years, I suppose it's natural. But I wouldn't tell your fiancé." She laughed.

Haley joined her. "I think you're right. We'll keep it to ourselves. Got your text, and I'm so glad you'll be here for Easter. Too bad you couldn't join us at Christmas, but I understood the need to crack the books even over the holiday. I had to do the same online." It'd be nice to talk and laugh with her again in person when she arrived.

"Yeah, but if I had to be stuck here with studies, I'm glad we could Skype, especially after Rob's accident."

"I can't thank you enough for being there for me, Kayla. All the late-night sessions, listening to me cry, the encouraging words, prayer, and Scripture. Rob looks forward to meeting you."

"Same here. Sorry I wasn't there with you, girl. I died inside every time you wept. But I knew our Lord would help you through it. So now on to wedding prep."

Haley adjusted her position in the swing. "We'll have so much fun putting our heads together. Auntie and Char have given me a ton of ideas. Lucy will be here too." Too bad she couldn't have asked both of them to be Maids of Honor. "You don't mind being a plain old bridesmaid, do you?"

"Of course not, silly. You and I were like sisters for almost three years, but Lucy's been your best friend since you were little. I can't wait to see you in three weeks. *And* that dazzling ring you've bragged on."

Haley cast an eye at the diamond. "It is lovely. Did I tell you Rob said he didn't trust himself, so he asked his mom to help him find the right one? She has exquisite taste."

"It's nice to hear of a guy who's comfortable enough in his manhood to know when he needs a woman's advice. I hope I find someone like that someday."

"I have a hunch, you will."

"You said Rob recovered from the accident with no lingering problems?"

"He's back to normal. But I'll tell you, that was the worst night I'd gone through in my life. Next to when Aiden showed up and told me what happened to Mom and Dad, of course. Aiden is sure someone tampered with Rob's brakes like they did with my parents'. Rob thinks so too."

The sheriff's office has investigated, but they still have no good leads on who. Our friend, Deputy Jason Schumaker, has his suspicions. He said whoever has caused all the problems around here is an expert at covering their tracks."

"Sheesh, Haley. They must be."

"It's enough to make me believe ghosts *are* responsible."

"Ghosts?"

Haley chortled. "Yes. You remember. From Drago's stories. One of the old legends I told you about?"

"The one with the pirate treasure?" Kayla's confusion came across in her voice.

"No. The other one. The myth about an Indian burial ground supposedly on our property."

"Oh, yeah." Kayla giggled. "Are you sure you want to live out there when all those crazy stories are connected to your place?" Her giggles continued.

Haley blew her bangs off her forehead. "*No one* will frighten me away from property that's been in our family for centuries. This is my home. And it'll be—" She gasped.

"It'll be what? Haley?"

"Something just occurred to me. I have to hang up and make another phone call. I'll talk to you again later. Gotta go."

While he unloaded his new Toyota Tundra, Rob's cell rang. He pitched a hay bale onto the ground and reached into the cab. A grin spread at the sight of Haley's adorable face. "Hi, gorgeous."

"Rob, I just thought of something," she said in a rush.

"Huh? What? No hello for the love of your life? Just jump right into another idea for the wedding?" He chuckled and strode to the discarded bale.

"Oh. I'm sorry, honey. But listen."

He snickered to himself. "Okay, I'm all ears. But wouldn't it be better to run this girly stuff by your bridesmaids, or aunt, or even my mom? Your sister-in-law?"

"This has nothing to do with our wedding plans. When I was on the phone with Kayla, she teased me about staying on the farm when such weird things have happened. I told her no one was getting me off this property. That made me think."

He sat on the bale. "Don't tell me you don't want Aiden and his family to move back to the farm and live there after our wedding." Her brother had gotten so excited about coming home.

"That's not it at all. But I'd rather not talk over the phone. Do you mind if I come over? I'll bring a picnic lunch."

"Hmm...a picnic in forty-degree weather? You won't be very comfortable unless you want to snuggle too." He laughed.

"Oh, Rob. Will you be serious for two seconds stuck together? I mean it."

"Then, I have an idea. We can eat in the loft. Should be warm enough up there."

"That'd be great. I'm aware you can't waste too much time when you have farm chores to do, but I *need* to talk to you."

"How's an hour from now? That'll give me time to finish with these bales."

"Perfect. Be there around twelve-thirty. Love you." She hung up before he could return the sentiment. "Love you, too, sweetie," he said to the cell.

What had gotten into her pretty little head? Guess he'd find out soon enough. Bet it did have something to do with the wedding plans. Rob finished unloading the truck and then took off for the field behind the barn.

In two months, she'd be his wife. His dream almost since she came back home. *Home.* It'd mean changes for everyone with Mom and Dad deeding him the farm when he and Haley got married. He recalled his mixed emotions when his dad told him their plans.

"Son, your mother and I are ready to retire. We want to turn the farm over to you and move into town. You can hire more farmhands and put the new ideas you've learned in college into motion. I know you've been itching to make those changes."

He *had* too. Their profit would increase significantly.

Yes, big changes in lots of areas were coming. Everything had happened so fast. When Mr. MacKenna's lawyer in North Bend found he needed a partner and asked Aiden, he jumped at the opportunity. Romans eight, twenty-eight in action, *"And we know that all things work together for good to them that love God, to them who are the called according to his purpose."*

After he rounded the backside of the barn, Rob waved at his dad, who climbed down from the tractor.

Mom and Dad had found a perfect little house in town, complete with an English garden. Dad could have his workshop out back where he'd tinker with his woodcarvings.

Thank You, Lord. Everything has worked out beautifully for us, so far. Drago'd continue to work the MacKenna farm. Char was excited over plenty of space and subjects for her artwork, and Everett would grow up on the farm with the animals he loved. They'd probably see plenty of the little rascal over here too.

"Let me give you a hand, Dad." Rob entered the barn behind his dad and filled a bucket with oats.

"What produced that smile on your face, Son? You must have talked to your girl."

As Rob helped his dad put feed in the horses' stalls, he laughed. "You guessed it. Haley called, and she's bringing me lunch. There's something she wants to talk over."

His dad raised his brows and nodded. "Son, you and Haley relax. Take a good, long lunch. You've worked extra hard around here since you recovered." He slapped Rob on the back. "Now, git."

"Thanks, Dad." Rob jogged out of the barn and perched on the stack of hay bales to wait. How many kids should they have? Boys or girls, or a farm full of both? He grinned. The girls should resemble their mom with soft red hair and light green eyes. The boys? Didn't matter.

Less than an hour later, Haley pulled her blue Hyundai Sonata into the Sheffields' yard and gazed at the house. She had loved this two-story clapboard farmhouse with its wrap-around porch ever since she first saw it as a kid. Who'd have thought it would be her future home? Only two months from now. Butterflies started up in her stomach.

Rob hopped off the haystack in front of the barn and ran to greet her. "Hi, gorgeous. What did you bring me?"

"You, men. Always thinking of your stomachs." She giggled and slid out of the driver's seat.

Rob took in an exaggerated breath. "How can you say that? I was *thinking* more about what you brought me in the way of *this*." He snatched her to his chest and covered her mouth with his.

Haley gave as good as she got for a moment, but giggled before the kiss ended.

He lowered his brows. "Is that any way to respond to your fiancé's kisses?"

"Your prickles tickle." She stroked his stubble and brushed back a lock of hair that rested on his forehead. The scar from the crash showed. She kissed the line of dark pink.

Rob ran his chin across her cheek, then reached into the back seat of the car and pulled out a picnic basket.

They headed into the barn, climbed the ladder, and stretched out in the hayloft. The smell of fresh hay brought back memories as Haley spread a cloth between them and set out ham on biscuits, chips, and apples. As a kid, she had loved the times they all ate snacks, and even lunch in the loft.

After prayer, Rob took a bite of biscuit. "So, what's this important topic you need to talk about?" He guzzled his cola, then wiped his mouth with a napkin.

She sighed. "All the crazy things that have happened on the farm, Mom and Dad's accident, and then yours. Everything has a connection to me. Or to the farm."

Rob sat up straight. "I'm not connected to the farm. Not really."

"Not directly, but don't you see, we're getting married. You're linked to me, and me to the farm. Something is going on here that has to do with our land. The MacKenna land, I mean. It's as if someone is determined to get me off of it. It made me wonder if they had tried the same thing with Mom and Dad. By attacking you, maybe they figured they'd scare me into leaving."

He scooted over and pulled her close with one arm. "But who'd want you to leave? For what purpose. If you left, Aiden would get the farm. He'd probably just have Drago take over the work."

"I'm not sure...but I...," she blew between her lips. "I haven't wanted to tell you this, but Craig's been sending me flowers again and asked me out after the lawsuit died. He also told me to drop my wedding plans, and that he's the man I'd marry."

"*What?*"

"Don't let that just-a-hair-short-of-an-Irish temper get the best of you. I no longer answer his calls, refuse the flowers, and avoid him whenever I see him in town. Since Drago threatened to haul him to the dump the last time he drove onto the property, he hasn't shown up again."

"He'd *better* stay away from you." Rob's face showed his fury.

"I'm sure he will now, but do you think I should talk to Jason about this? There's nothing to connect Craig with anything that's happened, but I can't get over this...hunch...I guess you'd call it."

Rob gazed at her for a moment without a word. He took her hands in his. "Your hunches have always been pretty much on target."

She nodded. "Oh, and get this. I saw our letter carrier at the gas station on the way back from town a couple of days ago. I parked on the other side of the pump from him. He spoke to the man in the car behind him loud enough for me to overhear. The mailman said he thought it strange that old man Lowell's son never received any posts from Italy after living there as long as he did. Especially when he had family still living in the country. That is peculiar, isn't it?"

"Why, Haley. You listened to gossip?" Rob's eyes grew round.

Heat flowed into her face. "Is it gossip if the man who delivers the mail is knowledgeable of what he carries...or doesn't, and makes a passing comment?"

Rob stifled a laugh. "Maybe not, but you eavesdropped." He grinned.

"I did no such thing." She folded her arms over her chest. "He talked loud enough for everyone to hear...including me. How could I not listen when I was right there...practically next to him?"

"I was only teasing you." He tapped her nose. "It is odd he doesn't get mail from Italy. They might communicate online. Many people do today."

Haley unfolded her arms and shook her head. "I'm not sure. Perhaps." She bit into an apple. "But all those things added together make me very nervous regarding *Mr. Craig Lowell.*"

Chapter Twenty-Six

With a grin, Craig's eyes traveled from Haley's ankles to her hips as she strolled in front of him on the downtown street of North Bend. "Good morning, Haley." He slinked up next to her. "And where is my curvaceous lady off to today?" At least she'd left the farm for a change.

Her step quickened, but he kept pace. "A fine morning it is, too, don't you agree, my dear? For a Monday. Why haven't you returned my messages?"

Haley stopped and faced him. "Mr. Lowell, I told you *not* to call me anymore. No more flowers, no more asking me out, no more anything. I'm engaged to be married. You have your nerve after all the trouble you caused for my family with your bogus claim against our land. I hope you've learned your lesson, now that you've lost. Leave—me—alone." She spun toward a dress shop.

He stepped between her and the entrance. "Come now, Haley. I only tried to get back what was lawfully mine. There should never be bad feelings between you and me. Let's go somewhere for coffee and talk. Or, perhaps a ride in the country. We'll spend a little private time together and discuss our future."

She glared and stepped around him, calling over her shoulder, "*We* have no future." She entered the shop.

So that was the way she wanted it. Hard to get. She needed to be convinced. That hick who'd attached himself to her couldn't satisfy a woman like Haley. *But I sure could.* And once he found the treasure, it'd be Lowell property. He'd get everything he ever dreamed of.

Through the shop window, Craig watched Haley as she searched through the dresses. She must want something special to wear for me. *Can't wait to see you in it.* He smirked.

As he turned from the store, he spotted Drago leaning on Haley's vehicle a few stores away. The farmhand's eyes bored holes into Craig's. What was that lowlife doing here? Did he want her for himself? He was too old for her. First Sheffield, now the hired help. *He'd better not try to threaten me in public.*

Craig strode down the street, away from Drago, and entered the building that housed his lawyer's office. He ran up the stairs, barged through the reception area, and sat in front of Mr. Doty's desk.

As the attorney explained why the court dismissed his case, Craig scowled. How did he botch this? Why had his father held so much faith in this incompetent man? Doty hadn't worked hard enough.

"I tried to explain this to you before, Mr. Lowell. Your claim to the land was weak. The MacKennas had everything in their favor. You've lost every battle, just as I predicted from the start. Now, you need to catch up on your payments to me. I'll expect a check by the end of this month, or I'll file a new lawsuit."

Craig gritted his teeth and leaned back in the leather armchair. "Don't worry. You'll get paid. But I didn't get my money's worth." He jumped up. The chair tipped backward, then banged back in place on the wooden floor.

Doty shook his head. "From what I've learned, the only way you'll acquire the *MacKenna* land is to marry the owner. And she's engaged to someone else. You couldn't have expected to win. I thought from the start, this was more of a vendetta against the MacKennas on your father's behalf. I tried to tell you not to waste your money."

With his hands flat on Doty's desktop, Craig leaned forward and glowered. "I *expected* you to do your job."

Mr. Doty slammed Craig's case file on the desk.

Craig stomped out of the office. He'd get the land all right—one way or the other. If Haley would cooperate, it would be so simple. With her as his wife, there'd be no problem with the excavation under the addition. It wasn't enough the treasure had been in the ground and forgotten by her family for years, her father had to cover the location with an added room. Stupid. But it meant no one had touched the chest. They had no idea what they were sitting on. He laughed as he took the stairs two at a time. The poor oblivious girl thought the legend was nothing but a children's fireside story. She'd made no attempt to hide her disbelief. It would be a big surprise when he showed her, it was real.

He should have left Italy when his father first mentioned the treasure. He and his father could have worked together to get the prize before he kicked off. But he had to take care of his mother first. The pittance he'd inherited from her estate hadn't lasted long. It was a good thing his father had investments that paid regularly.

The door to the building swung open, and an icy April wind hit Craig in the face. As cold as his mother's heart...and her family. He plodded to his Mercedes.

Craig envisioned Haley's angry face as he drove away. She needed to end this game of hers.

As they headed back to the farm with Drago at the wheel of Haley's Sonata, she fumed at the way Craig had ogled her. The most arrogant man she'd ever met. Delusional. Her woman's intuition had sure paid off when she asked Drago to accompany her to town. She had hoped to avoid Craig, but a run-in with him in their small community was inevitable.

What was she going to do? Craig still had not taken the hint. She couldn't tell Rob. He'd be furious. Angry enough to confront the man, and that was the last thing Rob needed. If they got into a fight, Rob would wipe the floor with Craig and be in all kinds of trouble.

"What's bothering you, Miss Haley?" Drago tilted his head forward to peer into her eyes as he drove.

She sighed.

"You don't have to tell me. It's that no account Lowell. If you hadn't gone into the building when you did, I'd 'ave escorted him out of town."

The vision of Drago dragging Craig out of North Bend by the shirt collar made her grin. A dump in the lake off Main Street would've cooled off Mr. Lowell. The idea should have made her happy, but she was too mad at Craig to crack another smile.

"Thank you for coming with me today, Drago. It was a comfort to have you nearby. Craig Lowell makes me nervous. He's like a bad dream you can't shake."

"I think you made the right choice in Rob Sheffield. He's a good man. As is his father. And your father."

They drove in silence for several minutes.

"I miss your dad, Miss Haley."

She reached over and patted his arm. "I do too." Haley swallowed a lump in her throat.

Drago pulled into the yard and parked the Sonata in front of the house. He stepped out and lifted her purchases out of the back seat. "You bought a lot today. Must have been a good sale."

She giggled and took the packages from him. "Not everything was on sale. But I needed new clothes for my trousseau."

"Your what?"

Haley stifled a laugh. "My trousseau."

Drago's brows and forehead wrinkled.

"A trousseau is something a girl gathers together when she's about to be married. New clothes, various items for the household, and personal belongings a bride may need for her...marriage." This conversation was awkward.

"I have Mom's linens for my new home, and they're not new, but she was very meticulous in their care. I'd rather have her things. But I have very little for the—nice things." Great! Heat flowed up her neck. "I've been too focused on school, my engagement, and...you know. With Easter and the wedding, I needed to pretty up my wardrobe." *Whew!*

"You're always pretty, Miss Haley. Ask Rob." He chuckled, turned, and headed for the bunkhouse.

"Thanks again for going with me."

He waved with half a turn. A flush of red showed in his face. Was he blushing? He must have figured out she was talking about the honeymoon. This was a side of Drago she'd never seen before. Would he ever find a lady of his own? It must be lonely out there every night. *Hmm.* He's never turned down an invitation to dinner when Aunt Debbie has been here.

As she climbed the stairs to the front porch, her thoughts returned to Craig. She'd told Jason about her *hunch*. It hadn't made a bit of difference. As much as he agreed something wasn't right when it came to Craig, there was nothing the sheriff's department could do if the man wanted to ask questions, send her flowers, or try to call her...even though she was engaged to Rob.

Jason said he'd give the guy a *friendly* warning. *I'm sure Jason will too.* Should she tell Rob about today's encounter? No. Not yet.

She placed her palm on her forehead. She felt warm.

Craig Lowell was one neighbor she'd never welcome here again. He'd not cross their property line either if she had anything to say about it. Maybe it was time to resume target practice. *A well-placed shot over the head speaks volumes*

Chapter Twenty-Seven

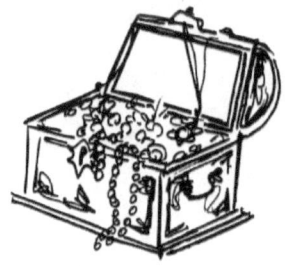

aley pushed the plate away. Her appetite was gone, her head throbbed, and she'd had chills most of the day. Must be a cold. She pressed Rob's speed dial number.

"Hi, gorgeous."

"I'll start believing it if you don't stop answering your phone that way...*handsome.*"

He laughed. "Do you want me to pick you up for church tonight since Drago had to drive to Omaha this afternoon?"

Haley placed her still full dish in the sink and dropped onto a kitchen chair. "How did you know he left?"

"Since I'd asked him to watch out for you, he stopped by to tell me. Didn't tell me where he was going, though, and I didn't ask. His business, not mine. But do you know where?"

She smiled. "First, don't pick me up. I think I'm coming down with a cold, so I'm staying home. And secondly, you wouldn't be asking me to *gossip*...would you?" A giggle escaped her.

"Are you okay, sweetheart? I'll come over and take care of you until Drago gets back."

Haley laughed at the alarm in his voice. "You mean mother hen me? No, Rob. It's a cold." She hoped. "And I don't want anyone else getting it, including you. *Achoo, achoo."* She sniffed. "Hold on." As she ran to the bathroom for a tissue, she dropped the phone on the couch.

She returned to the living room and picked up the cell. "Sorry. *Achoo.* That kind'a confirms it. Mom always told me, 'If you sneeze three times in a row, you have a cold.' Old wives' tale, but it seems to be true in my case." She lowered herself to the couch.

"A hot cup of tea with honey and lemon, then off to bed. That's what I have on my agenda for tonight." She sniffled and blew her nose again. "Hopefully, this will be gone before everyone descends upon me Easter weekend. I don't want to infect my guests. Everett had the flu last month, and Char's due to pop that baby soon."

"All right. I guess I was overreacting...a little. Sure wish Drago hadn't had to leave, though. And you haven't said if you know where he went."

She chuckled to herself. "No. I didn't."

"You won't tell me, will you?" A loud exhale traveled through the line.

"Oh well, if you're going to pout, I'll tell you all I know."

"Yes? Where?"

"I don't know." She giggled, then sneezed again.

"God bless you. You mean he didn't tell you either?"

"All Drago said was he had someone to meet. Someone he hadn't seen for a long time. And he was in a hurry, so I didn't try to make conversation. He told me he'd be back at the bunkhouse late tonight. Now don't worry."

"Me? Worried? About Miss Annie Oakley MacKenna? I've seen you with a rifle, remember?" He snickered. "Heaven help any polecat who wanders onto your property to steal those horses, chickens, and cows."

"Right." He wasn't fooling her one iota. The man had become a worrywart after Drago told him of her run-in on Monday with Craig. But it was nice to have someone care that much. "If you're worried about Mr. Lowell, don't be. He's aware we go to church on Wednesday night. He has no idea I'm not going. Enjoy the service. I'll be in bed by the time you get home, but call me anyway. The cell will be on the nightstand. I probably won't sleep until I know you're safe at home." Would she ever forget his wreck on Christmas?

"That's what I want to hear. I make you feel better."

She could imagine the grin on his face.

"But who's the worrier now? Can't wait to be married, so we'll be together all the time."

"*Robert Sheffield.* You mean you don't plan to work at all once we're married? You'll just lounge around the house?" That'd be the day. He'd always been a hard worker, even as a teen. Had the muscles to prove it too. Her man was built.

He huffed. "Not what I meant, Missy."

"I know you didn't, and I can't wait either. June isn't far off. Less than two months."

"Seems like forever to me. Oh, I received confirmation on our honeymoon plans. Want to know where we're going?"

Haley lifted her legs and propped her feet on the table. "Yes. Where? Tell me."

"Nope. It's a surprise."

"You'll never quit being a tease. Give me a hint."

"Somewhere...away from North Bend."

"Gee. Thanks, meanie."

They laughed.

She glanced at the antique grandfather clock in the corner of the living room. "Rob, it's almost time for church to start. You'd better go."

"You're right. Get some rest, and if you need me, call. I'll come a-runnin'."

"Thank you. You're the best. Now get to church, and don't worry about me. I'll expect your call when you get home."

After Rob said he loved her and clicked off, Haley strolled to the bathroom to get a couple of aspirins for her headache. She dropped her phone off on the nightstand in her bedroom, then ambled to the kitchen for a tumbler of water to wash down the medication.

Returning to the bedroom, Haley changed into her new black nightgown and matching robe.

She'd better check the weather station before she went to bed. She may want to change into sweats for the night. As she lowered herself to the couch, she pressed the TV remote button. She stretched her legs out on the sofa and dropped her head onto an accent pillow.

While the weatherman droned on, her eyelids drooped.

The front doorknob jiggled. Haley jumped. A glance at the clock told her there was still half an hour left of the mid-week church service. *Don't tell me Rob didn't go to church.* But he'd call before he came over. The pranksters again?

She shut off the television. The room plunged into darkness. No time to retrieve her gun from the locked case. Whoever is out there would have seen the light from the TV and when it went off.

Haley inched toward the entry. Had Drago returned? If so, he would have gone to church. And he wouldn't be checking the doorknob. She tugged her silk robe around her and tied the ribbon sash. From one side of the door, she peered out the narrow beveled-glass window. Nothing moved on the front porch.

She picked up a large clear vase of white and lavender roses from the foyer table, and drew out the flowers, laying them on the carpet. As she reentered the foyer, she dumped the water into the umbrella stand.

A sound from the rear of the house startled her. Haley tiptoed through the dining room and peeked into the kitchen. The mudroom door opened. A male figure stepped into the room. *Who is that?* He wasn't built like Rob. This man was smaller. And Rob wouldn't sneak into her house.

She flipped the kitchen light switch. "*Craig!* What are you doing here? How did you get in? That door was locked."

"Hello, Haley. I was passing your drive, and thought I'd drop these by." As his eyes roved her silk-covered form, he held out a bouquet of red roses in a fancy red vase. "I had intended to set the vase at the door, but saw your car, and then the glow from the TV. I figured you were home. I knocked, but you didn't answer. You look lovely."

"You did *not* knock. You tried the door. Now get out of my house." She held the clear vase over her left shoulder like a baseball bat.

"Come on, Haley." His gaze returned to her eyes. "I tried the knob when you didn't answer the door."

"I would have heard a knock. Leave."

His eyes narrowed. "You're not being very friendly. I only want to talk to you."

As Craig approached, she glared at him and backed up. "I have nothing to say to you, except get—out—of—here."

He glowered at her. "Let's talk about that ring you accepted from another man. You'll be my wife, not his. You're mine."

Without turning, Haley retraced her steps past the dining room table into the foyer. *Don't panic. Keep him talking.* She had to get out of the house.

Craig's stare drilled into her eyes as he narrowed the gap between them. "He'd tell you anything to have you for himself. You don't need a loser in your life. You need a passionate, virile man who'll see to *all* your needs and desires. And I know you want me."

He placed the vase of red roses on the dining room table and moved closer to her.

Haley threw the clear vase at his face. As he ducked, she lunged toward him, propelling her fists into his shoulders so hard he toppled backward. His head struck a chair with a loud thud. She spun and yanked the front door open.

She raced down the porch stairs and across the gravel drive toward the stable, ignoring the stones that stabbed through her satin slippers.

Footfalls sounded on the steps. She had to reach the building. Craig wanted more than a conversation. She had to find something to defend herself. Anything. Her eyes darted as she ran, but there was nothing to use as a weapon.

When she reached the stable, she slipped through the doors and closed them behind her. Haley shivered in her thin lingerie. As she felt her way along the stalls, her eyes adjusted to the darkness. The tack room should be next. Horses shuffled uneasily as she passed. Why hadn't she grabbed her phone? Dumb, Haley. Really dumb.

A door creaked open. She glanced back.

Craig's shadow stepped in, and he pulled the door closed behind him. "Come here, Haley," he called in a sickeningly sweet voice. "Let's not play games."

If she moved, he'd hear her. She crouched behind a tool bench. Maybe he wouldn't find her in the dark.

A lighter flicked on, and the glow illuminated Craig's face.

That face. Sinister. She gasped. The face in the window last fall. It must have been him.

He held the flame out and swayed his arm from side to side, lighting the stalls as he moved forward. *He's scaring the horses.* If she rushed by him, he might drop the lighter and cause a fire. She couldn't risk it.

There was no time to open the tack room and find a weapon. Why couldn't Drago have forgotten to lock the toolbox today? If she made it to the rear door, she could disappear into the woods.

As Craig neared, Haley retreated. One more step and he'd see her. She turned and ran for the rear exit.

The light went out, and Craig tore after her. He grabbed a fistful of hair and yanked her to his chest. As he thrust her into the rough planks of the wall, he pressed against her back with his torso. His arms pinned hers. "Now look, Haley. This is the way it'll be. You'll marry me. Understand?" He nuzzled her neck.

The rough wall scratched her cheek as she squirmed to free herself. "Get off me! You're crazy."

"*Don't* call me that." He shoved her against the wood with more force, yanked her head by the hair to the side, and whispered in her ear. "Eventually, you'll learn to cooperate. Once we're married, you'll find it's for the best. And, when we find the treasure, you'll be happy." He spun her to face him.

"What treasure?" She tried to push him away, but he didn't move.

"You can't fool me. I've known about it for years." His body forced her against the planks again. He smashed his lips onto hers.

Haley turned her head and screamed as she beat her fists on his shoulders and face. "*No!* Get your hands *off* me. You're deranged."

He backed away and slapped her mouth. "That's no way to talk to your husband." Before she could move, he seized another fistful of hair and slammed her head against the wall.

She winced and gulped in air. The room began to spin.

He released her hair and held her with one arm around her waist as he untied the ribbon of her robe. Her legs buckled.

The stable doors flew open, and a stocky shadow, backlit by the security light from the driveway, stood in the middle.

"*Drago! Help!*"

Drago flicked the light switch.

Craig jerked his head toward the figure. "This is none of the hired help's concern. Get out of here. We want our privacy."

"*No!* He won't let me go!" She scratched at the hand gripping her robe.

Drago didn't say a word but strode forward. While Haley struggled to get free, she watched his approach.

As Drago came within striking distance of Craig, he loosened his vise-grip on Haley and turned toward the stocky man. "I told you to get lost."

With a twist, Haley spun away from Craig to the other side of the aisle. She trembled as tears welled in her eyes, and nausea overcame her. She wrapped her arms around her midriff and doubled over.

Drago moved a step closer to Craig. "Are you okay, Miss Haley?" The brawny man's eyes remained on the intruder.

"I am—now." Rage filled her. "Please *escort* Mr. Lowell *off* the property."

"I'll be happy to do the honors." Drago reached for Craig's shirt but missed as the man bolted.

Drago took off after him, but Craig darted past the stable doors. Haley ran to the opening. He was across the yard and to his Mercedes before Drago reached the driveway. Craig jumped behind the steering wheel and sprayed gravel in a high arc as he made a hard turn and sped through the drive toward the road.

Haley drew in a deep breath and exhaled. She'd never been so happy to see Drago in her life. He jogged back to her. "Drago. I'm so glad you returned when you did. Craig got into the house. I ran, but he came after me."

"While I was in town, a thought kept nagging at me. I needed to go home. Something was wrong." Drago removed his jacket and threw it over her shoulders. "You sure you're all right?"

"I will be now that you're here...and Mr. Lowell is gone. Forever, I hope. From the expression he had on his face, I think you put the fear of God into him tonight."

Drago grinned. "The fear of *God*. That was it. It was *God* Who told me to go home."

As they headed across the grass to the house, Haley laid her hand on his arm to steady herself. Her knees wobbled. Fine thing. Seen in her nightgown by that jerk, and now Drago. And he'd be sure to tell Rob what happened tonight. *What will Rob do to Craig?*

Chapter Twenty-Eight

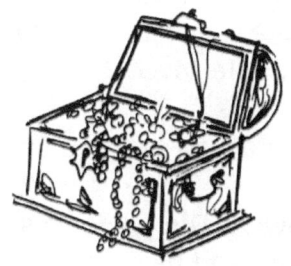

After the Wednesday night church service ended, Rob slipped behind the steering wheel of his truck. He should run by Haley's and see if Drago was back yet. Besides, he wanted to make sure her symptoms weren't worse. If the lights were out, he'd drive home and call her like she requested.

When he drove onto the MacKenna property, a Fremont Sheriff Department squad car was parked in front of the house. Jason Schumaker stood on the front porch talking to Drago while Haley sat on the porch double rocker dressed in jeans and a T-shirt with an afghan wrapped around her shoulders. His heart lurched. Now what?

He slammed on the brakes, and the tires screeched to a stop. Rob ran across the gravel. "*Haley.* Are you okay? What happened?"

Scratches on her right cheek glowed as if smeared with salve. He dropped into the rocker next to her and drew her to him.

"I'm fine. Just a little mishap that Jason will handle."

"Mishap?" Rob focused on Drago, whose forehead rutted like a country road after a washout. "Drago?"

The stocky man glanced at Haley, then at Rob.

She exhaled and rolled her eyes. "Oh, go ahead and tell him, Drago. Between you and Jason, he'll find out, anyway." Haley laid her hand on Rob's arm. "But promise me—" She backed away from his arms and pinned him with a warning look.

Through the years, she'd developed a way of speaking volumes without uttering a word. He loved that trait. It would be helpful when they had children. "Yes?"

"Promise me you'll stay away from him and let the sheriff's department handle this."

"Away from who? Lowell? Did he do this?" He touched her cheek below the scratches. "What did he do?"

Haley stood, threw her arms in the air, and turned away. "I give up." She spun back to face him. "The man wants to make trouble for us, Rob. Plus, he's nuts."

"I'd like to make a little trouble for *him*. Now, what did he do? I'll—"

"*Stop!* Not another word. Jason will handle it."

Rob opened his mouth to argue, but their deputy friend stepped in front of them. "All right, you two. That's enough. *Man.* A domestic dispute? And you're not even married yet. Can you save it at least until after the wedding? Don't make me throw you in the clink." He glared at Rob, switched to Haley, and then snickered.

She gaped at Jason. "You'd arrest us for this?"

Rob reached for Haley, pulled her back into the rocker, and wrapped her tightly in his arms. "Sweetheart, I think he's joking." He faced Jason and grinned. "You are joking, right?"

While he walked away, Jason chuckled. "This time. But settle down, both of you. I'll handle it." He turned back. "I'll send in the report and have a face-to-face with Mr. Lowell about his activities tonight. Also, the incident last fall."

"Wait a minute." Rob jogged over to Jason. "I still don't know what happened here. And what do you mean by last fall?"

"Enough with the twenty questions, man. Ask your fiancée."

Haley rushed to Rob's side. "Go ahead, Jason. Tell him. It'd be easier than explaining everything again when I'm not feeling well."

As Rob joined her on the double rocker, Jason read over the report. Rob's jaw tightened. His teeth clamped together, and heat rose in his neck. "That lousy, no good, rat." He eyed his friend. "You'll arrest him, right?"

Jason's brows furrowed. "Rob. Like I explained to Haley, we can't prove he broke the law. He came onto the property, but Haley has no restraining order against him. When we take his statement, I know he'll claim he dropped by to leave flowers for her, the excuse she told me he used. I'm sorry, but there's no law against a man trying to win the affection of a woman even if she is engaged to another man."

He addressed Haley. "Don't get me wrong. I believe every word you've told me, but it's still your word against his. And he'll no doubt say you encouraged him. It doesn't mean I can't give him a strong warning...again. And that will go into the record."

"But Jason, what about his slamming me into the wall?" She raised her hand to her cheek. "Isn't this assault?"

A heavy exhale came from the deputy. He closed his eyes and shook his head. "You don't have a witness. He'll say he didn't do it. That you had those marks on your face when he arrived. He may even accuse Rob. I wish you had a camera in the stable, but you don't, so there's nothing to prove he did it."

"What about his coming into the house uninvited. He had to have broken in through the back door."

"I'm sorry, Haley, but there's no evidence that he broke in. Are you sure you locked it?"

"I can't swear to it, but—I don't know." She slumped back against Rob.

Like a raging bull, Drago stomped from the corner of the porch. "But I told you—"

Jason held his hand up. "Same thing with your statement, Drago. I believe you, too, but you can't *prove* it. You didn't actually see him do anything to Haley but hold her. And she *is* your boss. He'll say she was consenting until you showed up. Although you and I both know a crime has been committed, and I truly believe it has, there needs to be proof." Jason exhaled loudly.

"Even if you had witnessed him doing more than holding Haley, it will be difficult to obtain a conviction without further evidence. A sleazy defense attorney could cast enough doubt on her testimony, and yours, to create reasonable doubt. I've seen it many times. Makes me sick. But our hands are tied."

Haley sniffled. Rob pulled her head against his shoulder.

Jason pocketed his report book. "And before you ask about him acting guilty since he ran away when Haley made her accusation...look at you, man. Compare your size with Lowell's. I'd run away from you too. That's the excuse he'll use." He spun toward his patrol car but stopped.

After an about-face, Jason said, "What I don't understand is the treasure he mentioned. What's that about?"

Haley shook her head. "I don't know. He said he's known about it all his life. It has to have something to do with that *stupid* legend our family has told for generations. But how would he have heard about it? And why on earth would he assume it's true?"

Rob kissed her hair. "Haley, forget it. Like you said, the man is nuts. His dad may have told him the story. But I do recall Craig Lowell hanging around the farm with us once or twice before his mother took him to Italy. And I think it may have been when your dad told us kids the legend. Lowell must have decided it was real back then."

Jason nodded. "Yeah. I remember your dad telling us the story at parties too. You're probably right, Rob. If someone gives too much thought to something they want, they lust after it. They become obsessed with it. When he came back to the States, it may have triggered the memory. When I talk to Lowell, I'll remind him it's only a legend, and to get *that* in his head."

The deputy took out his notebook and jotted another note, then rattled the book at Rob. "And you, my friend, remember to stay away from him. Let *us* handle this."

As the patrol car left the yard, Haley's headache kicked into high gear. Her stomach cartwheeled. When they stood, she hung onto Rob's forearm to keep from falling.

He swept her into his arms and carried her inside. Drago followed. Rob laid her on the couch in the living room. "Haley, look at me."

The room whirled. "I'm fine. Only dizzy. The stress, the congestion in my head. Could I have a glass of water?"

"I'll get it." Drago headed for the kitchen.

Rob's brows pinched together as he lowered to his knees next to her. "I should take you to the ER. You might be going into shock."

When Drago handed her the water, she lifted her head and took a long drink. The room stopped moving, and she sat up. "Not shock. Vertigo from my stopped-up head. I'll be okay."

Rob's expression of concern made her want to cry. She hadn't doubted he loved her, but now it was written all over his face. She lifted a hand to his cheek. "You need to go home. I need to take a couple of aspirin and go to bed."

"But Haley, what if that creep comes back. I can't leave you."

Drago rested his hand on Rob's shoulder. "It's all right, Rob. I have no intention of sleeping tonight. I plan to park my butt in the rocker on the front porch with my shotgun in my lap until the morning. If the louse shows his face, he'll have to pick lead out of his backside. He's already proved his cowardice when he ran from me."

Haley frowned. "No, Drago. You've worked hard today. You can't go without rest all night."

He laughed. "It won't be the first time. I'll take care of the animals before I take up a post outside, and when you wake in the morning, I'll get some sleep. The remainder of my work'll get a late start."

"I'll stand watch with you." Rob stood, hands on his hips, and peered at Haley. "And you're not going to tell me otherwise, Missy. If there's two of us out there, it'll be safer, and we can keep each other awake or take turns dozing. I'll call Dad to let them know I won't be home and why. He'll agree with me." He strode out of the room.

She sighed. "If you're both going to guard the castle tonight, the least I can do is make a pot of coffee."

Drago's eyes widened. "You better not stand yet. I can make it."

"Except for this headache, a stuffy nose, and a churning stomach, I'm good." She stood, lifted her chin, and took a deep breath. "See?"

He followed her into the kitchen. *Dear Drago.* He was as bad as Aiden when it came to hovering over her. And now Rob. At least, with the two of them around, she wouldn't wake up at every sound.

After Haley filled the water tank to the brim, she measured coffee grounds into the basket and turned on the machine. "There should be enough to last both of you until morning, although the heating element will go off after two hours. I could set it for four, but it might make the brew bitter. After this light goes off," she pointed to the red circle on the coffee maker, "fill your mug and microwave it on this setting." She indicated which button. "That will make one cup hot without spoiling the flavor."

"Check. Thank you, Miss Haley."

She opened the refrigerator door. "There's half a chocolate cake in this red container. And fruit in the crisper. But you can help yourselves to anything you find in here."

He chuckled. "We're not planning a party."

Rob strode into the house and joined them in the kitchen, his cell to his ear. "Mom and Dad are glad you're okay. And Dad agrees we should keep watch while you get your rest."

As Rob ended the call, tears filled Haley's eyes. She leaned against the counter.

"Sweetheart, are you feeling sick again? You'd better sit down."

"No. No more fussing. The dizziness is gone. Only the symptoms of the cold are left."

"But, you're crying."

"Rob. These are tears of joy. You and your family are not merely good people...you're *my* good people." She turned to Drago. "And that includes you. Now, I need to rest."

She headed toward the dining room. "Besides the refrigerator's bounty, you'll find chips and other snacks in the pantry when you get hungry." They walked her to the foyer.

Rob hugged her. "Sleep well. I doubt Lowell will return tonight, but we're not taking any chances. If you need anything, call out. We'll be right outside the front door."

He bent to kiss her, but she slipped her hand over her mouth and mumbled, "I don't want you to get sick." She winked at him. "Let's wait and see if this is a cold or not. It might just be a sinus issue from the spring pollen."

Rob grimaced.

She lowered her hand. "Quit being such a little boy." She threw him a kiss and headed him toward the front door.

Before she went to bed, she'd give her lips a good sanitizing from Craig's nasty mouth forced on hers. Then she'd get a good night's rest. *Lord, thank You for Rob and Drago. Keep them safe out there.* Who knew what Craig might try next?

Craig sulked as he sat alone in his living room. He blew a cloud of cigarette smoke at the ceiling. Things had not gone well tonight. Right when he was getting somewhere with Haley, the interfering farmhand had to barge in. Craig took in a long drag on the cigarette and blew the smoke upward.

She would have told him where to find the treasure, with a little more persuasion.

What nerve, pretending she didn't want him. She must have been embarrassed that the help saw her in her negligee. She sure had a fantastic figure. Craig's pulse raced. All the right curves.

What they did together was none of the hired help's business.

It was a stroke of luck that she hadn't gone to church tonight when he decided to drop off the roses. She must have been hoping he'd stop by for a chance to be alone and set things straight.

Why hadn't the farmhand gone to church? Craig frowned. From what he'd been told, even the hired help went to Haley's church on Wednesday night.

Craig ran his fingers over his lips. His passionate kiss should have told her how much he desired her. By her reaction, she'd never had a real man kiss her. *I'll make sure we're not interrupted the next time.* But when? He'd have to plan more carefully.

Women liked to play games, but he was getting tired of this one. He'd have to deal with her unwillingness to cooperate with his plans.

In a trance-like state, Craig stared at the stone fireplace, his thoughts back in the stable with Haley.

Call him crazy, would she? His mother had made the same mistake...once. He gritted his teeth at the memory. She'd never call him names again. And he'd teach Haley to have more respect too.

The front door chimes rang. Craig snapped back to the present and glanced at the clock over the mantel. "Who'd be at the door at this hour?" Craig opened the drawer in the end table, reached inside, and grabbed his father's revolver. He sauntered to the entrance and looked through the peephole. An officer? *What's he doing here?*

Craig reached behind him and slipped the gun into his belt.

Chapter Twenty-Nine

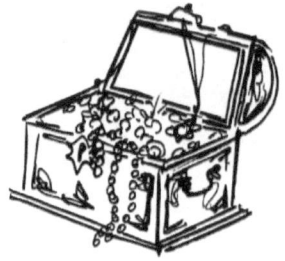

A s Rob and Drago settled into wicker chairs on the front porch, Rob watched the house go dark. He hoped Haley would be able to sleep after her ordeal with Lowell. "Good idea to leave the front porch and security lights off, Drago. If the snake shows up again, he'll wish he was back in Italy by the time he gets close enough to see us."

The older man chuckled and rested his head back on the chair, looking up at the stars. "It's great living out here where you don't have those bright city lights to blot out the view, isn't it?"

Rob stretched his legs and crossed them. "Country living is the best. I'm glad Aiden realized it and decided to move his family back home after all. Haley won't have to live here alone until the wedding."

Drago gave a solid nod. "Speaking of alone. I had good news yesterday myself. It's why I had to go to town today."

"What was it?"

"A call from my kid brother."

Rob's brows rose. "I thought you had no contact with your family after your folks disinherited you."

"Yeah. Almost fell over from shock when it was Markus on the other end."

"So, are they ready to accept you back into the family?"

"Markus is my only family now. That's what I meant by alone. Dad passed away first of the year, and I'd read about Mom's death a couple of years ago in the Gering newspaper I'd subscribed to. That's where my family...brother lives. Gering, Nebraska. Eight miles west of Scottsbluff."

"Why would you subscribe to the town paper after everyone treated you the way they did?" Rob shook his head.

"I'm not sure why, but I did. About a year after I came to work here. Since I didn't want my name on the subscription, Mr. MacKenna said he'd put it in his name. Paid for it yearly. I wanted to pay him back, but he refused. Called it a *bonus*." Drago grinned. "The paper stopped after the MacKennas' deaths, which came right before the subscription lapsed. I didn't have the heart to ask Haley or Aiden to renew it for me."

"I understand. So why did your brother get in touch with you now?"

Drago straightened in the chair. "Markus inherited everything. But he didn't think it was right that I'd been cut out of the will. He hired a private investigator to look for me. When he found out where I lived, and that I'd changed my life, he wanted to reconnect. He asked me to meet him in town for dinner."

"Wow. That's great."

"He plans to share the inheritance. Said he's missed me and wants me to come home. He was only ten when the folks kicked me out fifteen years ago. Markus is twelve years younger than me."

"Guess we'd better look for another farm manager." Rob rubbed his neck. He hated to see Drago go.

"Not at all. My life is here. Too many bad memories back in Gering. After I explained what Mr. MacKenna had done for me despite my arrest record, Markus understood. That's when I got the strange sensation that I needed to get home, and quick."

Rob took a sip of coffee. "I'm grateful you did. But you left your kid brother in town?"

"He had a hotel room. I told him something was wrong at the farm, and I had to go. He said he'd come with me. But not knowing what was going on, or what I'd walk into, I told him I'd rather he didn't. I promised I'd call in the morning to give him directions to the farm. I want him to stay with me for a while. Mr. MacKenna spared no expense when he had the old bunkhouse remodeled for me. It's like a ski lodge in there. Plenty of room."

"Yeah. When I was a kid, *I* wanted to live there."

They laughed.

"Sounds great, Drago. But you refused your inheritance?"

"Not exactly. Mark will set up things, so I receive an income. I'll have ample funds to take care of any repairs to the bunkhouse on my own, when and if needed." He glanced at Rob. "Did you know Aiden and Haley decided to put it in my name, along with the section of land it sits on? Including about an acre of the woods behind it."

Rob smiled at the stocky man who'd become more a friend than the MacKennas' farm manager. "Haley told me. I thought it was a fantastic idea. You've been as much of a blessing to this family as they've been to you."

After a few more cups of coffee and shared memories from the years Drago had worked for the MacKennas, a rustle of leaves caught Rob's attention. "Shh...I think we have company," he whispered.

Drago spun, aimed his shotgun, and stared like a deer frozen in place by headlights.

The porch light came on, and the door jerked open. Both men looked back at Haley, who stood in the doorway. A small coyote raced from the side of the house, sprinted across the gravel circle, and leaped into the brush.

Haley's jaw dropped. "What was that?"

Rob laughed. "A coyote Drago was about to pepper with buckshot."

"It could've been something else." Drago grimaced.

Haley pulled her fluffy white robe tight and stepped onto the porch. "Scratching from outside my window woke me. But when I looked out, nothing was there. I may have been dreaming."

"Everything's fine, sweetheart." Rob eyed the baseball bat resting on her shoulder and pointed. "What were you going to do with that?"

She took a deep breath and blew her bangs upward. "What do you think? Clobber the intruder. I, umm, if there was one. To be honest...I forgot you were out here."

He pulled Haley into his arms. "Sure glad you realized it was us." He snickered. "You can go back to sleep now. It's only two in the morning. Hopefully, no more critters will test our alertness tonight." He gave her a gentle kiss on the head and turned her toward the doorway.

Before shutting the door, she leaned against the frame. "Tomorrow, I'll get a restraining order against Lowell. I can't have you two sitting on the porch every night."

When Haley awoke, sunlight streamed through a gap between the drapes on the bedroom window. Her hand flew up to cover her eyes. Outside, crunching gravel announced a vehicle's approach. She threw on her jeans and T-shirt from the night before and rushed to the front door.

As Rob called out, "Lucy," Haley threw open the door. He waved from the porch.

Haley's friend slid out of the driver's side.

"*Lucy!*" Haley ran down the steps and wrapped her in a bear hug. "You're here."

Shaun stood with his paws on the steering wheel, his stump of a tail wagging so fast it was a blur. *"Yip. Yip, yip."*

Haley reached in through the window, and the canine jumped into her arms. "I'm happy to see you, too, little guy." The dog washed her cheek with kisses as she wiggled his ears back and forth.

Rob strode to Haley and slid his arm around her waist. "Hey, fella. No smooching my girl." He laughed.

When they approached the porch, Drago tucked the shotgun under his arm. "Guess I can go to sleep now. Miss Lucy, I'm happy you're back." As he skipped over the steps and headed for the bunkhouse, he waved in the air. "See you later."

Lucy's brows lowered. "What's he doing with that gun? He's going to sleep...now?"

"Haley'll fill you in. I need some shut-eye myself." Rob ruffled Shaun's head and lifted Haley's chin to kiss her. He stopped short. "Are you still contagious?"

She giggled. "I doubt it. Headache's gone, and I'm back to normal. It must have been my sinuses that made me sick yesterday, aside from the *jerk*." She frowned.

Rob planted a firm kiss on her mouth. "I'll call you when I wake up, sweetheart." He got in his truck and pulled away.

"Why do they need to sleep at this time in the morning? What's going on, Haley?"

Haley dragged Lucy up the stairs. "You must've driven through the night. Let's get coffee and breakfast going before I go into that."

"I did drive through the night. I love it, especially in Wisconsin. Less traffic. But what's with the shotgun?"

"While we eat breakfast. I'll tell you then. I'm so glad you've come back to North Bend for a good visit."

As soon as Haley put Shaun on the ground, he tore off to explore the premises. He yipped and tossed his head every few steps. His tail, held high, swished as if it were a flag in a parade. *Now there's one happy dog.*

After a leisurely breakfast, and Haley finished stowing the last dish in the dishwasher, the women sat at the kitchen table.

Haley sipped her coffee and lowered the cup. "So now you've heard the horrible story."

"Craig Lowell seemed like such a nice guy when I was here for Thanksgiving. I'd never have guessed he'd do such a thing. Although, he did ogle Char, and with her pregnant too. But I thought it was one of those "guy" things."

"Gentlemen don't, Lucy."

"You're right. I should have said something." She touched Haley's hand. "So, what're we doing today, girlfriend? Put me to work. My job hunt doesn't start until Monday."

"You should settle down...here...back home. Get steady employment instead of moving around the country all the time."

Lucy pulled her lips into a lopsided smile. "And miss the adventure?" She chortled.

"You, my friend, have wanderlust." Haley narrowed her eyes at Lucy. "Okay, the first thing on my list is to visit the Fremont Sheriff's Department to find out about a restraining order." Heat rose in her chest. She would not let thoughts of that man ruin her day with Lucy. "Then, we'll shop for wedding stuff."

A knock sounded on the back door. Haley jumped. "Hope I get over this edginess soon." She rose from the table and spotted Drago's happy face peeking through the window of the mudroom door.

He entered the kitchen with a tall, well-built man behind him. "Miss Haley, meet my brother Markus."

The brother's dark eyes sparkled with happiness as he shook her hand. "It's nice to meet you."

"Nice to meet you, too, Markus." He had the same eyes as Drago.

"Please call me Mark. I've never liked the name Markus. Reminds me of a Roman slave owner."

"Mark, it is, if you'll call me Haley. I've tried to get Drago to drop the *Miss* ever since I came home from college. Why don't you both sit and have coffee with us? Mark, this is my friend, Lucy Craft."

"Hello, Lucy." He held out his hand, and she placed hers in it without a word.

The poor girl had lost her voice. Haley giggled to herself. *I believe the love-bug has struck.* Mark's gaze remained on Lucy as he and Drago joined her at the table. Haley brought down two more mugs from the cabinet and poured the coffee.

As Mark took the chair next to Lucy, her face blossomed to a rosy pink.

Haley stifled a laugh. "Drago, you two don't resemble each other much, except for your deep brown eyes."

"My brother takes after our mother." He laid his hand on Mark's shoulder. "Except, she was pretty and refined."

Mark's jaw lowered. "Thanks."

Drago slipped his hand off Mark's shoulder as he guffawed.

For half an hour, the conversation centered on Mark and Drago's renewed relationship. Haley was so happy for him. She'd never seen Drago quite this joyful.

Drago finished his coffee and stood. "I've work to catch up on, and Mark said he'd give me a hand. So, little brother, let's hop to it."

Mark emptied his cup and pressed his lips into a straight line. "You introduce me to two lovely ladies and then drag me away. Is he always such a workaholic?"

"He is a hard worker. Tonight, I'd love to have both of you join Lucy, Rob, and me for dinner." *She might decide to stay in North Bend after all.* Her heart had been broken when Aiden chose Char. And Lucy'd never mentioned dating a man since. *Hmmm.* Maybe Mark could join them for Easter.

Mark held out his hand to Lucy again. "How long do you plan to stay?" She laid her hand in his.

"Miss Lucy," Drago broke in, "I hope you'll be here for at least a few days. With my workload here on the farm, I won't have much time to show my kid brother around. I'd like him to see what a great place North Bend is now that he's decided to stay for a visit."

Lucy broke out of her trance and blurted, "Yes. I'll be here for a while. My last contract in Wisconsin as a tour guide has ended, and I didn't renew it."

"While she looks for her next job," Haley peered up at Mark, "Lucy promised to stay on the farm with me. I'm sure she'll make a wonderful tour guide in her old home town." He was tall compared to Drago, but a good match for Lucy's height. "But can you start your tour early tomorrow morning? I need to stop at the sheriff's office this morning. Then we have a day of shopping planned."

The grin on Mark's face spread. "Tomorrow's a date. I'll look forward to learning all about my brother's home and community. Thank you, Lucy." His eyes didn't move from her for a second.

Haley watched Drago's brother and her friend. Yes, this could be a very interesting Easter. *And there'll be plenty of people around now to keep my mind off lecherous Lowell.*

Chapter Thirty

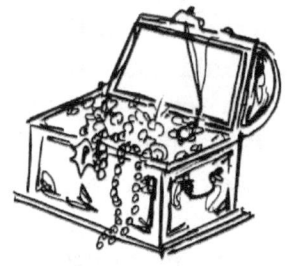

The next afternoon, Haley and Lucy went into town to meet the Greyhound bus from Colorado. As it pulled into the station, Haley waved at Kayla, who peered through a window near the front.

A sigh of relief escaped Haley. Kayla's fitting could be done on Monday, which would take care of all four attendants, including the flower girl's pastel-lilac princess gown complete with train. How beautiful the bridesmaids would look in orchid floor-length dresses. And Lucy in her Maid of Honor royal purple.

Haley scanned her surroundings. A chill snaked up her back. Since early morning, she'd had a premonition she might run into Lowell in town. But it was the Friday before Easter. Several businesses were closed. He probably wouldn't venture into town today.

Kayla stepped off the bus and rushed to Haley. "Roomie, I've missed you."

"Missed you too." Haley stepped back. "Lucy, this is my best friend from college, Kayla Ross." Haley held her hand out toward Lucy. "Kayla, meet my best friend from...forever, Lucy Craft."

Lucy stared at Kayla. "Have we met before?"

"I don't think so."

Here it comes. Haley grinned.

"You look so familiar. Wait a minute." She spun to Haley. "The movie we watched. The one about two friends who each get engaged and the two brides get into it because they both wanted the place on the same date for their wedding. The actress who played the blonde bride. Oh, what's her name? I'm so horrible at names." Lucy snapped her fingers while she thought.

Kayla's face turned pink. "Please don't say it."

Haley put her arm around Kayla's shoulder. "I can't remember her name either, but Kayla gets this response all the time. She's had people walk up to her on the street and ask for her autograph."

Kayla's nose wrinkled. "I'm so tired of people mistaking me for her. I just want to be me. Can you please forget who I resemble? I'm me, and me is all I want to be."

"Gotcha." Lucy chortled and pinched her index finger and thumb together, drawing them across her mouth. "My lips are zipped. But the resemblance is amazing."

"Unfortunately for me." Kayla sighed.

The driver dropped the last piece of luggage onto the ground, and Kayla picked up her bags. Haley grabbed the weekender from her hand. "Let me take this. Let's stop for a bite to eat before we head back to the farm. I'm starved."

"Sounds good. I didn't eat much on the trip here."

Lucy's eyes widened. "Are we going to Mom-and-Pop's?"

"Of course. You'll love this place, Kayla. A real mom-and-pop diner that's been in town for ages. The owners are friends...were friends of my folks."

Kayla and Lucy each squeezed one of Haley's shoulders.

How long would this heartache last?

Next to a window in the corner of an unimpressive diner in North Bend, Craig fumed over his lawyer's demand for the money owed him. The crook hadn't done a thing to acquire the MacKenna farm. But it'd be Lowell property very soon, anyway.

The bell on the entrance door jingled. Three women entered. Craig leered. *Well, well, well. My soon-to-be bride with a couple of luscious friends.*

The girls settled in a window booth next to the door. With her eyes closed, Haley inhaled slowly. "No fast-food burgers here. I only have to walk by this place to get hungry."

He cringed. She actually ate the food in this dump? She must be hungry since she hadn't noticed him yet.

A skinny teenage girl took the women's orders for cheeseburgers, onion rings, and chocolate shakes. The women handed the waitress their menus.

As they chatted, Craig slid out of his corner booth and strutted to their table. "Good morning, ladies." He smiled at each lovely face, stopping at Lucy's. "Ah, the pretty friend from Wisconsin."

Haley's jaw dropped. Her face blanched.

She deserved his giving someone else attention after her false accusations against him. It was all for show. To make him work harder to win her.

"Won't you introduce me to your new friend, my dear?" Craig pored over Kayla's features.

Haley sucked in a breath. Her jaw closed, and the muscles moved as she gritted her teeth.

He smirked. Maybe she didn't want to share him with anyone else. He liked that.

"Lucy, you remember *Mr. Lowell* from Thanksgiving. Kayla, this man is the one I mentioned. The one I had a restraining order filled out against. The man who has nerve even speaking to me."

When Craig held out his hand to Kayla, she glared at him, and he withdrew it.

Before he could say anything, Lucy stood. Her voice calm and low. "*Mr. Lowell*, we girls would appreciate our privacy. So get lost."

Where did she get off speaking to him that way? But he'd better not make a scene in the restaurant with others around. The tour guide may be helping Haley play hard to get, and who knew how far they'd take this little act. He gave a curt nod, left the table, strode to the counter, and paid for his coffee.

As Craig reached the door, he sneered at Haley. Hope he made it obvious to her he wasn't pleased with her game. But he'd get his payback. Soon.

"Thank you, Lucy." Haley's hands still shook. "Very well put. And you didn't cause a scene in front of the rest of the patrons. Now that he's gone, let's address those burgers and onion rings headed our way. Kayla, wait'll you taste the milkshake."

Haley took a deep breath, trying to push the bad experience to the back of her mind.

Kayla's eyes followed Craig as he passed them outside the window. "What a chameleon. So polite...but so...devious, from what you've told me. Like Satan himself."

Haley nodded. "Forget him. Let's enjoy lunch."

After their meal, they strolled toward the parking lot at the end of town. A man kept pace with them on the other side of the street. Haley's teeth clenched. *Lowell.* That weasel was like a bad cold that lingered.

When they came to the corner, he crossed the street to their side. Lucy stopped and faced him. "Mister, if you don't want to be arrested for stalking, you'd better leave."

"Who do you think you are? I'll follow my fiancée whenever and wherever I want."

Lucy's chin jutted out as she stretched to her full height, a couple of inches taller than Craig.

Haley grabbed her arm. "Come on. Ignore him. He's delusional."

"I'll say. He has a screw loose if he thinks you'll dump Rob to marry him. Let him explain himself to the sheriff." She waved at a squad car heading their way.

Lowell's brows lowered. He turned on his heel and dashed away.

The cruiser pulled over and parked. Deputy Jason Schumaker jumped out and hurried to them. "Can I help you, Haley?" His eyes widened. "*Lucy.* Didn't know you were in town."

"Hi, Jason. Just got here yesterday." She pointed to where Craig had turned the corner. "That Lowell guy is harassing Haley."

He turned to where Lucy indicated, but the street was empty. He glanced at Haley. "Lowell?"

"Yes. He came up to us while we had lunch at Mom-and-Pops. And a moment ago, he crossed over from the other side and stopped us here. But Lucy told him off both times, and he left. He's gone now, so don't worry. I'd like you to meet my friend, Kayla Ross." She stretched out her hand toward Kayla.

As the corners of Kayla's mouth lifted, her crystalline eyes sparkled, and her lips parted.

Jason's eyes locked onto hers as he extended a hand. She placed her fingers in his palm. He grasped her hand in his and held on. Her cheeks grew rosy.

"Kayla came to spend Easter with me and for her bridesmaid's dress fitting."

"That's great. Guess I'll see you Sunday." He let go of Kayla's hand and turned to Haley. "Regarding Lowell. Even though you've filled out a restraining order, don't go anywhere alone. I don't trust the guy. He wasn't the least bit phased by my warning after the barn incident."

"I'm not too worried with Lucy around. And she'll be here for a while. Rob spends as much time as he can at the farm with us. Drago's also around...along with his brother, Mark, who's staying with him. Mark decided," she peeked at Lucy, "to hang around at least for Easter."

"That's good, but remember, Lowell doesn't seem like he'll give up pursuing you. Be extra careful."

"I will, Jason. Thanks. If you're not busy tonight, why don't you have dinner with us?"

"Would love to." The deputy thanked Haley, gave Kayla a smile, and returned to his patrol car. He waved as he left.

Haley turned to Kayla, whose jaw had lowered and cheeks were still glowing. "You okay?"

"Ahh...he's...*cute.*"

Lucy and Haley tittered. Haley took Kayla's arm and led them to the parking lot.

Haley slid behind the wheel and started the engine. "I'd call myself a matchmaker. But I haven't done a thing to get you two to fall for these guys, except invite you to the farm." The girls giggled.

Ten minutes later, Haley pulled the car into the farmyard. "Oh look, Aiden's Honda. They're here."

As she parked the car, Aiden stepped out of the house onto the front porch. Shaun and Everett zipped past him.

"That little dickens always has to be first. He and Lucy's ball of white fluff are two of a kind."

Everett jumped into his aunt's arms. Shaun did the same with Lucy.

"We're happy you're here, Kayla," Aiden said as he stepped off the porch. "Char's inside planning dinner. Hope you don't mind her taking over the kitchen, Sis. She thought it would give you more time with your friends."

"She can take over the entire house any time she wants to. After all, it's about to become hers. Seven weeks, one day, and counting."

He grinned. "Where's Rob?"

"Working, as usual. He'll be here for dinner. So will Jason, Drago, and his brother. I'd better let Char know."

After a glance at the bunkhouse, Aiden stared at Haley. "Drago's brother?"

"I'll fill you in after I get Kayla settled. Do you mind getting her two bags?" The girls sauntered to the house.

While Aiden retrieved Kayla's weekender and carry-on from the trunk, Char waddled onto the porch. Haley introduced her to Kayla.

"It's nice to meet you, Kayla." Char gave her a sideways hug. "Haley's mentioned you so often. And Lucy, it's great to see you again too. You three relax. I'll handle dinner."

"Rob, Drago, his brother, and Jason will join us for dinner. Hope it's not a problem."

"None whatsoever. I had one of those MacKenna hunches, so I've planned on enough food for a small army." She smiled and turned to go inside but made a sudden stop. "Wait. Did you say Drago's brother?"

Haley nodded. "Yes. It's a long story. After Kayla's settled in, we'll join you and Aiden in the kitchen, and I'll tell you about it."

Aiden entered after the girls. "Kayla, you may only have two bags, but you didn't pack light. These weigh a ton." He lugged the weekender and carry-on upstairs with Haley, Kayla, and Lucy in his wake.

An hour later, the aroma of fresh coffee filled the room. While everyone sipped the brew around the kitchen table, Haley explained the presence of Drago's brother. Afterward, she studied the contented faces of the group with their cups in hand. "Now this is farm living—like Rob always says."

Aiden gave his sister a thumbs-up. "Why would anyone want to live anywhere else? Thanks for inviting Jason. An improvement over the likes of Lowell."

"I'll say," Lucy added. "Too bad he didn't arrest that creep this afternoon."

Aiden's brows furrowed. His phone rang.

"It's Jason. Hi there, buddy." He switched to the speaker. "What did you do, ping my phone and found out I was at the farm?"

"Hi." He laughed. "No. Thought I'd ask Haley if there's something she wants me to bring for dinner tonight since I was invited, but I decided to call you first to see if you made it in or not. Glad you finally got smart and moved home."

"Okay, okay. We got in a couple hours earlier than expected. Haley's friends, Lucy and Kayla, are here too. Kayla was Haley's roommate in college."

"Already met her this afternoon when Lucy flagged the squad down."

"She what? Why?" Aiden shot Lucy a look.

"Haley didn't tell you?"

"No." He faced his sister as he spoke. "What's happened now?"

"The girls had a run-in with Lowell. But you'd better ask her. From what I understand, Lucy took the matter in hand, and they were fine."

Char rose and carried her mug to the sink. "Just bring yourself tonight, and be here at least by six, Jason."

"Did you hear that, man?"

After a few more comments, they ended their call. Aiden's brows lowered, and he riveted Haley with an expression their dad had often used when he wanted the truth. "Now, what about the incident in town?"

She grimaced. Boy, he resembled Dad more each day. She stood. "I should help Char prepare for dinner first. With that baby as big as she is, your wife's feet must be tired."

"I'm fine. Tell your brother what the problem was." Char grimaced right back at her.

Haley sunk back into the chair and told Aiden what happened in town. "The restraining order our lawyer filed should be in effect any time. That will settle that."

Lucy added her take on the episode, then shook her head. "That man is evil. His attitude's beyond arrogant. Didn't you sense it?" She glanced at Kayla.

"I did." She touched Haley's hand resting on the tabletop. "Lucy's right, Haley. There's something wrong with that guy."

Chapter Thirty-One

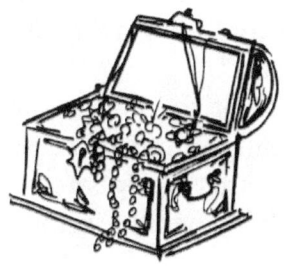

Early that evening, Rob pulled into the MacKenna front yard and parked next to Aiden's car. He'd been so relieved when Aiden called and told him they'd arrived. The girls wouldn't be alone in the house now. And Drago could relax more with his brother instead of being on watch for Lowell all the time. Although, Mark might want to keep an eye on at least one of the girls from what Haley had said. Rob chuckled and turned off the engine.

As he jumped out of the truck and retrieved two fresh apple pies from the passenger seat, Drago and Mark jogged up to him.

"What do we have here?" Drago lifted a pie from Rob's hands and took a deep whiff. "Umm. Apple. Your mom made them?"

Rob grinned. "She did. For us *tonight*, so don't get anxious."

Mark snapped his fingers. "For a minute, I thought it was an appetizer for us guys. They smell great. Bet they'll taste even better."

As the men headed to the house, Mark smiled and glanced at Drago. "I see why you're content here. Good food. Terrific people all around you. And Lucy's convinced me of what a great place North Bend is to live. I'll never get you out to Gering, Cary."

"Hey. If you want me to call you Mark instead of Markus, little brother, you'd better drop my old name. It's Drago now, thanks to these kids." He thumped Rob on the back. "But don't worry. I'll make time for a trip to the homestead. It'd be nice to see the old place again...just for a visit."

His brother nodded. "Not to change the subject, but I'd like to ask Lucy to dinner. I mean, on our own. Not on a tour date. I want to get to know her better this week before I have to go back to the ranch. Do you think Haley would mind if I steal Lucy for an evening?"

Rob grinned. "Great idea. She's been Haley's best friend forever. I'm sure she'd be thrilled if you and Lucy hit it off. It'd give her more reason to visit *us* when you visit Drago." Rob wiggled his eyebrows up and down.

When they entered the house, the aroma of fried chicken filled the air. Rob's mouth watered.

Drago knocked Mark's Stetson off his head and picked it up from the floor. He slapped it across his brother's stomach. "Where're your manners, boy?"

Mark laughed. "Sorry. Since Mom died, there's been a lack of social graces at home. Especially now that it's just me and the ranch hands."

As they entered the living room, Aiden and Jason rose from the couch. Aiden laid his hand on Jason's shoulder. "Mark, meet one of North Bend's finest, Deputy Jason Schumaker, and a longtime friend of ours."

Jason shook Mark's hand. "Sorry for the uniform. My shift ended at five, but I was in the middle of giving a lecture to a speeder. The kid needed a good talking to...*again*. Afterward, I remembered Char had warned me not to be late for dinner, so I didn't take time to change." He shrugged.

"Sure. Go ahead. Show the rest of us up in your spiffy uniform, Jason." Rob slapped him on the upper arm. "But, you won't have anything to do here tonight in the way of official business."

Rob left them to search for Haley.

After dinner, Haley cut the apple pies in the kitchen while her two best friends conversed with Mark and Jason in the living room. The joy in their voices drifted through the dining room and brought a tickle to Haley's heart. A chuckle slipped out.

"Why are you laughing?" Char carried the dessert plates from the cabinet to the table.

"Lucy and Kayla. Those two traveled over five hundred miles, from two different directions, to find guys they're head-over-heels about. Love, at first sight, is real."

"I've noticed the four of them are enraptured with each other." Char giggled.

A grin spread across Haley's face. "And here I fell in love with the boy next door, so to speak. Go figure."

"You and me both. Aiden and Rob have been friends since we were all little. Funny you and I never hung out. But, I am a little older than you."

"Yeah. A whole year. Wow!" Haley laughed. "Different interests. Different crowds."

Char nodded. She poured coffee into two carafes and loaded mugs, creamer, and the sugar bowl onto a tray. "It was nice that Mark had ranch hands to cover for him so he could stay for a while."

"I'm glad for both Lucy and Drago's sakes." Haley slid a server into one of the pie dishes.

She carried the desserts into the dining room. "Come and get it." She peeked into the living room. "What happened to Rob, Drago, and Aiden?"

Lucy placed a piece of pie on a plate for Mark. "They went out to the stable to check things. Said they'd be right back."

"I'll let them know we're serving dessert." Haley grabbed her sweater from the coat tree and rushed out the door. Shaun shot out onto the porch before she pulled the door closed. "Okay, little guy. Guess when ya gotta go, ya gotta go."

They crossed the circle drive and headed for the stable. Before they'd ventured a quarter of the way, Shaun stopped and barked toward the field. He raced into the dark.

"Come back here, boy."

The dog returned to Haley, giving a low guttural growl all the way.

"Good boy. You just gave me the willies."

Rob stuck his head out of the stable door. "What's all the ruckus?"

With Shaun right on her heels but still growling, Haley hurried to him. When they reached the door, Shaun turned and gave one more bark and growl.

"Was something out there?" Rob's brows lowered.

Shaun slipped through the doorway into the stable and sniffed like a bloodhound following a trail.

"I didn't see anything. He ran toward the field but stopped when I called. Then he growled as he came back to me."

"Maybe he sensed the coyote we saw." Rob led her through the stable to Aiden and Drago. The horses murmured and shuffled, hanging their heads over the rails of each stall for attention.

Drago secured a toolbox. "Strange how those thefts suddenly ended, Aiden." He gazed up at Haley and Rob. "Still can't help but think it was those Indian ghosts, no matter how many times Aiden assures me there's no such thing."

Aiden shook his head and stifled a laugh. "Drago, what would a ghost want with those tools?"

As Shaun followed a scent on the straw-covered floor, Haley and Rob watched. "Rob, you don't suppose Shaun can still smell the tracks of the perpetrator, do you?"

He ran his tongue across his lower lip. "I don't know. Maybe. It's strange how whoever was behind the petty thefts had singled out your farm. Must be a reason."

"If it isn't those old ghosts," Drago grimaced, "I'd vote for Lowell as the thief. Wouldn't put it past that scoundrel to be behind everything that's happened around here. Beats the tar out of me why the sheriff's department can't find any evidence against him. But it's probably those ghosts."

"Dra-a-go." She narrowed her eyes at him. "I don't believe in ghosts." She patted his back.

"So, men. If you're done rehashing old problems, the pie's on the table. Shaun and I are going in." Haley spun and headed outside.

As Craig drove away from the MacKenna property in the dark, he fumed. Now Haley entertained other men at her shabby house. He'd had enough. He'd settle things with her once and for all after her holiday company left. That would only leave the troublemaking handyman and Sheffield to deal with if they got in the way.

Why'd that smart-aleck *tour guide* have to flag down the sheriff this afternoon? He hadn't needed another run-in with them so soon, not after his visit from the deputy. Craig clenched his teeth.

And where did she get off with her remark about something being wrong with him? Screw loose, was it? If anyone had a screw loose, it was her.

Craig flicked the butt of his half-smoked cigarette out the window and sped down the road leading home. When he approached the gates to his drive, he slowed the car and turned onto the long, narrow lane leading to the house. He parked in the garage and stomped into the kitchen.

"Mr. Lowell!" Mrs. Yonge dropped a pot on the stone floor with a clatter. "You startled me." She retrieved the pot and placed it in the sink. "Dinner was ready an hour ago. As you asked. Do you want it served now? It's still warm. I've kept it wrapped in the warming oven."

Craig strode past Mrs. Yonge, through the kitchen, and out, as he snapped over his shoulder, "I'm not hungry." He clomped up the stairs to the master bedroom and threw himself across the king-size bed. The cook acted like his mother. She should have checked with him before she made dinner and wasted food. *He'd* asked her to have it ready by five? *He'd* asked no such thing.

Heat rose in his neck, and he gritted his teeth. He picked up a book from the night table and flung it at the dresser. Several pages of yellowed paper flew out and scattered across the room. Why were people always telling him he said things he didn't? Even his mother had done that. Had she tried to drive him insane?

After he lit a cigarette, he placed it in an ashtray on the nightstand. Craig cursed and retrieved the book and yellow pages. These were the papers he'd found hidden in his father's desk drawer when he first arrived. That's right. He remembered now.

He gazed at the old papers and fingered the treasure map. Right there. It had to be right there. In days, he'd have it in his hands.

A sudden pain surged from his forehead to the back of his head. He grabbed his temples, and dropped onto the bed, rolling to his side. Would these headaches never quit?

When the pain subsided, Craig rose and stumbled into the bathroom. He opened a bottle of aspirin and downed six, washing the bitterness from his mouth with a tumbler of water. If only he could find someone to sell him something stronger. He'd still made no connection in this backwater town. But he'd been given a new name when he visited the roadhouse late this afternoon. He'd call tomorrow. He wanted those pills. Something special was needed, too—to finish his plan.

Craig shuffled back to the bedside, lifted the old map, and lowered himself into a leather armchair. His father had believed the treasure was still there. The last time he'd called, he'd talked of nothing else. Then he said he'd hidden the map. Wouldn't say where. *But I found it.*

The treasure *must* be there. Craig dropped his head onto the back of the chair. He'd find it, once he married Haley. She could do nothing about it then. As his wife, the treasure would belong to him. He had no option but marriage, since he couldn't acquire the farm through the legal system and hadn't been able to scare her away.

Father's attempt to buy the MacKenna farmland from her parents had failed too. Craig frowned. As did his own attempt. He'd tried to scare them off. But when he'd adjusted the brakes on the MacKennas' vehicle, something went wrong. Their resulting deaths almost ruined everything. It was a good thing he was so skilled at leaving no evidence of his work.

He picked up the papers and surveyed them again. His ancestor found the treasure in the field with a MacKenna kid, or so his father had told him. Why would he make up something like that? No. It had to be real. That deputy lied when he said it was only a legend.

With his eyelids pressed together as hard as he could, Craig endured another wave of pain.

Several minutes later, he strode to the den, poured himself a tall glass of whiskey, and slugged it down. Another followed. He returned to the armchair in the bedroom and winced as he rolled his neck in circles to relieve the stiffness.

Craig examined the map again. Childlike scribbles. The X showed the treasure at the edge of a rough drawing of the field behind Haley's house. The addition of her bedroom pushed the field farther back. The X marked where the room stood. Yes. He had the location right. It *was* there.

The holes he'd dug under Haley's bedroom had produced nothing. But once they were married, and he pulled up the floor, he'd find the treasure without interference.

He stood up, doubled over, and landed on the bed. "Ohhh...I can't take this pain." Craig curled into a fetal position.

As the pain subsided once more, thoughts swam in his head. He didn't have to stay married to that farm girl for long. It wouldn't be any harder to get rid of Haley than it had his mother. His eyes closed.

Chapter Thirty-Two

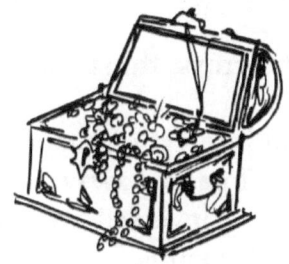

E aster Sunday evening, the aroma of savory lamb filled the room as Haley delivered the crowned roast with cranberry orange stuffing to the dining room table. This came out perfect, even though it was the first time she'd made the festive cut of meat by herself. The little white frills on each bone added an elegant touch, thanks to Auntie.

"Hope everyone likes lamb." Haley read joy and disappointment on the faces at the table. "But if you don't..." She held out her hand toward the kitchen doorway.

Right on cue, Char waltzed in with a platter of glazed ham, followed by Lucy and Kayla with scalloped potatoes, broccoli, homemade country white bread, and butter.

After Char set the ham on the table next to the crowned roast, she took her seat at one end. She pulled a kitchen stool next to her and helped Everett climb onto it.

Aiden gazed lovingly at his wife from the head of the table.

As she studied the friends and loved ones surrounding them, Haley seated herself next to her fiancé. Rob reached over and enveloped her hand in his.

She continued to study the people around her. Rob's dad eyeing the homemade bread while his wife smiled at him. Jason, brushing back a stray rust-colored curl from his forehead. Next to him, Kayla.

Drago took the seat across the table from Aunt Debbie and smiled at her.

Now *there* would be an interesting match. Auntie had been alone far too long since Uncle Jeff passed away.

Mr. and Mrs. Sheffield conversed with Lucy and Mark across from them. What a blessed evening.

Aiden clinked a crystal goblet. "Let's give thanks to our heavenly Father for the wonderful meal the ladies prepared today."

Everyone bowed their heads. "Father, we're grateful for the many blessings You've given us. Most of all, for salvation. Thank You for Your protection and provision. Please bless this food to our bodies. Bless the conversation tonight. In Jesus' Name, we pray. Amen."

Amens resounded, the food was passed, and pleasant discussions ensued.

Haley leaned back and searched each face once more. Her heart might burst with happiness. If only her best friends could always be this close to her.

While everyone chatted at the end of the meal, Shaun lifted his head from the floor and barked at the front door. The room silenced.

Char pointed toward the dining room bay window. "Someone's out there."

Shaun jumped to his feet and darted past the foyer to the living room window. Then he raced through the hallway toward Haley's bedroom.

Everyone jumped to their feet, and the men bolted out the front door.

Char grabbed Everett's shoulder.

"Let me go, Mama. I wanna see too."

"Everett, you stay here with me."

As Shaun barreled back through the hallway toward the front door, Haley, Kayla, and Lucy rushed out before him. Haley pulled the door shut before he could slip past her. He raised his objection inside.

Aiden pointed toward the field in the back. "Jason, Mark, Drago—check that side. Mr. Sheffield, will you stay with the girls?"

Rob's dad nodded.

"Come on, Rob." Her fiancé followed Aiden as he rocketed around the other corner of the house to Drago's place and the stable.

While the girls waited on the front porch, Haley's heartbeat and breathing increased. Penlights shone in every direction.

After what seemed an eternity, the men returned. She rushed down the stairs. "Did you find anything?"

Rob dropped to the steps, and she joined him. "We checked the bunkhouse, stable, barn, and tool shed. Flashed my light across the yards, corral, and fields. Nothing."

"What do you suppose Char saw?"

Aiden scratched his chin.

The hairs stood on Haley's neck. They hadn't checked the woods.

Rob held Haley in his arms in the foyer as the rest of the group settled in the dining room. Shaun had quieted and rested behind

Lucy's chair after his fit. Haley trembled and Rob kissed her forehead. "Sweetheart, we checked everywhere. Relax. Whoever it was, is gone. Maybe it was teens goofing off again." He hoped.

Char led Everett to the staircase. "It's been a busy day for you. Time to get ready for bed."

"Aw, Mommy. I wanna know what happened, and what about cake?"

Aiden strode to the steps and scooped his son into his arms. "The puppy may have sensed a rabbit out there. That's all." He winked at his wife. "Now you listen to Mama and get changed for bed. You've had enough Easter treats today. We'll save cake for tomorrow."

"Aww, Daddy." He hung his head as his lip protruded.

Aiden set Everett back on his feet and gave the boy a gentle swat on his posterior. Everett took his mother's hand, giggled, and rubbed his bottom as he climbed the stairs. His father followed.

Haley and her aunt took dirty dishes from the table. Lucy and Kayla carried platters and bowls into the kitchen.

Rob entered the living room and sat on the couch next to Drago. "Any idea what it was?"

He shook his head. "Not sure. Miss Char said she saw a face, which means it wasn't an animal. Bet it wasn't teens like you told Haley, either."

As Mark lowered himself into the armchair across from his brother, his brows furrowed. "Then what?"

"My guess is the same *what*, or *who*, that lifted those things from the stable." Drago slapped his leg. "I'll beef up security measures around here."

Rob's dad came in with a cup of coffee and eased onto the other end of the sofa. "Probably a good idea, considering."

Jason parked in the armchair next to Mark's. "I'll add this event to the list for my ongoing investigation. In the morning, I'll come back out. Maybe I'll find something we missed tonight in the dark." He sucked his lips between his teeth. "Could be pranks, but—we've never had this kind of weird goings-on in North Bend before. Not without finding any evidence of who's causing them, anyway."

At least Drago hadn't blamed ghosts this time. Rob clamped his jaw tight. They'd never had Craig Lowell in North Bend before either. Until last year.

Rob glanced at Aiden as he and Char came into the room and collapsed onto folding chairs. "Char told me the face in the window was pale. Reminded her of Craig Lowell."

"Although I couldn't swear to it." Char shrugged. "But as an artist, I'm good when it comes to noticing facial details."

Rob pinned Jason with his stare. Another clue for him to go on?

As Haley and her friends served coffee in the living room, Char and Aunt Debbie brought in plates with slices of Black Forest cake. Haley handed Rob a mug and then gave one to Drago. "Do you really still think we have ghosts out in the old field?" She raised her brows, and a twinge snaked up her arms.

"Not anymore. Someone's trying to make us *think* they're a ghost. But he can't stay invisible forever. I won't bring up the old Indian legend...*this time.*" He smiled at her.

Real smart, Haley. Why on earth had she asked?

Lucy accepted the armchair Mark had given up for her. "What about you, Mark? Do you believe in ghosts?"

He lowered himself to the folding chair next to her. "Only the ghosts that haunt my memories of past days without my brother. But we'll make up for it. Right, Car—sorry, Drago?"

A crash came from the kitchen. Haley's heart leaped into her throat.

Lucy jumped from the chair. Everyone's eyes bugged out. In a herd, they rushed to the scene.

In the kitchen, Everett, in his tractor PJs, stood barefoot on the top rung of the kitchen stool, fork in his hand, plate smashed on the floor. Tears ran over his chubby cheeks.

Aiden whisked him off the stool. "Are you all right?"

Everett nodded.

Aiden handed him to his mother. "What were you doing, Son?"

"I sowy. I wanted cake. But I bwoke Auntie's plate." He bawled.

Haley kissed Everett's cheek. "I'm not worried about the plate, sweetie. *You* could have been hurt. We can get more plates...but not Everetts." She ruffled his hair.

The tears stopped, and he swiped his nose with his hand.

"Mommy will get your cake, but promise us you'll never do this again." Char cut a tiny slice and put it on another plate, while Aiden tightened his lips. She whispered to him, "We'll discuss this later. It's Easter."

He nodded and left the room.

Haley bit her lip. Would she and Rob have moments like that too? Char won that time.

While Haley helped Char clean the floor, everyone else returned to the living room. Haley seated Everett in the dining room with his cake, and then she and her sister-in-law joined the rest of the group.

Kayla leaned back on the couch. "Haley, you said it was times like these, holidays, when your dad told the MacKenna treasure legend. Why don't you?"

And here she'd been so happy to have her old roomie around, until now. Haley narrowed her eyes at Kayla, who raised her brows. "Didn't you get enough over our three years together in college?"

"Nope. I find the story fascinating." She looked at Jason next to her. "Do you know the legend?"

"Sure. Aiden, Rob, and I hung out together as kids. Haley too. When we camped out at the old stone barn or by the pond behind Rob's place, Aiden's dad would build a campfire and tell us the story. Most people in town know the legend."

"Lucy, did you know it?" Kayla scooted to the edge of the couch.

"Of course, I did." She tittered. "Actually, Haley told it to me again when I came for Christmas after I bugged her about it. Until then, I didn't know all the details."

Mark turned to Aiden. "I'd like to hear the story."

"All right, Aiden." Haley crossed her arms over her chest. "Let's get this over with."

Her brother chuckled. "Here goes. The history of the treasure has been handed down for decades. It's impossible to say it hadn't changed over the years. But when I was a young teen, Dad showed me a copy of the legend written on a parchment from the eighteen hundreds, according to the date on the document. The paper used to be kept in a small chest in my parents' room. But I haven't seen it for years. As a kid, Dad had found what appeared to be a faded treasure map. He could only make out a tree, what resembled a wall, and some scratches forming an *ex*. Grandpa caught him with it and took it away. Dad never saw it again, but never forgot it."

Haley half closed her eyes and shook her head. What storytellers we MacKennas were.

Aiden continued. "The treasure came here on a ship headed to America which our ancestors had embarked on from Ireland. It was attacked by pirates and sunk in the Gulf of Mexico. Our ancestor, Gurth MacKenna, the only known survivor, made it to shore and later watched the pirates bury the chest in an overgrown area off the beach."

As Aiden related the rest of the details he could remember from the parchment, Haley's mind pictured each scene. She shuddered at the murder of the pirate's men onshore.

"The ancestor came to Nebraska from Florida and brought the treasure with him. He buried the chest in what's now the back field." Aiden paused for a sip of coffee.

"I'm intrigued." Mark leaned back. "This would make a great movie."

Lucy chortled. "Hear! Hear!"

Aiden nodded and went on. "Oh, yeah. Over the years, the treasure was forgotten, until another ancestor stumbled upon it, dug it up, and relocated the chest. That's when the map Dad discovered was supposedly drawn up, but no one has ever found the location of the reburied treasure. Or the map again."

"So was your ancestor a pirate?" Mark's eyes widened.

Aiden chuckled. "Gurth MacKenna was a passenger on the ship. He was terrified as a young lad and hid when the pirates attacked."

Lucy tilted her head to one side and pursed her lips. "It's hard to believe none of your relatives ever used any of the wealth in the chest. It would've been big news if they had. Did it have a curse on it?"

"The parchment didn't mention a curse." Aiden grinned. "From old family letters I've come across stored in the attic, our people were content with the lives they led here on the farm. Different from many people today. They didn't need treasure."

Murmurs of agreement filled the room.

Aiden placed his coffee cup on the table. "The story developed into a legend. Although, each generation of MacKennas hung onto those old papers."

"Where are they now?" Mark asked.

Aiden shrugged. "As I said, I haven't seen them since I was a boy."

"See?" Haley lifted her left eyebrow. "Legend. This great, great, however many greats, grandfather Gurth was obviously a prolific storyteller and handed his skill down. He made it believable enough that the story became a legend." She smoothed her skirt over her lap.

As his arm pulled her closer, Rob laughed. "You've never believed the story."

"Not a word. No more than I believe in ghosts." She glanced at Drago, who snickered.

Lucy placed her elbow on the arm of the chair, chin cupped in her palm. She tapped her lips with a finger. "Wait a minute. What about the Indian legend? The mound was in the same field behind this house, right? Didn't you say the treasure was found in that field? Are the stories connected?"

"Please stop with the legends," Haley pleaded. "We've had a beautiful day. Let's not spoil it with exaggerated tales of pirates and ghosts."

Jason crossed his legs and leaned back in the seat. "So, how are things going with the sale of your house in California, Aiden?"

Thank you, Jason. She could kiss him.

As if Rob had read her mind, he circled Haley's waist with his arm. "Haley, Lucy has a valid point. Two legends. Centered on the same field. It's possible the ghost stories were created to protect the treasure. What doesn't add up is the tree and wall Aiden said were on the map. There aren't any trees or signs of an old wall out in that field."

"Oh, Rob."

"And...I recall your dad once mentioned the friend who found the chest with your ancestor may have been related to the Lowells. Haven't they lived in the area about as long as your family?"

Haley clenched her jaw. "Ugh."

"Okay, I'll drop it...for now." He kissed her cheek.

She leaned on his arm. He was right. Lucy definitely had a valid point. So did he.

Chapter Thirty-Three

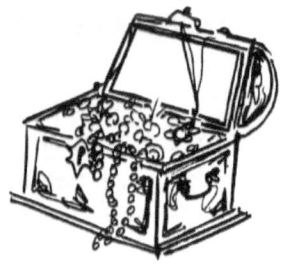

After a solid night's sleep for the first time in weeks, Haley awoke Monday morning and stretched. She glanced at the alarm clock. After seven. All quiet through the night, and not even a peep out of Shaun. She swung her legs over the edge of the bed.

As she threw back the curtains on the window, the sun beamed into her eyes. She blinked until they adjusted to the brightness, then gazed outside. Lucy squatted in the fallow field. What was she doing, looking for clues to the missing treasure? Haley chuckled.

Seconds later, Shaun bounded onto Lucy's side and knocked her over. She fell back to one hand and laughed. Silly dog. Haley shook her head. When Lucy rose from the awkward position, she spotted Haley at the window and waved. Shaun barked and ran off.

After the wedding, she'd talk to Rob about getting a dog. Neither of them had owned a pet for a long time, and Shaun had been so much fun these past few days. The little guy had proved himself a terrific watchdog. She spun and headed to the bathroom.

Haley washed and dressed, then went into the kitchen. She poured a cup of coffee and sat at the table. She'd wait until everyone came downstairs before she decided what to make for breakfast. After the late hours they kept last night telling treasure and ghost stories, the rest of the household might want to sleep in.

"Haley, I've been waiting for you to get up. There's a favor I need to ask of you," Lucy said as she strolled in through the back door and mudroom. Shaun scampered in behind her. She grabbed a mug and filled it with coffee.

"Sure, what is it?" Haley took a sip of her own.

Her friend laid a hand on her shoulder. "Wait until you hear me out before you say yes."

Haley nodded.

"Before I left Wisconsin..." Lucy dropped into the chair next to Haley. "...I applied for a job in Alaska as a tour guide, and I found an email from them this morning. They've asked if I'd come this coming weekend for an interview, and I'd really like to go. I've always wanted to take a trip to Alaska, so when this temporary contract came up...well, I want to check it out."

"Alaska?"

"Yes. They said I should plan to stay for a week. The current tour guide will show me the ropes and see how I do before the lodge owners offer me the job. The manager at the Dells sent them an outstanding reference letter for me. I'll be staying in the ski lodge for the week. My problem is, I can't take Shaun with me, not until I accept the job and find a place of my own to stay."

Haley waited while Lucy took a breath and lifted the mug to her lips. *Alaska?* Wow. So much for her homesickness for North Bend. "So, what's the favor?"

"I told them I'd drive my truck. Didn't want to fly there. So they offered to pay my gas. I have to leave on Friday."

Her mind was stuck on Alaska. "Okay, Lucy. So, again, what's the favor?"

Lucy peered over her cup. "Well...I wondered if Shaun could stay here with you while I'm gone. Is it too much of an imposition? Sort of like asking someone to watch your young child while you take a trip hundreds of miles away, huh? I'll understand if you'd rather not. It's just that I hate the thought of sticking poor Shaun in a kennel for more than a week while I'm gone. It'd stress him out to be with strangers and have other dogs barking all around him. With my parents living in Florida, and my brother in the service..."

Haley closed her eyes. She'd be leaving—this coming weekend.

"I'm sorry. I guess it's too much to ask with graduation and your wedding plans. I'll figure something else out."

"No." Haley's eyes popped open. "No. Not at all. I'll take care of Shaun for you. I love the little guy. I was just thinking of you leaving again."

The dog ran into the kitchen and jumped up on Haley's legs.

"What did you do, eavesdrop on our conversation?" His tail waved like it had a new motor. "So, little buddy, you'll bunk here while Mom takes her trip. But I'm afraid Everett can't play with you next week. He and *his* mom will leave for California on Thursday."

Haley smiled at Lucy. "Their house has sold, and Char wanted to be there to settle everything."

"I'm happy for them, Haley. And I'm glad they came home."

Leaning back in the chair, Haley studied Lucy's face. If only she would come home to stay and forget all this wandering.

Shaun bounced up on Haley's legs again. She scratched his ears. *You want to live here in farm country, don't you?* "Hopefully, you won't have to sound off any more alarms while you're here."

Craig stood by the old stone barn at the corner of the backwoods on MacKenna property. So this was the place of the old dispute. It would make more sense for the MacKennas' land to end farther back from here. But why had his father been so intent on this worthless piece of land cut out from what should be Lowell property?

What a wreck. Craig stuck his head through the door of the old barn. It should have been torn down long ago. He'd see it was done once it was his.

As he pulled his head out, his mind went to Haley's guests at the dinner table last night. He'd almost been caught peering into the dining room when MacKenna's wife looked straight at him. So cozy. Eating and laughing together. Craig sneered. Sheffield...holding Haley's hand. He'd pay for that. She'd be a Lowell, not a Sheffield. With the information he'd found online, he could now make the arrangements.

But when would he catch her alone? He'd have to bide his time and wait for the right moment. And he'd be more careful than he'd been last night.

Time spent with his friends in Italy had paid off. They were masters of stealth, and he'd been a good student. His mother never caught him listening in on her conversations with the doctor. Craig's blood boiled as he recalled her description of him. *Mentally unstable.* There was nothing wrong with him. "But Mother will never call me that again," he whispered.

Craig sat on an old stump, pulled out a pack of cigarettes, and lit one. As he drew in a mouthful of smoke, he sneered again. From what he'd heard in town, no one in the MacKenna family really believed the old treasure legend. Father knew it was real. *So do I.* It had to be.

A string of expletives erupted from Craig. "When will her guests leave?" He bolted from the stump and paced. "I'm tired of waiting." He had to find Haley alone...somewhere.

He kicked the rock-hard tree trunk. As he gritted his teeth from the discomfort in his leg, pain shot through his head. He grabbed his temples, doubled over, and fell to the ground. Stars flickered.

When he came to, the sun had dipped behind the trees. Craig trudged through the woods and across the field to his house. And his new supply of pills.

That night, as Haley ate dinner with Aiden, Char, and Everett, Lucy and Kayla's double date with Mark and Jason filled her mind. It'd be great if everything worked out for both couples. She hadn't prayed about it, but she'd spend serious time on it tonight.

Char waved her hand in front of Haley's eyes. "I've been trying to get your attention."

Haley blinked and stared at her. "I'm sorry. What?"

"Where's Rob this evening? He hasn't missed a meal here all weekend."

"At this moment, Rob and his parents are no doubt tackling their list of names for the wedding invitations." Haley giggled. "He dragged his feet until his mother made his presence mandatory. I was there this afternoon when she issued the command. Rob's eyes grew as big as saucers. It was so funny. His dad laughed and walked away. Mrs. Sheffield is a trip."

As she lifted a forkful of mashed potatoes to her mouth, she gazed at the chair where Rob usually sat. "His mother did have a point when she told him he'd hardly spent one night with them since Christmas, and they do have to get the wedding list done. I need to get those invitations addressed and sent out. He's also helping them pack for their move to town."

Aiden pointed his fork at Everett's plate. "Boy, you'd better eat those peas instead of playing golf with them."

Giggles erupted from Char. "Listen to Daddy, honey."

Everett pushed out his lower lip and peeked at Aiden. He pierced three peas with the fork and placed them in his mouth. His eyes widened. "Mommy, these are good."

After a stifled laugh, Aiden stabbed a piece of meatloaf. "Where did Drago go tonight, Sis? I thought for sure he'd have dinner with us since Mark had taken Lucy out to eat."

"He said he had other plans this evening." Haley sipped her milk. "Although he was secretive. Just like he was before we found out Mark had come to visit." Something told her Mark wasn't the only one Drago had met in town...on occasion. He'd spent quite a bit of time in quiet conversation with Auntie over Easter weekend, and she'd left for home right before he'd driven away this afternoon.

"Haley?" Char's voice cut into her thoughts. "You're a million miles away, again. You're not worried about that face in the window, are you? It could have been my imagination."

Aiden added another piece of meat to his second helping of potatoes. "It wasn't your imagination, dear. Even if we didn't find anything to suggest otherwise this morning when Drago and I helped Jason search the property. And it wasn't your imagination that set Shaun off on his barking spree either. Haley, after your friends leave and I'm at the office in town, you need to be watchful. Neither Rob nor Drago can be here all the time with the farms to run."

"Take seconds on vegetables with the meat and potatoes." Char gave Aiden a lopsided grin. "You don't want to be a poor example to your son."

"Yeah, Daddy. What's vegables, Mommy? Is it these green twee things?" Everett wrinkled his nose at the sprig of parsley on the end of his fork.

"Veg-tables, honey. But that one you don't eat. It's just a decoration on the plate."

"Oh." Everett pushed the parsley off his fork with an index finger. It dropped to the dish. "Ha!"

Haley bit her lips together to suppress a laugh. She shifted her eyes to Char. "No. I wasn't worried about the face. And yes, big brother, I will be careful."

"You're done with your studies at the end of this month, right, Sis?"

"Everything's already sent in and approved for my degree. I'll attend the graduation ceremony in Boulder at the end of May. It's too bad you and Char can't make it with the move back home and starting your new job. Not to mention Char's due date a week later. But Kayla and I will be there for each other. And Rob's coming."

Char reached over and patted Haley's hand. "Take lots of pictures."

"There'll be plenty. Don't you worry. Videos too. We'll all watch when Kayla and I get back to the farm."

Oops. She'd forgotten to tell them. "Ahhh...I neglected to mention that I invited her to stay here after graduation so she could make post-graduation plans. Hope I haven't overstepped."

"Sis, until after the wedding, this is still your home. You and Kayla are as close as you and Lucy." He shared a smile with his wife. "Kayla's no problem. We've enjoyed having her around. I take it she won't start a job right away."

"No. She has applications in several places who want someone with a degree in geology, but no interviews scheduled, yet. Since her parents died right after she entered college, and she's an only child, she had no one to go *home* to. So, I offered mine. She's like a sister to me."

Everett jumped out of his chair as soon as his mother finished wiping his mouth. "Thank you for dinner, Mommy." He bowed from the waist, courtier style, as though addressing royalty. "May I be excused now?"

"Yes, you may." As their son skipped into the living room, Char laughed and pointed at her husband. "He gets that dramatic flair from you, dear." She turned to Haley. "Kayla can stay as long as she wants. We have plenty of rooms."

After wiping her mouth on the napkin, Char propped her chin on her hand, elbow resting on the table. "It amazes me that you were studying both agriculture and computer science. And what will you do with your computer science degree?"

"First, I'll set up my own business website. Then I'd like to design a website for both farms to attract more customers. Drago plans to expand the horse breeding and hire more hands for everything else. Rob has a lot of new plans for the farms too."

"Farm." Her brother smiled. "It'll be *one* farm. We're only getting the house and yard, remember. Everything else is yours and Rob's."

After they'd finished their dinner, Aiden retired to the living room, and Char gathered the dirty dishes. Haley followed her sister-in-law to the kitchen with the platters of leftover food. "There are so many things I have to get done in such a short time. I hope I can finish before the wedding."

"Haley, be careful not to overdo. A wedding, graduation, and getting ready to move, even if it is only across the property line, is a lot of work. Don't worry. Everett and I will be back as soon as everything is settled in California and arrangements are made to move our things. Then I can help. So you relax."

Her sister-in-law's arms surrounded her. "What concerns me is that after I leave and your friends are gone next week, you'll be alone in the house while Aiden's at work. Drago will be tied up with Rob on new plans to manage the entire farm. Promise me you'll be very cautious when Aiden is in town."

"You're the best sister-in-law a girl ever had. I *promised* Aiden, and I *promise* you too. I'll even do check-in calls to him and Rob while Aiden's in town...as *Rob* made me promise." She giggled. "Now, don't worry. Nothing's going to happen."

Chapter Thirty-Four

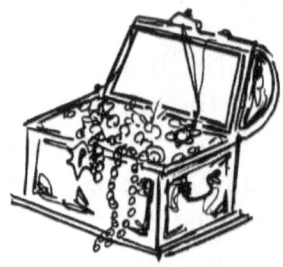

*L*ate Thursday morning, Haley sat at the dining room table, wrapping gifts for her bridesmaids and other wedding attendants. Kayla and Lucy would leave tomorrow. Mark too. Back to his ranch. It was nice of Jason to take a day off and invite everyone to go sightseeing before they left. And it was obvious the two couples had hit it off big-time—what a joy. The day's excursion might entice Lucy to come home and Kayla to seek employment near North Bend.

After Haley tied the bow around a bracelet box, she trimmed the ribbon and held the gift out for inspection. She'd found such beautiful silver filigree bracelets for the bridesmaids.

She laid the box on the table and leaned on one elbow, chin in hand. Too bad cleanup from the flood still swamped Rob with work.

They could have joined the group. But just as well. She had work to do too.

Though the MacKenna and Sheffield farms sat on higher ground than others in the county, there was still such a mess. So much to clean up in those soggy fields. Fence repairs had to be finished too. But...it'd keep Rob out of her hair and allow her to complete her tasks for the wedding and reception. Her man was *so* distracting. She giggled.

Char and Everett would be leaving any minute. But if everything went well with closing on the house and preparations to move their belongings home, perhaps they'd come back early. Soon they'd all be together again. Haley sighed. But she'd miss them while they were gone. Her heart pinched.

Aiden ran down the stairs with luggage in each hand. "Haley, are you sure you don't want to come with us to the airport? Isn't there something you can do in Omaha while I take care of my errands for work?"

"There isn't. Everything I need to tackle is right here. Another stack of invitations has to be addressed so they can go out tomorrow."

"I hate to leave you here alone, Sis. Wish Kayla and Lucy hadn't gone out for the entire day. Rob said he'd come by, but I'm not sure when."

"No doubt Rob and his dad are up to their hips in muck and mud right now, pulling debris and who knows what out of the flooded field at the back of their property. She shuddered. He'll come over the first chance he gets. Now, quit worrying."

"Drago won't be far away if you need anything. He's working with the horses today."

She grinned as Char and Everett descended the staircase. Would Char make it to the June due date? The baby was huge, but then, Everett had been too. A backpack hung from her forearm as she gripped the railing with one hand and clutched her son's arm with the other.

Aiden rushed to the stairs. "Honey, I told you to wait." He hastened up the steps and lifted Everett into his arms, along with his enormous teddy.

"Auntie, Auntie, I'm going on the big pwane." When Aiden put him on his feet, he skipped into the dining room and grabbed Haley around the neck.

"You'll have such fun watching the clouds float by the window." She leaned close to his ear. "See if you can get me one of those bags of peanuts they hand out. But only if you can get an extra."

He stepped back from her. "I will, I will." Then he came close as if to tell her a secret. He stretched and whispered. "I'll keep it in my PJ Teddy for when we come back here." He pointed to the zipper on his bear's back.

She pressed her lips together to hold back a laugh.

Aiden called from the foyer. "Come on, Son. We have to leave."

Everett skipped to the front door, then turned. "Are you coming, Auntie?"

"Awww, Everett, honey. I wish I could, but I have a lot of work to do here."

His face squished in disappointment.

She rose and joined him in the foyer. "When you get to California, you can call me on Skype and tell me all about your plane ride."

He smiled so wide, every tooth in his mouth showed. "Okay." He skipped out the door.

Shaun scampered down the stairs from the second floor. Everett screeched to a halt. "Wait. I forgot to say goodbye to Puppy." He jumped and spun.

A white blur bolted through the doorway. Shaun's little front paws jumped up onto the boy's stomach. Everett plopped to the porch on his bottom and giggled.

While the small dog bathed his friend with kisses, Everett wrapped his arms around the small fuzzy body.

Char stretched out her hand to help Everett to his feet. "Hey, you two, enough with the goodbyes." She turned to Haley, who stood in the doorway. "Remember your promise to be careful."

"Yes, I'll remember. Come on, Shaun. Your buddy will be back before long." Shaun whimpered and hung his head as he walked past her into the house. "Aiden and I will miss them too." As Haley slipped out to the porch, she shut the door behind her. Shaun made a noisy protest.

A second later, he jumped up on the bottom ledge of the dining room's bay window. Haley stood outside in front of him. She shook her finger. "You really think you belong there?"

"*Yip.*" He shook his head and disappeared.

That dog was almost human. If she guessed right, in a second, he'd be curled on Lucy's bed for a nap. She laughed and twirled to face the driveway.

Aiden's car roared to life. Haley waved until the car was out of sight.

She left the porch and strolled back to the living room. Now she'd have to concentrate on those invitations. From the desk in the corner of the dining room, she retrieved the lists of wedding guests and invitation envelopes and placed them on the table. Haley lowered herself into the chair and began.

As she wrote out the names, her mind wandered to Rob. Such a hard worker. And so loving. She couldn't have asked for a better man to marry.

Half an hour later, with only half the stack addressed, her hand ached. She twisted it in circles to loosen the muscles. Time for a break.

Aiden said Drago would work with the horses in the corral behind the stable today. She'd take him a couple of scones for a snack.

As she rose, the doorbell rang.

Rob glanced down at his clothes, covered from head to toe in splattered sludge. "That was what you call a tussle."

His dad slapped him on the back. "Enough for me today, Son. I couldn't lift a limb from a dry field, much less the muddy one we've been working on." As they trudged toward the barn, he pointed his thumb behind him at the white speckled black appaloosa he led on a rope. "Pulling Splash out of the mire did me in. It's a good thing you took a breather when you did. If you hadn't tread up that rise in the field and saw her right away..."

"That's for sure. She was sinking deeper with all her flailing to escape the mudhole. What I can't understand is how she got out of the corral and into that low, flooded area in the first place. The pen was secured before we came out to the field."

His dad scratched his head with his muddy hand. "Doesn't matter now. At least we managed to rescue her before she slipped further into the slimy goop."

"Yeah, after I rescued *you*." Rob snickered. "You resemble a chocolate-covered Easter bunny, minus its ears. But it's a good thing you didn't slide beneath her."

"Just for that, you can take her into the barn and clean her while I peel off these *chocolate*-caked clothes and shower. Your mother will kill me if I traipse through the house like this. Half your skin still shows, but you'd better do the same after you finish with Splash here."

He saluted his dad, accepted the rope, and led Splash to the barn.

When he finished with the horse, Rob jogged to the back of the house, discarded his outer clothing in the mudroom, and added them to the pile his father had dropped on the boot tray. He dashed up the back steps to his room and took a shower.

Clean and presentable, Rob entered the kitchen. He was starved after the mess he and his dad worked on all morning, not to mention the horse rescue.

His father hustled into the room. "Rob, Aiden called. He couldn't reach you, so he phoned me."

"Nuts. I left my cell in the barn this morning. Figured it would wind up buried in muck—along with you—if I had it with me in the field. What's up?"

"Char and Everett's plane just took off, and he's leaving the airport, but he's worried about Haley. He called to check on her, but she didn't answer. Thought she might be here."

Rob's brows furrowed. "The same thing happened when I tried her number on the house phone after my shower. I assumed she walked out of the house without her cell."

"Aiden said he tried twice, but both calls went to voicemail. He's called Drago's phone, too, but he doesn't answer either. You'd better get over there. Aiden will keep trying to reach them and let us know if he does."

Rob raced to the barn, grabbed his cell, and jumped into the truck. Gravel scattered from the tires as he sped out of the yard aimed for the MacKenna farm.

Haley's heartbeat went into overdrive as she tried to slam the door shut on Craig. He cackled and blocked it with his foot. She stomped his toes, then leaned into the door, determined to get it closed and keep him from entering the house. He pushed, inching the door back open.

She let go of the door and tore through the dining room toward the kitchen. He stumbled into the foyer. "Now, that's no way to act when I've come to pick you up for our wedding trip."

Haley ran into the mudroom, slammed the door shut, and pushed the linen cabinet from the corner to block the door. Every muscle in her body tensed. Her heart thundered like a thoroughbred at a gallop. Why hadn't she checked before she opened the front door? What a fool after everyone made her promise to be careful. But she thought it was Drago or Rob.

That horrible laugh as he'd pushed his way into her house. Nothing short of sinister.

What was he doing here? He was under a restraining order. He'd go to jail for sure this time. Had the man lost his mind completely? Leave with him to get married? Who'd marry them without her consent or a license? *He's crazy!*

Haley flattened her ear to the door and listened. Nothing. Her cell rang a fourth time. Why hadn't she grabbed it?

A crash and crunch sounded. Craig must have destroyed the phone.

Shaun barked from what sounded like the staircase. *Oh no!* A door slammed, and the dog's bark grew distant.

She sprung to the back door and peered out the window. No movement. She had to get out of the house. *God, please don't let him hurt Shaun.*

The door to the kitchen banged against the linen cabinet. Haley jumped. *He's pushing through.*

"Come on, Haley. We have to leave. Tomorrow's our wedding day."

Now was her chance. She unlocked the backdoor and streaked toward the stable.

Only a few more feet to the doors. Drago would be in the corral. She pulled the double doors open and sprinted to the other end. *"Drago! Drago!"* Where had he gone? His truck was still in the drive, so he hadn't left. *The bunkhouse.*

She darted to its back door and looked through the window. The door was locked. Haley beat on the wooden frame. If she went to the front door, Craig might see her. But if Drago was in there, he'd have come to the door.

As she peeked around the corner of the bunkhouse, she listened. No sound anywhere. If Craig had entered the stable, he hadn't come out yet. She peered across the field to the woods.

Drago must have gone to collect firewood. She bolted past the stable. At the far side of the toolshed, she took a quick glimpse around the corner. Still no Craig. *If only I can make it to the trees behind the field.* Drago had to be out there. She had to take a chance.

By the time she reached the trees, she was gasping for air. Haley hid behind a large clump of brush and checked for Craig. Maybe he'd gone home. She hadn't heard a car pull into the drive when he came...nor leave since. *Lord, help me find Drago.*

Chapter Thirty-Five

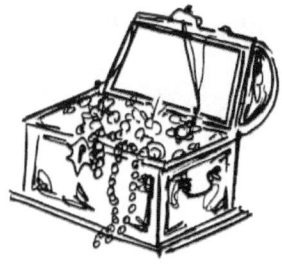

From the mudroom, Craig watched as Haley rose from a clump of bushes at the tree line and bolted into the woods. He knew she'd eventually show herself. She was headed right for the back road...and his car. Couldn't have calculated it better. In no time at all, they'd be in Las Vegas and married. No one would stop his plan now with the farmhand out of the way and meddlesome Sheffield busy for hours once the horse sank up to its belly in mud.

He smirked as he recalled leading Sheffield's horse out of the pen to the field and then slapping its rump. The dumb nag ran right into the flooded area in front of her. Pure genius. They'd need the fire department to get that mare out of the gunk once the stupid animal thrashed about.

As he stepped onto the back porch, Craig pulled a cigarette from his mouth and threw it onto the steps. He strode down the stairs and patted the plastic tube in his pants pocket. "These babies will ensure your cooperation, Haley." The pills rattled as he broke into a jog. Yes. She'd be very cooperative.

What a stroke of luck at the bank yesterday when he'd overheard Haley's brother telling some schmuck he'd be seeing his wife and son off for California today.

Craig jogged past the stable and along the edge of the corral.

Lady Luck had smiled on him. He should have read more about Las Vegas weddings, but he could find out the minute details when they got there. The place for quickie marriages. It'd be easy enough to phone and reserve a time for their ceremony once he and Haley were on the road. They'd spend the night in one of those swanky Las Vegas hotels once they arrived.

Angry barking sounded behind him. Craig turned to see Lucy's fluffy white canine come from the front of the house and race across the corner of the field straight for him. "Get out of here, you stupid mutt," Craig swore. He must have left the front door open after he pushed his way in.

The dog latched onto Craig's pants leg and growled, jerking his head back and forth, tearing a gaping hole in the material. "Crazy mongrel."

Craig kicked his foot out, flinging the canine away from him.

The dog yelped and rolled a few feet across the dirt. He whimpered for a moment but then jumped to his feet and shook himself. He bared his teeth and snarled.

"Too bad no one's around to hear you, cur." Craig glanced around for something to hit the pest with. Nothing but twigs and debris. Another string of expletives tainted the air.

He ran for the shed, yanked the door open, and ducked inside. When the canine neared, Craig opened the door a crack. The dog jolted into the dark. Craig slipped out the door and slammed it shut behind him. "Not so smart now, are you?" He flipped the hasp latch into the closed position and shoved two bent twigs through the loop. "You're small enough. That should keep you in. Now to find Haley."

Craig sped toward the woods. He'd have to hurry. She hadn't gone toward Sheffield's place, so she must plan to hide in that dilapidated barn near the road. He grinned. She'd pass the woodpile where he'd left that hireling fool. *With any luck, she'll stop to help.*

Haley vaulted over logs and patches of tangled brush. She raced between the trees for yards before she stopped to catch her breath. Why had she worn a skirt this morning instead of jeans? Her legs stung from the mass of cuts and scrapes. What had she been thinking? And she should have run to Rob's instead of this direction. But with practically nothing but fields between the two homes, Craig would have seen her. Too late now. She resumed her struggle through the overgrown section of woods. She needed to get to the stone barn. If only there were a way to reach Rob. And where was Drago?

She stopped for a second. Which way? She twirled as she tried to figure out which direction she should go, then stared through the thicket. That way led to the road. No. To the clearing where Drago chopped wood. *Yes. He might be there.*

A couple of minutes later, she skidded to a halt. "Oh, no. Drago." He lay face down in the woodchips next to a stack of cut logs, the back of his head covered with clotted blood. Tears poured from Haley's eyes as she dropped to her knees and touched his back. "Oh, Drago." Good. *He's breathing.* But for how long? *Craig! You fiend.*

She had to get help. It had to be Craig who did this. *That monster!*

Haley went through Drago's pockets to find his cellphone. What happened to it? Craig took it. Drago never left the house without the phone. She didn't dare move him. She'd have to run for help. But she couldn't go back toward the house. The back road. She'd take the long way around to the Sheffields' or flag a car. *Oh, Lord. Please help me. Help Drago.* No one traveled that way anymore since the flood.

She straightened, took a deep breath to clear her thoughts and get her bearings, and raced in the direction of the back road. Her side ached. She had to keep going. *Just keep running.*

When Haley reached the stone barn, she bent over the wall in front of the doors and gulped in air. Wrong direction. Her lungs burned. "Just a little further to the road." But everyone lived so far away, except Craig.

Hurried footfalls came from the woods. *Craig.* He'd come after her. Haley pushed off the wall, ran into the barn, and pulled the doors shut behind her. In the dim light, she searched for a place to hide.

A rickety ladder led to the loft. Would it hold her? No time to worry about that now. She climbed, testing each rung before she put her weight on it. *Hurry.*

At the top, she surveyed the dark planks stretching from the ladder to the far wall. If the ladder held her, the floor should. No signs of holes. Dad had warned them never to go up here. *Lord, help.*

After she gingerly stepped across the loft to a pile of old wooden boxes in the corner, Haley got on her scraped hands and knees behind them.

The door squeaked open, then slammed closed. Footsteps moved toward the ladder. Haley held her breath.

Rob slammed on the brakes and sprinted to the front door of Haley's house. Wide-open. Her car was there. He slipped into the house and listened. Silence greeted his ears. "Haley? *Haley!*" A graveyard couldn't be quieter. "Shaun?" Not here either. He'd try the cell again.

As he reached in his pocket for the phone, he turned toward the dining room. Pieces of a smashed cellphone littered the floor. Wedding invitations were scattered around the room. The door to the kitchen was closed. A chill ran up Rob's back. His call went to voicemail. The broken phone was silent.

He slipped his cell into his pocket and peeked into the kitchen. Empty. Rob breathed a sigh of relief. His imagination was worse than a horror film. The mudroom door was partially opened. He stuck his head in. The linen cabinet was out of place. Rob flung the back door open, stepped out to the porch, and scanned the surrounding area. Drago's truck sat where he always parked in front of the bunkhouse. No sign of Drago or Haley in the area.

Entering the house again, Rob ran into the hall that led to her bedroom. "Haley, are you in here?" He entered the room. Nothing out of place. He zoomed back to the foyer and thundered up the stairs to the second floor, searching each room. Seemed normal, except for his missing fiancée...and the mess in the dining room? *Where was she?* And where was Shaun?

Rob vaulted down the staircase and tore back into the kitchen. Had she taken the dog out for a walk? But what happened to her phone and the invitations? His scalp tingled. Could she be at Drago's? But he hadn't answered his cell either.

As Rob burst out the back door and stepped off the porch, he spotted a half-smoked cigarette on the bottom stair, still smoldering. *Lowell.* Rob sprang over the stairs and barreled across the backyard toward the bunkhouse. He opened Drago's front door. It was always unlocked when he worked close by. Rob stepped in. "Drago!" More silence.

He searched the barn and stable. Out of breath, he faced the back field and gazed across to the trees. Drago might be chopping firewood. Rob dashed for the woods.

Chapter Thirty-Six

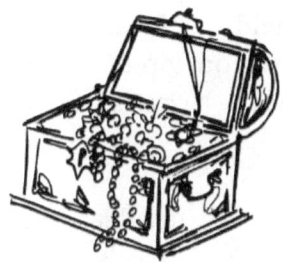

Craig scanned the darkened inside of the stone barn. In a far corner, a shaft of sunlight angled into the darkness from a broken board in the back wall and illuminated debris as it drifted down from the floor above. As he surveyed the loft, he smirked. So, she'd hidden in the corner like a mouse. He'd have fun playing the cat. He moved forward and lifted his foot to the first rung of the ladder. For such a rundown place, it seemed sturdy enough.

He laid his hand on a higher rung. "Come on, Haley. I know you're up there. I have my bag packed, ready to leave. You won't need any extra clothes. We'll get what *little* you'll need in Las Vegas." He laughed. "We have a long trip ahead. You can come willingly...or you can come the easiest way...for me."

Craig reached the top of the ladder and focused on the corner from where the debris had fallen. Boxes. She was behind them.

The floor creaked and groaned as he crossed. "Come out, come out, wherever you are," he sang. Once he got those pills in her, she'd be willing enough. Excitement surged through his body. His pulse increased.

He stretched an arm over the boxes and grabbed the back of her blouse.

Haley rolled away from the crates to the wall, breaking free of his grip. She rose to one knee, but Craig pushed her onto her back. He sat astride her and held her forearms to the floor. She thrashed and kicked. He eased down on top of her, wrapping his legs around hers, so she couldn't move. "That's it. I relish a little fight in my women."

She screamed.

"Mustn't make such a fuss, my dear." He kissed her neck. "We'll save the rest for Las Vegas. There's not enough time for you to enjoy the experience now." When he released one of her arms to push himself upward, she smashed a fist into the side of his face.

Craig got up and yanked her to her feet. He laughed. "Was that supposed to hurt?" He glared at her. "Enough of this nonsense. Another scream, and you'll wish you hadn't."

He pulled the bottle of pills from his pocket.

Rob passed the toolshed, but a scratching sound from inside stopped him. He turned back. As soon as he removed the twigs which held the latch shut, Shaun leaped out and bounded across the field, barking and snarling. Lowell must have locked the poor dog in there. Rob took off after the four-legged blur of white.

As they neared the clearing in the woods where Drago chopped firewood, Rob saw a body on the ground. "Drago!" Shaun sniffed at the blood-clotted hair on the back of the man's head. That jerk must have hit him. But how did he get close enough?

After Rob checked Drago's pulse, he exhaled. There was a steady beat. He pulled his cell out and punched in Jason's number.

The call connected after one ring. "Hey, buddy. Change your mind? You and Haley joining us?"

"No, Jason, listen. Drago's been attacked, and Haley's gone. It has to be Lowell. You said to call you if Lowell did anything."

"Where are you?"

"In the woods behind Haley's. The clearing where Drago chops wood."

"Hang on, Rob."

Rob waited while Jason asked Lucy to call the sheriff.

Come on, Jason.

His deputy friend came back on the line. "Lucy's phoning the office for me. We're not but five minutes away. I'll let my supervisor know what's happened while you call nine-one-one. Stay put and watch out." The call disconnected.

Rob tapped in 9 1 1. The dispatcher took the information and told him to stay where he was and on the line until the paramedics got there. Rob's heart throbbed. How could he stay here when Haley was in danger? But he couldn't leave Drago.

He turned on the speaker, but when he slipped the cell in his shirt pocket, his finger hit a button and accidentally disconnected the call. They'd call him back if needed.

Rob searched the area for any sign that Haley had been there but found nothing. He balled his hands at his sides and let his head drop back. His eyes closed as he took in a deep breath. He glanced at Drago. At least he hadn't lost any more blood.

A memory from last year came to Rob. He'd panicked when his dad cut the back of his head while working under the tractor. So much blood. But his dad told him head wounds bleed a lot because of the blood vessels near the surface of the skin. He'd refused to go to the hospital. Mom treated it in the kitchen. Maybe Drago's wound wouldn't be any worse.

As Rob paced, he envisioned the scene that might have taken place. No sign of a struggle. The coward must have hit Drago from behind. If he'd seen Lowell, the jerk would be the one on the ground. At least he hadn't used—*where's the ax?*

Rob found it propped against a tree in the open circle. "Thank God." He brought the tool back to where Drago lay and sank it into the pile of stacked logs. No sign of blood on it. What had that mental case used on Drago? He must have parked the ax here and taken a break before he was attacked.

Another search produced wireless headphones stuck on a nearby bush. "Man, you must have been listening to music and didn't hear Lowell approach." Rob lifted them out of the shrub and dropped them next to the ax. "Guess they flew off your head when you were hit."

In his peripheral vision, Rob spotted a large branch with a red mark on one side. The weapon. Better not touch it.

Shaun darted several feet beyond Drago and sniffed the ground. "Come here, boy." He obeyed and sat in front of Rob. If ever an animal looked worried, this one did. "What did you smell? Was it Haley?" The dog whimpered.

Rob called Jason's number again. "Jason, I can't just sit here. The paramedics are on their way. How far are you? I have no idea where Haley is or what's happening to her. I've got to find her."

"We just pulled into the end of the field at the woods. Getting out of the car now. It should only take me a couple of minutes to reach the woodpile. Hang tight."

"No. Drago's breathing, and his pulse is steady. If you'll be here in two, I have to find Haley."

"No, Rob. You need to wait 'til I get there. Another unit's on the way."

A crushed, empty cigarette pack lay next to a tree trunk in the direction of the stone barn. "Gotta go, Jason. I'll check the old barn first. If she's not there, I'm headed for Lowell's. Hurry." Rob hung up.

He raced into the woods, Shaun on his heels. *Lord, please protect Haley. Help me get to her in time.*

When Craig scooped Haley into his arms, she shouted. He clamped his hand over her mouth and carried her to the ladder while she twisted and fought. She was a feisty one.

Haley bit his hand, and he jerked it away, dropping her onto the floor. He grabbed her again before she could get on the ladder.

"Let me go." She slapped and scratched him. "You can't make me take those pills."

He pushed her to the floor and pulled his gun from a side pocket. "Oh, really? You *will*, whether you want to or not. All we need is a little liquid to wash them down. I have what's called for right here." He produced a silver flask of whiskey from his hip pocket. "This should help the pills go down nice and smooth, and boost their power at the same time. Now climb down that ladder, slowly."

"You're crazy. I won't take them. I won't go to Las Vegas. And I won't marry you." She rolled to her knees and stood, then inched back toward the ladder. "You're insane."

He backhanded her across the mouth.

Haley staggered and fell from the loft.

As Craig gaped over the edge, her limp body tumbled off a stack of hay bales below.

He returned the pistol to his pocket and hustled down the ladder to her side. *She broke her neck.* He turned her head. It bled from near the temple. Blood also marked the rim of a barrel half-surrounded by the bales.

"Now look what you've done, stupid woman." He stood. "You've ruined everything." If only she'd have cooperated with him. He shifted from one foot to the other. This hadn't gone as planned.

He paced to the doors and back. His mother had been so easy. He'd made it appear an overdose of her medication. But this. What should he do now? Why hadn't she listened to him? "This is all your fault." He narrowed his eyes at Haley and kicked her ribs. "Stupid woman. Why couldn't you do as you were told?" Now he had to get rid of her body. But where?

If he started a fire in the doorway, this relic would go up in flames. He glowered at Haley. And she'd go up with it.

Rob picked up Shaun as the stone barn came into view through the trees. "Quiet boy," he whispered. "We need to be careful. Find out if Haley is in there. Don't make a sound. Can you do that?"

The dog let out a soft whimper as if he understood.

"Haley told me she thought you were part human. I can see why. Now you stay here. Understand? Stay!" He put Shaun on his feet and faced a palm toward him. "Stay."

The dog sat on his haunches, then lowered himself to the ground. He lay his muzzle on his front paws, watched Rob, and gave a soft whine.

Rob crept through the last several feet of trees, careful not to step on anything that might herald his approach. He neared the edge of the clearing and stopped.

Craig squatted in front of the partially opened barn doors. No sign of Haley. Rob inched closer and crouched. The reprobate had made a pile of debris. Craig flicked on his lighter and lit the mound.

He's setting the barn on fire. In a flash, Rob sped toward him. The ground crunched and snapped under his feet. Craig jumped up, his eyes wide. Rob grabbed Lowell's shirt at the shoulders, flung him out of the way, then stomped on the flames licking the air.

Craig charged Rob from behind and propelled him through the opening, into the barn. The doors slammed shut. A loud clunk sounded. The jerk dropped the wooden plank that secured the door from outside.

Rob leaped to his feet and barreled into the doors, but they didn't budge. Running footsteps faded into the distance. The flames hissed and crackled as they licked upward from the bottom of the old doors and spread to the straw scattered on the floor. The wind fanned the flames from the narrow space under the doors. Smoke billowed toward him. He hunted for something to smother the flames but found nothing useful. If only the entire barn had been made of stone.

As Rob coughed, he squinted and looked through the dim light for another way out. There was the opening in the loft where the farmers used to take in hay.

He ran to the ladder as the smoke thickened. On the other side, bare legs protruded from the pile of hay bales. "*Haley!*"

Dropping onto his knees next to her, he bent to check for breath. He lifted her hand and found a pulse, then let out a heavy sigh. *She's alive.* "Wait'll I get my hands on that—" A large bloody knot on the side of her head near her temple made him grit his teeth. He shouldn't move her, but he couldn't leave her here with the fire growing.

Rob pulled Haley to the back of the pile and rolled her onto her stomach. He yanked off his shirt and covered her nose and mouth. That should keep the smoke from filling her lungs. *Now to find a way out.*

Behind her, a broken piece of wood at the bottom of the wall sent a patch of sunlight onto the floor. Rob kicked the panel, and it splintered. He sat next to her and pressed on the rotten boards until he'd broken off a large enough section to crawl through. Gathering an armful of scattered straw, he threw a path into the open area, then retrieved his shirt from Haley and spread it over the straw. After he moved Haley's head and arms toward the hole, Rob slid through, feet first. He grasped her wrists and the material and dragged her on top of the shirt to the outside.

He carried Haley several feet to the woods behind the barn. "That snake will pay for this." Rob snatched his phone and called Jason.

"Rob! Thank God, it's you. I'm at the old barn, trying to beat out a fire. Where are you?"

"I had the cell off. I found Haley. We're at the edge of the woods on the other side of the barn, and she's hurt bad."

"The paramedics just left with Drago. I'll call nine-one-one and tell them about Haley and the fire."

Rob kneeled next to Haley and brushed the hair from her face. "Sweetheart, hang on. Help's coming." She didn't move.

Jason rounded the corner of the barn.

"They'd better hurry, Jason. She's not responding." Rob grabbed his forehead. Had he done the right thing by moving her?

His friend dropped to his knees beside Rob and Haley and prayed.

A bark came from the woods. *Shaun.* "Come, boy."

The little dog bounded over the brush and stopped next to Rob and Haley. He whimpered and licked her face. Rob kissed her fingers. "Haley, it's me. Please wake up. Please."

She groaned. Her eyes fluttered and opened. She flung her arms out and slapped at Rob.

"It's okay. It's me, Rob. You're okay now."

Jason helped Rob restrain her. "You're all right, Haley. Rob has you."

Tears flooded her eyes. "Where's Craig? He's lost his mind."

Rob wrapped his arms around her. "Don't worry about him. He's gone." For now. After Haley was taken care of, he'd deal with that psycho.

Chapter Thirty-Seven

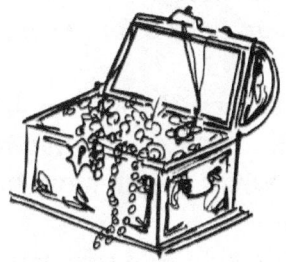

*R*ob hopped up from the ground and braced himself against a tree. "Jason, someone's coming. Lowell may have returned to make sure his dirty work's done."

"Relax, Rob. Didn't you hear the EMS siren?" A siren faded, and another wailed as it neared. "Paramedics and the fire truck are on the back road."

Rob squinted. The road wasn't a half-mile from them, and yet he could only see several yards through all the brush. He hoped Jason was right.

"There they are, buddy." Jason pointed.

The paramedics entered the small clearing and attended to Haley. Rob let out the breath he held and leaned with one hand on the tree to thank the Lord.

A few seconds later, firefighters hustled their equipment toward the front of the barn. Mark, Kayla, and Lucy rushed around the corner and almost collided with them. Shaun dashed to Lucy and leaped into her arms.

As the medical team worked, Rob's and Haley's friends surrounded him and bowed their heads.

The paramedics strapped Haley onto a gurney and carried her toward the back road. Rob and his friends followed close behind. They stood on the dirt road and waited until the back doors of the ambulance closed on Haley.

As the vehicle left, Jason patted Rob's shoulder. "Let me give you a ride to the hospital."

An icy shock wave crashed through Rob's body, and heaviness filled his stomach as the reality of what had happened to Haley struck him. Worse yet, what might have happened. He bent with both hands on his knees.

Jason pulled Rob to his side. "Mark, you and the girls stay here with Rob while I run back for the car?"

Rob straightened. "I'm okay now. Thanks, Jason."

The firefighting team exited the woods and hauled their equipment back to the truck. The last man stopped in front of Rob and his friends. "Fortunately, the flames couldn't ignite most of what was in the barn. Everything was still damp and moldy from last year's flood and all the storms that followed. And the fire was still small enough to be contained. It's out now. Only the doors are charred."

Rob clasped his hand. "Thank you. That'll make my fiancée happy. This old place has been here forever. It means a lot to her family."

With a two-fingered salute, the firefighter hurried away.

Jason smiled. "It means a lot to all of us, Rob. Lots of good memories here." He rested his hand on Rob's shoulder again. "Remember when we played cowboys and Indians around the barn and woods? You stole your first kiss from Haley there too."

"Oh, really?" Kayla's eyes widened. "She never told me *that* story."

Rob smiled. "Boy, was she mad at me. I was what, seven years old back then?"

"Yeah. Bet you didn't know Aiden and I were spying. For a six-year-old, she must have packed a pretty good wallop. Knocked you on your butt."

"It did. But I deserved it." Rob grinned wider and drew in a deep breath. "I've been in love with her ever since."

"I'll be back in a flash, as they say." Jason raced off through the trees. Rob watched as his friend disappeared into the thick copse, heading for the MacKennas' field.

Rob turned back and gazed out over the Lowell property on the other side of the road. His blood boiled.

Sitting in the passenger seat of Jason's car, Rob's thoughts were still on Lowell as Jason stopped in front of Haley's house to drop off Kayla and Lucy en route to the hospital.

Rob's parents got out of their vehicle. He hopped out of Jason's car and jogged to them. "Thanks for coming to stay with Haley's friends, Mom...Dad. Mark and I need to get to the hospital."

"Of course, you do." His mother hugged him, then walked to the house with Lucy and Kayla.

His dad's brows pinched into a straight line. "We're glad you called to let us know what happened. Mother was beside herself with worry when you sped out of the yard like you did."

As Rob slipped back into the car, his dad waved and shouted, "Be safe."

Jason pulled away and drove out of the farmyard.

Rob seethed inside as the car sped down the country roads. Better calm himself before they got there, or he'd upset Haley more. Prayer. *Need to pray. Serious prayer. Lord, help me control my anger.*

Jason broke the silence. "What happened, Rob? How did Haley get hurt and the fire start?"

Mark leaned forward in the back seat. "Craig Lowell, right? Jason mentioned him when you called the first time, but he was too focused on getting to you to give details." He glanced at Jason. "It was probably a good thing you didn't tell me about my brother," his voice hitched, "until we got there."

In a hushed voice, Rob said, "Don't know what went on before I got there. Haley will explain when she feels up to it. But Lowell was setting fire to the barn as I came from behind him. I threw him out of the way and started to put the fire out. While I stomped on the blaze, he shoved me inside. The door slammed shut, locked, and I heard the creep run away." Rob fought tears and swallowed hard. "Haley was on the floor behind a pile of hay bales with a blood-covered lump on her head."

Rob, Jason, and Mark arrived at the hospital and got out of the vehicle.

Aiden drove into the parking lot, jumped out of his car, and sprinted toward them. "When I got to the house and saw the sheriff's cruiser, my heart went into my throat. Your dad told me what happened."

"Aiden, I'm sorry I didn't phone you." Rob shook his head. "Couldn't think clearly."

His soon-to-be brother-in-law stretched his arm over Rob's shoulders. "Don't worry. I understand. Haley was on your mind."

Jason followed Rob, Mark, and Aiden but stopped at the ER entrance. "I suppose I should get to the office and make my report. I'll stop to check on your folks and the girls first, and see what the other deputies have found out." He jogged backward a few steps. "I'll call you in a while, Rob. Tell Haley and Drago we'll pray for them."

"I will. Thanks again."

Rob, Aiden, and Mark entered the ER. Tears threatened to spill from Rob's eyes again. *What if Haley has serious injuries? Lowell will pay for this, one way or the other.*

As Aiden strode through the ER's sliding glass door entrance, he gritted his teeth. Rob and Mark followed him to the check-in desk. Aiden filled out the paperwork the girl gave him.

She pointed to the waiting room. "Please have a seat while I let the doctor know you're here."

After learning from Rob all he knew of what had transpired, Aiden fumed. If he got his hands on Lowell, he'd answer for what he did to Haley and Drago. But first, he had to make sure they were all right. That reprobate had his comeuppance ahead.

The men sat and waited in silence.

After an unbearable length of time, Mark leaned forward, elbows on knees, and propped his head on his fisted hands. "When they were loading my brother into the ambulance earlier, he had regained consciousness and wanted to find your sister. The big lug. That's the way he used to be when I was a kid too. Always worried about me, always protective. Then, he passed out. I can't stand the idea of losing him again."

Aiden smiled at Mark. "We won't lose either of them. They'll be fine. Have faith." He grabbed Rob's arm. "That means you too." *Let's pray.*

A little before midnight, Rob's anger still smoldered as Aiden drove them back to the farmhouse. At least Haley and Drago were out of danger, and they'd recover...in time.

As they exited the vehicle, Aiden touched Rob's shoulder. "It'll be okay."

"Thanks, man. When Jason called me earlier, he said they had the situation in hand. The department had already started a thorough investigation of Lowell after his first attack on Haley." Rob turned to Mark. "Your brother's testimony, added to Haley's, will end Lowell's crime spree. Good thing Drago didn't pass out before he saw who hit him."

Mark nodded. "Also good that Lowell didn't notice. And with your encounter at the barn, he's sunk."

Lucy, Kayla, and Rob's mom stepped out onto the front porch, his father right behind them. Shaun scampered to greet Rob.

Aiden extended his hand. "Mr. Sheffield, thanks for staying while we were at the hospital."

"No problem. Happy to do it. So, how are Haley and Drago?"

A squad car rolled into the yard, and Jason got out. Rob grabbed Jason's hand. "Thanks for everything. What will happen now?"

"No problem, buddy. Part of my job." Jason followed everyone to the house. "Lowell's been arrested."

"Thank heavens!" Rob's mom exclaimed.

Lucy raised her hands in the air. "Thank You, Lord."

"What a relief!" Kayla covered her chest with her hand.

Jason circled her other hand with his. "You betcha. Would it be okay if we went inside and sat down? My feet are killing me."

Kayla suggested coffee and headed to the kitchen with Lucy and Rob's mother. The rest of the group sat at the dining room table, waiting for the women to return. The machine finished gurgling, and the aroma filled the house.

Kayla strolled into the dining room with two carafes. "Haley's cell is dead, Aiden, but the wedding invitations are fine." She pointed to the stack on the sideboard and smiled at Rob, then sat next to Jason.

After Rob's mom brought in the cream and sugar with spoons and napkins, everyone helped themselves to the brew. Rob updated them on Haley and Drago's wounds and recovery, according to the doctor.

Mark sipped and then grinned. "It's a good thing Drago's so hard-headed. But I guess Haley's head is as well." He peered at Rob.

Rob chuckled. "Thank God He protected both of them." He faced Jason. "Did Lowell put up a struggle when they found him? And *where* did they find him?"

"At his house." Jason leaned back in the chair. "You won't believe this, but they found him in front of the TV with his feet propped up, eating a piece of cake, as if nothing had happened."

Rob slammed down his fist. "Nothing happened! He almost killed Haley and Drago. She's right. Lowell's insane."

"That may be true, Rob. When they arrived and questioned his housekeeper, she appeared scared. She told them she'd decided to quit because he frightened her. She said Lowell had been acting strangely and even hostile. He went berserk when he was taken away in handcuffs."

Aiden lowered his mug with a clunk. "Since Haley was able to give an account of what happened to her, will Lowell be charged with attempted kidnapping *and* attempted murder?"

Jason leaned in and lifted a brow. "And possession of drugs. But he'll be tried for a lot more than that. As I said, he's been under investigation."

Rob nailed Jason with a stare. "What do you mean, 'more than that'?"

"During interrogation, Lowell confessed. But some things he said contradicted others. He was calm as could be at the station when he said he had no choice in his actions because no one cooperated with him. He'll be evaluated by a psychiatrist next."

Jason lifted his mug for a drink. "Our town ace reporter somehow got wind of the arrest. He gets information from somewhere before we're ever ready to release it." He shook his head. "This'll be in the news tomorrow morning, no doubt. Rohypnol was found in Lowell's possession."

Kayla's eyes widened. "Roofies?" Her jaw dropped.

"And GHB, another club or date rape drug." Jason nodded. "It substantiates what Haley said about him trying to stick pills in her mouth and telling her she was going with him to Las Vegas, whether she liked it or not. But Lowell told us a different story."

Rob sipped his coffee as he burned inside. He'd end up in jail alongside that creep for what he'd like to do to him.

Jason continued. "He said drugging Haley was the only way for her to relax, and that she agreed to it. Lowell claims she wanted to marry him and get away from here and Rob. Said she told him you'd tricked her into your engagement. He was a real teller of tall tales with that one. He actually thought an official in Vegas would overlook Haley being drunk. Not to mention drugged."

"That's absurd," Lucy interjected. "Who'd perform a wedding with Haley in that condition? Things aren't like they show in the movies." Her forehead and brows rumpled. "I'm sure they have laws in that town about forcing someone to marry you."

Rob's neck muscles tensed.

"Exactly." Jason took another drink. "When Lowell was confronted with his attempt to kill Haley, he lost it. Not sure what was going through his brain by then, but he swore up a storm and blurted out that his mother deserved what she got for calling him crazy, and so did Haley. He thinks he had every right to do what he did to both of them. Worked himself into a frenzy, grabbed his head, and almost passed out."

Rob jumped from his seat. *"He had every right?"* He *was* insane, but he'd better not get off with that plea. After a long breath, Rob reseated himself.

"Narcissism." Jason gave a sharp nod. "A few months ago, my cousin Tammy, who's a psychologist in Omaha, gave a talk on the subject." He folded his hands and leaned in with his elbows on the table. "She'd been at my mom's birthday party when I overheard her mention the lecture. It intrigued me. Tammy said narcissists believe they're entitled to anything they want and to get it any way they choose."

"Even attempted murder?" Kayla's eyebrows rose.

"I don't know everything about the subject, but I guess so, in extreme cases. Our team of investigators has been in contact with the authorities in Italy over the death of Lowell's mother. They'll also dig deeper into your parents' accident, Aiden. Also, Rob's accident. It seems that Lowell had been a very good mechanic while in college. He'd know how to make a tampered brake system appear to have failed on its own. The team suspects he's responsible for every strange event on your farm too."

Mark half-smiled. "I'm not sure you'll convince Drago of that."

Rob narrowed his eyes. "That rat has enough money to hire another sleaze of a lawyer." *He'd better not get away with this.*

Chapter Thirty-Eight

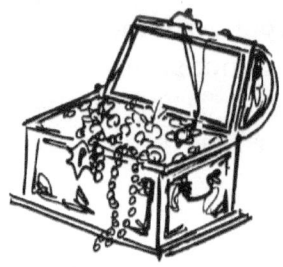

On the third Saturday morning of May, Haley awoke to birdsong outside her bedroom window. Sunbeams streamed through the curtains. She rolled onto her side.

Her hospital stay seemed as though it were yesterday, not weeks ago. But she'd finally recovered. Good thing she was back to normal, too, with graduation next week.

Drago had returned to work with only a scar where Craig had slammed the branch against the back of the poor man's head. Mark had stayed an extra week to help his brother get back on his feet before he left for the horse ranch. As a bonus, Mark and Lucy got to spend more time together.

Ah, Lucy. Thank goodness she gave up Alaska and listened to her heart. She and Mark were so right for each other. And Mark's home outside Scottsbluff wasn't that far away. He planned to visit here often. Haley sighed. After her wedding in three weeks, maybe a couple more would follow before too long. She couldn't be happier for Lucy and Kayla.

Haley rolled from the bed and threw open the curtains, startling a bluebird that sat on the sill. "Sorry, little guy. Thanks for the wake-up song."

While she watched, Drago strode from the bunkhouse to the stable. Hmmm, Uncle Drago soon. She chortled. Auntie had hinted last week about their budding romance. And the dates they had gone on, both of them keeping everything so hush-hush. As if we wouldn't have approved. At least, the mystery of Drago's unexplained trips was solved.

Haley washed, dressed, and joined Char and Everett in the kitchen. "Good morning. I take it, Aiden slept in."

Her sister-in-law turned, tongs in hand. "Still is. After he unpacked the moving boxes last night, he was bushed. I told him I'd send Everett up to get him when we were near ready to eat." She spun to the stove. "One egg or two?"

Back to her trim shape already. "You sure are spry after delivering a nine-pound baby a little over a week ago. Two eggs, please. Rob and I plan to assist in his parents' move to the new house in town this afternoon. I'll need protein."

Haley poured herself a cup of coffee. "Can I do something?"

"I have everything under control." When a piece of bacon popped and spattered grease on her apron, Char jumped back. "Well, everything but the bacon grease. And why shouldn't I be spry? Everett was a nine-pounder too." She covered the griddle with a spatter shield. "Speaking of things under control, I'm glad Lowell's behind bars."

"No kidding. It was a blessing when Aiden assured me he'd be in custody one place or another for a long time. Did you read the follow-up article in the news last week?"

"No. Never found time with my new little bundle. What did it say?"

"Let me get it." Haley sprinted to the magazine rack. She reentered the kitchen and spread the newspaper on the table. "Here it is. I'll summarize for you. Nothing this big ever happens around here." She read the initial information and stopped for a breath.

"Lowell faces charges of attempted murder and kidnapping...blah, blah, blah...confessed to numerous crimes...blah, blah...including crimes committed overseas..." Haley turned the page to find the rest of the article.

"Here we go. The reporter tells how Craig managed to overdose his mother with her own medications to inherit her money. It goes on to mention how he's responsible for the apparent supernatural incidents on our farm."

Haley took a drink of her coffee. "A tumor found on Craig's brain explains the headaches and passing out Jason told us about." She lowered the paper. "Guess he'll be in the hospital for a while before trial."

Char removed the bacon and placed it on paper towels to drain. "He sure is a mess. Why did he want you to marry him, though? Not that any man wouldn't."

"Jason also told us about that. Craig claimed ownership of the treasure because the land where it was buried, as he alleged, used to be Lowell property. But because he failed to legally obtain the farm, he decided to marry me to get it." She blew the raspberry sound from her lips and scanned the paper.

"The combination of his narcissism, the tumor, his drug abuse, and alcohol played havoc with his system. It almost makes me feel sorry for him, Char."

Aiden strode into the kitchen with Rob behind him. "Haley, did you invite this lunkhead for breakfast?"

Rob punched him on the upper arm. "Yes, she did." He pulled out the chair next to Haley and gave her a hug.

"How many eggs can you eat, Rob?" Char brought an almost empty egg tray out of the refrigerator.

"Three would be great." He perused the newspaper in front of Haley. "This is quite the article."

"It is." Haley kissed him on the cheek. "But it hardly mentioned the heroes of the story. Our knight in shining armor and his tiny white Bichon sidekick."

Rob chuckled. "Shaun deserves hero status. He led me to Drago and to you that day. And you're right, sweetheart. The pooch does have a touch of human in his DNA."

As Aiden read over Haley's shoulder, he put his finger on the article. "You know another thing they didn't mention? Jason's promotion. He was a bulldog about the investigation."

Haley leaned into Rob. "Kayla's so proud of him. She's waltzed around here for days."

"Has she found a job?" Rob got up and poured a mug of coffee.

"Not yet. But when Lucy moves back from Wisconsin next week, she and Kayla plan to rent an apartment together...at least until things change." She peeked at Rob.

He mouthed a silent, "Oh." One corner of his lips rose. "That's good. I was afraid Aiden would get tired of an extra woman on the farm, and you'd have her move in with us. And that means our privacy..."

"*Rob!*" Heat flowed through Haley's neck into her face.

He pressed his lips together and gave her a sheepish grin.

Char giggled as Aiden snatched his son's hand. "Mom needs more eggs, Son. We'll collect them. The conversation in this room is a little too—er—before you ask questions."

As they left, Kayla came in from her morning run. "When did Aiden get a sunburn? His face was beet red when he passed me."

Char hurried out of the room with her hand covering her mouth.

Kayla stared at Haley. "Did I say something wrong?"

"Not a thing." Rob slid his arm around Haley. "My beautiful bride here plans to write a comedy based on a boy and his dog who discover a treasure and defeat the bad guy. Char thought it was funny."

Kayla stole a crumb of bacon. "Wonderful. But make it a mystery. You'd be good at it, after hearing that treasure story for so long."

"Well, if I do, it won't include Craig's crazy theory."

"Theory?" Kayla's face showed confusion.

"Yes. Jason told us Craig planned to dig up the floor in my bedroom once he forced me to marry him. He swore the treasure was there."

Coffee in hand, Kayla lowered herself to a chair at the table. "So, it might be under your room?"

Haley blew her bangs upward. "Not a chance."

That evening, Rob relaxed in the MacKennas' living room with Aiden and Jason before dinner. Soon he'd relax at night in his own home with his new bride.

Everett sprawled on the floor and spread out several yellowed papers next to the coffee table. He carefully arranged his farm vehicles and ran the tractor on the pages. Rob rubbed his chin. "That son of yours has imagination. He's using those sheets of paper for a field."

"He has a good one." Aiden furrowed his brows. "Not sure where he got those papers, though. From the attic, I'd wager." He peered at Everett from under his brows.

Everett frowned.

Rob rested his head on the couch. His thoughts shifted to the field in the back of the house. He lifted his head and faced Jason. "Didn't you say Lowell insisted he had proof the treasure was buried under Haley's bedroom?"

"Yeah. He claimed he had papers, but they were hidden. The man's delusional."

Rob nodded. "Aiden, remember the story? The treasure chest was first found at the edge of the field behind the house."

"Yes." Aiden cocked his head at Rob.

"Isn't that spot *now* under Haley's bedroom? The field used to come within feet of the house, but it wound up yards away when the room was added."

Aiden whistled. "You're right."

"However..." Rob scooted forward in his seat. "The chest was dug up and relocated long ago. The map you saw showed it was buried between a tree and what looked like a wall. What if it's the stone wall by the old barn at the back of your property?"

Aiden observed his son running the toy over his pretend field. "I found old papers in a trunk full of family pictures in the attic. Everett had ventured up there and had hidden behind the trunk. When he popped up, it fell off the box it sat on, and everything scattered on the floor, including the stack of old documents." He glanced again at the yellowed pages on the carpet. "I planned to examine them, but Char called us to dinner, and I forgot."

The boy peeped at his dad from behind the table.

"Everett? Did you go back upstairs for those?" Aiden pointed at the papers.

The boy nodded.

While Aiden reprimanded his son about his trip to the attic without permission, Rob reached for the page Everett's tractor rested on. He jerked his head toward Aiden. "It's a map."

Several minutes later, the men thundered into the kitchen, the drawing clutched in Rob's hand. "Haley!"

She spun from the counter with a half-peeled potato. "What?"

"We have to run out to the stone barn." He waved the map in front of her nose. "Everett found the map."

"What map?"

As Rob laid the paper on the table, Haley, Char, and Kayla gathered around.

"Wait a minute." Haley pinned her fiancé with a stare. "Is this about that crazy legend again?"

"Sis, it may be real." Aiden wrapped his arms around his wife. "Honey, dinner will be a tad late."

The women followed the men into the living room. Everett sat on the floor and peered over the edge of the coffee table at his dad.

"It's okay, Son. But promise me you won't go in the attic without permission again."

"I won't, Daddy. I pwomise. But those were good fields for my twac-to."

Everyone smiled and took a seat while Rob laid the weathered, hand-drawn map next to the other old papers across the coffee table. "Haley, do you remember the part of the legend where your ancestor dug up the treasure and reburied it?"

"How can I not?" She pursed her lips. "I've lived with the story my entire life."

Aiden held a rolled-up paper in one hand and pointed to the map with his other. "I'll bet anything Lowell found a map his ancestor drew up matching this one when they found the treasure way back then." He unrolled a faded blueprint on top of the old map. "This was drawn up for the addition on the house, your bedroom. Check it out."

She studied the page.

"Now the map." Aiden lifted the blueprint.

Haley's brows lowered as she focused on the map. Her gaze darted to meet her brother's. "You mean it's real?"

Rob slid a newer map over the first one. "Now look at this one. Note the line." He circled his arm around her waist and pointed. "And what does this remind you of?" He traced the rectangular drawing close to the line.

Her eyes widened. "The stone barn? And the stone wall?"

Rob surveyed the room. "Anyone want to go on a treasure hunt?"

Haley pressed her hand to her heart. Could it be?

"I wanna go." Everett hopped to his feet.

Char grabbed the back of his pants. "No, you don't. It's getting too dark for you to be outside. You, your baby sister, and Mommy will stay here."

"I found it." He stuck out his bottom lip.

Haley stifled a laugh. "There may be *coyotes*." She raised her brows.

"I'll stay with Mommy and baby sissy."

"Good decision, Son." Aiden winked at his sister.

Kayla's brows furrowed. "I'll stay too."

Jason squeezed her shoulders. "This shouldn't take too long."

Fifteen minutes later, Rob stopped the truck on the back road where the ambulance and firetruck had parked weeks earlier. Rob, Haley, Aiden, and Jason flicked on their lanterns and flashlights and headed into the woods toward the old barn with shovels and a pick.

Haley's eyes followed the crazy branch shadows that moved above them from the lanterns as they passed through the trees. Did everyone get a feeling of someone watching them in the woods?

As they reached the structure, a screech owl flew inches above their heads and let out a blood-curdling shriek. Haley grabbed Rob's arm.

"No time for smooching now, sweetheart."

She backed away and slapped his bicep. *Smart-aleck.* At least it wasn't one of Drago's Indian ghosts. But she wasn't so sure they *didn't* exist now.

Rob checked the map as they approached the barn. "As best I can tell, this is the spot the *ex* indicates. Between the stump and the wall."

Jason set his shovel on the ground. "All those years we played back here, leaped off that stone wall and stump. We could have been landing on the treasure. Incredible."

Aiden grinned. "Let's find out." His pick bit into the dirt.

Rob and Jason pitched out the loosened ground. Before long, they'd dug a five-by-five hole, three feet deep.

"It was worth a try, Rob," Aiden said as he knocked a clump of dirt off the pick. "Could be long gone."

Haley grimaced. *Yeah.* Just as she thought.

Rob grimaced and threw the shovel as if it were a lance into the hole. A thump sounded. The group gaped at one another.

"Don't get too excited." Rob gripped the shovel. "It may only be a tree root." He flung dirt out of the hole until he struck a hard surface. "This isn't a root."

Aiden eased himself into the hole opposite Rob, and they extracted dirt from the sides of a two by one-foot rectangular object. Jason lifted the lantern higher.

Haley held her breath.

After tugging and pulling, the resting place let loose of its weighty box. Rob and Aiden placed it on the stump. The four gawked at the dirt-encrusted chest.

A chill traveled up Haley's arm. *After all this time.* The treasure was real. Would the Indian ghosts turn out to be real too?

Rob put his hand on Jason's shoulder. "You're the armed guard, man. Should we take it home first, or open it here?"

Jason patted his hip and around his waist. He whispered, "Hate to disappoint you, buddy, but I'm not packing. Let's get it back to your house quick, then worry about what's inside."

"Right." Rob grasped one end of the heavy box, and Aiden lifted the other. They hurried to the truck, swung it onto the bed, loaded the tools, and closed the tailgate.

Haley slipped into the passenger seat without a word. She still couldn't believe it.

When they reached the house, they placed the coffer on the back porch and brushed off the remaining dirt.

Kayla stepped out onto the back porch. "Aiden, Char is putting the baby to bed, she'll be right down. What did you find out there?"

"Thanks, Kayla. We think we've found the missing treasure."

They all gathered around the dark wooden chest. The rusted lock was immovable, stuck to a metal strip.

Aiden retrieved a toolbox from the trunk of his car and whacked the latch with a hammer several times before it broke off.

As Rob lifted the lid, an audible gasp filled the air.

Haley's hand went over her mouth. Her knees buckled.

Chapter Thirty-Nine

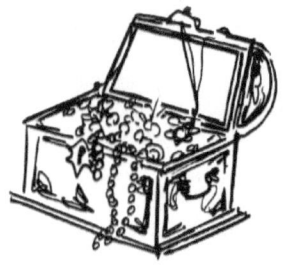

aley slowly dropped her hand from her lips. "Aiden! What are we going to do with that?" Her heart pounded. She surveyed the open-mouthed faces surrounding the chest. No one uttered a word.

Her brother let out the breath he'd drawn in. After a few seconds, his eyes met hers. "I'm not sure, Sis."

Jason jumped over the backstairs railing and raced around the side of the house. Five pairs of eyes blinked at each other, but no one spoke. A minute later, he careened around the corner again, back to the porch, and hurtled up the steps. He adjusted his belt and pulled it tight.

Haley eyed the gun on his hip. "What's that for?"

He shrugged. "I'm not taking any chances." He glanced at Rob. "You did say I was your armed guard."

Rob's eyes were still on the contents of the old wooden box. "I did."

Kayla's jaw wilted as she gazed at the chest.

Char stepped out the back door, Everett's hand clutched in hers. She sucked in a breath. *"Oh!"*

"Wow! A weal piwet chest." Everett pulled on his mother's arm as he leaned. He stretched out a hand, but his mother drew him back before he could touch anything.

Haley whispered. "Bracelets, rings, necklaces, tiaras. Where did it come from? This can't be the MacKenna treasure."

Rob circled his arm around her shoulder. "What else can it be, sweetheart? It was exactly where *ex* marked the spot on the map."

Aiden shook his head. "Pirate booty. But it was supposed to be the family's wealth. I expected some form of currency. Maybe gold. Never this." He tapped his index finger on his lower lip. His eyes narrowed. "When I was a kid, Grandpa MacKenna told Dad a story. I listened from the other room. Grandpa said an ancestor...way, way back...had appropriated a great fortune of unknown origin from the nobles who invaded Ireland."

Jason grabbed Aiden's shoulder. "Hey, buddy. Before you start into another legend, shouldn't we get the loot inside?"

Rob bent, closed the lid, and raised one end. "Good thinking, man. Come on." He bumped Aiden's arm.

They hoisted the coffer and inched their way toward the back door.

"Wait!" Char shouted. "Don't put that down anywhere until I get papers under it." She bolted through the doorway.

Haley rushed into the house after her. "Take it into the dining room. I'll shut the curtains. We don't need prying eyes, if any are out there."

Rob and Aiden followed her.

As they entered the dining room, she pulled the drapes closed. Char dashed in from the living room, her arms full of newspapers.

Aiden groaned. "Hurry. Spread them on the table before Rob and I get hernias."

When the papers were down, the men deposited the chest in the middle. Aiden reopened the lid. Everyone took a seat around the table and gawked at the box and its contents. Jason stood with his hand on the holstered pistol.

Haley chewed the inside of her mouth.

Rob glanced at Aiden. "So, tell us the rest of this Robin Hood tale you overheard from your Gramps."

"Well, I thought it was one of Grandpa's made-up sagas. He said one of our many-times-removed relatives had been party to raids on castles, carriages, and who knows what else."

While Aiden spoke, the group kept their eyes on the jewels of every size, shape, and color.

"When Grandpa told Dad the story was true, Dad said he'd never heard the tale before. Grandpa told him it was a forbidden subject."

Haley shifted her gaze to her brother. "Is it true?" She fingered a tiara of white stones, studded with smaller reddish-purple gems.

"I don't think Dad believed him." Aiden's brows furrowed. "But what else could this be?" He cocked his head at her.

Kayla touched the tiara. "If I'm not mistaken, these are half-carat diamonds and the highest quality amethyst set in gold. What a beautiful piece."

Haley gulped, although her mouth was bone dry. Kayla'd know. She had loved the study of precious gems in her geology class. *It would be stunning with my wedding veil.* Haley took the tiara in her hand to have a better look. "The treasure is real. It's been at the old stone barn the entire time."

Everett tugged on her arm. "Are you gonna wear that when you get married, Auntie?"

Char tousled his hair. "Your auntie would look like a queen."

"No, little guy." Haley replaced the tiara in the coffer and then lifted her nephew onto her lap. "This belongs in a museum."

He placed one chubby hand on each side of her face. "You pwetty, anyway."

"Thank you, sweetie." She kissed his cheek and lowered him to the floor. Then she turned to Aiden. "What do you say?"

"You'll have to include Rob in that decision, Sis. He's the one who figured out where it was, and he'll soon be your husband." Aiden winked at his wife, who nodded her agreement.

Haley shifted to face her fiancé. "So?"

Rob pulled her chair closer to him and took her hands in his. "It needs to be in a museum. We don't need this stuff any more than your ancestors did. Obviously, that's why it remained buried." He leaned to look past Haley at Aiden. "Can you take care of the legalities, Counselor?"

"I'll work on it Monday morning. But for now..." He eyed Jason, who stood behind Kayla's chair. "What are we going to do with it? It's unnerving to have this *booty* on the property."

"I agree." Haley stared at Jason, then at Rob. Her brows rumpled. The lengths that Craig had been willing to go to for the treasure filled her mind. "What if someone found out about it?"

Jason pulled out his cell and held up a finger. "Hang on." He punched in a number. "Hello, Chief? I have a favor to ask."

Haley breathed a sigh of relief as she, Rob, Aiden, and Jason left the Douglas County jailhouse where they'd handed over the chest of jewels, cleverly disguised in a large ice chest, for safekeeping. "I'll bet this is the first time you've ever locked up a treasure chest in jail."

"I'll bet you're right." Jason laughed as he pulled into the drive leading to the MacKenna farm.

Rob let out a guffaw. "We'll all have stories to tell our grandkids someday—especially you, Jason. You found the culprit behind the mysterious events on the MacKenna farm and had a hand in arresting him. Helped us find the legendary treasure. And then on top of it, you arrested said treasure and hauled it off to jail."

"It'll match any story our ancestors ever told," Aiden added.

Jason chuckled and parked in front of the house.

As she unlatched her seatbelt, Haley shook her head. As beautiful as the gems were, and as excited as they'd been to find the treasure, she was relieved to have it out of the house. Even when Rob called his parents to tell them they'd located the treasure, Mr. and Mrs. Sheffield were happy Jason had thought of a safe place to keep it for now. The MacKennas and Sheffields had experienced enough excitement and trauma to last a lifetime.

Char and Kayla greeted them on the front porch. "Dinner's ready," they both called.

As they ate, Jason asked, "So, how were those jewels kept secret from the English before your ancestors left the country?"

Haley gaped at him. "One of many facts about the legend we'll never know unless we find more old pages like the ones Aiden read as a kid. Or, a book written by someone in the family who recorded everything. Pass the potatoes, please."

It was too good to be true. The legend wouldn't die. What a bunch they all were. She could only imagine the stories that would emerge in the future about the rediscovered treasure.

After dinner, Char chased Haley and Rob out of the house. "We have plans to discuss without the bride or groom listening."

"Uh-huh." With a smile, Haley peeked over her shoulder at her sister-in-law. Bridal shower? No doubt, Aiden and Jason had their heads together in the living room, planning a bachelor get-together.

Rob led Haley to the double rocking chair on the front porch. As they reclined, Haley let out a long breath. It sure had been some week.

She studied Rob's face. So serious. He'd been as quiet as a mouse since they left the jail. But then, so had she. She folded her hands in her lap. All the information Jason had found out about Craig Lowell. Could that be why Rob was quiet? As terrible as the events caused by Craig were, she couldn't help but feel sorry for him.

"Rob?"

He pulled her into his arms. "Yes, sweetheart."

"You'll think I'm crazy, but I feel bad for Craig Lowell. After what Jason told us about the man's childhood. Dragged away from his father, raised by an oppressive mother, and led astray by his father's obsession with the MacKenna treasure."

"You're not crazy. The same thing's been on my mind this evening. I've added Craig to my prayer list."

She snuggled closer. "I'm glad. We need to pray that Craig accepts the Lord as His Savior."

Rob kissed her forehead.

Haley sat upright and faced him. "Are you sorry I suggested we give the jewels away?"

"No. And Aiden's idea to split it among area museums is terrific. Besides, I found a *real* treasure in a field long ago." He kissed her nose. "Correction. In the stone barn." He beamed.

She poked him in the ribs. "The day I decked you for stealing a kiss? I smacked you good, didn't I? For years, that kiss stayed on my mind. Even in high school, when I was so angry."

He dropped his head against the back of the rocker. "You'll never forget my error in judgment, will you?"

She snuggled back into his arms, tilted her head back, and gazed into his deep blue eyes. "Let's change the subject." Haley stifled a giggle. "Aiden shouldn't have kept out the diamond and amethyst tiara for me to wear on our wedding day." She dipped her head forward and tittered. "But I really did want to keep it."

"We gathered as much. Nothing wrong with a family heirloom, sweetheart." He squeezed her.

She nodded. "But something that costly."

"Don't give it a second thought. Remember, Jason will be your personal armed guard. At least until we lock it in the bank after the wedding." He whispered in her ear. "He said he'll be packing."

Haley chortled. "I still wonder about those gaps in the family history. Precisely where the jewels came from. And about the Indian burial mound legend. If the MacKenna treasure is real—"

"Aha!" Rob held her at arm's length and narrowed his eyes at her. "Don't tell me you've sided with Drago on the ghost issue."

"No." She bit her lip and admitted, "Okay. It has crossed my mind. One or two of the events on the farm would have been impossible for Craig to pull off. Don't you think? And the sheriff's department hasn't come up with any answers."

Rob set the rocker in motion. "True. And it'd be nice to know the answers. I wonder who the pirate was."

"Not to mention why Dad warned us to stay away from the Lowells' property and the stone barn. Maybe fear that old man Lowell was deranged or narcissistic himself? But why the barn? Do you suppose Drago got those Indian ghosts superstitions from my dad?"

Rob shrugged. "I remember your dad warned us to steer clear of the old barn, but he never said why. We assumed it was because it was unsafe."

She peered into his eyes and bit her lip again. "A pirate ghost wouldn't come all the way to Nebraska. Even if he did exist."

Drago stepped out of the bunkhouse and waved at them. He strode across the grass. "Hi, kids. Just three weeks left as a free man, Rob." He winked.

"From what I hear, you're next."

Haley jabbed Rob in the ribs with her elbow.

Drago snickered. "Discussing the treasure?"

"What?" Her jaw slacked.

"Aiden told me. In case anyone comes snooping around. Where there's a good story, those news reporters have radar."

Rob nodded. "Right. Speaking of stories, are you convinced it wasn't Indian ghosts that caused the ruckus around here?"

"I'll admit *those* spirits were not responsible for everything, but I'm still not persuaded they don't exist. And it wasn't only Indian ghosts that concerned me. Your aunt saw something run out to the back field that one night. Looked like it held a sword. Bet she didn't tell you that, did she? Then the glow appeared. No one's figured out how. Not even the fire department. The only thing they found was that cigarette butt. But they established it as an old one of mine before I quit."

Haley's skin crawled.

"Bet that shadow of a ghost ran into the woods in the direction of the old stone barn."

"What are you saying?" Haley leaned forward.

"You mean about the ghost with the sword? I mean..." Drago's eyes widened. "Ah...I mean...nothing. Your dad must have been teasing your mom when I overheard him talk about it years ago. That's it. He was only teasing."

Rob peeked at Haley.

She grabbed Drago's wrist. "What ghost?"

He twisted his arm out of her grasp and backed away. "It was just a joke. I was only kidding. Well, I need to turn in, kids." Drago headed back toward the bunkhouse with a wave.

Haley watched him cross the grass. *No.* There couldn't be a pirate ghost. Not possible.

Rob grinned at her. "Now you have more fodder for a story, thanks to Drago's imagination. You can write a tale about the sacking of castles, the trip across the ocean on a vessel, the attack by pirates." He pulled her back against him. "The buried chest, the legend that resulted, the Indian burial mound, the maps, the hunt for the treasure in the dark...and possibly, a haunting by the pirate himself. You'll fill in the gaps."

She slapped his leg. "*Stop it!* Stop trying to scare me. You're as bad as my dad was." She smiled at him. "But how's this for a title. *Buried Treasure in Nebraska.* Or, *The Nebraska Pirate Treasure.* Sound good?"

Rob tightened his arms around her. "I think you need to work on that title." He grimaced. "But you won't have time to write until *after* our wedding. Make that after the *honeymoon.* Or even later...much later." His lips covered hers.

Haley melted into his embrace and returned his kisses. She'd write the story, all right. Pirate ghost indeed. Not hardly. *I hope.*

But lay up for yourselves treasures in heaven, where neither moth nor rust doth corrupt, and where thieves do not break through nor steal: Matthew 6:20

The End

About The Author

Sharon K Connell writes stories about people who discover God will allow things in their lives to bring them to a saving knowledge of Jesus Christ and/or increase their faith. Her genre is Christian Romance Suspense, always with a dose of humor and very often mystery. She also writes short stories in other genres (soon to be published).

Although born in Wisconsin, Sharon was raised in Illinois and went to school through college in Chicago. She has also lived in Missouri, California, Florida, and Ohio. Her travels have taken her to all but six states in the United States, and she has visited Canada and Mexico. She is now a resident of Texas.

Sharon is a member of the American Christian Fiction Writers organization, Houston Writers Guild, 2 Elizabeths Literary Magazine, CyFair Writers, and the Christian Womens Writers Club (CWW). She runs the Facebook Christian Writers & Readers Group Forum and puts out Novel Thoughts, a monthly newsletter for writers as well as readers.

She is a graduate of the Pensacola Bible Institute in Florida and holds a certificate in fiction writing from the International Writing Program through the University of Iowa.

Let the words of my mouth, and the meditation of my heart, be acceptable in thy sight, O Lord, my strength, and my redeemer.
Psalm 19:14

Links

Website: www.authorsharonkconnell.com

Amazon Author Page:

http://www.amazon.com/author/sharonkconnell

Author's book page on Facebook:

https://www.facebook.com/averypresenthelpbook1

Author's Page on Facebook:

https://www.facebook.com/ChristianRomanceSuspense/

Group Forum on Facebook:

https://www.facebook.com/groups/ChristianWritersAndReadersGroupForum/

Twitter: https://twitter.com/SharonKConnell

Goodreads: https://www.goodreads.com/SharonKConnell

LinkedIn: https://www.linkedin.com/in/sharonkconnell

Pinterest: https://www.pinterest.com/rosecastle1/

Other Works

Novels
A Very Present Help
Paths of Righteousness
There Abideth Hope
His Perfect Love

Novella
Icicles to Moonbeams

Short Stories in Anthologies
Ding-A-Ling Holiday Blues
In *Tales of Texas*, Vol. 2

Spirit Lake
In *Dark Visions*

Thank You for Reading